Chapter 1: The Une

The café door swung open with a chime, ushering me into a world draped in warmth and the rich scent of freshly ground coffee beans. As I stepped inside, the comforting buzz of conversation wrapped around me like a favorite blanket. I made my way to the counter, my usual spot, where the barista, an affable fellow named Jake, knew my order by heart. A glance at the menu was merely a formality. My eyes flicked past the chalkboard of daily specials and landed on a window seat, sunlight spilling in like liquid gold, illuminating the worn wood and the delicate steam rising from ceramic mugs.

My thoughts drifted, just like the steam, to the same predictable patterns—work, errands, the unremarkable cadence of my life. I was a collector of moments, capturing them in my mind like fireflies in a jar. But that morning, there was an unusual energy in the air, a sense of adventure waiting just beyond the horizon. I sighed and shook off the thoughts, focusing instead on the scent of cinnamon and caramel wafting from the counter, where Jake was expertly crafting my drink.

"Coming right up, Harper!" he called, a grin playing at the corners of his mouth. His voice was a familiar comfort, like the sound of the rain against my window on a lazy Sunday.

"Thanks, Jake," I replied, leaning against the counter, my fingers tracing the grain of the wood, lost in thought.

Just as my order was set before me, a figure stepped through the door, cutting into my reverie. He was tall, with an effortless kind of grace that seemed to challenge the very laws of physics. His dark hair fell just so, framing a face that could only be described as striking—strong jawline, cheekbones carved by an artist's hand, and an easy smile that hinted at mischief. My heart stuttered in my chest, a flutter I hadn't felt in a long time.

I barely registered how close he was until, with a careless step backward to survey the room, I collided with him. My drink teetered perilously on the edge of disaster, and I flung my hands out in a wild attempt to catch it. "Oh no!" I gasped, half-laughing, half-apologizing.

"Whoa there," he said, catching my elbow just in time, steadying me as I regained my footing. His touch sent an unexpected thrill racing through me, like the jolt of a rollercoaster on its first drop. "Didn't mean to be a hazard."

"I should have looked where I was going," I said, my cheeks warming as I met his gaze. There was something in his eyes, a flicker of recognition or maybe just amusement, that made me feel seen in a way I hadn't anticipated.

"I'm Ethan," he introduced himself, a slow smile spreading across his face as he held my gaze. "And I'm definitely not a hazard, just a coffee enthusiast."

"Harper," I managed, a bit flustered, as my heart thumped like a drum in my chest. "I guess I'm a little clumsy around my caffeine."

"Clumsy can be charming," he quipped, his voice low and smooth, like the finest chocolate. "At least you didn't spill your drink all over me."

I chuckled, the tension in the air dissolving like sugar in hot coffee. "I'll try to keep it that way. You might not find my 'charm' so charming if I ruin your morning."

"Try me," he shot back, eyes twinkling with a challenge. "I've faced worse hazards in life—like ordering a 'surprise' at a brunch place."

We fell into an easy rhythm, the surrounding bustle of the café fading into background noise. It felt as though the universe had conspired to throw us together, two unlikely characters in this small-town drama. As he recounted his disastrous brunch experience, I found myself laughing harder than I had in ages. The way he gestured animatedly with his hands made every story seem alive, the vibrant details painting pictures in my mind.

"I still can't believe they thought a 'mystery egg' was a selling point," he said, rolling his eyes dramatically. "I'm not here to play food roulette, you know?"

I giggled, shaking my head. "Next time, maybe just stick to the basics. Scrambled eggs are a safe bet."

"Maybe. But where's the fun in that?" he countered, a playful glint in his eye. "Life's too short for boring breakfast choices."

As our conversation flowed effortlessly, the world outside seemed to dim, the autumn leaves fluttering in the wind like confetti celebrating this unexpected encounter. We discovered shared interests, everything from books to movies, and a mutual disdain for pineapple on pizza, which seemed like a perfect bonding point. With every laugh, every shared secret, I felt a warmth spreading through me, an exhilarating sense of connection I hadn't realized I was missing.

"Do you come here often?" Ethan asked, his gaze fixed on me, as if he were searching for hidden depths beneath my unassuming exterior.

"Most mornings," I replied, feeling a little bolder. "It's my ritual—coffee, a bit of people-watching, then off to face the world."

"Sounds like a solid plan. Mind if I join you next time?"

My heart raced at the thought, and for a moment, I hesitated. "You're asking to join my ritual?"

"Seems only fair," he replied, a teasing smile dancing on his lips. "I've already invaded your space today. Might as well make it official."

"I guess that's how friendships are forged—over clumsy encounters and coffee," I replied, laughing nervously as I tried to gauge the intention behind his words. Was he really interested in being friends, or was there something more?

"Friendship, or perhaps something more," he mused, his voice dropping an octave, sending a shiver of anticipation through me. The playful banter had shifted, the air thickening with possibilities. "We could explore this town together, start a whole new ritual."

The prospect of spending more time with him sent a thrill through me, igniting a spark of hope. "I'd like that," I found myself saying before I could overthink it.

And just like that, in the bustling warmth of a coffee shop filled with laughter and familiar faces, the mundane contours of my life shifted, rearranging themselves around this unexpected encounter. The ordinary had been painted over with vibrant strokes of the extraordinary, and for the first time, I felt the stirrings of adventure beckoning me forward.

The following morning, the sun peeped through the curtains of my bedroom, casting warm golden beams across the quilted comforter. I awoke to a fluttering of excitement in my stomach, as if a dozen butterflies had taken up residence, and the thrill of the unexpected encounter with Ethan played on repeat in my mind. I swung my legs over the side of the bed, the wooden floor cool against my bare feet. I stood there for a moment, gathering the courage to confront the day, a day that held a promise I hadn't realized I craved.

A quick shower and a few choice selections from my closet later, I found myself ready to face the world. I had always favored soft, muted colors—navy blues and gentle grays—but today, I chose a bright mustard cardigan that hugged my frame just right, paired with my favorite jeans. There was something liberating about the color; it felt like a subtle declaration that I was ready for whatever was to come.

As I walked to the coffee shop, the leaves crunched beneath my feet, their vibrant hues swirling like confetti. I felt alive, buzzing with energy. The familiar scent of roasted coffee beans welcomed me as I stepped inside, and I immediately scanned the room for Ethan. I didn't know what I expected; perhaps a wave, a smile, or even a chance encounter to confirm that yesterday wasn't a dream.

My heart sank slightly as I spotted an empty table by the window. I made my way to the counter and ordered my usual, hoping the familiar ritual would ground me. Jake flashed a knowing smile as he prepared my drink, the kind that said he was well aware of my little crush, even if I wasn't quite ready to admit it to myself. I could feel a rush of warmth creeping into my cheeks.

"Looking for someone?" Jake asked, his eyes twinkling mischievously.

"Just... wondering if Ethan might be around," I replied, attempting to sound casual but failing miserably.

"Ah, the tall, dark, and charming type," he said with a smirk, setting my drink down. "He comes in at random times, but I saw him here yesterday. Maybe you should just take a seat and see if he pops in."

I nodded, clutching the warm cup as I made my way to the window. Settling into the chair, I let out a sigh, half contentment and half impatience. The café bustled around me, filled with laughter and chatter, but my focus was on the door, my heart doing a little dance every time it swung open. I lost myself in thoughts of yesterday, each moment replaying like a movie—his easy laugh, the way his eyes sparkled with mischief. I was completely unprepared for the way I had felt, like I had stepped into a scene from a rom-com.

Time ticked by, and just as I began to wonder if I had imagined the whole encounter, the bell above the door jingled, and in walked Ethan. He stood in the doorway for a moment, scanning the room, and my heart leaped. His dark hair was tousled, the sunlight catching the strands and creating an almost halo effect. He spotted me, and that smile—oh, that smile—bloomed across his face, a bright spot amidst the café's warmth.

"Looks like my favorite coffee shop hasn't burned down yet," he said as he approached, his voice playful, effortlessly charming.

"Not yet, but I can't promise anything if you order something adventurous," I teased, gesturing for him to join me.

"Adventurous? You're looking at the guy who once tried a mystery egg," he countered, taking a seat across from me.

I burst into laughter, the kind that made my cheeks hurt, and suddenly, it felt as though we had picked up right where we had left off. We fell into conversation as if the world outside had vanished. I shared my most embarrassing food experiences, recounting the time I tried sushi for the first time, only to realize I had bitten into a piece of ginger thinking it was a bizarre fruit. He roared with laughter, eyes sparkling with amusement.

"You're a culinary rebel," he declared. "Ginger as a fruit? Bold move. I'd say we should team up for a cooking show. I'll be the charming host; you can handle the ingredients."

"And what will you do, stand around looking pretty?" I shot back, grinning.

"Exactly! It's a full-time job," he replied, pretending to adjust an invisible bowtie.

As we continued to banter, I couldn't shake the feeling that I was learning more about him in these lighthearted exchanges than I had in years of half-hearted small talk with acquaintances. There was depth in his humor, a hint of vulnerability beneath the surface that intrigued me.

"So, Harper," he said, leaning back in his chair, studying me with an intensity that made me slightly self-conscious. "What's the story behind the cozy cardigan and the coffee shop ritual? There must be a more exciting side to you than this charming coffee lover facade."

I hesitated, the moment feeling heavier, the playful banter taking on a new layer. "I guess I've always been... safe. Comfortable. My life has revolved around routine, and I like my little rituals. They're predictable and... peaceful."

"Peaceful is overrated," he countered. "What if I told you I could introduce a little chaos into your life?"

"Chaos? Like what?" I raised an eyebrow, intrigued.

"How about we start with a spontaneous adventure?" he suggested, his eyes dancing with mischief. "No coffee shop rules, no safety nets. Just us, exploring whatever the day throws our way."

The challenge in his voice made my heart race, but a sliver of hesitation wormed its way in. "Spontaneity has a way of backfiring, you know."

"Or it could lead to the best stories. How many memorable tales do you have from your safe little coffee rituals?" He leaned in, his tone earnest. "Life isn't meant to be lived in a cozy corner. Sometimes you've got to jump into the unknown."

A flicker of desire for adventure ignited within me. I'd spent too long being the quiet observer in my own life. Maybe it was time to step into the light, to embrace the chaos Ethan was offering. "Fine," I said, a grin breaking across my face. "But if we end up on some wild goose chase, I'm holding you responsible."

"Deal," he replied, his smile wide and infectious, a silent promise hanging in the air between us.

Just as I was about to consider the implications of my decision, the café door swung open, and an unexpected figure stepped inside—a woman with fiery red hair and an air of confidence that demanded attention. I recognized her instantly as Natalie, the café's most ardent socialite, known for her extravagant parties and matchmaking prowess.

"Ethan! There you are!" she called, striding over, a beaming smile plastered on her face. "I've been looking everywhere for you!"

My heart dropped slightly as she turned her attention toward me, her gaze assessing. "And you must be the infamous Harper. Ethan's been talking about you."

"Infamous?" I echoed, feigning a casual tone as I glanced at Ethan, who looked caught off guard.

"Yes, the one who nearly spilled coffee all over him!" she laughed, her voice like a bright chime, though the undertone of curiosity sent a slight chill down my spine.

"Guilty as charged," I replied, forcing a smile, trying to navigate the sudden shift in the air.

Ethan cleared his throat, glancing between us. "Natalie, we were just—"

"Planning your next adventure, I hope?" she interjected, her enthusiasm bright but edged with an intensity that made me wary.

"Something like that," Ethan said, his gaze lingering on me for a brief moment, a flicker of something unreadable in his eyes.

"Well, don't let me interrupt! But just so you know, the annual Harvest Festival is coming up this weekend. You should both come! It'll be a riot," she declared, her excitement palpable.

"Sounds... fun," I said, my heart racing as I tried to gauge Ethan's reaction. The festival would be crowded and chaotic, the perfect breeding ground for unexpected twists.

Ethan met my gaze, a slight smile on his lips that hinted at mischief. "How about we make it our first chaotic adventure?"

Natalie beamed at the suggestion, her enthusiasm infectious, but I felt the weight of uncertainty settle over me. A festival? Crowds? Was I truly ready to plunge headfirst into the unknown?

But as Ethan's warm gaze held mine, the promise of excitement and unpredictability shimmered like autumn leaves in the breeze, beckoning me to embrace it all. With a deep breath, I decided to let the winds of spontaneity carry me wherever they would lead.

The evening of the Harvest Festival arrived like a long-awaited promise, the air electric with anticipation and the scents of cinnamon, caramel, and crisp autumn leaves swirling together in a delightful embrace. As I stood in front of the mirror, I fiddled with my hair, trying to find a balance between looking effortless and actually feeling it. My mustard cardigan had become my favorite, but tonight, I wanted something different—something that whispered adventure while still feeling like me. I finally settled on a cozy flannel shirt, the soft fabric wrapping around me like a reassuring hug, and a pair of well-loved jeans.

With a final glance in the mirror, I grabbed my phone and texted Ethan, my fingers hesitating slightly before hitting send. "Ready for our chaotic adventure?" The words felt like a leap into the unknown, my heart pounding with the thrill of what might come next. The reply was almost instantaneous.

"Absolutely! Meet you at the square in ten?"

"See you there!" I replied, a grin stretching across my face. I could hardly contain the flutter of excitement bubbling inside me. I had no idea what the night would hold, but the thought of experiencing it with Ethan made me giddy.

As I stepped outside, the street was alive with festivity. Strings of twinkling lights crisscrossed above, casting a soft glow that made everything look like a scene straight out of a storybook. The laughter of children filled the air, accompanied by the tantalizing aroma of popcorn and roasted chestnuts. My heart soared with each step toward the square, the sounds and sights blending into a perfect symphony of autumn magic.

When I arrived, Ethan was already there, leaning casually against a lamp post, looking effortlessly charming in a navy jacket that complemented his tousled hair. He looked up just as I approached, and his face broke into that warm, inviting smile that had ignited a spark in me since our first meeting.

"There you are! I was starting to think you might be too afraid of a little chaos," he teased, his eyes glimmering with mischief.

"Me? Afraid? Never," I shot back, trying to match his playful energy. "I'm just fashionably late."

"Fashionably late is my favorite kind of late," he grinned, gesturing toward the heart of the festival. "Ready to dive into the madness?"

With a nod, we made our way into the throng of people. The square was a kaleidoscope of color—brightly colored booths showcasing handmade crafts, the tantalizing sizzle of food stalls, and laughter that floated through the air like confetti. It was a feast for the senses, and as we wandered through the festivities, I felt a sense of freedom washing over me, mingling with the rush of adrenaline.

"First stop—carnival games!" Ethan exclaimed, pointing toward a booth where a line of eager participants stood, trying their luck at knocking down cans.

"Do you really think you can win me a prize?" I challenged, raising an eyebrow.

"Watch and learn, Harper," he said confidently, striding toward the game. He paid for his turn and stepped up, his focus laser-sharp as he picked up the heavy beanbag. With a swift flick of his wrist, he sent it flying, knocking over all three cans with one perfect throw. The crowd erupted in cheers, and my heart raced not just from the excitement but from the way he beamed at me afterward.

"Your prize, madam," he said dramatically, handing me a plush bear that looked suspiciously like it had just emerged from the '90s.

"A bear? You're really going for the charm factor, huh?" I teased, unable to stifle a smile.

"Hey, it's vintage! And it matches your style," he replied, a glimmer of amusement in his eyes.

We wandered from booth to booth, sampling everything from caramel apples to warm cider. Each new experience felt like an unwrapping of layers, revealing more of the genuine Ethan beneath the effortless charm. He had a way of making even the most mundane moments feel special, transforming simple bites of food into gourmet experiences through his laughter and storytelling.

As night began to fall, we found ourselves near the center of the square, where a small stage had been set up for local performers. A folk band was tuning their instruments, the rich sound of guitars and banjos weaving through the crisp evening air. I leaned against the railing, mesmerized by the scene unfolding before me, but even more so by the way Ethan stood beside me, his presence comforting yet exhilarating.

"What do you think?" he asked, his voice a low rumble that vibrated through me.

"It's beautiful," I replied, my gaze lingering on the flickering lights that danced in the darkening sky. "It feels like something out of a dream."

He turned to me, his expression shifting, something deeper glimmering in his eyes. "You know, it's funny. I never used to think I'd enjoy these kinds of things. I was always the guy who preferred quiet nights in, a book, and takeout. But... there's something about this, about sharing it with someone."

My heart fluttered at his words, an unexpected warmth blooming within me. "Maybe that's the magic of it. Sometimes the best experiences come from stepping outside your comfort zone, right?"

"Exactly," he said, his gaze steady on mine. "And I'm glad I stepped outside mine."

Before I could respond, the band struck up a lively tune, and without a word, Ethan grabbed my hand, pulling me toward the makeshift dance floor.

"Wait! I can't dance!" I exclaimed, laughter bubbling up inside me as I tried to resist, but he was relentless.

"Just follow my lead!" he said, spinning me around, and before I knew it, I was caught up in the rhythm of the music, laughter spilling from my lips as I twirled and stumbled, the world around us fading into a blur of color and sound.

The joy of the moment enveloped us, a cocoon of shared exhilaration. We danced as if no one was watching, our movements becoming a conversation of their own—playful, spontaneous, and free. I felt alive in a way I had never experienced before, the weight of my usual worries lifted in the air around us.

As the song came to an end, I breathed heavily, exhilaration coursing through my veins. We stood close, our faces flushed, and in that fleeting moment, the noise of the festival faded, leaving only the two of us in our bubble of warmth and laughter.

"You're an amazing dancer, you know," he said, a breathless smile plastered across his face.

"Flattery will get you everywhere," I joked, my heart racing as I met his gaze, feeling the air thicken between us.

"Good to know," he replied, his voice dipping to a more serious tone, the moment shifting subtly. "But really, you're incredible. I can't believe how easy it is to be with you."

Just as I was about to respond, the sound of fireworks exploded above us, vibrant bursts of color lighting up the night sky. The audience around us oohed and aahed, but my focus was solely on Ethan. The light reflected in his eyes, and for a heartbeat, it felt like the world had stopped spinning.

In that moment of shared wonder, the air hummed with unsaid words, the connection between us palpable and electric. But before I could let myself dive into the depth of what I felt, a loud commotion erupted nearby, shattering the fragile bubble of intimacy.

"Did you see that?" a voice shouted, cutting through the music. I turned to see a crowd gathering around a booth at the edge of the square, faces twisted in shock.

"What's going on?" I asked, anxiety creeping into my voice.

"I don't know," Ethan said, his eyes narrowing as he scanned the gathering crowd. "Let's check it out."

We pushed our way through the throng, my heart pounding in my chest for a different reason now. As we reached the front, I froze at the scene before me. A young man stood atop a table, wild-eyed and disheveled, waving his arms. "Someone stole my wallet!" he shouted, voice tinged with panic. "I swear I just had it!"

Gasps spread through the crowd, and I exchanged a glance with Ethan, the playful atmosphere suddenly clouded by tension.

"Should we help?" I asked, my instincts kicking in.

Before he could respond, a sharp scream pierced the air, slicing through the chatter like a knife. My stomach dropped as I turned to see a figure darting away from the chaos, weaving through the crowd, a flash of something shiny in their hand.

"Hey!" Ethan called, instinctively starting to chase after them, adrenaline coursing through him. "Wait!"

I hesitated for a brief second, my heart racing as I weighed my options. Should I follow him? Should we get involved? The festival, with all its magic and warmth, suddenly felt like a storm brewing.

With a determination fueled by instinct, I took off after Ethan, the thrill of the chase igniting something fierce within me. But as I ran, the figure slipped into the shadows, and my breath caught in my throat as I realized that this night of adventure might lead us down a path neither of us could have predicted.

Chapter 2: The Invitation

The late afternoon sun cast a golden hue over Cedar Hill Community College, illuminating the sprawling campus like a scene from a vintage postcard. Students drifted from one lecture hall to another, their laughter punctuating the air with warmth. Yet, in that moment, I felt like a solitary star in a galaxy bustling with vibrant constellations, still finding my orbit. The gentle rustle of leaves added a soothing backdrop as Ethan and I emerged from Ms. Delaney's art class, our conversation swirling around the latest assignment like paint on a palette.

Ethan's light brown hair danced in the breeze, and his green eyes sparkled with mischief as he spoke. He was effortless in a way that made my heart race—a mix of charm and wit that left me both exhilarated and bewildered. "So, you'll come to the gallery opening then?" His question lingered, almost teasing, as if he already knew my answer but relished the thrill of coaxing it out of me.

The invitation felt weighty, like a prized possession. I blinked up at him, caught off guard by the warmth radiating from his genuine smile. I could have easily deflected, could have smiled politely and offered some excuse about prior commitments or my fear of crowds. Social anxiety gripped me, whispering all the familiar doubts. But nestled beneath that apprehension was a defiant spark, a voice that dared me to take the leap. "Yeah, I think I will," I said, my voice steadier than I felt.

His grin widened, and for a moment, the world around us faded. "Great! I promise you'll love it. The featured artist is incredible, and the atmosphere will be... well, let's just say it's always a bit chaotic. Just like Ms. Delaney's classes." He chuckled, his laughter rich and warm, and I found myself laughing too, surrendering to the lightness of the moment.

As we walked toward the parking lot, the thrill of acceptance pulsed through me, mingling with a sense of vulnerability. Ethan fell into step beside me, his presence steadying. "You okay?" he asked, his brow furrowing slightly. The concern in his voice washed over me like a balm, easing the knot in my stomach.

"Yeah, just... I guess I'm not used to these things." I shifted my gaze, focusing instead on the ground beneath my feet, the cracked pavement marking our path.

He tilted his head, a teasing smile playing on his lips. "The art gallery? Or the part where you get to spend time with me?"

I couldn't help but laugh, the sound bubbling up from a place I had almost forgotten existed. "Both," I admitted, the honesty spilling out as easily as the autumn leaves danced in the crisp air.

His expression turned serious for a heartbeat, a flicker of something deeper sparking in his eyes. "Well, consider it an adventure, then. You'll never know what you're missing if you don't try." The weight of his words hung in the air, a promise laced with mystery.

That night, I stood in front of my closet, assessing my options like a painter contemplating a blank canvas. I rifled through the hangers, discarding anything that felt too casual or too formal. I settled on a deep emerald green dress that hugged my curves just right, its fabric shimmering like a secret I was eager to share. Standing in front of the mirror, I twisted my hair into soft waves, adding a touch of lipstick that was bold enough to make a statement but subtle enough to feel like me.

As the clock inched toward seven, I felt a rush of excitement mingle with nerves, turning my stomach into a tight coil. The prospect of stepping outside my comfort zone loomed large, but I steeled myself with the thought of Ethan. His enthusiasm was contagious, and if I could keep pace with him for just one night, perhaps I'd discover a piece of myself I hadn't realized was missing.

The gallery was a charming little venue, a brick building adorned with twinkling fairy lights that danced in the gentle evening breeze. I pushed open the heavy door, and the soft hum of chatter washed over me like a warm embrace. My heart raced as I stepped inside, the mingling scents of paint and wine wrapping around me. Vibrant canvases adorned the walls, splashes of color and emotion drawing me in like sirens beckoning sailors to shore.

"Hey! You made it!" Ethan's voice cut through the clamor, and I turned to find him striding toward me, radiating that effortless charm that made my heart do somersaults. He looked stunning in a fitted black shirt and jeans, the casual ensemble somehow highlighting his every feature, making him look like a piece of art himself.

"I didn't want to miss your grand adventure," I quipped, feeling a thrill at the banter.

"Good choice," he replied, leaning in slightly, his breath warm against my ear. "Now, let's see if we can find the artist before the crowd devours them whole."

Together we wove through the throng of people, the atmosphere vibrant and alive. Laughter and animated discussions filled the air, a symphony of voices that made me feel both overwhelmed and exhilarated. I caught glimpses of abstract pieces, their colors clashing and blending in ways that made my heart race—each canvas telling a story I yearned to decipher.

Ethan led me to a particularly striking piece—a large canvas splashed with swirls of blue and gold, reminiscent of a stormy sea kissed by sunlight. "What do you think?" he asked, leaning closer, his shoulder brushing against mine.

"I think it looks like chaos waiting to be understood," I replied, the words tumbling out before I could second-guess myself.

He chuckled, clearly pleased. "I love that perspective. Art should make you feel something, right? And if it doesn't, it's just a pretty picture."

We continued to explore the gallery, and with each passing moment, I felt the walls of my comfort zone begin to crumble. The warmth of his presence buoyed me, allowing me to take risks I usually avoided. For the first time in a long while, I felt seen, truly seen—not just as the anxious girl trying to blend into the background, but as someone who had a voice, a viewpoint worth sharing.

"Let's grab some wine," he suggested, guiding me toward the makeshift bar set up against the far wall. The clink of glasses and the laughter of strangers created a symphony of mirth that surrounded us, amplifying the thrill in my chest.

"Here's to stepping outside our comfort zones," he toasted, raising his glass with a glint of mischief in his eyes. I clinked my glass against his, feeling a rush of exhilaration as the wine glided smoothly down my throat, igniting a spark of courage deep within me.

I was ready for this adventure, for whatever twists awaited us in the enchanting chaos of the night.

The hum of the gallery buzzed around us, the air thick with anticipation and creativity. I had spent years hiding behind the safe walls of my own self-doubt, and yet here I was, caught in a whirlwind of color and laughter. Ethan's easy demeanor made it all feel manageable; I was acutely aware of every laugh we shared, every sideways glance that hinted at a connection deeper than mere friendship.

We stood side by side, examining a piece that seemed to pulsate with life. The colors—vivid oranges and purples—battled for attention, a dance of chaos that mirrored my swirling thoughts. "What do you think?" I asked, my voice almost lost amidst the clamor of the crowd.

Ethan leaned in closer, his shoulder brushing against mine, sending an electric thrill through me. "It looks like a sunset trying to escape a storm. Isn't it beautiful?" His gaze flickered from the painting to me, his green eyes sparking with enthusiasm. "It's like the artist captured the struggle, you know? That moment before everything goes dark."

"Or the moment right before everything changes," I replied, surprising myself with the depth of my observation. "It's a reminder that even chaos has its moments of brilliance."

"Exactly!" he exclaimed, his expression lighting up like a thousand-watt bulb. "You should consider taking a stab at painting. You've got a way with words that could translate beautifully to the canvas."

"Me? Paint?" I laughed lightly, half-flattered, half-terrified. "The last time I tried, I ended up with more paint on my hands than the canvas. Let's just say I'm better with words."

"Words can be art too, you know," he said, a playful glint in his eyes. "But let's not turn this into a poetry slam just yet. How about we find that wine?"

He navigated through the crowd with a confidence that made me wonder if he had been here before, but then again, I was still discovering the layers of Ethan, each one more intriguing than the last. We reached the bar, and I watched as he ordered two glasses of red wine, his casual charm disarming the bartender who seemed momentarily entranced.

"I didn't know you had that kind of influence," I teased as he returned with our drinks.

"Just a little charm goes a long way," he replied, winking as he handed me a glass. "Or maybe it's just the shirt."

I rolled my eyes playfully. "Ah yes, the infamous 'Bartender Magnet' shirt."

We raised our glasses in a toast that felt surprisingly intimate, the clink echoing like a promise between us. As I took a sip, the rich flavors enveloped me—smooth with a hint of something daring.

Ethan watched me, a soft smile playing on his lips. "So, tell me about yourself. What else do you do besides surviving art classes and looking fabulous in green dresses?"

The question caught me off guard, but I was ready to plunge deeper. "Well, I'm a bit of a bookworm, to be honest. I could lose myself in a library for days, devouring everything from contemporary fiction to ancient mythology."

"Fiction? Oh, now you're speaking my language. Give me a character with a dramatic backstory, and I'm hooked," he said, leaning against the bar with a relaxed grace that made my heart flutter.

"Then you would love the protagonist in my latest read," I said, launching into a description of a fierce woman battling her inner demons and societal expectations. "She's flawed and complicated, but that's what makes her so relatable."

Ethan listened intently, nodding as I spoke, his gaze steady and encouraging. "I think flawed characters are the most fascinating," he mused. "They show us that perfection is overrated."

"Sounds like you're an aspiring writer too," I shot back, a playful challenge glinting in my eye.

"Only if we can co-write a dramatic story about a girl who takes on the art world and accidentally stumbles into a romance," he replied with a grin that could light up the darkest of rooms.

"Oh, I can see it now—an epic saga of love and paint splatters. But we should probably include a rival artist who tries to sabotage our hero."

"Only if the rival artist is ridiculously attractive," he quipped, a mock-seriousness enveloping his expression. "Just for the sake of tension, you know?"

We both burst into laughter, the sound blending seamlessly with the chatter around us. In that moment, everything felt right, as if the universe conspired to align our paths just for this evening.

Our conversation flowed effortlessly, each story exchanged weaving a stronger bond. We explored the gallery together, discussing each piece with a passion that illuminated our shared love for creativity. When we reached a haunting portrait of a woman with eyes that seemed to follow us, I turned to Ethan. "What do you see?"

His brow furrowed as he studied the painting. "A woman who knows secrets, maybe? There's a depth in her gaze that suggests she's been through more than we can imagine."

"Or perhaps she's waiting for someone to discover those secrets," I added, intrigued by the layers of interpretation unfolding before us.

"Now that's a twist," he said, grinning. "A mystery wrapped in an enigma."

But just as the night unfolded with promise, a sudden commotion caught my attention. A group of rowdy patrons gathered near a particularly abstract installation, their laughter turning into shouts. My heart raced, the atmosphere shifting like the air before a storm. "What's going on?" I asked, instinctively stepping closer to Ethan.

"Looks like some excitement over there," he said, eyes narrowing with curiosity.

Before I could voice my concerns, a loud crash shattered the laughter. A painting, previously secured to the wall, teetered dangerously before plunging to the ground with a resounding thud. Gasps erupted from the crowd, and I felt a knot tighten in my stomach.

"Oh no," I whispered, the reality of the situation sinking in.

Ethan stepped forward, instinctively leading the way as people began to gather, their faces a mix of shock and concern. I followed, my heart pounding as the atmosphere shifted from celebratory to chaotic. The gallery owner hurried over, his face pale as he surveyed the damage.

"What happened?" I murmured, my mind racing with the consequences of such a mishap.

"It's part of the opening, I suppose," Ethan said, glancing at me. "But it looks like a few people are more interested in drama than art."

As the crowd buzzed with excitement, I couldn't shake the feeling that this was more than just an accident. Something about the tension in the air, the way people leaned forward with greedy anticipation, made me feel like we were on the brink of something larger.

Ethan turned to me, the shadows of concern in his eyes deepening. "Stay close. I have a feeling we're about to witness a masterpiece of chaos."

And just like that, the night shifted again, the anticipation crackling like electricity, hinting at twists I had yet to uncover.

The unexpected crash of the painting sent shockwaves through the gallery, snapping me back to the chaos surrounding us. The crowd buzzed with a mix of curiosity and horror, people jostling each other for a better view as if this was a performance art piece instead of an unfortunate accident. My heart raced, caught in the tension of it all. Ethan's hand found mine, a reassuring gesture that grounded me in the whirlwind.

"Let's see what all the fuss is about," he urged, guiding me through the throng of bodies. The air felt electric, charged with anticipation and an undercurrent of gossip that swirled around us like confetti. I was acutely aware of our hands clasped together, the warmth of his skin sending delightful shivers up my arm.

We reached the center of the commotion just as the gallery owner, a short man with a dramatic flair in his every gesture, began to address the crowd. His face, usually flush with excitement, was now pale as he assessed the fallen artwork. "Ladies and gentlemen, please remain calm! This is not part of the performance," he declared, though a hint of desperation crept into his voice.

I leaned into Ethan, our shoulders brushing as I whispered, "What do you think happened? Was it really an accident?"

"Who knows? Maybe someone was overly enthusiastic about the piece," he replied, his eyes twinkling with mischief. "Or perhaps it was sabotage. The art world is full of drama."

My curiosity piqued as the owner gestured toward the shattered frame lying on the ground. The painting itself had miraculously remained intact, its vibrant colors untouched, but the chaos around it spoke of a different story—one of rivalry and unspoken tensions hidden beneath the gallery's polished surface.

As we stood there, the crowd's chatter crescendoed, voices mingling in a symphony of speculation. "Do you think it's the artist?" someone shouted, and the murmurs grew louder, igniting a fire of intrigue that crackled in the air.

Ethan turned to me, excitement lighting up his features. "What if it is? We could be witnessing the birth of an art scandal right before our eyes."

"Let's not get too dramatic," I said, half-serious, though I couldn't suppress a smile at the idea. "We'll need a good story to tell afterward."

As if on cue, a tall woman with striking red hair and an air of confidence strode forward, commanding attention. She wore a flowing black dress that billowed around her like the smoke of a recently extinguished candle. "Excuse me! I am the artist," she announced, her voice cutting through the murmur like a knife through butter. "And while I appreciate your enthusiasm, I assure you, I did not authorize any such theatrics."

Ethan raised an eyebrow, an expression that mirrored my own intrigue. "Now this is getting interesting," he murmured, his voice low enough that only I could hear.

The gallery owner stepped back, his eyes wide with shock. "But the painting—"

"It was meant to be hung at eye level, not as an example of your slapdash installation skills," she interrupted, her tone sharp and unapologetic. The tension in the room shifted; now, it wasn't just about a fallen painting but a clash of egos on display.

The crowd buzzed with excitement, and I felt the adrenaline of the moment pulse through me. "This isn't just a gallery opening; it's a soap opera," I whispered to Ethan, who chuckled softly in response.

"Don't underestimate the power of art to stir emotions," he said, leaning closer to catch my eye. "But this is all very theatrical. I can't wait to see how it unfolds."

The artist continued, her voice rising with a fervor that echoed through the room. "I poured my soul into that piece! It speaks of resilience and beauty in the face of chaos, not of your negligence!"

I couldn't help but admire her fiery spirit. "She's certainly passionate," I remarked, glancing sideways at Ethan, who nodded in agreement, his eyes gleaming with amusement.

"Passion makes for good art—and even better drama," he quipped, nudging my shoulder playfully.

"Does this mean we get front-row seats to a creative meltdown?" I replied, matching his playful tone, relishing the thrill of the evening's unpredictability.

Suddenly, the artist's gaze darted around the room, her sharp eyes landing on us. I felt a jolt of surprise as she locked onto me. "You!" she exclaimed, striding toward us with purpose. "What do you think?"

I stammered, caught off guard. "Me?"

"Yes, you! You seem to have a sense of what art should convey. Speak!" She gestured toward the fallen piece, her expectant expression leaving me momentarily speechless.

Ethan's grip on my hand tightened slightly, as if to ground me, but there was an undeniable thrill in the challenge. "Um, well," I began, collecting my thoughts. "I think it captures a struggle, but it also embodies hope. It's about the light breaking through the storm."

The artist's eyes widened, and I couldn't tell if my response had impressed her or simply surprised her. "Interesting," she said slowly, as if she were weighing my words. "You might have a good eye for this after all."

Her praise stirred something within me, a flicker of confidence I hadn't expected to feel in such a tense moment. I glanced at Ethan, whose approving smile encouraged me to continue.

Before I could gather my thoughts to say more, the crowd erupted into applause, surprising us all. The artist straightened, seemingly invigorated by the unexpected support, and I felt a rush of exhilaration course through me.

"Thank you, thank you!" she called, her demeanor shifting from defensive to engaged. "But let's not forget the real reason we're here—the art!"

Suddenly, the atmosphere shifted again, a wave of anticipation rippling through the crowd as they resumed their chatter, weaving new stories about the unfolding drama. Ethan leaned closer, whispering, "You've got a way with words. Who knew you'd be the star of the night?"

"Right, because this is definitely how I envisioned my evening going," I replied, rolling my eyes dramatically. "All I wanted was a quiet night surrounded by art, not to be thrust into the spotlight."

"Who doesn't love a little excitement?" he teased, his eyes twinkling mischievously.

Just then, a commotion erupted from the back of the gallery. A figure in a dark hoodie rushed toward us, weaving through the crowd with a frantic energy that caught everyone's attention. My heart skipped as I realized it was the gallery's security guard, his face a mask of urgency.

"Everyone, please!" he shouted, cutting through the chatter. "We need to clear the area. There's been a theft!"

Gasps rippled through the crowd, and I felt the world tilt slightly on its axis. A theft? My pulse quickened, and I exchanged a startled glance with Ethan, who looked equally bewildered.

"What do they mean, a theft?" I asked, but before he could respond, the guard continued, his voice rising above the chaos.

"It appears that one of the artworks has gone missing, and we need everyone to cooperate!"

An electric tension filled the room, mingling with confusion and curiosity. My instincts kicked in, and I felt a mix of excitement and dread. As if the night hadn't been unpredictable enough, now we were on the brink of a mystery far more intriguing than I could have imagined.

Ethan leaned closer, his voice barely above a whisper. "This just got way more interesting. Are you ready for a real adventure?"

I nodded, a thrill racing through me as the gallery buzzed with whispers and speculation. I wasn't sure where the night would lead us, but as Ethan's eyes locked onto mine, I felt an undeniable pull, an adventurous spark that ignited the air between us.

And just as I thought the unfolding chaos couldn't escalate further, the lights flickered ominously, casting eerie shadows that danced along the walls. A moment later, the power went out entirely, plunging us into darkness.

Panic surged through the crowd, gasps echoing off the walls, and I could feel Ethan's hand tighten around mine, grounding me amidst the chaos. In that moment, my heart raced with anticipation, not just for the mystery unfolding but for the undeniable connection I felt with him.

Then, a single spotlight flickered back to life, illuminating a figure standing at the far end of the gallery. The air crackled with suspense, and I held my breath, ready for whatever revelation awaited us in the shadows.

Chapter 3: The Gallery

The gallery opening was an explosion of color and sound, a symphony of art that had been carefully curated to evoke emotions I couldn't quite name. I stepped through the entrance, the doors swinging open to reveal a world steeped in anticipation. The scent of freshly mixed paints lingered in the air, mingling with the rich aroma of red wine and artisanal cheese, each note drawing me further into the vibrant scene unfolding before me.

 I smoothed down the fabric of my red dress, feeling its soft silk against my skin, a stark contrast to the cool air of the gallery. It hugged my curves just right, providing a sense of confidence I had thought long lost. My reflection shimmered in the glass as I turned, the warmth of the color complementing the flush of my cheeks, and I whispered a small promise to myself: tonight would be different.

 As I crossed the threshold, the noise enveloped me like a welcoming embrace. Laughter danced through the air, twinkling like stars caught in a whirlwind of conversation. Brightly lit canvases hung on stark white walls, each piece a universe unto itself. I could feel the pulse of the crowd, their energy electrifying, and my heart raced in sync, an echo of both excitement and trepidation.

 Ethan was already a few steps into the crowd, his presence a beacon. He turned, his smile cutting through the cacophony like a lighthouse guiding a lost ship home. "You made it!" he called, his voice warm and inviting. The way his eyes sparkled made me feel like I was the only person in the room, even amidst the swirling chaos.

 "Wouldn't miss it for the world," I replied, attempting to sound nonchalant while inwardly battling a whirlwind of nerves.

 As he introduced me to his friends, I felt a wave of awkwardness wash over me, threatening to drown my confidence. Each handshake felt like an initiation, and every friendly smile came with an unspoken scrutiny. The conversation ebbed and flowed around me, but I struggled to catch the rhythm, feeling like an outsider peering in on a secret dance.

"Don't worry," Ethan whispered as he leaned closer, his breath warm against my ear. "You're doing great. Just be yourself."

"Right, because being myself is so easy," I quipped, my voice laced with sarcasm that surprised even me. But his laughter, a rich and genuine sound, lifted the tension. It was a reminder that I wasn't alone.

The night unfolded in delightful layers. We moved through the gallery, exploring each piece together, our discussions weaving a tapestry of thoughts and ideas. One piece, an enormous canvas splashed with vibrant blues and deep purples, caught my eye. It was chaotic yet beautiful, evoking the tempestuousness of the ocean. "It's like a storm you can't look away from," I mused, stepping closer to admire the texture.

Ethan nodded, his eyes reflecting the colors as if they had seeped into him. "It reminds me of those nights we'd sit by the beach, watching the waves crash. Beautiful and terrifying all at once."

I turned to him, surprise flickering in my chest. "You have a way with words. I'm almost jealous."

He chuckled, a soft, rumbling sound that sent a thrill through me. "Just a side effect of being an artist. We like to find the poetry in chaos."

As we wandered, he shared stories of his journey as a painter, his passion for capturing the world in colors and strokes, a fire igniting in his eyes. Each word he spoke was a brushstroke, painting a portrait of his dreams and struggles. I felt myself leaning in, enraptured by his enthusiasm, my heart beating a little faster with each story he told.

Just when I thought the night couldn't become more magical, we stumbled upon a particularly perplexing piece—a sculpture composed of twisted metal and shattered glass. It was both haunting and beautiful, embodying a chaos that made me feel understood. "What do you think?" Ethan asked, a challenge glinting in his gaze.

I examined it, feeling the weight of my thoughts. "It's like a reminder that beauty can come from destruction. Sometimes you have to break apart to become something new."

His expression shifted, a mixture of surprise and admiration dancing across his features. "That's deep. I love how you see things."

Before I could respond, he leaned in, lowering his voice conspiratorially. "Did you know this piece was made by a local artist who had a massive life change? They transformed their pain into art."

The warmth of his breath tickled my ear, a shiver of excitement rushing through me. "That's incredibly inspiring," I replied, feeling a connection bloom between us like the colors splashed across the canvases around us.

As the night deepened, laughter echoed, and the buzz of conversation enveloped us like a warm blanket. We continued to drift from one piece to another, our banter sharp and witty, reminiscent of characters in a romantic comedy. I found myself opening up more, sharing snippets of my life, while he countered with anecdotes of awkward gallery experiences and the occasional mishap with paint that left his clothes splattered in a rainbow of colors.

"Next time you visit my studio, be prepared for an adventure. It might end with you covered in paint," he teased, his eyes dancing with mischief.

"I'll hold you to that," I shot back, my heart racing at the thought. The connection we were forging felt electric, vibrant as the art surrounding us. I could sense the night shifting, a palpable tension lingering in the air between us—a spark waiting for the right moment to ignite.

As the evening wore on, I couldn't help but steal glances at Ethan, noticing the way his laughter lit up his features, the way he effortlessly engaged everyone around him. But it was when he turned to me, his expression softening, that I felt a warmth blossom in my chest—a blend of admiration and something deeper.

It was in those moments, amidst the chaos of the gallery, that I realized I didn't just want to be part of this world; I wanted to be part of his.

Ethan's laughter echoed in my ears, a warm and inviting sound that sliced through the ambient chatter of the gallery like a well-aimed dart. His playful jabs about the abstract painting—a chaotic explosion of colors that resembled a toddler's temper tantrum—had a way of disarming my nerves. "Look at that one," he said, gesturing dramatically. "I think I could replicate it using only the crumbs from my last pastry. You know, art for the people!"

I laughed, the tension in my chest easing as we stood side by side, our elbows almost touching. "Maybe we should submit it as a collaboration. I could provide the crumbs; you can work your magic with the colors. Together, we'll start a new art movement—'Post-Pastry Realism.'"

His eyes sparkled, and I felt that familiar flutter in my stomach. The gallery was a whirlwind of colors and personalities, but in that moment, it was just the two of us, cocooned in our own playful banter.

With each painting we studied, I found myself drawing closer to him, our shoulders brushing like magnets pulling us together. We drifted from one piece to another, discussing each artist's intent and the emotions they tried to evoke. "Art is like dating," I declared as we moved to a striking portrait of a woman with hauntingly beautiful eyes. "At first glance, you're drawn in, captivated by the surface. But the more you learn, the more layers you uncover—some pleasant, some... not so much."

Ethan chuckled, leaning in conspiratorially. "So, is this where I confess that I'm a complex masterpiece waiting for someone to appreciate my depths?"

"Or a glorified paint-splattered mess," I shot back, feigning seriousness. "It could go either way."

He threw his head back in laughter, and I couldn't help but smile, feeling like a sunbeam had slipped through the clouds. The world around us melted away, leaving only the colors of his laughter and the warmth of his gaze.

We moved to a corner where a striking installation—a twisted maze of mirrors—caught my eye. Each reflection played tricks on the viewer, distorting our features in an amusing, yet oddly profound manner. "This is how I feel at parties," I admitted, stepping closer to the installation. "Like I'm trying to find my way through a funhouse, but every turn leads me further away from the exit."

Ethan stepped beside me, peering into the mirrors. "You're not alone. I think everyone feels like that sometimes, especially in a sea of unfamiliar faces." He tilted his head, his expression turning playful. "But I have to admit, you look fantastic in that light. It's almost like it was made for you."

A warmth flooded my cheeks, a mixture of embarrassment and something sweeter. "You're just saying that to make me feel better."

"Guilty as charged," he said, feigning a dramatic confession. "But also, it's true. You light up this place more than any of these pieces."

Just then, a loud crash from across the gallery broke the moment. We turned to see a small group of patrons gathered around a fallen sculpture—an abstract piece that had somehow managed to topple over, sending shards of art and awkward laughter echoing through the room.

"See?" I nudged Ethan, grinning. "That's the kind of chaos I'm talking about. Even art has its bad days."

"True," he replied, amusement dancing in his eyes. "But I suspect the artist intended for it to evoke the fragility of existence. Or perhaps just an unfortunate encounter with gravity."

As the crowd buzzed with excitement, I caught sight of the gallery owner, a tall woman with a vibrant scarf wrapped around her neck, making her way toward us. "Ethan!" she called, her voice sharp and authoritative. "We're about to begin the artist talk. Can you round up some people?"

"Duty calls," he said, a hint of mischief in his tone. "Are you up for a little more chaos?"

"Lead the way," I said, my heart racing at the prospect of more time with him.

Ethan wove through the crowd with confidence, gesturing for people to gather. I followed closely, my heart still dancing in rhythm with the evening's energy. As the group settled in, the gallery owner introduced the featured artist, an enigmatic figure clad in all black, her short hair framing her face like a halo of rebellious creativity.

She spoke passionately about her work, her hands animatedly slicing through the air as she described the inspirations behind her pieces. "Art is about connection," she declared, her voice ringing clear. "It's a dialogue between the creator and the observer, and tonight, I want you all to join in. Ask questions, share your thoughts. Let's get messy together."

Ethan leaned toward me, his voice a conspiratorial whisper. "See? Just like life, it's about engagement and unpredictability."

I grinned, my pulse quickening as the artist invited questions from the crowd. For the next hour, we bounced ideas back and forth with the other guests, the energy crackling as we debated the meaning behind various artworks. Each question posed seemed to bring Ethan and me closer, our shoulders brushing more frequently, our laughter rising above the din.

"Tell me," he said at one point, tilting his head with that playful spark in his eyes, "if you could create a piece of art that captured this moment, what would it look like?"

I paused, imagining the vivid chaos around us—a riot of colors, laughter, and conversation. "A giant kaleidoscope," I said finally. "Every time someone steps in front of it, they see a different version of themselves, depending on their mood. Some days, it's a burst of joy; other days, a spiral of confusion."

"Now that's an idea worth exploring," he said, his tone serious yet playful, as if he were contemplating a new artistic venture.

As the night wore on, the gallery glowed with an ethereal light, the artworks illuminated like stars in a dark sky. I found myself lost in the beauty of it all, entranced by the way Ethan's energy complemented my own. Every shared glance, every laugh, felt like a step deeper into a connection that neither of us had anticipated.

Just as I thought we were heading toward a more intimate moment, the artist finished her talk and encouraged mingling again. Ethan's gaze caught mine, a flicker of something unspoken lingering in the air between us. But before we could delve deeper into whatever had sparked, a wave of people surged toward us, eager to engage with him.

"Ah, the joy of being popular," he joked, casting an apologetic glance my way. "I'll find you in a bit?"

"Of course," I replied, a twinge of disappointment threading through my voice, but I smiled, determined to savor the magic of the night.

As he mingled, I took a step back, allowing myself to breathe in the vibrant atmosphere. I watched him charm those around him, his charisma undeniable. But amidst the laughter and chatter, I felt a knot of uncertainty creeping back in. Would I ever truly fit into his world, or was I just a fleeting moment of color in the grand tapestry of his life?

And as the night stretched on, I couldn't shake the feeling that, somehow, this evening was just the beginning of a story far more complicated than either of us had bargained for.

Amid the whirl of conversation, I spotted Ethan across the room, his laughter ringing out like a favorite song. I couldn't help but smile, even as a part of me fought to shake off the lingering doubts that had clung to me all night. His magnetic energy drew people in, and I felt like a moth orbiting a brilliant flame, captivated and terrified all at once.

"Excuse me," I muttered to the group I had gravitated toward, stepping away to get a better view. The sounds of the gallery faded as I approached Ethan, who was animatedly discussing art with an older couple. They seemed enchanted, leaning in as he animatedly described one piece—a bold, chaotic sculpture that appeared to be half-constructed, like a puzzle missing its last few pieces.

"You have to see it from this angle," Ethan insisted, gesturing dramatically. "It's like the artist wanted you to question what's real and what's not. It's the embodiment of indecision!"

The couple nodded, clearly enthralled. I lingered, waiting for a lull in the conversation, eager to rejoin the laughter that felt so vibrant and alive when we were together. Just then, a gust of air swept through the gallery as the main doors swung open, revealing a group of latecomers who entered like a flock of excited birds, chirping and flapping their arms, eager to join the party.

In the flurry of movement, I caught a glimpse of Ethan's gaze drifting toward me, that same warm spark igniting between us. He smiled, and the rest of the world faded into a blur. I felt a surge of energy, a swell of hope that perhaps tonight would mark the turning point I had been longing for.

"Hey there, artistic maven!" he exclaimed, finally breaking away from his conversation as the couple wandered toward the refreshments. "What did I miss? Did someone try to take over my throne as the gallery's favorite?"

"Only the usual suspects," I teased, flicking my hair back in mock defiance. "But I've declared you the reigning champion of charming art enthusiasts. Your title remains secure."

"Ah, I knew it. I'll need a crown." He feigned a serious look, brushing his fingers through his hair. "How about a beret? It's more artistic, right?"

I burst into laughter, and his smile widened, that spark of connection flaring brighter. "Okay, but only if it's a really flamboyant one. You've got to fully commit to the artist persona."

"Deal." He leaned closer, his voice lowering conspiratorially. "But if you find a beret with sequins, I might just have to wear it to every event from here on out."

"Just remember, you can't blame me when people start to avoid you out of sheer jealousy."

As we bantered, a familiar figure approached—a tall, impeccably dressed man with striking silver hair and an air of confidence that seemed to draw people toward him like moths to a flame. It was Victor, the gallery owner, a man who could command attention just by stepping into a room. "Ethan, my boy!" he boomed, his voice rich and warm. "You've outdone yourself with the energy tonight. And you!" He turned to me, his eyes bright. "Who is this lovely muse gracing us with her presence?"

"Just someone who's trying to keep up with the artist," Ethan replied, his gaze darting to mine, a hint of mischief in his eyes.

Victor raised an eyebrow, clearly amused. "Well, I hope she's taking notes, then. You're quite the conversationalist."

"Only when I'm in the presence of greatness," I chimed in, finding my confidence buoyed by their banter.

"Ah, flattery will get you everywhere," Victor replied, a knowing smile playing on his lips. "But remember, it takes more than charm to survive in this world. You must be prepared for the unexpected."

"Like a surprise abstract sculpture crashing to the floor?" Ethan quipped, gesturing playfully behind him.

"Exactly! Or late arrivals stealing your spotlight!" Victor laughed, and just as I was about to respond, a commotion erupted on the other side of the room.

A figure stepped into the gallery, their presence palpable and electrifying. She wore a flowing black gown, her hair cascading like a waterfall of midnight. The moment she entered, conversation paused, and all eyes turned toward her, drawn in by an unseen magnetism. I couldn't help but feel a shiver of recognition—she was a local artist known for her striking work and enigmatic personality. Her name escaped me, but the energy in the room shifted, the air thick with anticipation.

Ethan straightened, glancing at her, and for a fleeting moment, a flicker of something darker crossed his face—was it apprehension? Uncertainty? I couldn't tell. "Is that..." he started, but Victor interrupted.

"Yes, it is. She's been a bit of a recluse lately," he said, his voice laced with intrigue. "Rumor has it she's been working on something new. Something... groundbreaking."

Ethan's gaze remained fixed on her, a tension building between us. "She's incredible, but..." His voice trailed off, as if he were wrestling with thoughts he didn't want to voice.

As she strode toward us, the crowd parted like the sea, a path forming in her wake. I felt an inexplicable pull to her, a mix of curiosity and concern. What was she here to unveil? What impact would she have on this night, on Ethan?

"Ethan!" she called, her voice melodic yet firm, drawing nearer with each step. The world around me faded, the colors of the gallery dimming as I focused on the space between them.

"I need to speak with you," she continued, her gaze unwavering, penetrating.

My heart raced, a storm of emotions churning within me. Who was this woman, and what did she want? In that moment, I felt the first stirrings of jealousy mixed with a strong urge to step between them. To protect whatever fragile connection had begun to weave itself between Ethan and me.

"Excuse me," I murmured to Victor, who raised an eyebrow in surprise. I stepped back, wanting to give them space but feeling an undeniable pull to stay close. This wasn't just another gallery opening; something significant was unfolding, and I could sense the electric charge in the air, the weight of unspoken words and unresolved tension.

As I turned to watch, the moment stretched like a taut string, ready to snap. Ethan's expression was unreadable, caught between surprise and a flicker of something darker. I couldn't shake the feeling that tonight was about to shift in ways none of us could have anticipated.

The air hummed with possibility, tension crackling like static electricity before a storm. And as I stood there, caught between two worlds, I couldn't help but wonder: was this the beginning of a new chapter, or would it unravel everything we had just begun to build?

Chapter 4: The Revelation

Rain drummed steadily against the windowpanes, the sound a soothing backdrop as I sat cross-legged on the floor of Ethan's apartment, surrounded by a disarray of textbooks and scattered notes. The air was heavy with the scent of brewed coffee and the faint hint of cinnamon, courtesy of a candle flickering on the small table nearby. I often wondered if his apartment was a reflection of him—a little chaotic, but undeniably warm and inviting. It felt safe here, like a sanctuary tucked away from the world's incessant noise, where I could lose myself in the comfort of our shared silences.

Ethan was sprawled out on the couch, laptop balanced precariously on his knees, a frown etched on his forehead as he typed. He had a way of looking intensely focused, his brow furrowing slightly as if he were solving the world's most pressing problems. I admired him from my corner, his dark hair tousled just so, and his blue eyes darting back and forth across the screen, illuminated by the soft glow of the laptop. It made me think of summer skies and clear waters, the kind of blue that promised adventure, yet could also swirl into a storm without warning.

The rain outside picked up, each drop a reminder of how isolated I often felt. It stirred something inside me, a bubbling urge to break free from the careful layers I'd wrapped around my heart. "Do you ever feel... lonely?" I blurted out, surprising even myself with the question. It hung in the air, a vulnerable echo amidst the patter of rain.

He glanced up, a shadow of surprise flitting across his features, and set the laptop aside. "Lonely? All the time," he admitted, his voice steady but softened by sincerity. "It's like everyone around me is doing their thing, and I'm just... floating."

My heart raced at his honesty, a gentle thrill igniting in my chest. "Really? You seem so put together. I always thought you had it all figured out."

Ethan chuckled softly, a rich sound that filled the room, the tension of my confession melting away. "Believe me, I'm a mess. It's all a facade. I just learned to wear a mask that keeps the chaos at bay." He leaned forward, resting his elbows on his knees, his gaze penetrating and earnest. "What about you? You've always been so... composed."

I shook my head, my cheeks warming with the weight of my admission. "Composed? More like petrified. I don't know how to connect with people. Every time I try, it feels like I'm speaking a different language." The floodgates of my vulnerability swung wide open, and I found myself sharing the deep-rooted insecurities that had clung to me for years—the awkwardness at social gatherings, the crippling fear of rejection, and the shadows of past failures that haunted me like specters.

Ethan listened, his expression shifting from curiosity to empathy. "You know, I was the same way in high school. I felt like I had to fit into this mold—be the smart kid, the athlete, the guy who had it all together. But inside, I was terrified of being found out." He leaned back, arms crossed, his smile tinged with a hint of sadness. "It's exhausting pretending to be someone you're not."

I could feel the weight of his words settle between us, a shared understanding binding our hearts in an unexpected way. The walls I had so carefully built around my insecurities began to crumble, revealing a vulnerability I hadn't dared show anyone. "How do you deal with it?" I asked softly, seeking a thread of hope in his experience.

He paused, glancing toward the window, where the rain fell in sheets, blurring the world outside. "I guess I just try to embrace the mess. It's not easy, and some days, I fail spectacularly. But I remind myself that everyone has their struggles, even the ones who seem to have it all figured out."

"Like you?" I teased, injecting a playful lilt into my tone, desperate to shift the mood away from the weighty topic.

"Touché," he replied, smirking back at me, the twinkle in his eye returning. "I suppose I'm more of a masterpiece in progress."

Our laughter mingled, a harmonious melody against the rain's relentless percussion. I found comfort in this exchange, a shared moment of authenticity that felt like a new beginning. It was liberating to connect in this way, peeling back the layers that had hidden my true self.

"I think I'm falling for you," I said before I could stop myself, the words tumbling out, unfiltered and raw. The room fell silent, the air thickening with the weight of my confession. My heart raced as I watched his expression shift, surprise flickering across his face, followed by an undeniable warmth in his gaze.

He studied me for a moment, his smile growing softer, more genuine. "You're not the only one," he admitted, his voice low and intimate. The atmosphere between us charged, crackling like static, and I could feel the undeniable pull of our connection intensify.

As the rain continued its steady symphony outside, I realized that perhaps this wasn't just a moment of vulnerability but the beginning of something beautiful. Two souls, both imperfect, clinging to the hope of understanding and acceptance, ready to face the uncertainties of life together. And as Ethan's eyes locked onto mine, I knew that whatever storms lay ahead, I was ready to embrace them—especially if he was by my side.

The rain drizzled on, its gentle cadence a comforting backdrop as Ethan and I sat on the floor, the remnants of our earlier conversation still lingering in the air. It was like we had stepped into an alternate universe, one where the weight of our insecurities had lifted, leaving behind only the electric current of connection. I could hardly believe how effortlessly we had delved into the depths of our vulnerabilities, as if sharing our flaws was an art form we were both just beginning to master.

As the light faded outside, casting a warm glow through the window, Ethan reached for a mug, the steam curling like whispers of secrets around us. "Do you believe in fate?" he asked, taking a sip, his eyes glinting with mischief. "Because I have this theory that the universe conspires to throw us together with the people we need most."

I raised an eyebrow, a playful grin creeping across my face. "Is that your romantic side talking, or is it just the caffeine kicking in?"

"Maybe a bit of both," he replied, chuckling. "But seriously, it feels like we just clicked, you know? Like two puzzle pieces that somehow fit together, even if we both have a few edges that are a bit rough around the corners."

The warmth in his gaze ignited something in me, a blend of laughter and something deeper that settled in my chest. "Or maybe we're just two quirky misfits, trying to figure out how to play nice in a world that keeps tossing us around."

"Quirky misfits, huh?" He grinned, and the corner of his mouth quirked upward in that way that made my heart race. "I like that. Sounds like a bestseller waiting to happen."

We exchanged light-hearted banter, the room suffused with an easy intimacy, but beneath the laughter, I could feel the tension of something unspoken lingering just out of reach. As the rain continued its serenade, I found myself contemplating the shift in our dynamic. Ethan and I were no longer just acquaintances sharing study sessions; we were kindred spirits, navigating the maze of life together.

But the deeper connection we'd forged also brought with it an unexpected wave of apprehension. I couldn't shake the feeling that I was standing at the edge of a cliff, the ground beneath me both solid and treacherous. What if I was falling for him? What if this blossoming relationship was destined to crash and burn? I could almost hear the echoes of past failures whispering in my ear, urging me to tread carefully.

As I wrestled with my thoughts, Ethan's laughter broke through my internal turmoil. "You look like you just solved a Rubik's Cube in record time. What's going on in that brilliant head of yours?"

I exhaled, the tension in my shoulders easing a fraction. "Just trying to navigate the emotional minefield I seem to have stumbled into," I admitted, my voice a little shaky. "I mean, it's one thing to feel a connection, but it's another to acknowledge that I'm falling for you."

His expression shifted, the playful glint in his eye morphing into something serious, almost tender. "And what if I told you I'm falling for you too?" The words hung in the air, heavy with promise and possibility.

My heart stumbled over itself, the fluttering sensation both exhilarating and terrifying. "Really? You're not just saying that to make me feel better, are you?" I shot back, half-joking, half-anxious.

"No, I'm serious," he replied, his gaze unwavering. "This isn't just about shared awkwardness; it's about how easy it is to be around you. I feel like I can let my guard down, and that's rare for me."

I couldn't help the smile that spread across my face. "So, we're officially a couple of quirky misfits on the same emotional rollercoaster?"

"Exactly," he laughed, a rich sound that echoed off the walls. "And just think about all the therapy bills we'll save by doing this together."

The tension that had been building began to dissolve, replaced by an infectious energy that surged between us. I felt a lightness, as if the very air in the room sparkled with newfound possibility. "Well, if we're doing this, we might as well embrace the chaos, right?"

"Absolutely. And if we crash and burn, we'll do it with style," he said, his eyes glinting with mischief. "Besides, what's life without a little adventure?"

Just then, a loud clap of thunder rumbled outside, startling us both. I burst into laughter, and Ethan joined in, our shared joy echoing through the apartment. "See? Even the universe approves of our quirky misfit romance," he said, his grin infectious.

The atmosphere shifted again, a blend of lightheartedness and an unspoken understanding wrapping around us like a cozy blanket. The rain continued to pour, each drop a reminder of the world outside, but here, in this moment, it was just the two of us, dancing to the rhythm of our own story.

As the evening wore on, we delved deeper into conversation, sharing dreams and aspirations that had once felt too vulnerable to voice. Ethan spoke of his desire to travel the world, to seek out the beauty in places untamed and unspoiled, while I confessed my longing to write, to create stories that would resonate with others in the way our connection had resonated with me.

With every word shared, the invisible bond between us strengthened, weaving a tapestry of shared dreams and mutual understanding. I felt like a flower unfurling in the sunlight, its petals reaching out to embrace the warmth, and I knew I had found something rare and precious.

But just as I was ready to lose myself entirely in this moment, a small voice in the back of my mind whispered warnings. What if I opened my heart too wide, only for it to shatter again? I glanced at Ethan, caught in a soft laugh, the light playing in his eyes, and I realized that perhaps, just perhaps, I could allow myself to trust this burgeoning connection. After all, we were two flawed souls navigating the same fears, and maybe it was time to stop holding back and start embracing the beautiful mess of life together.

The evening unfolded like a scene from a film, where two characters found themselves caught in a moment of serendipity, illuminated by the soft glow of lamplight and the rhythmic drumming of rain against the windows. Laughter bubbled between Ethan and me, flowing as freely as the coffee that filled our mugs. The easy banter had morphed into something deeper, a shared sanctuary where our insecurities felt less daunting.

I watched him as he animatedly recounted a story about a disastrous attempt at a cooking class that ended with him accidentally setting off the fire alarm. "I swear the chef was glaring at me like I had committed a culinary crime," he said, his eyes sparkling with mischief. "He was more dramatic than a soap opera villain."

"Were you wearing a beret and a striped shirt too?" I shot back, feigning a serious tone. "Because that sounds like a classic 'chef has had enough' moment."

Ethan threw his head back in laughter, the sound warm and inviting. "I wish! But I looked more like a flustered raccoon trying to figure out how to use a spatula. Honestly, it was a disaster, but at least I didn't burn down the place."

"Yet," I teased, nudging him playfully. "Give it time. I can see a whole series of Ethan the Culinary Catastrophe in your future."

He leaned closer, his expression shifting from playful to earnest. "You know, it's those little moments of failure that make life interesting. If everything went according to plan, we'd have no stories to tell."

There was a truth in his words, a resonant chord that struck deep within me. I thought about my own experiences, the missteps that had shaped me. "Maybe that's what we need—more missteps and less pressure to be perfect."

"Agreed. Here's to gloriously imperfect adventures," he declared, raising his mug in a mock toast. I clinked my cup against his, the sound echoing softly in the room.

The air grew heavier, thick with unsaid words and lingering glances that seemed to dance between us like sparks in the night. My heart raced, a steady drumbeat against my ribs, and the warmth of our connection wrapped around me like a soft blanket. I could sense the shift, the palpable tension that buzzed in the air as our laughter faded into a comfortable silence.

"What are you thinking about?" Ethan asked, tilting his head slightly, his eyes searching mine with an intensity that made my breath hitch.

I hesitated, the weight of vulnerability pressing down on me. "I was just thinking about how easy it is to talk to you, how different it feels from... well, from everything else."

He nodded, his gaze unwavering. "It's refreshing, isn't it? No pretenses, just us being... us."

I swallowed hard, the moment hanging delicately between us. "What if we kept being us, like... beyond the study sessions? I mean, what if we went on an actual date?"

Ethan's eyes widened in surprise, and for a heartbeat, I feared I had misread the signals. But then, a slow smile spread across his face, lighting up his features. "You mean like a proper date? With real clothes and everything?"

"Absolutely. No aprons or fire alarms this time," I replied, my heart fluttering as hope ignited in my chest.

"Count me in," he said, leaning back with a satisfied grin. "I'll even dress up if that's what it takes. I'm willing to risk it all for a chance at romance."

"Now you're just being dramatic," I laughed, though I felt a thrill at the thought of venturing into this new territory with him.

The rain continued its steady patter, but I hardly noticed it anymore. Instead, my thoughts spun around the idea of our first date—what it would be like to step beyond the comfortable confines of friendship and into the exhilarating unknown. The possibilities felt endless, tinged with excitement and just a hint of apprehension.

As the evening wore on, we swapped stories of our childhoods, revealing bits of ourselves that had long been tucked away. Ethan spoke of summers spent exploring his grandfather's farm, while I reminisced about the books that had filled my childhood with magic and wonder. The conversation flowed effortlessly, a dance of words that felt both thrilling and familiar.

But as the clock ticked toward midnight, an unsettling thought crept into my mind. I couldn't shake the feeling that something was lurking just beyond the periphery of our perfect little bubble, a storm brewing on the horizon that could threaten to upend everything we had started to build.

Just as I was about to voice my concerns, Ethan's phone buzzed on the coffee table, cutting through the delicate atmosphere. He glanced at the screen, and the smile that had lit up his face faltered. "It's my sister," he said, his brow furrowing. "She's been dealing with some stuff lately."

I nodded, a lump forming in my throat as I sensed the shift in his mood. "Is everything okay?"

He sighed, running a hand through his hair. "I'm not sure. She hasn't said much, but when she does reach out, it's usually not good."

The air thickened with unspoken worries, and I wanted to reach out, to comfort him, but the distance of impending trouble loomed large. "Do you want to take it?"

He hesitated, glancing between the phone and me. "Yeah, I should. But I don't want to ruin our moment."

I reached for his hand, squeezing it gently. "Family first, Ethan. We can pick up right where we left off."

He nodded, though I could see the worry etched on his features as he answered the call. "Hey, what's up?" His voice shifted, becoming more serious, the lightness from moments before slipping away.

I leaned back, trying to give him space, yet my heart raced as I watched him. The way his expression changed, the tension in his shoulders—it was as if the world outside our cozy sanctuary was intruding, threatening to pull him away from me.

"Yeah, I'm here. What happened?" he said, his tone sharp. My breath caught, a knot of anxiety forming in my stomach as I strained to hear the muffled conversation.

I caught snippets of words—"hospital," "accident," and "urgent." Each one felt like a dagger to my chest, the looming reality that something was terribly wrong sinking in. My mind raced with questions, a whirlwind of fear and uncertainty.

As Ethan's face paled, I could see the familiar walls he had built begin to rise, a protective barrier shielding him from the vulnerability we had just shared. It felt like a dam breaking, threatening to wash away all we had built in this space of openness.

When he finally hung up, his face was a mix of confusion and fear. "I have to go. My sister—she was in an accident. I don't know the details, but I need to be there."

The moment felt fragile, teetering on the edge of something monumental. I opened my mouth, ready to offer comfort, to assure him that he wasn't alone, but the words lodged in my throat.

Ethan stood, a whirlwind of energy and urgency. "I'll call you as soon as I can," he promised, though his eyes were already distant, focused on something beyond our evening.

"Ethan, wait!" I called, reaching out as he grabbed his jacket, the warmth of our connection fading in the face of uncertainty.

But he was already slipping away, the weight of the world pulling him from our fragile bubble of joy. As he stepped into the rain-soaked night, I was left standing in the doorway, the echo of his absence ringing louder than the storm outside.

A chill crept into the air, and I knew that everything had changed in an instant, the serene comfort we had built now shattered by the unexpected chaos of life. As the rain poured down, I couldn't shake the feeling that the storm was only just beginning.

Chapter 5: The Misunderstanding

Ethan and I had carved out our own little universe. It was one where coffee-scented mornings merged seamlessly with evenings painted in the hues of sunset, where laughter danced through the air like the fireflies we used to chase in childhood. The soft glow of the lamp in my small living room had become our sanctuary, the pages of my scattered project notebooks strewn around like the memories we were crafting together. I reveled in this newfound companionship, where each stolen glance felt like a promise and every brush of his hand against mine set off delightful sparks.

But that serenity shattered the moment Lila walked through my door, her presence crashing into our bubble with all the subtlety of a freight train. One moment, we were tangled in a discussion about my latest project, and the next, she was standing there, looking like she had just stepped off a fashion runway. She radiated effortless elegance, a reminder of everything I could never be. I could feel my stomach knotting, my heart racing, as the warmth between Ethan and me felt suddenly precarious.

"Ethan!" she chirped, her voice ringing out like a bell, summoning all the memories I wished I could forget. "I thought you'd be at the bar with the guys!"

He turned, surprise flickering across his face before settling into a soft, easy smile that sent a wave of resentment crashing over me. "Hey, Lila. I didn't think you'd come by."

The conversation flowed between them like a gentle stream, their laughter echoing in my ears as I stood frozen in the doorway. My heart thudded ominously, each beat reverberating with jealousy and insecurity. I wanted to scream, to shove her out the door, but instead, I felt the blood drain from my face as I quietly retreated into the safety of the bedroom, shutting the door behind me with a deliberate click.

In the dim light, I could hear them, their voices muffled but still piercing through my solitude. I pressed my forehead against the cool surface of the door, trying to tune out the sound of her laughter. What was she doing here? My mind spun with wild accusations, painting scenarios where he was still tangled up in his past, where Lila was the one he really wanted.

As the minutes stretched into an eternity, I felt my emotions morph into something darker, something that began to consume me. With each shared joke, each familiar inflection in his voice, I could almost see the tender way he used to look at her, and I hated it. My own vulnerability felt like a weight pressing down on my chest, stifling any rational thought.

I finally emerged from my self-imposed exile, the hallway stretching before me like a chasm. I found Ethan in the kitchen, his back to me as he and Lila exchanged playful banter, her hand brushing against his arm as she leaned in closer. I felt like an intruder in my own home, an unwanted shadow flickering at the edge of their light.

"Ethan," I said, the word catching in my throat as I approached.

He turned, his expression shifting to one of surprise mixed with concern. "Hey, everything okay?"

I swallowed hard, the weight of the unspoken emotions pulling me down. "Can we talk?"

His brow furrowed, and I knew I was asking for something monumental, a crack in the fragile facade we had built. Lila's laughter faded into silence as she glanced between us, her eyes narrowed in curiosity.

"Of course," he replied, his voice steady despite the tremor in my heart. "Lila, can we take a rain check?"

She smiled, that infuriatingly perfect smile that made me want to hurl something. "Sure, I'll just... be in the other room."

As she sauntered away, I braced myself for what was about to unfold.

Once the door clicked shut behind her, I felt an involuntary shiver course through me, nerves thrumming like a live wire. "I overheard you two," I started, my voice quivering with raw emotion. "You looked... happy."

Ethan's expression shifted, confusion etching his features. "What? Is this about Lila?"

A swell of anger and hurt rushed to the surface, and before I could stop myself, the words tumbled out like an avalanche. "I don't understand why she's here, Ethan. Why now? It feels like I'm competing with a ghost, and I can't... I can't do that."

He stepped closer, concern in his eyes. "You're not competing with anyone, Celeste. I care about you. Lila's just—"

"Just what? Your ex-girlfriend? The one who broke your heart?" I interrupted, my voice rising in pitch. "It's easy for you to say that, but I can't help feeling like I'm just a consolation prize. You were happy with her once."

"Celeste," he said, a note of desperation creeping into his tone. "You have to trust me. Lila and I are done. She just showed up out of nowhere. I was trying to be polite."

I crossed my arms defensively, refusing to look at him, the swell of emotion making my eyes sting. "You could've just told her to leave. Instead, you let her charm you back into your past."

A tense silence filled the space between us, thick enough to cut. I could see the conflict flickering in his eyes, a battle of understanding and frustration. "You're pushing me away," he finally said, his voice low. "I don't want to fight. I want to be with you."

"But you don't even know what you want," I shot back, the hurt spilling over into bitterness. "What if you just want to find comfort in the familiar?"

With that, I turned away, retreating back into my chaotic thoughts as the air between us crackled with unresolved tension. In that moment, I felt as if I were standing on the precipice of everything we had built, and I was terrified I might just tip over the edge.

The days that followed felt like I was moving through a fog, each step heavier than the last. It was as if the air had thickened around me, wrapping my heart in layers of doubt and regret. I drifted through my routines, exchanging pleasantries with friends and family, my mind a constant whirlpool of thoughts. Ethan was like a shadow, always just out of reach, the memory of our last confrontation lingering like an unwanted echo. My heart ached for his laughter, the warmth of his presence, yet I found myself recoiling from the possibility of facing him again.

We avoided each other, a silence filling the spaces where our laughter once danced. I would catch glimpses of him in the hall, his face set in concentration as he worked on his own projects. The sight would send a pang through my chest, a sharp reminder of what I had so foolishly thrown away. Each time I saw him, I felt the weight of my own decisions. How had I allowed jealousy to twist my feelings into something so ugly?

One evening, while I was buried in a particularly grueling assignment, the doorbell rang, sending a jolt of anxiety through me. I hesitated, glancing at the clock. It was late, too late for anyone but the mailman or a lost soul in need of directions. When I opened the door, I was met not with a stranger but with the unmistakable figure of Ethan, his hands shoved deep in his pockets, his expression caught between resolve and uncertainty.

"Celeste," he began, his voice a mixture of hope and trepidation, as if he were stepping onto a tightrope stretched above a chasm. "Can we talk?"

I almost closed the door again, the impulse to hide overwhelming, but I fought it back. Instead, I stepped aside, letting him enter. The moment he crossed the threshold, the atmosphere shifted, charged with unspoken words and unresolved tension. The familiar scent of his cologne enveloped me, and I almost felt dizzy from the longing that surged through me.

"I miss you," he said, his voice low, the confession hanging in the air between us. "I don't know how to fix this, but I want to try."

I opened my mouth, ready to spill the doubts I had been harboring, the insecurities that had kept me from him. But instead, silence poured from my lips. What could I say? That I felt unworthy of his affection? That every time I thought of him and Lila together, it twisted like a knife in my gut?

He must have seen the storm brewing in my eyes because he stepped closer, the warmth of his body radiating like sunlight breaking through a dark cloud. "I care about you, Celeste. I wish you could see that."

"Care doesn't erase the past, Ethan," I replied, bitterness creeping into my tone. "You and Lila... there was something there once, and I can't help but wonder if I'm just a placeholder."

"Do you really believe that?" he asked, a mix of disbelief and pain in his eyes. "I'm not with Lila. I'm here, with you. I want to be here with you."

"But you don't have to—" I started, but he cut me off, frustration coloring his features.

"I want to. I want to know you. Not just the surface stuff, but everything. You're not just someone to fill the gap. You're... you. And I want that."

His earnestness was like a balm to my wounded heart, but I still felt the prick of fear at the edges of my resolve. "Then why does it feel like every time I turn around, you're still tangled up in her shadow?"

"Because you're letting her shadow you," he shot back, passion igniting his words. "You're the one who keeps pushing me away, and I don't understand why."

For a heartbeat, we were suspended in a moment that felt both fragile and electric, the weight of our emotions teetering on the brink of revelation. I wanted to reach out, to bridge the distance between us, but my fear clung to me like a second skin.

"You think it's easy for me?" I finally said, frustration lacing my voice. "Every time I see you two together, it feels like I'm fighting a losing battle. I'm not sure I can measure up."

He shook his head, his eyes intense. "This isn't about measuring up. It's about being real. About letting each other in, flaws and all."

I took a deep breath, my resolve wavering. "You have to understand. It's hard for me to trust. After everything, I've built these walls to protect myself."

"I get that," he replied, his voice softening. "But those walls will only keep you trapped. I can't promise I'll never hurt you, but I can promise I'll always be honest with you. I want to understand your fears. I want to be there for you."

His words were like a lifeline, tugging at the part of me that yearned to let go of the fears that had held me captive for so long. I wanted to believe him, to let him in, but the scars from my past whispered caution into my ear.

Before I could speak, he took a step closer, closing the distance between us, his eyes locked onto mine. "Celeste, if you want to walk away, I won't stop you. But know that I'm not going anywhere. I'm here, whether you like it or not."

His determination swept through me, stirring emotions I had buried beneath layers of uncertainty. My heart raced as I fought against the desire to retreat, to shield myself from potential pain. Instead, I leaned into that uncomfortable space, taking a chance on the promise of what could be.

"I don't want to walk away," I finally confessed, my voice barely above a whisper. "I want to figure this out. Together."

His relief was palpable, a wave of warmth flooding the space between us. "Together," he echoed, a smile breaking through the tension that had surrounded us.

And in that moment, with everything hanging in the balance, the walls I had built began to crack, the first glimmers of hope breaking through the fog of misunderstanding that had clouded our hearts. We were standing on the brink of something new, and for the first time in days, I felt a flicker of possibility lighting the way forward.

The moment we agreed to take this leap, to figure things out together, a cautious relief washed over me. It was as if the storm clouds that had shadowed my heart began to dissipate, revealing the tentative sun that had been hiding behind them. I wanted to believe in Ethan, in us, but the echoes of our past misunderstandings lingered like a stubborn chill. I needed to show him that I was more than just my insecurities, that I could be strong enough to embrace the unknown.

"Okay, so where do we go from here?" I asked, attempting to inject a semblance of normalcy into the swirling emotions around us. "Do we, like, sit down with a PowerPoint presentation of our feelings?"

Ethan laughed, the sound sending delightful shivers down my spine. "PowerPoints? Not my style. But how about we start with a coffee? It's a good icebreaker."

"Ah, yes, caffeine—the universal remedy for existential crises." I smirked, pushing aside the remnants of my doubt. "I'll brew a pot, and we can pretend we're discussing world domination over lattes."

We moved to the kitchen, and I set about preparing the coffee while Ethan leaned against the counter, watching me with that familiar mix of admiration and bemusement. It was reassuring, his presence grounding me as I poured the water and scooped the fragrant grounds into the filter. The comforting scent filled the space, curling around us like an embrace.

"You know," Ethan said, a mischievous glint in his eye, "I think we might just make a fantastic team—if only to ensure our coffee doesn't explode."

I looked over my shoulder, raising an eyebrow. "You don't think I can handle my caffeine, do you?"

"Let's just say I have a vivid imagination," he teased, crossing his arms with that signature playful smirk that made my heart flutter. "Remember the last time you tried to make spaghetti? I'm just looking out for our kitchen's well-being."

"Hey, that was a cooking experiment! Besides, I thought we agreed to forget that incident," I shot back, a smile breaking through my lingering tension. "I was trying to create an avant-garde dish."

"And you succeeded! It was the first time I'd ever seen noodles actually try to escape their fate," he laughed, and the sound was like music, washing away the remnants of our previous conflict.

With the coffee brewing, the atmosphere shifted into a lighter, more playful zone. I took a moment to watch him, the way his eyes sparkled when he laughed, how effortlessly he filled the space around him with warmth. My heart softened. This was the Ethan I knew, the one who made every moment feel alive.

As I poured two steaming mugs, I turned to him, feeling a surge of gratitude. "Thank you for being patient with me. I know I can be... a bit much sometimes."

"You're not 'a bit much,'" he countered gently, taking a sip of his coffee. "You're passionate, and that's one of the things I admire about you. Just don't forget that I'm here, no matter how chaotic it gets."

We settled onto the couch, the coffee warming our hands as we settled into a more comfortable rhythm. For a while, we exchanged light banter and shared stories about our childhoods—his embarrassing dance recitals and my unfortunate bowl haircut phase. Laughter came easily, and it felt as if we were weaving back together the threads of our relationship, each shared memory stitching us closer.

But just as I began to relax, my phone buzzed on the coffee table, pulling me from the moment. I glanced at the screen, and my stomach dropped. A text from Lila.

"Hey, just wanted to check in. I'm back in town and would love to catch up with you and Ethan."

I felt my heart race, anxiety flooding my system. The sweetness of the moment with Ethan evaporated as the message loomed over me, casting a shadow I couldn't shake. "Um, Ethan," I said, my voice trembling slightly. "It's Lila. She's back."

His expression shifted, tension threading through the warmth of our earlier exchange. "What does she want?"

"Just to catch up, apparently," I replied, trying to keep my voice steady. "She's back in town and wants to see us."

He ran a hand through his hair, a gesture that indicated his frustration. "Why now? After everything that happened?"

I set my coffee down, a new wave of unease washing over me. "I don't know. But you need to tell her how you feel. You can't just let her waltz back into your life. Not after everything."

Ethan sighed, his brow furrowing as he wrestled with his emotions. "I thought we were moving past this. I don't want her to come between us again."

"Neither do I!" I shot back, the sharpness in my voice surprising even me. "But if you don't set boundaries, it'll be like she's still a part of our lives. You need to be clear about where you stand."

He leaned back, crossing his arms, the frustration emanating from him like a storm cloud ready to burst. "You're right. I just—she has this way of pushing all the right buttons, and it makes it hard to think straight."

The coffee table suddenly felt like a battlefield, both of us navigating a landscape fraught with landmines of unspoken fears and insecurities. I wanted to tell him that it was okay, that I was ready to stand by his side through this chaos, but my own anxiety crept back in. The worry gnawed at me, a persistent whisper that I was unworthy of this kind of connection.

"Let's not go back there," I murmured, frustration slipping into my tone again. "I can't handle another round of misunderstandings. It's exhausting."

"I get it. Trust me, I do," he replied, his voice softening, but the tension still lingered in the air. "But if she reaches out, I need to know how you feel about it. I don't want to keep anything from you."

A silence enveloped us, heavy with uncertainty, and I found myself weighing my words carefully. "I want to support you, Ethan. But I can't shake the feeling that she's trying to drive a wedge between us. Maybe she's not done with you."

His expression hardened slightly, and I could see the gears turning in his mind. "She won't come between us if we don't let her. But I need to make that clear."

The thought of him confronting her sent a mix of apprehension and resolve through me. "What are you going to say?"

"I'll tell her that I'm with you now," he replied, his voice steadying. "That I don't want her to intrude into our lives."

"Good," I said, feeling a flicker of hope. "That's what you need to do."

Just then, a sudden crash outside jolted us both from our thoughts, the sound echoing like a warning bell. I shot a glance at the window, my heart racing.

"What was that?" I asked, my pulse quickening.

Ethan stood up, moving towards the door, a protective instinct flaring in his eyes. "I'll check it out."

"Wait, let me come with you!" I protested, but he waved me off, already opening the door.

As he stepped outside, the evening air wrapped around him, shadowed and uncertain. I watched from the threshold, a knot forming in my stomach.

"Ethan?" I called out, my voice trembling.

He turned back, just as a figure emerged from the darkness, a familiar silhouette that sent a chill coursing through me. I squinted into the night, recognition crashing over me like a wave.

It was Lila, standing there with an enigmatic smile, her presence casting a long shadow over everything we had just built.

"Ethan, I was hoping we could talk."

The words hung in the air like a weight, and I felt my heart plunge. Suddenly, the fragile peace we had found felt precarious, teetering on the edge of chaos, and I couldn't shake the feeling that everything was about to unravel.

Chapter 6: The Distance

The rain fell in soft sheets, blurring the edges of the world outside my window as I sat hunched over my desk, a fortress of textbooks and highlighters built to shield me from the emotional storm brewing within. The scent of damp earth and crisp leaves wafted in, a reminder of the autumn that had crept up without my noticing. The trees outside were caught in a dance, their leaves swirling in a chaotic ballet, mirroring the tumult inside me. I flicked through the pages of my notes, my mind wandering despite the words that leapt off the page, vibrant and full of promise. Each formula I memorized was a distraction, a bandage for the gaping wound in my heart.

Ethan had always been my tether to reality, the gentle pull that grounded me when my head spun with uncertainty. But after that fight, the one that had shattered our unspoken understanding, the distance between us stretched like an endless chasm. I replayed our last heated words, each syllable echoing like a distant thunderclap, and every time I did, I felt the ache of regret tighten its grip on my chest. He had tried to reach me, text after text lighting up my phone like a beacon, but I had stifled that flicker of hope, burying it beneath layers of stubborn pride.

The campus had transformed into a kaleidoscope of colors, but I saw it through a muted lens. Friends gathered under the oak trees, laughter mingling with the sweet scent of cinnamon from the nearby café. I watched them from a distance, the warmth of their camaraderie a stark contrast to the chill that settled over me. It felt as if the world had moved on, and I was left standing still, caught in a moment that felt both interminable and fleeting. My heart ached for the simple comfort of Ethan's presence, the way his laughter could slice through my darkest thoughts like a knife through butter. But admitting that would mean stepping out from behind my barricade, and I wasn't ready for that.

The chill of the lecture hall was a welcomed distraction, the professor's voice a steady hum that wrapped around me like a blanket. I found solace in the rhythm of academic life, where problems had clear solutions and emotions were kept neatly at bay. Yet even here, whispers of Ethan lingered, woven into the fabric of my memories. I could almost feel his playful nudges as we sat shoulder to shoulder, his excitement contagious as he unraveled complex theories. I bit my lip, forcing my focus back to the professor, but my mind betrayed me, conjuring images of Ethan leaning back in his chair, his eyes sparkling with mischief, always ready with a quip that sent my heart racing.

Lunch was no longer the joy it used to be. The cafeteria buzzed with life, but I sat at the edge of a crowded table, a ghost among the living. My best friend, Clara, had taken to hovering around me, her eyes flickering with concern as she tried to draw me into conversations that felt like splashes of cold water on a sunburn. "You can't hide forever, you know," she teased gently, her voice softening as she leaned in. "Ethan will break down your walls, one way or another. You two are like that magnet thingy—opposites attract and all that."

I snorted, more out of habit than humor, and shook my head, pushing my salad around the plate. "I'm not hiding. Just... taking a break from the chaos." But even as I spoke the words, I could hear the lack of conviction in my tone. Clara's eyes narrowed, piercing through my facade.

"Right. Because avoiding him will magically fix everything," she replied, arching an eyebrow. "You miss him, admit it."

"I miss how things used to be," I countered, the defensiveness creeping into my voice like the autumn wind sneaking through the cracks of my armor. "Things were... simple."

"Simple isn't the same as happy," Clara replied, her tone turning serious. "You two have something special. Why throw that away?"

"Maybe because it's easier?" I shot back, my frustration bubbling over like a pot left too long on the stove. "Confronting emotions is messy, and I'm not ready to clean up the aftermath."

Clara sighed, exasperated yet affectionate. "You're smarter than this. You know that avoiding him will only make it worse. You're just prolonging the inevitable."

Her words sank into me like stones, heavy and unyielding. I glanced around the cafeteria, watching as couples shared quiet whispers, their hands entwined, warmth radiating between them. The sight twisted my stomach, and I turned back to my untouched food, trying to suppress the growing urge to scream.

The day wore on like a slow-moving tide, the minutes dragging as I navigated through my classes with the weight of unspoken words hanging over my head. I needed to confront Ethan, to address the fissures in our relationship, but every time I considered it, the fear of vulnerability tightened around my throat like a noose. What if I couldn't find the right words? What if my attempts at reconciliation only dug the wounds deeper?

I retreated into myself, drowning in study sessions that felt both futile and necessary, drowning out the world as I buried myself in textbooks. I needed a plan, a way to break through the silence that had settled between us. But even as I devised strategies, the truth loomed over me, a shadow that refused to be ignored.

I glanced at my phone, the screen illuminating my face in the dim light of my room. Ethan's name lingered in my notifications, a ghost of what used to be, teasing the edges of my resolve. I hesitated, fingers hovering over the screen, wrestling with the urge to reach out. But then I thought of his laughter, the warmth of his presence, and I felt that familiar crack begin to widen once more.

The rain pattered gently against my window, a soothing lullaby that echoed the turbulence within me. I closed my eyes, imagining the warmth of his hand in mine, the way our fingers fit together like puzzle pieces. I had to find a way to bridge the distance, to let him back in, even if it meant facing the parts of myself I had kept hidden.

The weekend loomed like a tempest on the horizon, threatening to upend my carefully constructed routine. As Friday slipped into evening, the chill in the air mirrored the frost that had settled in my heart. I sat curled up on the couch, wrapped in a blanket that smelled faintly of lavender and past arguments, the flicker of candlelight casting shadows on the walls. Clara had insisted on a movie night, but as the film played—a whimsical rom-com that had once made us both laugh until we cried—I found my mind drifting, far away from the antics of the screen.

"Are you even watching?" Clara tossed a popcorn kernel at me, her voice dripping with mock irritation.

"Of course! This is a cinematic masterpiece," I replied, my tone dry. I turned my gaze back to the screen, forcing a smile at the antics of the lead couple, but every scene felt like a reflection of my own reality, bright and painfully unattainable.

"I swear, you're like a zombie. Can you at least pretend to be alive? You could be binge-watching the latest Netflix series instead of moping around with me." She poked my side, her playful annoyance a thin veneer over genuine concern.

"I am alive! Just... contemplating the complexities of cinematic love," I retorted, shooting her a half-hearted glare that softened at the corners. "You know, the kind where everyone is beautifully flawed and the problems magically resolve in two hours."

"Yeah, well, real life is messier than that," Clara said, her eyes narrowing with purpose. "Just like your situation with Ethan. If you don't talk to him soon, you'll be stuck in this love-limbo forever."

"Love-limbo?" I laughed, the sound foreign and rusty, but her words struck a chord. It was true; I felt trapped, caught in a limbo that was both self-imposed and agonizing. "Is that even a thing?"

"It should be! You're living proof," she shot back, tossing another piece of popcorn my way, this time landing squarely on my lap. "Seriously, you need to give him a chance to explain, to make things right. You might find that he's just as scared as you are."

"Scared? Please. He was the one throwing around accusations like confetti," I said, the words tumbling out, more wounded than I intended.

"Then maybe he deserves to be heard," Clara replied softly, her eyes steady on mine, searching for something beyond my defenses. "And you deserve closure. Or, you know, an open door."

Her gaze held me captive, and for a moment, I wanted nothing more than to shake off the weight of indecision and leap into the unknown. I closed my eyes, picturing Ethan's face, the way it lit up when he laughed, the warmth of his hand brushing against mine. The memory felt like a warm tide, washing over the cold landscape I'd built around my heart.

"What if he doesn't want to talk?" I whispered, the fear creeping in, prickling like the autumn wind against my skin. "What if he's moved on?"

Clara shook her head, a determined glint in her eye. "Ethan is a persistent guy. You know that. If he wanted to move on, he would've already. Trust me, he's probably just as miserable as you are."

"Or he's out living his best life, with someone else," I countered, my heart sinking like a stone thrown into a still lake.

"Stop it! You're spiraling," Clara said, her tone turning firm, as she plucked the remote from my hands and paused the movie. "Listen to me. You both need to sort this out. It's like a bad pair of jeans—you can either keep wearing them and hope they magically fit, or you can make a change and find something that actually works for you."

I opened my mouth to argue, but the truth of her words settled in the pit of my stomach. The jeans analogy was ridiculous, yet oddly fitting. The longer I held onto the familiar, the more uncomfortable I became.

"Fine. I'll text him," I said, the resolve surprising even myself. The moment I said it, a surge of adrenaline coursed through me, as if I'd leapt from a high dive, feeling both terrified and exhilarated.

Clara clapped her hands in delight, her eyes sparkling with mischief. "Yes! Now you're talking. Just remember, you're both adults. Adult conversations can be hard, but they're worth it."

I grabbed my phone, my fingers trembling as I opened a new message. The blinking cursor seemed to taunt me, a small reminder of the weight of words. What do I say? Sorry for being a brat? Or maybe, Hey, let's put this whole awkward situation behind us and just be besties again? I blinked at the screen, feeling the panic rise like bile in my throat.

But Clara leaned closer, her encouragement palpable. "Just be honest. Tell him how you feel. It's not rocket science."

As the seconds ticked by, the tension in my shoulders eased slightly. I could do this. I had to do this. With a deep breath, I began typing, my heart racing with every word.

"Hey, Ethan. I've been thinking about our fight..." I paused, fingers hovering, unsure of how to continue. The enormity of my emotions felt almost tangible, filling the room like the scent of baked cookies—warm, inviting, and slightly overwhelming. I pressed onward, my mind racing. "I'm sorry for how I reacted. I miss you."

There. It was out in the universe, floating between us like a fragile balloon, and I sat back, heart pounding, breath hitching. I hit send, the sound echoing in the silence of my living room.

"Done!" I said, a little breathless.

Clara beamed, a mixture of pride and mischief dancing in her eyes. "Now we wait. Do you think he'll respond immediately, or will he take his sweet time to drive you crazy?"

"Probably the latter," I replied, the anxiety creeping back as I remembered our last exchange. But just as I prepared for the familiar rush of nerves to consume me, my phone buzzed in response, an unexpected jolt of electricity racing through my fingertips.

I snatched it up, heart racing, and there it was, Ethan's name flashing on the screen.

"Looks like someone's eager," Clara teased, leaning in.

My heart was pounding so loudly I was sure she could hear it. With a deep breath, I opened the message, anticipation mixing with dread. "I've been thinking about you too. Can we talk?"

The simplicity of his response shattered the walls I had constructed, and for the first time in weeks, a sliver of hope ignited within me. "Tomorrow?" I typed back, my fingers flying across the screen as if racing against time.

"Sounds perfect. Let's meet at our spot."

My breath hitched at the thought of that familiar bench by the river, where we'd shared secrets and dreams under the canopy of stars. The memories rushed back, flooding me with warmth and nostalgia.

"Okay," I replied, a nervous excitement bubbling beneath the surface. "See you then."

As Clara and I resumed the movie, my heart danced in rhythm with the plot unfolding on screen. I felt lighter, the oppressive weight of uncertainty beginning to lift as the anticipation coiled around me like a vibrant spring, ready to burst forth. Tomorrow would be a turning point, a chance to mend what was broken, to leap into the unknown and reclaim the laughter that had slipped through my fingers.

The morning sun broke through the clouds, casting a golden light that danced on the surface of the river, where the water rippled gently, reflecting the trees dressed in hues of amber and crimson. I arrived at our spot early, the bench nestled beneath a sprawling oak that seemed to cradle secrets in its gnarled branches. I wrapped my arms around my knees, feeling the cool metal beneath me, a chill that matched the flutter of nerves in my stomach. The air was crisp, tinged with the scent of damp earth and falling leaves—a reminder of the change that was coming, inevitable and transformative.

As I sat there, waiting, the world around me felt alive with possibility, each rustle of leaves and chirp of birds echoing my racing heart. I wondered if Ethan was feeling the same anticipation, or if he had been able to move on, leaving our moments behind like the leaves falling from the trees, free and unencumbered. What if this meeting only solidified the distance? What if it was an exercise in futility, a conversation destined to spiral into another fight?

"Hey," his voice broke through my swirling thoughts, warm and familiar, causing me to glance up.

Ethan stood a few feet away, hands shoved deep into his pockets, his expression unreadable. He looked just as I remembered—his tousled hair framing his face, eyes reflecting the autumn sky—yet something felt different, as if the air between us buzzed with unspoken words. My heart did a little leap, a mix of joy and trepidation.

"Hey," I managed, the single syllable feeling inadequate to capture the tempest of emotions swirling inside me.

He stepped closer, the weight of our silence thickening around us. "Thanks for coming," he said, his voice low, almost tentative. I could see the shadows under his eyes, hints of sleepless nights and worry, and my heart softened at the sight.

"I almost didn't," I admitted, my voice barely above a whisper. "But I figured... it was time."

His gaze flickered to the ground, then back to me, uncertainty etched across his features. "Yeah, it feels like we've been avoiding this for too long."

I nodded, my pulse quickening as I fought the urge to fill the space with idle chatter, to deflect from the real conversation looming ahead. But this wasn't just any conversation; it was the one we both needed, the one that could either pull us together or push us apart for good.

"Do you want to sit?" I asked, motioning to the bench.

"Sure." He sank down beside me, the familiar scent of his cologne mingling with the earthy aroma of fallen leaves, igniting memories of late-night study sessions and laughter that felt like home.

A heavy silence enveloped us, punctuated only by the rustling of leaves above. I took a deep breath, my resolve strengthening. "I'm sorry for what happened the other day. I shouldn't have reacted the way I did. I guess I was just... scared."

Ethan turned to me, his expression shifting. "Scared of what? Of me?"

"No!" The denial burst forth before I could reign it in. "I mean, yes... maybe. I'm scared of losing what we had, of what it could become."

He leaned back, staring at the sky as if searching for answers among the clouds. "You think I wanted to fight? It was never about you, you know? I was just trying to make you see how important this was for both of us. For our future."

"Future?" I echoed, feeling the word weigh heavy between us. "What future? I thought we were just taking things one day at a time."

"Exactly. One day at a time. But if we're always worried about the next step, we'll never get anywhere," he replied, a hint of frustration creeping into his voice. "And I want to get somewhere with you. But it feels like you're pushing me away."

My heart clenched at his words. He was right; I had built walls, convinced they would protect me from the hurt of potential loss. Yet here he was, offering a glimpse of something beautiful, a path forward. "I know I've been distant, but I was just... trying to figure things out," I confessed, my throat tightening. "I didn't want to feel vulnerable. I thought if I avoided you, it wouldn't hurt as much."

He turned to me, his eyes searching mine, the intensity of his gaze making my breath hitch. "But it does hurt. And avoiding it won't make it go away."

A lump formed in my throat, the truth of his statement resonating deep within me. "You're right," I whispered, my voice trembling slightly. "It hurts like hell."

"Then why not let me in?" he pressed gently. "You don't have to face this alone. I'm here, waiting, hoping you'll let me be part of whatever this is."

I blinked back the moisture threatening to spill from my eyes, overwhelmed by the sincerity in his tone. "I want to," I said, my heart racing, "but I don't know how."

Ethan reached for my hand, our fingers intertwining naturally, as if they had been meant to fit together all along. The warmth radiating from his touch sent shivers up my arm, igniting a spark of courage I hadn't realized I'd been lacking. "Then let's figure it out together," he said softly, his voice laced with determination. "One step at a time."

In that moment, the world around us faded into insignificance. The trees swayed, the river murmured, and all I could focus on was the connection forming between us, a delicate thread that could either mend the rift or unravel entirely. "I want that," I said, squeezing his hand.

As we shared a tentative smile, a sense of hope blossomed in my chest. Maybe this conversation would lead us somewhere beautiful, a new chapter brimming with promise. I leaned in, feeling the weight of his presence, my heart echoing the unspoken desire for reconciliation.

But just as the warmth of his gaze wrapped around me like a blanket, a sudden rustle in the bushes caught my attention. I turned my head, tension coiling in my stomach.

A figure emerged from the thicket, a familiar silhouette that sent my heart plummeting.

"Ethan? I thought you'd be here," she said, a bright smile plastered on her face, oblivious to the storm brewing in the air.

My breath hitched, the realization crashing down on me like an unexpected wave. It was Ava, Ethan's ex-girlfriend, the one person I'd hoped wouldn't intrude on this fragile moment. The air thickened with unspoken words, and my heart sank, torn between the sweet promise of connection and the looming shadow of doubt. I glanced at Ethan, searching his eyes for answers, but all I saw was surprise mirrored in his expression.

And as the world shifted around us, I could feel the fragile thread of hope begin to fray, leaving me teetering on the precipice of uncertainty, wondering if this was the moment that would change everything.

Chapter 7: The Awakening

The sun hung low in the sky, casting a warm, golden hue that wrapped around me like a comforting shawl as I stepped into the bustling community center. A scent of freshly brewed coffee wafted through the air, mingling with the sharp tang of paint from a nearby art class. The chatter of familiar faces filled the room, each conversation a thread woven into the fabric of our small town. I slipped into a seat at the back, my heart racing slightly as I took in the atmosphere. The poetry reading was always a safe harbor for me, a place where emotions flowed like the very words being shared.

As the first poet approached the mic, their presence transformed the mundane into something electric. They stood with an air of confidence that I envied. Dressed in a loose, bohemian shirt that swayed with every movement, the poet cradled a notebook in one hand, their fingers dancing nervously along its spine. I leaned in, curious, my own struggles fading into the background as their voice broke the silence.

"I once thought love was an all-consuming fire," they began, eyes sparkling with unshed tears. "But it's more like a candle—warm, flickering, and at times, vulnerable to the slightest breath." Each word they uttered washed over me like a wave, both comforting and unnerving. The crowd hung onto their every syllable, collectively holding its breath as the poet delved deeper into their story.

With each stanza, I felt my heartstrings tighten, resonating with themes of longing and heartbreak that echoed my own life. I could almost see the memories swirling around me—fragments of laughter shared with Ethan, the warmth of his hand in mine, and the cold aftermath of our last fight that felt like a distant, bitter winter. The poet spoke of the ache of unspoken words, the haunting echo of what could have been, and I realized how much I had been running from my own truths.

The room pulsed with emotion, a shared understanding binding us together in that moment. I could feel the flicker of hope igniting within me, bright and stubborn. My mind raced back to Ethan—the late-night conversations under the stars, the silly arguments over pizza toppings that felt trivial yet significant. I had let fear drive a wedge between us, allowing silence to fill the gaps where communication should have thrived.

As the poet concluded, the audience erupted into applause, a tidal wave of appreciation for the raw vulnerability shared. I sat, momentarily frozen, caught in the undertow of my own thoughts. My gaze drifted toward the exit, where the soft light spilled in, beckoning me to step outside, to confront the very feelings I had been so desperately avoiding. It was a call to arms, an invitation to emerge from my cocoon.

Taking a deep breath, I stood up, the decision firming in my chest. I needed to face Ethan—not with accusations, but with the honesty that had eluded me. I imagined his surprised expression, the way his dark hair fell into his eyes when he was deep in thought, and I felt a surge of determination. Love was not just a series of perfect moments; it was the messy, unpredictable dance of two souls navigating through the chaos of life.

The energy of the room buzzed as I slipped outside, the cool air a refreshing contrast to the warmth of my earlier emotions. My heart thudded against my ribcage, a frantic drummer echoing my resolve. I had no plan, just a sense of urgency driving me forward. I walked briskly, the sound of my footsteps a steady rhythm against the pavement, each step a mantra of intention. I wanted to tell Ethan that I had seen the light, that I was ready to meet him in the space between our misunderstandings.

When I reached his apartment building, the familiar sight struck me with nostalgia. The peeling paint, the crooked mailbox—it was all too reminiscent of the happy chaos we had built together. I hesitated for a moment, the shadow of doubt creeping in. What if he didn't want to see me? What if he had moved on? But then I recalled the poet's words, how they had spoken of the courage it took to love fully, to risk everything for the sake of connection.

With a resolute nod to myself, I walked through the front door and climbed the worn staircase, each step steeped in memories of laughter and heartache. I paused outside his door, my hand hovering above the brass knocker, the cool metal grounding me. I could hear the faint strumming of a guitar from within, the sound a siren's call to my heart.

Finally, I knocked, the sound resonating through the silence that followed. Moments passed, each second stretching painfully long, until I heard shuffling inside. My breath hitched, nerves coursing through me. When the door creaked open, I was met with Ethan's surprised face, his eyes wide with disbelief and something else—was that hope?

"Hey," I managed, my voice barely above a whisper. The warmth of his presence flooded over me, pulling me into a whirlwind of emotions. It was like coming home. "Can we talk?"

His gaze softened, and for a moment, the world fell away, leaving just the two of us suspended in that fragile moment of possibility.

The sun hung low in the sky, casting a golden hue over the community center as I settled into a creaky chair among a sea of eager faces. The atmosphere was alive with anticipation, a kaleidoscope of emotions woven together in the shared experience of artistry. It was a far cry from my reality, where the cacophony of self-doubt and regret played on a relentless loop. The poets took to the stage, each voice distinct, yet woven from the same fabric of human experience—love, loss, longing.

As the first poet spoke, their words danced through the air, wrapping around me like a warm embrace. They painted vivid pictures of joy intertwined with sorrow, each verse a delicate thread binding the audience together. "Love is a fleeting melody," they said, their voice trembling with raw emotion, "sometimes a symphony, sometimes a whisper. It can leave you breathless or break you entirely." I could feel the truth in those words resonate deep within my chest, awakening a part of me that I had buried beneath layers of fear and shame.

The next poet stepped up, their demeanor confident, yet their words spoke of vulnerability. "We wear our scars like medals," they declared, a wry smile crossing their lips. "Each one tells a story, an adventure of survival in this chaotic journey called life." I couldn't help but chuckle softly at the irony—survival felt more like a distant memory to me than a current adventure. Yet, somehow, their humor anchored me, reminding me that even the most painful moments could yield laughter.

Then, the final poet took the stage, and I leaned forward, captivated. They spoke of rekindling lost connections, of grappling with choices that lingered like ghosts. "Sometimes, the hardest battles are the ones we fight within ourselves," they said, their gaze piercing through the crowd. "But it's in those moments of doubt and despair that we find our true strength. Embrace the discomfort; it's the gateway to growth."

My heart raced as the weight of their words settled upon me. In that moment, I knew I couldn't retreat any longer. The spark of hope that had flickered within me was now a flame, igniting my resolve to confront Ethan, to mend the fracture between us. The air hummed with unspoken possibility, and I felt an overwhelming urge to step outside, to breathe deeply and reclaim the narrative of my life.

The poetry reading concluded, and as applause erupted, I slipped out of the crowd, feeling invigorated yet terrified. My fingers trembled slightly as I typed Ethan's number into my phone, the screen illuminating the path to him. He answered on the second ring, his voice a familiar melody that sent butterflies fluttering in my stomach.

"Hey," he said, a hint of surprise lacing his tone. "What's up?"

"I... I think we need to talk," I stammered, my mind racing with possibilities, each more daunting than the last.

"Okay," he replied, the weight of that word hanging in the air like a promise. "When?"

"Now? I'm at the community center."

"I'll be there in ten," he said, and just like that, the world tilted slightly on its axis.

The minutes felt like hours as I waited, heart pounding in my chest. The very walls of the community center seemed to close in around me, amplifying my anxiety. The chairs that had once felt inviting now loomed like judgmental specters. I glanced out the window, watching the sun dip lower, casting long shadows that mirrored my uncertainty.

Finally, I spotted him, his figure a familiar silhouette against the evening sky. The moment his eyes met mine, a rush of memories flooded back—laughter shared over ice cream, whispered secrets in the dark, and moments of tenderness that had felt eternal. He approached, uncertainty etched on his face, yet there was a flicker of hope in his eyes, a reflection of the flame I felt igniting within me.

"Hey," he said again, softer this time, stepping closer. "What's going on?"

"I—" My voice faltered, the weight of unspoken words pressing down on me. "I realized I've been running away from everything, from you. I've let my fears drown out the things that matter most."

His brow furrowed slightly, and I could see the gears turning in his mind. "What do you mean?"

I took a deep breath, forcing myself to embrace the discomfort. "I mean, I want to be honest about how I feel. I miss you, Ethan. I miss us. And I know I messed things up, but I'm ready to fight for it. For us."

His expression softened, and for a moment, the world around us faded, leaving just the two of us suspended in that moment. "You're not alone in this," he said, his voice steady. "I've been struggling too. But we can figure this out together."

As the shadows began to stretch and the sky darkened, I felt the walls I had built around my heart begin to crumble. Together, we stood at the edge of something new—a chance to rewrite our story, a possibility laden with uncertainty yet brimming with hope. The future was unwritten, but for the first time in a long while, I felt ready to embrace whatever came next, hand in hand with the one who had always understood me best.

The air thickened with the weight of our shared past, the scent of possibility mingling with the remnants of unresolved feelings. "So, what now?" I asked, a teasing lilt to my voice, trying to lighten the atmosphere.

"Well," he said, a playful smile creeping onto his lips, "how about we start with dessert? I know this little place that makes the best tiramisu in town. It's impossible to be sad with that in front of you."

I laughed, the tension melting away as I nodded, feeling lighter, more alive than I had in weeks. "Only if you promise not to get lost on the way. You know my sense of direction is worse than a compass in a thunderstorm."

He chuckled, the sound reverberating through the evening air. "Deal. But if I get us lost, it's on you for not having a backup plan."

As we walked side by side, the laughter flowed easily between us, weaving a thread of connection that felt both familiar and new. The path ahead was uncertain, but together, we would navigate it.

As Ethan and I strolled through the quaint streets, our laughter punctuated the warm evening air, weaving a tapestry of sound that mingled with the distant hum of conversation from nearby cafés.

The sun dipped lower, painting the sky in hues of orange and pink, casting a golden glow that felt almost surreal against the backdrop of our renewed connection. The aroma of freshly brewed coffee and baked pastries wafted through the open doors of a small Italian café, pulling us toward it like a moth to a flame.

"Are you sure this place has the best tiramisu?" I asked, my curiosity piqued. "I mean, that's a pretty bold claim. What's your basis for comparison? Did you conduct a thorough taste test?"

He shot me a grin, his eyes sparkling with mischief. "I might have taken a few too many 'research trips' to various cafés. But this place? It's like a love letter to my taste buds."

"Careful, or I might start getting jealous of your desserts," I teased, bumping my shoulder against his as we entered the café, the inviting warmth wrapping around us like a comforting blanket.

We found a cozy table by the window, the soft glow of overhead lights illuminating the menu. As I perused my options, I could feel the anticipation swirling between us, a blend of excitement and unspoken tension. Our conversation flowed effortlessly, touching on everything from our favorite childhood movies to embarrassing first dates, each revelation drawing us closer together.

Ethan leaned in, a teasing glint in his eyes. "So, did I ever tell you about the time I accidentally wore two different shoes to a meeting? One was brown, the other black. Let's just say I was the talk of the office for a week."

I laughed, picturing the scene vividly. "You? Disheveled? I can't imagine it. You're always so put together."

"Looks can be deceiving. It's all part of my charm," he replied, his tone mock-serious, and I couldn't help but roll my eyes, amused.

When the waiter approached, I ordered the tiramisu, fully embracing the indulgence, while Ethan opted for a slice of lemon tart. As we waited, the conversation turned to our dreams, the unfiltered hopes we rarely voiced aloud. "I've always wanted to write a novel," he confessed, a shy smile gracing his lips. "Something that captures the chaos of life, the beauty in the messiness."

"Really? You? I wouldn't have guessed. You seem far too practical for that." I leaned back, crossing my arms playfully.

"Just because I love spreadsheets doesn't mean I can't appreciate a good story," he retorted, laughter dancing in his voice. "What about you? Any secret ambitions?"

"Honestly? I've thought about it, but it always felt like an unattainable dream. I mean, who would read my story?"

"Anyone who's ever felt lost and found themselves again," he said, his gaze steady, igniting a warmth in my chest.

Before I could respond, the waiter returned with our desserts, placing them in front of us like treasures unearthed from a hidden trove. The tiramisu looked divine, layers of creamy goodness teasing me with their promise.

"Dig in," Ethan encouraged, his enthusiasm contagious.

I took my first bite, the flavors exploding in my mouth. "Oh my God, this is amazing!" I exclaimed, a little too loudly, earning a few curious glances from nearby tables.

"See? I told you it was worth the trip," he said, his grin widening. "I'm practically a dessert connoisseur now."

"Maybe you should open a food blog," I suggested, wiping a bit of cream from the corner of my mouth, my heart racing at the playful banter that felt so natural.

"I don't know. What if no one reads it? That would be worse than my two-shoes debacle."

"Then I'll read it! I'll be your number one fan," I declared, our eyes locking in a moment that felt charged with something deeper.

As we finished our desserts, the conversation shifted, a subtle shift in the atmosphere as the weight of unaddressed feelings loomed over us. "So, what happens now?" I asked, my voice softer, the lightheartedness giving way to something more serious.

Ethan hesitated, running a hand through his hair. "I think we both know we can't just pretend everything is fine. There's still a lot we need to unpack."

I nodded, the vulnerability in his gaze making my heart race. "You're right. I've been avoiding this conversation for too long. I—"

Suddenly, the door swung open, and a gust of wind swept through the café, drawing my attention. A figure entered, cloaked in shadows. As they stepped into the light, I felt a jolt of recognition mixed with dread. It was someone from my past—someone I had never expected to see again.

My heart raced as I locked eyes with the newcomer, their expression unreadable. "What are you doing here?" I whispered, the words barely escaping my lips.

Ethan followed my gaze, confusion clouding his features. "Who is that?"

Before I could respond, the figure approached our table, an inscrutable smile dancing on their lips. "Fancy seeing you here. I was hoping we could have a chat, just the three of us."

The tension in the air shifted, a palpable charge filling the space around us as I fought to regain my composure. "Now? Here?"

"Why not?" They leaned against the table, their presence casting a shadow over what had just felt like a fragile moment of reconnection between Ethan and me. "After all, it's about time we had an honest conversation, don't you think?"

Ethan's brow furrowed in concern, the carefree banter evaporating like steam from a hot cup of coffee. "Do you know this person?"

I swallowed hard, the weight of the past crashing down on me like a wave. "Yes, but it's complicated."

"Complicated? You could say that again," the newcomer interjected, their tone dripping with sarcasm. "How about we get to the bottom of it?"

The air grew thick with unresolved tension, and the laughter that had once filled the café felt like a distant memory. I glanced at Ethan, searching for reassurance in his eyes, but instead, I found uncertainty. The delightful moment we had shared began to slip away, replaced by an impending storm of confrontation and revelation.

As the three of us sat in that small café, the stakes felt higher than ever, and I realized that this unexpected encounter could change everything. The fragile thread of hope I had begun to weave with Ethan now dangled precariously, teetering on the brink of uncertainty. My heart raced as I faced the specter of my past, uncertain of what would unfold next, knowing that the truth could shatter the delicate balance we had begun to restore.

Chapter 8: The Apology

I parked my car beneath the glow of a flickering streetlamp, its light barely piercing the curtain of dusk that had settled over the city. The air was thick with the mingling scents of rain-soaked asphalt and blooming jasmine, wrapping around me like a comforting shawl. I could almost convince myself that the world outside was an enchanting place where nothing was amiss. Yet, as I stood on the threshold of Ethan's apartment, my pulse thrumming in my ears, the reality of the evening pressed down like a weighty stone.

With each knock on his door, the sound reverberated through my chest, a reminder of all the things left unsaid between us. My mind spiraled through every possible scenario: what if he had moved on? What if he opened the door only to turn me away? But there was no turning back now; I had come too far. I shifted my weight from foot to foot, wishing I could harness the courage that had propelled me here, just as a gust of wind howled down the street, almost daring me to flee.

And then the door swung open.

Ethan stood there, his hair tousled as if he had just rolled out of bed, an expression of genuine surprise illuminating his features. The warmth of his smile ignited something deep inside me, dispelling the chill of doubt that had wrapped around my heart. "I didn't expect to see you," he said, his voice a soft rumble, like the distant echo of thunder. It was a welcome sound, grounding me amid the chaos of emotions swirling within.

"Yeah, well, I figured I should... um, talk," I stumbled over my words, the weight of them heavy on my tongue. My fingers twisted nervously at my side, betraying my anxiety. "Can I come in?"

He hesitated for a heartbeat, eyes narrowing slightly as if weighing my presence against the tumult of our recent past. Then, with a subtle nod, he stepped aside, allowing me entry into his world—one I had so recently found myself locked out of.

The apartment felt cozy, yet stark; a reflection of Ethan himself. It was filled with the soft glow of golden lamps and the faint aroma of coffee lingering in the air, an alluring reminder of the mornings spent wrapped in our own little universe. But the silence that enveloped us was suffocating, thick with the memories of our last encounter—hurt and misunderstanding swirling around us like a stubborn fog.

I took a step inside, my heart racing as the door clicked shut behind me. "Ethan, I've been thinking," I began, my voice barely rising above a whisper, yet trembling with urgency. I could feel the familiar flutter of vulnerability creeping in, urging me to shield myself, but this time, I would not retreat. "I'm sorry. For everything. I let my insecurities get the better of me. I pushed you away when I should have been fighting for us."

His expression softened, eyes glimmering with something unnamable—a mix of hope and apprehension, perhaps. "You didn't have to come all this way just to say that," he said, his tone teasing yet sincere, as if trying to lighten the weight of the moment.

"I know," I replied, a laugh escaping me, surprised at how easily it came. "But it's true. I was scared, and instead of talking to you about it, I let my fears dictate my actions. I didn't want to drag you down with my issues."

"Letting fear drive a wedge between us wasn't a solution," he said, stepping closer. The warmth radiating from him pulled me in, urging me to keep speaking. "You think you were the only one feeling vulnerable? I missed you. Every day without you was like living in black and white."

His admission struck me, igniting a flicker of warmth in my chest. "I missed you too, more than I can say," I confessed, my voice thick with emotion. "But I was scared of losing myself in you, of losing my independence."

He nodded slowly, processing my words. "I get that. But I wanted to be there for you, to support you, not to consume you. We could've navigated it together."

I felt the walls I had built around myself start to crumble. "I know now that I need you. I need us. I'm done pretending I don't want that."

He took a step closer, his gaze piercing through the remnants of my defenses. "You're stronger than you think. You just need to trust yourself, and trust me. We can figure this out."

My heart swelled, and for a brief moment, the noise of the outside world faded into the background. Here, with him, everything felt right. The connection we shared—raw, honest—began weaving a tapestry of understanding between us.

"Can I just... can I hold your hand?" I asked suddenly, the words tumbling out before I could think better of them.

His lips curled into a playful smirk, a spark igniting in his eyes. "Only if I can steal a kiss too."

"Are we negotiating now?" I teased, but my heart raced at the prospect. "Okay, but just one kiss first. Then the hand-holding."

"Deal," he said, his tone light yet serious, the air around us thickening with a palpable tension.

As he leaned in, the world around us melted away, and I felt the warmth of his lips brushing against mine—a spark igniting a fire long dormant. The kiss deepened, weaving threads of comfort and desire, the kind of kiss that spoke of promises and new beginnings.

When we finally pulled away, breathless and wide-eyed, I could feel the remnants of fear evaporating, replaced by something electric. "Wow," I murmured, still lingering in the glow of his touch.

"Wow indeed," he replied, a grin breaking across his face. "Now, about that hand..."

With a laugh, I entwined my fingers with his, feeling an overwhelming sense of belonging wash over me. Here, in this moment, all the chaos faded, and the future stretched before us—bright, uncertain, but full of promise.

The moment hung in the air, heavy with the unspoken. I could feel the warmth of Ethan's hand wrapped around mine, an anchor in the swirling chaos of emotions. Our laughter lingered, a gentle reminder that amid the heartache and fear, there was still joy to be found. Yet, beneath the surface of our newfound intimacy, a disquieting thought tugged at the edges of my mind. Could this really be the beginning of something solid, or were we merely playing at fixing what had cracked between us?

"Okay, so," I began, attempting to clear the air with a teasing tone, "what now? I've confessed my deep, dark secrets. Do I get a cookie or something?"

Ethan chuckled, shaking his head as if I had suggested something preposterous. "You think a cookie can fix our relationship? That's adorable. But I do have a better idea."

"Oh?" I leaned in closer, intrigued, feeling a spark of excitement flaring between us. "Do tell."

"Let's take a trip," he said, his eyes twinkling with mischief. "Just you and me. Somewhere we can talk without distractions. How about the lake house? The one my family owns?"

The mention of the lake house sent a ripple of apprehension through me. We had shared countless memories there, laughter echoing off the water and lazy afternoons spent in the sun. But those memories came bundled with the weight of the past, and I wasn't sure I was ready to unpack all of that yet. "That sounds... amazing," I replied cautiously, trying to mask my unease. "But are you sure? I mean, it could stir up a lot of old feelings."

"Exactly," he said, his voice firm yet gentle. "And it could also help us figure out what we really want. I want to be all in, and if you're willing to take that leap with me, I think we can make it work."

His conviction washed over me like the warmth of the sun breaking through clouds after a long storm. "I think you might be right," I admitted. "But we need to be honest with each other about everything. No more walls, no more misunderstandings. I don't want to go back to the way things were."

"Agreed," he said, his grip tightening slightly around my hand. "Let's make a pact. No secrets, just honesty and—"

"And cookies?" I interjected playfully, my heart swelling with hope.

"Fine, cookies too," he laughed. "But only if you promise to bake them."

"Oh, I see. You're just trying to get free baked goods out of me. That's your plan all along!" I quipped, feigning indignation.

"Hey, they'll be worth it," he shot back, grinning. "You're a culinary genius."

As we bantered, a sense of normalcy enveloped us, and the laughter felt like a balm to my bruised heart. The hesitation that had once choked our connection slowly began to dissolve. We talked late into the night, sharing stories and dreams, each revelation building a bridge where fear had once laid its heavy stones. It felt good to share those moments again, to explore the corners of each other's lives that had been overshadowed by our insecurities.

Eventually, we settled into a comfortable silence, the kind that spoke volumes without the need for words. It was then that the vulnerability returned, creeping in as I turned serious. "Ethan, what if we try and it doesn't work?"

He released a deep sigh, his expression thoughtful. "Then we'll deal with it. Together. That's what we're doing, right? Not running away this time?"

"Right," I whispered, my heart swelling with a mixture of hope and trepidation. "I want that. I really do."

"Then let's start fresh. Just you and me, without the shadows of our past," he said, his voice low and earnest.

With a sudden rush of determination, I nodded. "Let's go to the lake house. We can leave tomorrow. Just give me a little time to pack."

Ethan's face lit up with excitement, and I couldn't help but mirror his enthusiasm. The thought of escaping the noise of the city for a few days, surrounded by nature and water, felt like a promise—a chance to rekindle what had been lost.

We spent the rest of the night planning our escape, our laughter intertwining with the hum of distant traffic outside. I even found myself picking out ingredients for the cookies we had jokingly promised to bake. It felt liberating, to think of nothing but the two of us and what lay ahead.

As dawn crept into the world, painting the sky in hues of gold and lavender, I packed my bag with a mix of anticipation and nerves. Every item I selected held a weight of significance—the sunhat I loved for lazy afternoons, the worn journal where I scribbled my thoughts, and a pair of old sneakers that had seen better days but were perfect for wandering along the lake's edge.

When I arrived at Ethan's place, his eyes lit up at the sight of my bag, brimming with promise. "Ready for adventure?" he asked, pulling me into a playful hug.

"Ready as I'll ever be," I laughed, my spirit soaring as we hopped into his car, the warmth of the morning sun bathing us in golden light. The engine purred to life, and as we drove away from the city, leaving behind the tangled web of our lives, I couldn't help but feel that we were on the brink of something transformative.

The highway unfurled before us, each mile pulling us farther from our past and closer to whatever lay ahead. We spoke of everything and nothing, our conversations flowing as easily as the landscape shifted outside the window. With every twist and turn, I felt the weight of my insecurities lighten, replaced by a burgeoning excitement that echoed in my chest.

As we approached the lake house, the familiar silhouette of the trees danced against the sky, their leaves shimmering like emeralds in the sunlight. I took a deep breath, the crisp air filling my lungs and invigorating my spirit. It felt like returning home, but also venturing into a new frontier, one filled with endless possibilities.

Ethan parked the car and turned to me, his expression serious yet soft. "Whatever happens here, we're in it together."

"Together," I echoed, my heart pounding with hope and a hint of uncertainty. This was our chance to redefine everything, to move forward without the shackles of fear. I stepped out of the car, and as I inhaled the sweet scent of pine and water, I knew this was just the beginning.

The air buzzed with the scent of pine and the gentle lapping of waves against the shore as we approached the lake house, each step igniting a sense of nostalgia in me. It felt as though the world around us had taken a collective breath, waiting to see what would unfold. The familiar cabin, with its rustic charm and weathered wood, loomed ahead, bathed in the soft light of the late afternoon sun. I could almost hear the echoes of laughter and the sound of splashing water from summers past, a blend of memories that seemed to dance on the surface of the lake.

"Just think of it as a weekend retreat for our souls," Ethan said, breaking the silence as he gestured toward the cabin with a flourish. "A cozy little slice of serenity where we can sort through our baggage and maybe bake some cookies. Lots and lots of cookies."

I chuckled, shaking my head at his playful optimism. "You're really banking on those cookies, aren't you?"

"Absolutely. They are the key to emotional healing." He winked, his grin infectious, as we crossed the threshold into the cabin.

The interior was warm and inviting, a mix of rustic charm and cozy comfort. Sunlight streamed through the windows, illuminating the dust motes dancing in the air. A familiar couch, upholstered in a patchwork of warm colors, sat facing a stone fireplace, ready to embrace us after a long day. A small kitchen tucked away in the corner promised the potential for culinary disasters and delightful treats.

Ethan dropped our bags on the floor with a dramatic thud, clearly relishing this moment. "Welcome to paradise!" he declared, as though he were unveiling the wonders of a five-star resort rather than his family's simple getaway.

"Paradise indeed," I replied, taking a moment to soak it all in. The laughter of our shared history wrapped around me, soothing the remnants of anxiety that clung like a shadow.

As evening fell, we set about preparing our first meal together in the cabin. Ethan assigned himself the role of sous chef, while I commandeered the stove, determined to create something worthy of our reunion. The air filled with the aroma of sautéed vegetables and garlic, a comforting backdrop to the banter that flowed between us.

"Are you sure you know how to cook? That smells suspiciously good," Ethan teased, leaning against the counter, arms crossed, watching me with an amused expression.

"Oh, please! I'll have you know I am a culinary mastermind in the kitchen," I retorted, pretending to be affronted. "These sautéed vegetables are but a warm-up for my world-famous cookies."

"World-famous, you say? I'd better be careful. I could end up having to put them on my menu," he quipped, making a mock serious face.

We laughed as I plated our meal, the shared humor breaking down the last vestiges of tension between us. Eating together felt like an act of reconciliation, an unspoken agreement that we were moving forward. As we sat across from each other, the flickering candlelight casting soft shadows on our faces, I felt a warmth blooming inside me, a promise of what could be.

After dinner, we cleared the dishes, the conversation drifting effortlessly between memories of childhood adventures and our hopes for the future. The stars twinkled outside, creating a canvas of silver that felt impossibly romantic.

"Do you remember that summer when we tried to build a raft?" Ethan asked, his eyes sparkling with mischief.

"Only the part where it sank and you fell in!" I shot back, laughter bubbling up as I recalled that hilariously disastrous day.

"Hey, I was trying to be resourceful!" he protested, holding up his hands in mock defense. "We were pioneers!"

"Pioneers who needed a life jacket and a boat," I replied, smirking.

As the night wore on, we found ourselves on the couch, wrapped in a shared blanket, the warmth radiating between us more than just the fabric. I could feel the comfort of his presence, the way it settled like a gentle tide, washing over the jagged edges of my anxiety.

"Can I ask you something serious?" I said, my voice quieter now.

"Sure, hit me with your best shot."

I hesitated, but the urge to voice my fears pushed through the hesitation. "What if we try to make this work and it still falls apart? What if I can't let go of the fear that brought us here in the first place?"

Ethan turned to face me, his expression shifting from playful to serious. "You have to trust me. We can't predict the future, but we can be honest with each other. If it starts to feel like we're slipping back into old patterns, we talk. No more secrets, right?"

I nodded, grateful for his earnestness. "You're right. I'm just scared of losing what we have."

"Then let's not lose it," he replied softly, brushing a strand of hair behind my ear, his touch lingering. The world outside faded away as we locked eyes, a promise hanging between us like the stars outside.

A sudden rustle broke the spell, the noise pulling my focus away from Ethan's gaze. The sound seemed to come from the direction of the door, like a whisper in the dark. "Did you hear that?"

Ethan's brow furrowed. "Yeah, I did. It sounded like—"

Before he could finish, the front door creaked open, sending a chill racing down my spine. The moonlight spilled into the cabin, casting eerie shadows that danced on the walls. My heart raced as I glanced at Ethan, confusion etched on his face.

"Who's there?" he called out, his voice steady but edged with concern.

There was a pause, then a figure stepped into the light, their silhouette blurred by the darkness outside. My breath caught in my throat as recognition settled in. It was someone I had never expected to see again, someone whose presence threatened to unravel everything we had just begun to rebuild.

"Surprise!" the figure said, a sly grin spreading across their face, the kind that promised trouble and turmoil.

Ethan stood up, his stance shifting into a protective posture, eyes narrowed with suspicion. "What are you doing here?"

The air crackled with tension, the warmth of the cabin suddenly feeling stifling. I could feel the ground shifting beneath us, uncertainty blossoming like a dark flower in the night. What had started as a hopeful reunion was now teetering on the brink of chaos, and as I exchanged glances with Ethan, I knew this was just the beginning of something much bigger—and possibly more dangerous—than either of us had anticipated.

Chapter 9: The New Beginning

The sun dipped low in the sky, casting a warm golden hue over the streets of downtown, illuminating every corner like a freshly polished gemstone. I felt the cool evening breeze tugging gently at my hair, lifting strands of it like playful spirits eager to dance. Beside me, Ethan's fingers entwined with mine, and I couldn't help but marvel at how simple gestures felt monumental now. Every brush of skin against skin sent a ripple of warmth through me, igniting a kind of spark that made me believe in magic—our magic.

We wandered aimlessly, lost in the glow of the streetlights and the laughter of late-night revelers. It was as if the city had transformed overnight, shedding its mundane skin to reveal something vibrant and alive beneath. Street vendors called out cheerfully, their voices mingling with the rhythmic pulse of music drifting from nearby cafes. The aroma of grilled meats and spicy tacos hung in the air, tantalizing my senses, beckoning us to explore every nook and cranny.

"Let's grab a bite," Ethan suggested, his gaze flickering toward a taco stand adorned with string lights and a hand-painted sign that swayed gently in the breeze.

"I'll race you," I declared, sprinting ahead before I could second-guess myself. My laughter danced in the air as I dashed toward the stand, adrenaline surging through me. It was exhilarating, a feeling I hadn't indulged in for far too long. I glanced back, finding Ethan's expression a mix of amusement and admiration, a smirk tugging at the corners of his mouth.

"Cheating already, Harper?" he teased, catching up to me with a grace that made me envious. His competitive spirit was as infectious as his smile.

I pretended to consider the question seriously. "What can I say? I've always been a fan of strategic advantages."

He chuckled, shaking his head, and I reveled in the sound. There was something undeniably delightful about how easily we had slipped back into this rhythm, a comforting familiarity laced with the excitement of new beginnings.

As we approached the counter, the vendor greeted us with a grin that crinkled the corners of his eyes. "What can I get for you, lovely people?"

"Two tacos—one spicy and one mild, please," I said, eyeing Ethan as he raised an eyebrow, clearly skeptical of my adventurous choice.

"I'll stick with the mild," he said, a hint of teasing in his tone. "Someone has to be sensible in this relationship."

"Sensible, huh?" I shot back, rolling my eyes playfully. "That's a bold claim for a guy who just raced after a girl to a taco stand."

"Touché," he replied, a smile breaking across his face. "I'll admit, that was pretty impulsive."

The vendor placed our tacos on the counter, each one wrapped in shiny foil, steaming and fragrant. We grabbed them, the warmth radiating through the foil as we stepped aside to devour our dinner beneath a canopy of twinkling stars.

With every bite, my taste buds erupted in a fiesta of flavors. The spicy taco packed a punch, igniting a fire that made me gasp in delight. Ethan laughed at my reaction, taking a careful bite of his own, and the sound of his amusement filled me with warmth.

"Too spicy for you?" he asked, the corner of his mouth lifting into a smirk as he wiped a stray morsel of salsa from my cheek with the tenderness of a lover who had just unlocked a secret door to my heart.

I grinned, wiping my mouth with the back of my hand. "You should know by now, I don't back down from a challenge."

As we continued our playful banter, I felt a sense of relief wash over me. This was what I had wanted—an easy companionship, where laughter flowed as freely as the evening breeze, where every moment felt like a cherished memory in the making. I had spent too long hiding in the shadows, second-guessing every move, every word. But with Ethan, I felt like I was stepping into the spotlight, ready to shine.

"Want to see something cool?" he asked, mischief glimmering in his eyes.

"What do you have in mind?" I replied, curiosity piqued.

"Follow me," he said, leading me down a narrow alley, the bustling street fading behind us. The air was charged with anticipation as we rounded a corner, revealing a hidden courtyard adorned with vibrant murals. It was a living canvas, each stroke bursting with color and life, as if the walls themselves were breathing.

"This is amazing," I whispered, completely entranced. The murals told stories of love and loss, dreams and despair, each image woven together in a tapestry of emotion. I stepped closer to one mural, a breathtaking depiction of a phoenix rising from the ashes, the colors vibrant against the night sky.

Ethan stood beside me, his presence comforting and warm. "I come here when I need to clear my head," he said softly. "It reminds me that even in darkness, there's beauty waiting to emerge."

His words resonated deep within me, stirring something long dormant. I had spent so much time buried under layers of doubt and fear, but here, under the flickering glow of the courtyard lights, I felt those layers peeling away.

"You're right," I replied, my voice barely above a whisper. "It's beautiful, just like... well, everything feels different now."

His gaze locked onto mine, the intensity making my heart race. "I'm glad you see it, Harper. We're just getting started."

The promise in his voice wrapped around me like a warm blanket, filling me with an exhilarating sense of hope. Together, we stood amidst the murals, embracing the magic of this moment and the potential of what lay ahead.

The evening air was a symphony of sounds, laughter, and distant music blending into a harmonious backdrop as Ethan and I ventured further into the city. The murals we'd stumbled upon felt like a portal, and I was eager to see where this newfound adventure would take us. Each step we took revealed another corner of the vibrant tapestry that was our surroundings.

"What do you think is the story behind that one?" I asked, pointing to a mural that depicted a woman reaching toward the sky, her hair flowing like rivers of gold.

Ethan leaned closer, his breath brushing against my cheek. "It looks like she's trying to escape, doesn't it? Like she wants to break free from something holding her back."

I nodded, entranced by the way his voice carried a depth of thought that made even the simplest observations feel profound. "Maybe she's searching for something she's lost."

"Or perhaps she's found it," he suggested, his gaze lingering on the mural. "Sometimes it's not about escaping but embracing what's ahead."

His words echoed within me, igniting a sense of purpose I hadn't known I needed. I was done running from my fears, my insecurities. With Ethan beside me, I felt empowered to leap into the unknown.

"Let's make a promise," I said, turning to him with a mix of earnestness and playful determination. "No more hiding. We embrace whatever comes next."

"Deal," he replied, extending his pinky in a childlike gesture that made me laugh. I linked my pinky with his, sealing our vow with a light-hearted seriousness that belied the weight of our commitment.

As we wandered on, a little coffee shop caught my eye, its rustic charm drawing me in. A hand-painted sign declared it the best place for "cozy conversations and caffeine-induced epiphanies." I tugged

Ethan toward it, and he complied, his enthusiasm matching mine as we stepped inside.

The scent of freshly brewed coffee enveloped us, and I felt an immediate sense of comfort wash over me. The interior was adorned with mismatched furniture, each piece telling a story of its own. A worn velvet couch beckoned from the corner, while fairy lights twinkled overhead, casting a soft glow over everything.

"Two coffees, please!" I called out to the barista, a cheerful woman with a colorful apron. Ethan leaned against the counter, his arms crossed, a relaxed smile gracing his face.

"What's your go-to?" he asked, tilting his head.

"Definitely a caramel macchiato," I replied. "It's sweet, but with a bit of bitterness to keep things interesting. Kind of like me."

Ethan's laughter echoed in the cozy space, rich and warm. "I'd say that's pretty spot on. But let's hope you're not too bitter. I'd like to keep our new agreement intact."

"Touché," I said, feigning offense. "But I'll have you know, I'm mostly sweet, with just a hint of sass."

He leaned in, feigning seriousness. "I can work with that."

After placing our orders, we settled onto the couch, sinking into its embrace like a pair of weary travelers. As we sipped our drinks, we continued to exchange stories—each revelation pulling us closer, revealing the layers beneath the surface.

"I've never really been one for coffee shops," Ethan confessed, a thoughtful look crossing his face. "I used to think they were just places for people to pretend they're working while scrolling through their phones."

"Okay, but what about the people-watching? That's half the fun!" I replied, gesturing around the shop filled with various characters—a couple lost in their own world, a group of friends laughing raucously, and a solitary figure furiously typing on a laptop.

"True," he conceded, eyes sparkling with mischief. "And I do love a good people-watching session. But I have to admit, I'm more of a bookshop guy. It's like stepping into a different universe."

"Books are definitely magical," I agreed. "But coffee shops have their own kind of charm. It's like an atmosphere of creativity and inspiration."

Ethan leaned back, contemplating my words. "So, which universe do you belong to? Coffee shop girl or bookshop girl?"

"Hmm, a little of both, I think. I'm the one who sneaks a coffee into the bookstore and loses track of time while getting lost in pages," I said, the warmth of the moment wrapping around us like a favorite blanket.

"Perfect," he said, raising his cup in a mock toast. "Here's to the best of both worlds."

As our drinks vanished, the conversation flowed freely, turning from playful banter to more serious topics—our hopes, our dreams, and the inevitable fears that loomed like dark clouds. I felt the weight of my own insecurities lift as I shared my aspirations of starting my own business, something I had dreamed of for years but never quite had the courage to pursue.

"I want to create a space for others, somewhere they can feel safe and inspired," I said, the words pouring out as if I'd been holding them back for too long. "But the thought of failing terrifies me."

Ethan's expression softened, the flicker of understanding evident in his gaze. "You're stronger than you think, Harper. And you've already made it this far. What's stopping you?"

"I don't know," I admitted, my voice barely above a whisper. "Maybe I just need a little push."

"Consider me your designated cheerleader," he said, his tone light but with an undercurrent of sincerity. "We'll tackle it together. I can help you brainstorm ideas, and you can help me figure out my next big move."

I laughed, the sound echoing with genuine delight. "Now that sounds like a dangerous proposition."

"Dangerous or not, I'm in," he said, leaning closer, his eyes gleaming with excitement.

In that moment, the café faded away, the world outside falling silent as we existed in our little bubble of inspiration and promise. I could feel the bonds between us tightening, weaving a tapestry rich with potential. The uncertainties that had once held me back felt lighter now, like feathers in the wind, and I found myself leaning toward the possibility of what lay ahead.

As we prepared to leave, the bell above the door chimed softly, a gentle reminder of the world outside. I stood, feeling a mix of anticipation and nervous energy coursing through me, wondering what adventures awaited us next.

As we stepped back onto the bustling street, the world outside felt electrified, pulsing with a rhythm that matched the quickening beat of my heart. The evening sky was painted with strokes of lavender and deep indigo, the stars beginning to twinkle like mischievous fireflies ready to share their secrets. I glanced at Ethan, who was gazing at the sky with an intensity that made me wonder what dreams danced behind his eyes.

"Do you ever think about what you want to be when you grow up?" I asked, half-joking but genuinely curious.

Ethan turned his attention back to me, a playful smirk curling his lips. "Harper, I'm already an adult. I'm pretty sure I've missed that boat."

"Please. You're only as grown-up as you feel," I shot back, nudging him playfully with my elbow. "So, what do you want?"

He paused, his expression shifting as he considered my question. "Honestly? I've always wanted to be a storyteller—someone who can weave tales that linger long after the last page is turned."

I couldn't help but admire his passion, the way his eyes sparkled with possibility. "That's incredible! What's stopping you?"

He shrugged, his smile faltering for a moment. "Life, I suppose. Adulting has a way of distracting you from what really matters."

"I get that," I replied, my heart tightening at the thought of my own dreams hovering just out of reach. "But what if we helped each other find our way?"

His gaze met mine, a silent understanding passing between us. "You mean, I help you with your business, and you help me with my stories?"

"Exactly! We could keep each other accountable," I suggested, feeling the thrill of possibility surge within me. "Who knows what could happen?"

"Let's do it," he said, the enthusiasm in his voice igniting a spark in me. "But if I'm going to help you with your business, you'll have to promise me one thing."

"What's that?"

"No boring meetings. If I'm going to spend time discussing plans, there better be coffee and maybe a few snacks."

I laughed, a lightness flooding my chest. "I can promise you that! My meetings will be more like brainstorming parties."

"Now that sounds like something I could get on board with."

Our conversation flowed effortlessly, the energy around us crackling with excitement. We strolled past street musicians, their melodies dancing in the air, luring us closer. A small crowd had gathered to watch a guitarist strumming a soulful tune, the notes lingering in the night like whispers of romance.

"Should we?" I asked, my eyes sparkling with mischief.

"Absolutely," Ethan replied, leading me toward the gathering.

As we settled on the edge of the crowd, the musician's voice washed over us, and I felt my heart swell with every note. The world around us faded, leaving only the music and the warmth of Ethan's presence. His shoulder brushed against mine, a simple touch that sent shivers down my spine.

"You know," he said, his voice barely audible above the melody, "this is one of those moments I wish I could freeze in time."

"Agreed," I whispered, leaning closer, intoxicated by the atmosphere. "Moments like these don't come around often enough."

The song ended, and the crowd erupted into applause, their cheers echoing through the streets. Ethan turned to me, a playful gleam in his eyes. "Now we have to find a way to make our lives this captivating. No pressure."

"I accept the challenge," I replied, matching his intensity with a grin. "But first, let's grab dessert. I hear that place on the corner has the best pastries in town."

He raised an eyebrow, clearly intrigued. "Lead the way, pastry queen."

As we made our way toward the dessert shop, I couldn't shake the feeling that something significant was unfolding between us—like a delicate tapestry being woven thread by thread. Each laugh, each shared glance felt like a promise of what could be, igniting a yearning deep within me.

The dessert shop was a treasure trove of sweet delights, the display case overflowing with colorful confections and decadent pastries. "What's your poison?" I asked, my voice filled with playful mischief.

Ethan's eyes darted around the shop, taking in the choices. "How about we get a few things and have a taste-testing extravaganza?"

"Perfect!" I clapped my hands in delight. "We can be the official judges of dessert."

After selecting an array of treats—rich chocolate éclairs, fluffy raspberry tarts, and a couple of macarons—we found a cozy spot outside. I took a bite of the éclairs, the creamy filling bursting in my mouth. "Oh wow," I gasped. "This is heavenly."

"See? I knew you'd appreciate the finer things in life," Ethan teased, taking a bite of the raspberry tart. "And this is pretty amazing too. I might just declare this our official dessert destination."

We continued to taste and share, laughter punctuating our exchanges, weaving our own little world amidst the chaos of the street. I felt a rush of happiness wash over me, each moment solidifying our connection.

But just as I was about to suggest another round of pastries, my phone buzzed insistently in my pocket. I pulled it out, my heart sinking as I read the message.

"Emergency meeting with the board. Can't miss it. Call me."

It was from my boss, the tone terse and demanding, an all-too-familiar urgency echoing within the words.

"Harper?" Ethan asked, concern knitting his brow as he noticed my sudden change in demeanor.

"I... it's work," I stammered, trying to mask the disappointment creeping into my voice.

"An emergency meeting?" he prodded gently. "Is everything okay?"

"Yeah, just the usual," I said, forcing a smile. "You know how it is—sometimes they want to talk about things that could have been an email."

He raised an eyebrow, clearly not buying my facade. "Sounds serious."

"It is," I said, my heart racing. "But I'll be back before you know it. I promise."

He studied me for a moment, the depth of his gaze unsettling, as if he could see right through my bravado. "Okay," he said slowly, "but don't let it ruin your night. We just made a pact to embrace life, remember?"

"Of course," I said, the weight of my phone pressing heavily in my hand. "I'll keep that in mind."

With one last lingering look, I slipped my phone back into my pocket, not wanting to mar this perfect evening with the worries of my job.

"Let's finish up and get back to enjoying the night," I said, forcing the lightness back into my tone.

"Right," he said, but I could tell he wasn't convinced.

As we wrapped up our treats, I felt a strange pull in my chest, a tension that hinted at unresolved issues lurking just beneath the surface. We walked back toward the heart of downtown, the laughter of passersby ringing in the air, but my mind was a swirl of worry and anticipation.

Ethan tried to maintain the light-heartedness, but I sensed an undercurrent of concern brewing in him. I needed to find a way to ease the tension, to keep this moment unspoiled.

"Tell me more about those stories you want to write," I said, desperate to shift the focus.

Just as he opened his mouth to respond, a loud crash echoed from the alley beside us, followed by frantic voices. We turned to see a figure stumbling out, wild-eyed and disheveled, clearly in distress.

"Help! Someone! Please!" the voice cried, and the laughter and lightness of our evening shattered like glass.

Ethan's expression hardened, his instincts kicking in. "Stay here," he said, his tone serious.

"No way," I protested, following him as he moved closer to the chaos unfolding in the alley.

As we approached, the figure—a woman—collapsed onto the pavement, her hands clutching a small bag tightly. The air shifted, charged with a new tension, as a sense of urgency filled the night.

"What happened?" Ethan asked, crouching beside her.

"They took it!" she gasped, her eyes wide with fear. "They took everything!"

The chaos of the night morphed into something darker, and a sense of foreboding settled over us like a heavy fog. Just as I was about to step closer, a shadow loomed behind Ethan, and I felt a chill creep down my spine.

In that moment, I realized our evening had taken a sharp turn, and the adventure we had embraced was spiraling into something entirely unpredictable. The sound of footsteps echoed behind us, and the stakes were suddenly higher than I could have imagined.

Chapter 10: The Turning Point

The first hint of winter nipped at the air as I sat at my favorite corner table in the coffee shop, my hands wrapped around a warm mug of cocoa. The rich aroma enveloped me like a cozy blanket, with steam swirling upwards, creating ephemeral shapes that danced and vanished into the overhead lights. I stared into the depths of the creamy concoction, lost in a whirlpool of thoughts. My heart raced as I replayed the recent months, each moment laden with uncertainty and fear. The window beside me framed the world outside, where leaves, tinged with burnt oranges and deep russets, fluttered down like whispered secrets, settling onto the cobblestone streets below.

I had chosen this spot for its charm, the worn wooden table that had seen countless conversations and the mismatched chairs that held a peculiar kind of comfort. The gentle hum of chatter around me formed a soft backdrop, punctuated by the occasional clinking of mugs and the hiss of the espresso machine, yet I was in my own world, teetering on the precipice of self-discovery. The patrons around me became mere shadows, their laughter and voices blending into a soothing melody that further ensnared me in my reverie.

Then, he appeared. Ethan, with his tousled dark hair that fell over his forehead and those captivating hazel eyes that held a spark of mischief. He was my anchor, the steady force in the turbulent seas of my insecurities. As he slid into the seat across from me, a familiar smile lit up his face, instantly warming the chilly space. "You look like you've just solved the world's problems," he teased, leaning forward, his playful demeanor disarming me in an instant.

I shrugged, a shy grin creeping onto my face. "Or maybe I'm just contemplating how to get my cocoa to stay warm long enough to finish it." The teasing tone between us felt like a lifeline, pulling me out of my spiral. He chuckled, the sound rich and full, like music on a crisp autumn day. Our conversations had always danced between light banter and deeper musings, but today felt different—charged with an electric anticipation that hinted at change.

"Let's talk about dreams," he said, tapping his fingers on the table rhythmically. "What's the biggest one you haven't chased yet?" His question pierced through the layers of my hesitation, stirring the dormant aspirations I had tucked away for far too long.

I hesitated, fingers tracing the rim of my mug as I pondered his words. "I've always wanted to write a book," I confessed, a flicker of vulnerability dancing in my chest. "But I keep putting it off, waiting for the right moment. I guess I thought I'd have to be someone else first—someone more confident, more... I don't know, worthy?"

Ethan tilted his head, his expression softening as he absorbed my words. "You're already worthy. You just need to believe it." His sincerity was a balm to my fraying nerves. "What's stopping you?"

I chuckled, though the sound was laced with bitterness. "Fear. Fear of failure, fear of putting myself out there. It's easier to hide behind my insecurities."

"And what if you didn't?" His challenge hung in the air, bold and unyielding. "What if you embraced all those quirks you think are flaws? Those are what make you uniquely you."

The warmth in his voice and the intensity of his gaze stirred something within me. Perhaps it was the cocoa or the gentle autumn light streaming through the window, but a spark of defiance flickered to life. "You know, maybe you're right. I'm tired of being afraid."

"Good." His smile deepened, revealing that adorable dimple on his left cheek that I could never resist. "You should fight for what you want. Not just for us, but for yourself."

The words hung between us, heavy with significance. I felt as if the universe had shifted, allowing me to see a path illuminated by possibility rather than shadows of doubt. "What about you?" I asked, my curiosity piqued. "What's your biggest dream?"

Ethan leaned back, his expression contemplative. "I've always wanted to travel the world. To experience different cultures, to write about them. But life gets in the way—work, responsibilities... the usual."

"Sounds familiar," I said with a wry grin. "Maybe we should make a pact. You inspire me to chase my dream, and I'll help you make yours a reality."

He raised an eyebrow, intrigued. "A dream team? I like the sound of that."

"Deal," I said, feeling an unfamiliar confidence swell within me. "But I need you to hold me accountable. I can be, well, prone to procrastination."

"Count on me," he replied, a teasing glint in his eyes. "But you have to promise to send me updates. I want to hear about every word you write, every moment you spend crafting that masterpiece."

His encouragement ignited a fire I hadn't realized was smoldering inside me. I could picture it now—the pages filled with my thoughts, my fears, my triumphs. It was intoxicating. I would no longer hide behind my awkwardness but embrace it, allowing it to shape me into a stronger version of who I was meant to be.

As our conversation meandered into lighter territory, filled with laughter and witty banter, I felt the weight of the past begin to lift. Each joke we shared chipped away at the walls I had constructed around my heart, walls built from years of self-doubt and insecurity. I realized this moment was not just about chasing dreams; it was about believing in myself, in us, and in the journey ahead.

The coffee shop buzzed around us, an ever-changing backdrop to our unfolding story, as the chill of winter crept closer, promising fresh beginnings and uncharted territories. The world outside faded away, leaving just the two of us, laughter intertwined with the warmth of shared aspirations, forging a path forward that felt exhilaratingly uncertain yet impossibly right.

The sun dipped lower in the sky, casting long shadows across the cobblestones as we left the coffee shop, the familiar bell above the door chiming in a cheerful farewell. Ethan and I stepped into the cool embrace of the late afternoon, and the air crackled with possibilities. I pulled my scarf tighter around my neck, the fabric a comforting reminder of the warmth I had found not just in our conversation but in my newfound determination.

"Where to next?" Ethan asked, his hazel eyes sparkling with mischief as he glanced around. The streets were alive, people bustling by, their laughter punctuating the crisp air.

"Let's wander," I suggested, feeling spontaneous and daring, as though I were shedding more than just my coat. "I've always wanted to explore the alleyways around here."

His smile widened. "A secret adventure? I like the sound of that. Lead the way, fearless explorer."

With a laugh, I gestured dramatically for him to follow. We turned down a narrow passageway lined with brick buildings that told stories of time and weather, their surfaces adorned with creeping vines and the occasional splash of graffiti art that brought splashes of color to the otherwise muted landscape.

The alley opened up into a small courtyard, a hidden gem with ivy-covered walls and a lone bench sitting beneath a gnarled tree. The sunlight filtered through the leaves, casting playful patterns on the cobblestone beneath our feet. I sank onto the bench, feeling like I had stumbled upon a secret hideaway. "This is perfect," I sighed, letting my head fall back against the cool wood. "It feels like a scene from a movie, doesn't it?"

Ethan sat beside me, his shoulder brushing against mine. "You mean a movie where the main character has an epiphany and realizes they can be the hero of their own story?" He nudged me playfully. "Because I'm all in for that."

"Exactly! I'm ready for my montage sequence where I write my book, travel the world, and maybe save a cat from a tree or something equally heroic," I shot back, my voice dripping with sarcasm.

"Just don't forget to include the dramatic love interest," he quipped, his expression turning mock-serious. "Every great hero needs one."

My heart raced at the suggestion, but I feigned indifference. "Oh, I don't know. It might distract from my epic journey. I mean, can you imagine trying to write a bestseller while also battling intense romantic feelings?"

"Intense romantic feelings can lead to great stories, though. Think about it. Tension, longing, perhaps a dramatic storm where everything comes to a head." He leaned closer, his voice dropping to a conspiratorial whisper. "And don't forget the inevitable kiss in the rain. It's a classic."

"Why is it always rain?" I asked, feigning frustration. "What's wrong with a sunny day?"

"Sunny days are for picnics and ice cream. Rain is for passion and angst," he declared, his voice playful, yet there was an earnest glint in his eye that sent my heart racing.

We lapsed into laughter, the sound melding with the distant echoes of city life around us. I could feel a warmth spreading in my chest, a sense of belonging I hadn't fully recognized before. It was exhilarating, knowing I was sharing these moments with someone who not only understood my aspirations but actively encouraged them.

As our laughter faded, a sudden thought struck me like a bolt of lightning. "What if I just... started writing right now? Like, here, in this moment?"

Ethan's eyes widened with excitement. "Do it! I'll be your audience. Just think of me as your very own literary critic, minus the beret and the pretentious air."

With an amused roll of my eyes, I pulled out my phone, determined to capture this surge of inspiration. I opened a notes app, staring at the blank screen, words swirling around my mind like leaves caught in a windstorm. "Okay, okay, here goes nothing."

I began typing, letting the thoughts flow without overthinking. "In a world where dreams felt unattainable, a girl discovered the power of embracing her true self..."

"See?" Ethan interjected, feigning a gasp of awe. "The magic has already begun! I can feel the award for Best Original Screenplay coming your way!"

I chuckled, my confidence growing with each keystroke. "If only I had your talent for charming words, I'd have a bestseller in no time."

"You already do, just in your own way," he said softly, the sincerity in his voice grounding me. "It's all about believing in yourself. You're the one holding the pen, after all."

His words washed over me, a reminder that I was more than just the girl who hid behind her insecurities. I was a dreamer, an adventurer, and now, perhaps a writer. The sun dipped lower, casting an amber glow that ignited the courtyard, and for the first time in a long while, I felt like I was exactly where I needed to be.

Lost in the moment, I barely noticed the shadow that drifted across our little haven. A sudden figure emerged from the shadows, breaking the spell: a woman, tall and commanding, with an air of confidence that was both alluring and intimidating. Her sharp features softened only slightly by the golden hues of the fading light.

"Excuse me, but is this where the award-winning author hangs out?" she asked, a teasing lilt in her voice.

I blinked, momentarily thrown off. "Um, well, not yet. I'm still working on my first draft."

She chuckled, her laughter ringing like chimes in the wind. "I admire the ambition. I'm Lila, by the way. I couldn't help but overhear your charming banter."

Ethan grinned, ever the social butterfly. "Charming? That's a strong word for what we've got going on. It's mostly just ridiculous nonsense."

"Ridiculous can be entertaining. I write a blog about local spots, and I think this little corner could use some exposure," Lila said, her gaze flitting between us. "Mind if I take a photo?"

I exchanged a glance with Ethan, the mix of curiosity and caution swirling within me. "Sure, but only if you promise to capture our good side."

Lila laughed, and in that moment, it felt like the world around us shifted again, as if this unexpected encounter could lead to something entirely new. I leaned closer to Ethan, our shoulders brushing, my heart thrumming in sync with the excitement buzzing in the air.

"Say cheese!" Lila chimed, her camera clicking as she captured the moment, the sound echoing in the stillness of our secret courtyard. The flash momentarily blinded me, but I couldn't help but smile. Ethan and I leaned into each other, our laughter bubbling over as we struck exaggerated poses, channeling our inner goofballs. I felt the warmth of his arm brushing against mine, grounding me in a way I hadn't anticipated.

"Perfect!" Lila exclaimed, reviewing her shots with the intensity of a director examining film dailies. "You two have a chemistry that's palpable. Are you sure you're not hiding a rom-com script in your back pocket?"

Ethan shot me a sidelong glance, a smirk playing at the corners of his mouth. "Not yet, but I'm taking notes for when she finally gets that book deal."

Lila grinned, tucking a strand of hair behind her ear. "You should definitely consider it. The world needs more lighthearted tales that don't shy away from genuine emotion. Speaking of which, I'd love to feature your story on my blog."

My heart raced at the unexpected offer. "You want to write about us? The spontaneous adventure duo?"

"Why not?" Lila replied with a shrug, her enthusiasm infectious. "There's something about your dynamic that feels refreshing. Plus, who wouldn't want to hear about two people diving into their dreams together?"

"Diving? More like flailing," I laughed, but deep down, her words struck a chord. The thought of sharing our journey felt thrilling yet terrifying, like standing at the edge of a diving board with no guarantee of a graceful splash.

Ethan leaned closer, his voice low and conspiratorial. "I think you'd be great at it. You have a story worth telling, and Lila seems like she could give it the spotlight it deserves."

"Okay, but what if I sound ridiculous?" I replied, uncertainty creeping back in. "What if my journey is filled with embarrassing moments and failed attempts?"

"Then that's what makes it real," Lila chimed in. "Authenticity resonates with people. They'll connect with your struggles, and trust me, every writer has embarrassing moments. It's what makes you relatable."

My mind raced with possibilities, a cocktail of excitement and fear swirling within me. The idea of baring my soul to strangers felt daunting, yet the prospect of inspiring others kept beckoning. "Fine. Let's do it," I declared, surprising even myself. "But you have to promise to soften my more ridiculous moments."

"Deal!" Lila clapped her hands together, a spark of enthusiasm lighting her eyes. "Now, give me the juicy details—how did you two meet?"

The sunlight dipped lower, casting a warm glow around us as we settled into our impromptu storytelling session. Ethan and I exchanged glances, our past blooming vividly in my mind like a well-worn novel, each page filled with quirky moments that led us to this very point.

As we recounted our meet-cute at a local art gallery, where I had nearly knocked over a priceless sculpture while attempting to impress him with my knowledge of abstract art, laughter bubbled between us. "And you still came back to talk to me afterward!" I exclaimed, shaking my head in disbelief.

"Of course! I couldn't resist the charming girl who nearly brought down the gallery. You had this fearless spark," he replied, his voice laced with fondness.

Just then, a familiar figure caught my eye, striding purposefully toward our courtyard. My heart dropped as I recognized Marissa, my ex-best friend. Her long, wavy hair flowed behind her like a cape, but today, the usual confidence radiating from her seemed tinged with something darker.

"Great, just what we need," I muttered under my breath, tension creeping back in. I had avoided Marissa for months since our falling out, and now she appeared, a storm brewing behind her stormy eyes.

"Uh-oh. Do we need to hit the escape route?" Ethan whispered, a hint of concern etched across his face.

"Not yet," I replied, hoping to project confidence I didn't quite feel.

"Hey! Mind if I join?" Marissa's voice cut through the laughter, her gaze locking onto me, assessing. There was an edge to her tone that made me uneasy.

"Actually, we were just—" I began, but she brushed past me, plopping down on the bench with a decisiveness that left no room for debate.

"I heard you two talking about dreams and all that. Thought I'd see what the fuss was about," she said, her smile stretched thin like a rubber band ready to snap.

"Lila was just offering to feature us on her blog," Ethan said quickly, his eyes darting between us, sensing the tension thickening the air.

Marissa's smile faltered for a fraction of a second before she regained her composure. "How quaint. A little blog, is it?" she said, the words dripped with a hint of mockery. "I suppose you're going to turn your lives into a fairytale now?"

Her words sliced through the moment like a knife, and I felt my pulse quicken. "What's that supposed to mean?" I shot back, my cheeks flushing with indignation.

She leaned back, crossing her arms, her gaze piercing. "Just that you've always had a knack for making everything seem more glamorous than it really is. You and your dreams."

"Dreams are what make life worth living," I retorted, my voice firmer than I felt. "Isn't that right, Ethan?"

"Absolutely," he replied, shooting me a supportive smile that momentarily steadied my resolve.

Marissa rolled her eyes, her expression unreadable. "Sure, but don't forget reality has a funny way of reminding us who we really are. Not everyone can just write their way into a happy ending."

Her words hung in the air, heavy with unspoken tension, and a knot tightened in my stomach. Was this a warning, or was she simply trying to regain her place in my life? I didn't know, but as I glanced at Ethan, I could see he was just as perplexed.

"Look," he said, attempting to diffuse the situation, "we're all about authenticity here. Sometimes it's messy, and that's okay."

"Messy? That's an understatement," Marissa shot back, her voice rising slightly. "What happens when the real world catches up to your little fantasies?"

Before I could respond, the ground beneath us seemed to shift, as if the universe itself had decided to intervene. A sudden crack of thunder rumbled overhead, and we all looked up to see dark clouds swirling ominously above us, blotting out the warm sunlight.

"Looks like a storm's coming," Lila said, her tone shifting to one of unease.

A gust of wind whipped through the courtyard, sending leaves spiraling and sending a shiver down my spine. I felt the air change, crackling with energy and tension, mirroring the brewing conflict among us. Marissa's gaze was fixed on me, and I sensed an unspoken challenge in her eyes.

Before I could voice my thoughts or confront her head-on, the sky opened up, releasing a torrential downpour that soaked us within seconds. The sound of rain pelting the ground was deafening, drowning out everything else, and chaos erupted as we scrambled to find shelter.

"Let's get inside!" Ethan shouted, tugging me toward the nearest doorway, but just as we started to move, I caught one last glimpse of Marissa, her eyes narrowed, a smirk playing on her lips.

As the rain cascaded around us, I couldn't shake the feeling that this storm was only the beginning. The tension hung thick in the air, and as we raced for cover, a thought gnawed at me: what had Marissa truly meant with her words? And as the clouds roared above, I realized that sometimes, storms were more than just weather—they were harbingers of change, and I could feel that something significant was about to break.

Chapter 11: The Challenge

The air buzzed with a palpable energy as I stood backstage, the cacophony of laughter and clinking glasses spilling from the bar like a vibrant tide. My heart raced, a frantic drumbeat against my ribcage. Each rhythmic thud reminded me of what lay ahead—an open mic night at The Rusty Nail, a dive known for its eclectic mix of talent and unwavering support for the brave souls willing to bare their souls on stage. I was terrified, yet there was something intoxicating about the anticipation, the kind that crackled like static in the air.

Ethan leaned against the wall, casually flipping through his notecards, a mischievous grin playing on his lips. "You know, if you trip over the mic cord and fall flat on your face, I'll definitely catch it on video," he teased, his blue eyes sparkling with mischief.

"Thanks for the vote of confidence," I shot back, rolling my eyes, but I couldn't suppress a smile. Ethan had this magical way of transforming my nerves into something lighter, something that felt almost manageable. "Just don't trip on your own brilliance when you step up there."

"Brilliance, huh? I like the sound of that," he quipped, leaning in closer, his voice dropping to a conspiratorial whisper. "But I'd settle for just not embarrassing myself."

I had to admire his casual swagger, his innate ability to make everything feel like an adventure, even when the prospect of standing in front of a room full of strangers made my stomach twist into knots. He was a magnet of energy, drawing everyone in with a charm that was as effortless as it was infectious. I felt like a moth, fluttering closer to a flame I both craved and feared.

With every passing moment, I felt the anticipation morph into something more profound—a bittersweet cocktail of fear and excitement that sent my thoughts spiraling. What if they didn't like my poetry? What if I froze, mouth dry and mind blank, under the unforgiving glare of the spotlight? I tried to quell the anxiety swirling in my stomach, reciting the lines I had practiced a hundred times, yet the words felt like butterflies flitting out of reach.

Ethan clasped my hand, grounding me, his touch warm and reassuring. "Are you ready?" he asked, his voice a steady anchor amidst the chaos.

"Ready as I'll ever be," I said, though doubt seeped into my voice like ink spreading across paper. The low hum of chatter faded as we approached the stage, and I squinted into the bright lights that washed over the wooden floor like a river of gold. The crowd appeared as a blurred mass, faces illuminated by the soft glow of candles flickering on the tables. A sense of vulnerability enveloped me, but Ethan's confident presence beside me ignited a flicker of hope.

"Remember, it's just you and me out there," he said, his eyes locking onto mine with a fierce intensity. "We've got this."

The MC called our names, and the moment stretched, a taut wire ready to snap. As we stepped into the spotlight, the laughter faded, replaced by an expectant silence. I could feel the heat radiating from the stage lights, and it mingled with the coolness of the night air that slipped through the bar's open door. I could almost taste the anticipation—the promise of something thrilling just beyond my reach.

Ethan grinned at the crowd, his confidence shining like a beacon. "Hey, everyone! We're here to share a few poems. I promise they won't bite," he joked, and laughter erupted from the audience, a wave of sound that washed over me, momentarily easing my nerves.

I leaned into the mic, feeling the cool metal against my lips, my palms damp against the paper in my hands. The first few lines slipped out, tentative at first, but as I saw Ethan nodding encouragingly, the words began to flow like a river unbound. My heart settled into a rhythm, and I lost myself in the verses that spoke of longing and discovery, each line a fragile thread connecting me to the audience.

I glanced at Ethan, who watched me with an expression that mixed pride and admiration. The world around us blurred into insignificance as I poured my heart into the poem, revealing pieces of my soul I rarely shared. The warmth of the crowd's reception wrapped around me, a blanket of acceptance that urged me to continue, and with every stanza, I shed layers of fear, like a snake shedding its skin.

As I finished, a wave of applause crashed over me, a tidal force that threatened to sweep me off my feet. I looked over at Ethan, who beamed like a proud father, and I couldn't help but laugh, exhilarated and surprised by the burst of emotion within me.

"You were incredible!" he exclaimed as we switched places, and I felt buoyed by his enthusiasm, my own heart racing alongside his.

He stepped to the front, his charm captivating the crowd as he shared his own piece, a poignant reflection on vulnerability and connection that struck a chord deep within me. The way he wielded words was an art, each syllable woven with passion and sincerity.

His performance resonated with the audience, their laughter mingling with murmurs of appreciation, and I felt a swell of pride. This was the man who had challenged me to confront my fears, and in this moment, it was as if we were both laying bare our hearts under the spotlight, unveiling the raw edges of our souls to a room full of strangers.

When he finished, the applause swelled again, this time a chorus of appreciation that enveloped us like a warm embrace. I reached for his hand, squeezing it tightly, and the look he gave me—a blend of excitement and gratitude—took my breath away. It was a moment suspended in time, a reminder that facing our fears together could forge an unbreakable bond.

As we stepped off the stage, laughter and chatter resumed around us, but the world felt different, softer. The knot of anxiety had unraveled, replaced by a newfound confidence that pulsed through my veins. I had stepped into the spotlight, yes, but more importantly, I had stepped closer to Ethan, who stood beside me, a partner in this exhilarating dance of life. Together, we had faced our fears and emerged stronger, ready to embrace whatever came next, no matter how daunting it might seem.

The night air outside The Rusty Nail felt charged with electricity, like the calm before a storm. After our electrifying performance, Ethan and I slipped into the bar's back patio, a hidden gem adorned with twinkling fairy lights that draped over the wooden beams like stars caught in a net. The chatter from the inside faded, replaced by the distant strum of an acoustic guitar and the comforting sounds of clinking glasses and laughter that floated in from the bar's interior. It was a far cry from the tension of the stage, and for a moment, the world felt softer, wrapped in the warm glow of lanterns that flickered gently against the darkening sky.

I took a deep breath, trying to inhale the sense of accomplishment that buzzed in the air like the last notes of a song. "I can't believe we did that," I said, my voice tinged with disbelief and exhilaration. I tucked a strand of hair behind my ear, a nervous habit that seemed to linger, even in moments of triumph.

"Did you see the way they reacted?" Ethan's eyes sparkled, his enthusiasm infectious. "You had them eating out of the palm of your hand! They were hanging on every word."

I laughed, the sound bubbling out of me like champagne. "That might be a bit of an exaggeration. I mean, there were people ordering drinks during my poem. I can't compete with cocktails."

Ethan leaned closer, a teasing grin on his face. "Maybe you should write a poem about cocktails. 'Ode to the Margarita'—it could be a hit!"

"Oh please, I'd probably just end up spilling half of it on myself in the process," I replied, shaking my head, imagining the catastrophe of sloshing drinks while trying to recite my work.

He nudged my shoulder, his laughter intertwining with the warm breeze. "Well, if that's the case, we could always do a dramatic reading with props. I'll be your trusty bartender, and we can improvise."

"Just what I need—a comedy duo act for my poetic endeavors," I shot back, my heart soaring as I took in the way his smile lit up his face. There was something so wonderfully refreshing about being in his orbit, a warmth that spread through me like sunlight breaking through the clouds.

As the night wore on, the sky deepened into a navy blue, the stars glimmering like diamonds scattered carelessly across velvet. We found a secluded corner at the far end of the patio, where the chatter from the bar became a low hum, almost a soothing background. The laughter and music created a kind of soundtrack to our conversation, wrapping around us like a comforting blanket.

"So, what's next on this adventure of facing our fears?" I asked, curiosity piqued. The night had sparked something in me, a desire to embrace the unpredictability of life and take more leaps of faith.

Ethan tapped his chin thoughtfully, the moonlight casting playful shadows across his features. "How about we take a dance class? You know, just the two of us—nothing like some awkward footwork to bond us even more."

"A dance class?" I raised an eyebrow, half-laughing at the idea and half-excited. "What's next, tangoing in the park?"

"Hey, you never know! We might be the next big dance sensation," he said, mimicking a dramatic pose, his arms outstretched as if leading an imaginary partner in a grand waltz.

I giggled, imagining us spinning wildly across a floor, colliding into other couples while desperately trying to remember the steps. "I can see it now: 'Dancing with the Stars' comes calling, and they're all like, 'What is this chaotic whirlwind?'"

"Exactly!" He laughed, his delight infectious. "We'd be a sensation for all the wrong reasons."

"Or we could just stick to the poetry and leave the dancing to the professionals," I suggested, the thought of twirling around a floor with Ethan sent a mix of excitement and trepidation through me.

"Oh come on, where's your sense of adventure?" He nudged me again, his eyes twinkling. "Besides, I'll be right there with you. We can't be any worse than those two people who were practically doing the cha-cha in the corner just now."

I turned to glance inside, where indeed, two individuals were making a valiant, if not awkward, attempt at dancing to a lively tune, their movements both spirited and chaotic. The sight made me laugh again, and it struck me that perhaps we could dive into something as light-hearted as dance.

"You make a compelling argument," I conceded, feeling the thrill of potential adventures ahead. "But if we're going to dance, you have to promise not to step on my toes."

"Cross my heart," he promised, raising his right hand dramatically. "And if I do, I'll make it up to you by cooking dinner one night."

"Now that's a deal I can get behind," I said, the prospect of an evening with Ethan—a candlelit dinner and the aroma of something delicious wafting through the air—made my heart flutter.

As we chatted and laughed, the night unfolded, layers of connection unfurling between us, building something beautiful and fragile. Each shared moment felt like a stepping stone, and I could sense that we were weaving a tapestry of memories that would linger long after this night.

Suddenly, Ethan's expression shifted, the warmth replaced by a hint of vulnerability. "You know, this whole challenge thing? It's not just about the activities. It's about pushing each other, growing together. I'm really glad we're doing this."

His sincerity hit me like a soft breeze, stirring something deep within. I nodded, the weight of his words settling over me. "Me too. I never thought I could share my poetry like that, let alone feel so… free."

"I think we're just getting started," he said, his voice low, holding a promise that made my pulse quicken. "Whatever comes next, I'm ready if you are."

The night wrapped around us, a cocoon of possibility, as laughter and music danced in the background. In that moment, I knew that with Ethan beside me, there was no fear we couldn't face, no challenge too daunting. Together, we were crafting our own adventure, one unexpected twist at a time, and it felt like the beginning of something wonderfully, beautifully new.

The evening air around us held a delicate chill, wrapping us in a cozy embrace as we lingered on the patio, where the laughter and chatter from the bar created a warm backdrop. I leaned back in my chair, a dreamy smile lingering on my lips, the echoes of our performance still dancing in my mind. Ethan leaned forward, elbows on the table, his gaze sharp with mischief. "Okay, so about that dance class—when are we signing up?"

I pretended to ponder, swirling my drink as I fought the urge to laugh. "Only if you promise not to wear those awful neon dance shoes I saw you eyeing the other day."

"Those shoes have personality!" he retorted, feigning offense. "Besides, it's all about expressing oneself. They'd make me unforgettable!"

"Oh, you're definitely unforgettable," I shot back, rolling my eyes playfully. "More like, 'Oh my God, who dressed that guy?'"

Ethan chuckled, his laughter blending seamlessly with the sounds of the night. The moment felt light and free, the shadows of uncertainty that had previously loomed over me retreating like a tide. I was grateful for this connection, this unexpected camaraderie that blossomed amidst the chaos of our lives. But just as I began to relish the thought of future adventures, the shadows returned, creeping into the edges of my mind.

"I mean it, though," Ethan continued, his tone shifting slightly, a hint of sincerity threading through the joviality. "I want us to do more things together. I think we're growing as a team."

The way he looked at me, a mixture of warmth and determination, sparked something in my chest—a yearning to dive deeper into this newfound bond. "You know what?" I said, leaning in, "I'm up for it. Let's be the craziest pair in town. Dance classes, poetry slams—bring it on."

Just as he was about to respond, the bar door swung open, a gust of laughter spilling onto the patio like confetti. An older gentleman with a thick white mustache and a playful twinkle in his eye strode towards us, clutching a well-worn guitar. "Did someone say poetry slams?" he bellowed, his voice booming with enthusiasm. "I used to be a poet in my day, you know! And I still have some tricks up my sleeve."

Ethan's grin widened, his eyes sparkling with excitement. "We just did our first one tonight!"

The man's brow shot up, a hint of respect mingling with the mischief. "And how did it go? Please tell me you weren't reciting haikus about the weather!"

I laughed, shaking my head. "I'll have you know, I'm way more complex than that. I tackled some deep existential themes."

"Ah, a modern-day Shakespeare! Next, you'll be telling me you write sonnets on the side," he teased, plopping down at our table with an exaggerated flourish.

"Only when the mood strikes," I replied, feeling surprisingly comfortable with this newcomer. "What about you? Do you have any poetic aspirations?"

He chuckled, plucking a few strings on his guitar absentmindedly. "Just the aspiration to keep my fingers moving and my heart singing. Would you care for a demonstration?"

Ethan and I exchanged glances, a spark of adventure igniting between us. "Absolutely! Let's hear what you've got," Ethan encouraged, leaning back in his chair, clearly ready for anything.

The man, whose name turned out to be Charlie, strummed a gentle melody, the notes curling through the air like smoke from a freshly lit fire. "This one's called 'The Night's Embrace'—an ode to the unpredictable joys that creep up on you when you least expect them," he said, a twinkle in his eye as he began to sing.

His voice was gravelly yet warm, wrapping around the lyrics like a favorite blanket. The song danced through the air, vivid images springing to life with each line. I couldn't help but smile, enchanted by his talent and the unexpected bond forming right before my eyes.

As he finished, the bar erupted in applause, and I joined in, clapping enthusiastically. "That was incredible!" I exclaimed, genuinely impressed. "You've got some serious talent, Charlie."

"Thank you, thank you!" he grinned, taking a dramatic bow. "But enough about me! What are you two planning next? An album? A tour?"

"Maybe just a dance class," Ethan replied, winking at me. "Nothing too ambitious."

"Oh, I can see it now!" Charlie leaned in, his eyes alight with mischief. "You'll be the toast of the town—dancing and reciting poetry, winning hearts and minds. But here's a challenge for you both: How about a song challenge?"

"A song challenge?" I repeated, intrigued. "What does that entail?"

"Simple! You each have to write a short song about your favorite subject, and then you perform it right here next week!" Charlie announced, his excitement palpable. "I'll provide the guitar. What do you say?"

Ethan turned to me, a teasing glint in his eye. "Are you up for it, poetess? Think of it as our next step in fear-facing. It could be fun!"

"Fun? Or utterly terrifying?" I shot back, pretending to contemplate while the flutter of nerves danced in my stomach. "What if I blank out in front of everyone?"

"Then you'll just have to improvise! That's what I did when I forgot my lines during my first performance," Charlie said, his tone encouraging. "You'll find your rhythm. Trust me, it's all part of the experience."

I sighed, the weight of the challenge settling heavily in my mind. A song? The very thought made me tremble. Yet, deep down, a flicker of excitement ignited, mingling with the anxiety. "Fine. I'm in," I said, feeling the rush of adrenaline coursing through me.

"Yes! And I'll join too!" Ethan declared, his enthusiasm infectious. "Together, we'll create an unforgettable masterpiece."

I laughed, the weight of my fears momentarily lifted by the thought of facing them alongside him. "Unforgettable, indeed," I mused, glancing at Ethan. "More like a disaster in the making."

"Or the best thing we've ever done," he countered, his smile unwavering.

The energy at the table crackled as we mapped out ideas for our songs, the evening transforming into a whirlwind of creativity and laughter. But just as I was about to share an idea about combining elements of nature with romance, a commotion erupted from the bar, cutting through our banter like a knife.

I turned, my heart racing as the door swung open again, revealing a flustered waitress and a group of patrons hovering around the entrance. "Hey, is everything okay?" I called out, concern washing over me.

The waitress, her face flushed, looked frazzled. "There's been an incident! Someone's lost a wallet, and they think it might have been stolen!"

A hush fell over the patio, the laughter and music fading into the background. The bar's atmosphere shifted abruptly from carefree to tense, and a sense of unease began to weave its way into our gathering. My heart raced, the weight of uncertainty pressing down as the patrons exchanged worried glances.

Ethan's hand tightened around mine, and I could feel his pulse quicken. "Do you want to check it out?" he asked, concern etching his features.

I nodded, the intrigue drawing me closer to the unfolding drama. "Definitely. Let's see what's happening."

As we rose from our seats, the atmosphere buzzed with uncertainty, the air thick with unspoken questions. The challenge we had embraced suddenly felt overshadowed by a much darker threat, as we stepped back into the bar, ready to uncover whatever mystery lay ahead. My heart thudded in my chest, a mix of excitement and apprehension, as I prepared for whatever revelation awaited us on the other side of the door.

Chapter 12: The Performance

The stage lights glared down on us, a blazing halo that turned the world into a soft blur. I could barely see the faces of the audience through the haze of the spotlight, but I could feel their energy buzzing in the air like static before a storm. My heart raced in time with the pulsing beat of the music that played in the background, but it wasn't fear that propelled me; it was an electric thrill, a sweet anticipation that coursed through my veins. I shifted my weight from one foot to the other, trying to tame the nerves dancing in my stomach, but as I looked at Ethan beside me, I found an anchor in his unwavering gaze.

Ethan stood tall and confident, his messy curls catching the light in a way that made him look almost ethereal. He wore that signature lopsided grin, the kind that had a way of igniting warmth in even the coldest of hearts. The smell of his cologne—a mix of sandalwood and something fresh, like rain on asphalt—wrapped around me, grounding me in the moment. We were here, together, ready to bare our souls to the world through our words.

"Are you ready?" he whispered, leaning slightly closer, his breath brushing against my ear, sending a shiver down my spine.

"As ready as I'll ever be," I replied, attempting to inject confidence into my voice, but the slight tremor betrayed my nerves. We had rehearsed this a thousand times, yet standing here, with the weight of everyone's eyes upon us, felt like standing on the edge of a cliff. The thrill of the unknown beckoned, daring us to leap.

With a shared nod, we took a collective breath, and then it was time. The music faded, and the stage was ours. I stepped forward, the cool wooden floor beneath my feet anchoring me, and began reciting my poem, my voice steady and clear. The words flowed out of me like a river, rich and deep, carrying with them echoes of my experiences, my loves, and the lessons learned along the way. I painted a picture of vulnerability, each line a brushstroke that laid bare the layers of my heart.

Ethan joined in, his voice a deep, melodic counterpoint to mine, weaving seamlessly into the fabric of my verses. As we spoke, our eyes locked, creating a bridge between us that felt like an unbreakable bond. The audience leaned forward, engrossed, and I could almost hear their collective heartbeat syncing with ours. Each stanza fell into place, a dance of rhythm and emotion that swirled around us, wrapping us in an intimate embrace that felt both exhilarating and terrifying.

The rush of performing was intoxicating. The audience responded with rapturous applause as we finished, a wave of sound that washed over me like a warm embrace. I beamed, my cheeks flushing with joy. We had done it. We had conquered our fears, taking a leap into vulnerability and landing triumphantly on the other side. The moment hung in the air, suspended in time, a testament to our shared courage and creativity.

Once we stepped off the stage, adrenaline surged through me. I could still feel the heat of the spotlight on my skin, and the echo of applause rang in my ears like a beautiful symphony. We were quickly enveloped by friends, their cheers and laughter blending together in a joyous cacophony. I spotted Jenna, her vibrant red hair like a beacon in the crowd, waving enthusiastically as she navigated her way towards us.

"Did you see that? You two were amazing!" she exclaimed, throwing her arms around both of us. "You had the entire room eating out of the palm of your hands!"

"Did you think they would applaud?" Ethan chuckled, nudging me playfully with his elbow. "I thought I might hear crickets."

"Please," Jenna scoffed, rolling her eyes. "With the way you two performed, I wouldn't be surprised if they were dreaming of encore performances."

As laughter erupted around us, I felt the weight of the world lifting off my shoulders. In this moment, surrounded by friends who understood the hard work and dedication we had poured into this performance, I was buoyed by an overwhelming sense of belonging. We made our way to the bar, where drinks flowed like the very poetry we had just shared.

I ordered a cocktail—a concoction of gin and elderflower, refreshing and light. The first sip danced on my tongue, a delicious spark of flavor that mirrored my mood. Ethan leaned against the bar beside me, his arm brushing against mine, and I caught a hint of his warmth radiating through the fabric of my shirt.

"Next time, let's do something even more daring," he proposed, his eyes glinting with mischief. "What do you think about a spoken word competition? Just you and me against the world?"

"Are you trying to kill me?" I laughed, shaking my head. "You know I'm not exactly a competitive person. What if we embarrass ourselves?"

"Or we could become local legends!" He grinned, his enthusiasm infectious. "Think of the stories we'll tell. 'Once upon a time, in a tiny little bar, two poets captured the hearts of everyone present and ended up in the local paper.'"

As he spoke, I couldn't help but be swept away by his imagination. There was a spark in his eyes that mirrored the excitement bubbling within me. I imagined it: our names in print, our words reaching beyond this small venue and into the world.

"Alright, you have yourself a deal," I replied, a playful glint igniting in my own gaze. "But if we're going to do this, I want to write something that really challenges us. Something raw."

"Now you're speaking my language," he said, raising his glass to toast. "To challenges and adventures!"

As our glasses clinked, I felt a sense of determination settle within me. This was just the beginning, and I was ready to embrace whatever came next—fear, vulnerability, and all.

The energy in the bar pulsed like a heartbeat, vibrant and alive. Friends encircled us, each of their faces lit with joy, and I felt as though we had woven ourselves into a tapestry of shared triumphs and dreams. Laughter mingled with the clinking of glasses, creating a symphony of celebration that reverberated through the room. I savored the sweet tang of my cocktail, the elderflower dancing lightly on my tongue, while the atmosphere buzzed with excitement and the promise of new adventures.

"Alright, people!" Jenna called, her voice cutting through the merriment like a clarion bell. "It's time for a toast! To our fearless poets—may they never run out of words, inspiration, or cocktails!"

Laughter erupted again, and I raised my glass, feeling the warmth of the moment settle around us like a cozy blanket. Ethan stood beside me, his eyes shining with an enthusiasm that was utterly contagious. I could see him already mentally crafting our next performance, the gears of his creative mind spinning faster than I could keep up. He had an uncanny ability to turn every idea into an adventure, no matter how wild or daunting.

"Here's to our next big leap," I added, my voice ringing clear above the laughter. "And may we not embarrass ourselves too terribly!"

"Oh, come on," Ethan said, his eyebrows raised in mock disbelief. "If we're going to embarrass ourselves, let's do it spectacularly. The kind of flops that'll go down in history!"

"Good thing I'm not aiming for history. Just survival," I shot back, a smirk playing at the corners of my mouth.

As the evening unfolded, the energy only intensified. Friends shared stories of their own creative endeavors—Jenna had recently started painting again, inspired by a whimsical dream she had about dancing flamingos, and Alex was gearing up for an open mic night, where he planned to unveil his newest stand-up routine. The possibilities seemed endless, and I could almost feel the creative pulse of the room pushing us all forward, daring us to reach for something more.

But amid the laughter, a flicker of unease tugged at the edges of my mind. What if my next performance didn't live up to the expectations we had just set? I caught Ethan's gaze again, and the spark of determination in his eyes reassured me. He seemed to sense my hesitation.

"Hey," he said, leaning in closer, his voice low but firm, "you okay? You seem a little distant."

"I'm fine," I lied, shaking off the self-doubt that threatened to creep in. "Just thinking about what comes next."

"Next is whatever we make it," he replied, his confidence unwavering. "This is our moment, and we're going to ride it as far as it takes us. Don't let the 'what ifs' drown out the 'what can be.'"

His words wrapped around me like a comforting hug, and I couldn't help but smile. "You really believe that, don't you?"

"Of course! I mean, look at us!" He gestured broadly, encompassing our friends, the bar, the entire universe. "We just took the stage and shared our hearts. What could possibly be more exhilarating than that?"

"Riding a rollercoaster without the safety bar?" I teased, nudging him lightly with my elbow.

"Okay, maybe that one would be worse," he laughed. "But it wouldn't be nearly as fun without you."

As the night wore on, we found ourselves outside, the cool evening air refreshing against our flushed cheeks. The stars twinkled overhead, shimmering like scattered diamonds against a velvet backdrop. It felt as though the universe was celebrating with us, and

I could almost hear the echoes of our performance in the rustling leaves.

"Let's go for a walk," Ethan suggested, his tone light yet inviting. "We can plan our next masterpiece under the stars."

"Are you sure you can handle my creative genius? It can be overwhelming," I replied, feigning seriousness.

He snorted, a laugh escaping before he could stop it. "Please. I thrive on your genius. It's like rocket fuel for my imagination."

"Then strap in, because I'm about to launch us into orbit!" I declared, my spirits soaring higher with every step we took down the quiet street, the soft glow of streetlights guiding our way.

The world felt different, charged with possibility. The sidewalks were familiar, yet tonight they sparkled with a sense of newness. As we strolled, we discussed everything from themes for our next performance to the possibility of including props—a brilliant idea, if I did say so myself. I imagined the two of us on stage, surrounded by whimsical items that added layers to our poetry.

"Picture this: a giant inflatable flamingo in the background while we recite a poem about summer love," Ethan proposed, his eyes lighting up with mischief.

"Oh, I love it! And we could wear matching beach hats!" I countered, my laughter mingling with his.

"Clearly, we're going to take the poetic world by storm," he grinned, shaking his head as if trying to rein in his excitement. "But you know what? I think it's time we explore something darker. A poem about heartbreak, maybe."

My heart sank slightly at the mention of heartbreak, a topic I had avoided since we began this journey. "But do we have to? I mean, who wants to relive the worst parts of life?"

"Sometimes those 'worst parts' lead to the most beautiful creations," he said, his tone gentle but insistent. "It's a part of the process, and we can't ignore it."

I sighed, staring at the ground as we walked. "You might be right, but it's not easy to revisit those memories."

"I get that," he replied, his voice softening. "But you're not alone. Whatever we create will be ours, together. We'll face it side by side, just like we did tonight."

His sincerity washed over me, and I felt a swell of appreciation for the bond we were forging. "You make it sound so simple," I murmured.

"Maybe it is. Or maybe it's just a little messy," he said with a shrug, a hint of a smile creeping onto his lips. "Life is messy, and we're just two artists trying to make sense of it all."

I looked up at him, my heart fluttering at the depth of his understanding. "Alright, then. Let's dive into the mess together."

With renewed determination, we continued down the street, our laughter mingling with the night air. The weight of my earlier insecurities faded away, replaced by the exhilarating prospect of exploring new depths in our poetry and, perhaps, in ourselves. There was something powerful about vulnerability—an unspoken promise of growth that lay waiting just beneath the surface. And as we wandered, I couldn't shake the feeling that the best was yet to come.

The night air shimmered with a cool, inviting freshness, an antidote to the warmth of the bar we had just left. As we strolled, our laughter echoed off the cobblestone streets, a sweet reminder of the joy that had filled the performance. The flickering glow of streetlights cast playful shadows, turning our every step into a small adventure, each moment a brushstroke on the canvas of the evening.

Ethan's exuberance was infectious. "I can't believe we just did that! The rush! The applause!" He was practically bouncing beside me, the energy radiating off him like a supernova. "We need to channel this feeling into our next piece. I mean, if we can do that, we can do anything!"

"Like rob a bank?" I suggested, grinning mischievously. "I hear poetry is great for disguises."

"Oh, I'll wear a beret. That'll throw them off." He chuckled, pretending to adjust an invisible hat, striking a pose that was equal parts ridiculous and charming.

I couldn't help but laugh, the warmth of the evening embracing us. But as we turned a corner, a darker shadow flitted across my mind. What if our next performance fell flat? What if I couldn't dig deep enough to share my truth? My smile faltered, but I masked it with another playful jab. "Just remember, if we do rob a bank, I'm not sharing the loot."

"Fair enough. I wouldn't want to spoil our friendship over stolen cash." He paused, catching my gaze, his expression shifting to something more serious. "But seriously, let's make sure we tackle something real for the next piece. We can use this energy to break down walls."

"Okay, okay," I conceded, feeling the weight of his earnestness. "But you realize you're setting the bar really high, right? What if I'm not ready to go there?"

"You're more ready than you think," he replied, a softness in his tone that made my heart flutter. "We've got to embrace the messy bits. That's where the good stuff hides."

Our conversation spiraled into the art of poetry and performance, each idea flaring into life between us like fireworks. The night unfolded as we wandered through a maze of thoughts, each more exhilarating than the last. Just as we reached a particularly enchanting little square, where flowers spilled from window boxes and laughter floated from nearby cafés, I felt the stirrings of confidence bubbling up within me.

"Alright," I said, pausing to take in the beauty around us, "let's put together something that captures this moment. Something that speaks to the excitement of now."

Ethan's face lit up. "Yes! A celebration of everything—the laughter, the fear, the joy, the connection! We can do it together."

Before I could respond, a familiar voice sliced through the serene atmosphere like a blade. "Well, well, if it isn't the dynamic duo of angst and ambition."

I turned, spotting Mark, my old classmate, leaning casually against a lamppost. He wore a smug grin, one that dripped with the kind of condescension that made my stomach twist.

"Mark," I said, forcing my voice to remain steady, "nice to see you."

"Is it really?" he shot back, his tone laced with mockery. "I must say, I'm surprised to see you performing poetry. You always seemed more of the, oh, I don't know, the 'I'll just keep my thoughts to myself' type."

Ethan stiffened beside me, the air growing thick with tension. "And yet here we are, performing for a captivated audience," he replied, his voice cool. "What have you done lately, Mark? Besides lurking in the shadows?"

"Lurking? I prefer the term 'observing,'" he said with a wave of his hand, brushing off Ethan's jab. "I just thought I'd drop by to witness the spectacle. It's quite the change from the shy girl I remember."

The way he spoke cut deeper than any knife. It reminded me of old insecurities, the fear that I'd never truly break free from the shadows of my past. I could feel Ethan tense beside me, ready to pounce on Mark's venomous comments.

"Is that really all you've got?" I asked, forcing my voice to be light despite the sting of his words. "You should know by now that growth isn't linear. I'm not afraid to share my story anymore."

Mark's smirk faltered for a heartbeat, replaced by a flicker of something that resembled curiosity. "Oh, so we're sharing stories now? What's next? A cozy book club in someone's basement?"

Ethan stepped forward, standing protectively at my side. "You might be surprised at how much sharing can inspire, Mark. But I guess that's hard for someone who thrives on cynicism."

Mark crossed his arms, leaning back as though he was watching a play unfold. "Touché. But let's not forget that your words can fall flat too. That stage can be a harsh mistress, and I'd hate for you to find out the hard way."

"Or maybe it's just a stepping stone," I said, trying to reclaim the power in this exchange. "A platform to reach new heights."

"Interesting perspective," Mark replied, his smirk returning. "Just make sure you don't fall too far."

With that, he pushed off the lamppost and sauntered away, leaving an unsettling silence in his wake. The lingering tension felt like a cold draft, but Ethan remained steadfast beside me, the warmth of his presence a comforting contrast.

"Are you okay?" he asked, concern etched on his face.

"I'm fine," I said, my voice steadier than I felt. "Just... it's frustrating to have someone like him show up right now, isn't it?"

"It's infuriating," he replied, his gaze hardening. "But you know what? His words don't define you. You're stronger than you realize."

I took a deep breath, the air filling my lungs with a refreshing clarity. "I just want to prove to myself that I can be brave enough to share my truth without letting his doubts seep in."

"Then let's make that the heart of our next piece," Ethan suggested, his eyes brightening with inspiration. "We'll use his negativity as fuel. We'll write something that will echo long after he's forgotten."

His determination lit a fire within me, but the embers of uncertainty still flickered at the edges of my mind. As we began walking again, I felt the need to shake off the remnants of Mark's disdain. The streets felt oddly constricting, the flowers around us losing their vibrancy. I glanced sideways at Ethan, drawing strength from his unwavering presence.

"Let's write something unforgettable," I said, my voice firm. "Something that makes all of this worth it."

"Absolutely," he replied, his grin returning. "We'll show him and everyone else what we're capable of. Just you wait."

As we turned another corner, an idea began to form, intertwining with the pulse of my heart. The creative spark ignited within me, and for a moment, I felt invincible. But just as the excitement built, a loud crash shattered the peaceful evening.

We stopped, exchanging startled glances as the sound echoed down the street. I strained to hear above the distant chatter, my pulse quickening. Then came shouts—urgent, frantic, an alarming cacophony that sent a jolt of adrenaline coursing through me.

"What was that?" I asked, dread curling in my stomach.

"Stay here," Ethan instructed, his voice firm but calm, as he moved toward the sound.

"No! I'm coming with you."

He hesitated for a moment, then nodded.

Together, we moved toward the source of the commotion, our steps quickening, curiosity and fear melding into one. As we rounded the corner, the scene unfolded before us—a crowd had gathered, their faces a mixture of shock and concern. A small shop had been broken into, glass littering the ground like shattered dreams.

Ethan's expression shifted to one of urgency. "Let's find out what's happening."

But before we could step closer, a figure darted from the broken window, clutching a bag that bulged suspiciously. They froze as they spotted us, their eyes wide and wild, caught in a moment that felt like time had stretched into eternity.

"Ethan!" I gasped, my heart racing, every instinct screaming for us to move.

The figure's gaze darted around, and without a second thought, they bolted in our direction. The world narrowed to a single focus as adrenaline surged through me, and in that instant, everything shifted. The night had taken a dark turn, and whatever awaited us felt like a storm brewing just beyond the horizon, threatening to engulf everything we had just begun to build.

Chapter 13: The Secret

The sound of Ethan's voice, usually so warm and comforting, wrapped around me like a thick fog, obscuring the clear path I thought we had been walking. I stood in the kitchen, the aroma of roasted garlic and thyme wafting through the air, as I sliced into a ripe tomato for our evening salad. It was a quiet Saturday, the kind that begged for lazy conversation and playful banter, but the tension clung to me like a second skin.

I could hear him in the other room, his words muffled yet sharp enough to slice through the blissful veil of my culinary efforts. I leaned closer to the open doorway, pretending to be engrossed in my task, but every slice of the knife felt heavier than the last. "What do you mean they found out?" he said, his tone low and urgent. My heart quickened, a feral beat against my ribs as fragments of a conversation spiraled into a dark cloud of uncertainty.

My fingers trembled slightly as I placed the knife down, willing myself to step back into the comforting embrace of ignorance. But I couldn't. The snippets wove a tapestry of unease that wrapped tighter around my chest. "You need to handle it. I can't be involved in this," he continued, his voice threading through the silence of our home like an unwelcome gust of wind. I wanted to burst into the room, to shake the truth out of him, but I stood paralyzed, a statue caught in a moment of dread.

What was this secret that made his voice quiver with a mix of anger and fear? My mind raced through the possibilities, each scenario more twisted than the last. A former love? A financial disaster? Was he in trouble with the law? All the laughter we had shared, the plans we'd made to travel to the coast next month, and the evenings spent wrapped in each other's arms began to feel like the fleeting shadows of a dream I was waking from too soon.

The clattering of pots startled me, yanking me back to the reality of my kitchen. I picked up the knife again, though it felt foreign in my hands. With every chop, I forced the rhythm to drown out the chaos brewing in my mind, but it only amplified the tension brewing between us. I could feel the weight of the secret stretching like a tightrope strung above a chasm, and with each heartbeat, I felt myself teetering closer to the edge.

Ethan's footsteps echoed in the hallway, and I busied myself with tossing the salad, though the greens seemed to lose their vibrant hue as if reflecting my growing despair. When he entered the kitchen, the atmosphere shifted. He flashed me a smile, but it didn't quite reach his eyes, which held a shadow I had never seen before. "What are you making?" he asked, his voice deceptively light, like a fragile bubble ready to pop.

"Just a little something to keep us fueled for our movie marathon later," I replied, my tone steady even as my heart raced. I tossed in the dressing with more force than necessary, the clink of the spoon against the bowl echoing my inner turmoil.

He stepped closer, and I could see the tension coiling in his shoulders, a silent battle raging behind that charming facade. "Smells great," he murmured, leaning in, his breath mingling with the aroma of fresh basil and cracked pepper. I wanted to lean into him, to breathe him in and forget the heavy conversation I had eavesdropped on, but my body resisted, held captive by the question I dared not voice.

As we sat down to eat, the silence between us thickened, each bite punctuated by the unsaid. I tried to engage him with questions about his day, hoping to draw him out, but his responses were clipped, as if each word had to battle through an invisible wall he had built. My fork clattered against the plate as I finally lost my patience. "Ethan, are you okay? You seem... distant," I blurted out, the question tumbling from my lips like a secret waiting to be freed.

He hesitated, a fleeting moment where I could see the struggle dance across his features. "Yeah, just work stuff," he replied too quickly, his gaze flitting away, avoiding mine like it was a hot ember.

I felt my heart sink, frustration bubbling just below the surface. "You know you can talk to me, right? Whatever it is, we can figure it out together." The words felt heavy, a plea more than a reassurance, but it was true. I wanted him to let me in, to share whatever burden he was carrying.

He sighed, a long, heavy breath that seemed to draw the very air from the room. "It's complicated," he admitted finally, running a hand through his hair, an endearing habit that always tugged at my heartstrings. "I just... I don't want to drag you into it."

"Drag me into what?" I pressed, feeling a mix of urgency and worry swell inside me. "You can't keep shutting me out. It feels like you're building a wall, and I'm on the outside, wondering what's happening inside."

His gaze flicked back to mine, and for a moment, the tension shifted; there was something raw and vulnerable in his eyes. "I promise, it's not what you think. I just need to handle this myself," he said, his voice low and edged with frustration, as if he were wrestling with demons I couldn't see.

I opened my mouth to respond, to argue my case, but the moment hung suspended, like the fragile balance between us was teetering on the brink. Instead, I fell silent, feeling the air thicken with unspoken words and half-formed thoughts. The joy we had found together felt delicate, like a paper lantern glowing softly in the dark, and I was terrified of a sudden gust of wind that would snuff it out.

Dinner passed in a blur of mundane conversation and stolen glances, but I could feel the divide between us widening, an invisible gulf filled with secrets. When I climbed into bed that night, the sheets cool against my skin, I couldn't shake the feeling of unease that lingered in the air. I lay awake, staring at the ceiling, wondering how the warmth of our shared moments could transform into such an icy distance in the blink of an eye. Ethan's secret was a silent specter in the room, whispering shadows of doubt that twisted and turned, pulling me further into the dark.

The days dragged on like a slow-moving train, chugging toward an uncertain destination while I sat in the passenger seat, heart racing with every inch. I wanted to bring it up, to shred the curtain of tension hanging between us, but every time I opened my mouth, the words fled like startled birds. Instead, I immersed myself in my daily routine—work, coffee dates with friends, and a few too many late-night binge-watching sessions. Yet, even the simplest joys felt muted, like the sound had been turned down low on my life's remote.

Ethan and I maintained our usual rhythm, but it was as if the music had turned discordant, each note a reminder of what remained unsaid. I noticed little things—the way he held his breath when I asked about his day, how his laughter seemed forced, like an actor struggling to remember their lines. And then there were the moments when I'd catch him staring into space, an unreadable expression clouding his features, leaving me wondering if I was staring at the man I thought I knew or a stranger cloaked in shadows.

One chilly evening, I arrived home to find Ethan standing in the living room, his back turned to me as he stared out the window. The city sprawled below us, a shimmering sea of lights, yet he looked lost in a tempest of his own making. I set my keys down, the soft chime echoing in the quiet, and took a deep breath, the air laced with the familiar scent of our favorite candles. "Hey, you," I said, trying to inject warmth into the coolness between us.

He turned slowly, a flicker of a smile crossing his lips before it faded into something more somber. "Hey." The way he said it was cautious, like he was treading on thin ice. I hated it. I wanted the old

Ethan back—the playful one who could make me laugh with a single look or tease me with an eyebrow raised.

"Want to talk about your day?" I asked, my voice softer than I intended. The last thing I wanted was to make him retreat further into his shell. He rubbed the back of his neck, a gesture I had come to recognize as a sign of discomfort.

"It was fine," he replied, though the tension in his shoulders told a different story. "Just the usual stuff."

"Uh-huh." I leaned against the kitchen counter, crossing my arms, hoping the nonchalance would convince him to open up. "You know, I've always believed that 'the usual stuff' is never really that usual. It's more like the tip of the iceberg."

He chuckled, but it sounded strained. "You always did have a way of making the mundane sound profound."

"Call it a gift," I said, smiling to lighten the mood. "But really, Ethan, if there's something bothering you, I'm here. I promise I won't bite."

"Maybe just a nibble?" He offered a lopsided grin that almost felt real. I appreciated his attempt at humor, but it only highlighted the divide between us.

"Seriously. You can't keep hiding whatever this is. You're not just my boyfriend; you're my best friend," I said, forcing the vulnerability to edge closer to the surface. "I can't help you if you don't let me in."

He looked at me, and for a moment, the mask slipped. The pain in his eyes was unmistakable, a crack in the armor he had built around himself. "It's complicated, okay? I'm just trying to handle it, and I don't want you to worry."

"Not worry?" I laughed, though it came out more bitter than I intended. "How can I not worry when you're pulling away? It's like I'm watching you drown, and I can't throw you a lifeline if you won't even tell me where it hurts."

The words hung between us, heavy and potent, and for a heartbeat, I thought he might break. Instead, he inhaled sharply, straightening his back as if bracing for an impact. "You don't get it. This is my mess to deal with. I don't want you getting dragged into something you can't control."

That struck me like a slap, and I took a step back, the sting of his words echoing in my mind. "So, what? I'm just supposed to stand by while you fight your battles alone? That's not how this works. We're supposed to be a team."

His expression darkened, and I could almost hear the gears in his head turning, calculating risks and outcomes, until finally, he let out a shaky breath. "You really want to know?"

"More than anything." I crossed my arms tightly, summoning courage I didn't quite feel.

He hesitated, glancing away, as if searching for the right words amidst the storm brewing inside him. "Okay, but promise me you won't freak out."

"Freak out? I make no promises," I replied, trying to lighten the mood, but my heart was racing, a frantic rhythm urging him to speak.

"I've got some... complications with work." His voice lowered, as if the walls might eavesdrop on our conversation. "A project I took on that didn't exactly go according to plan."

My stomach twisted, anxiety bubbling to the surface. "What kind of project?"

"It's about some... sensitive data," he said, running a hand through his hair again. "I didn't realize how deep I was getting in until it was too late."

My brow furrowed. "Sensitive data? What does that even mean?"

"It's more than just numbers and spreadsheets. There are people involved, powerful people. I thought I could manage it, but now... I don't know. There are implications that could reach beyond just me."

The air crackled with uncertainty, and I felt the pieces start to click into place. "Ethan, are you in some kind of trouble?"

"I'm trying to make sure I'm not," he replied, his gaze flickering to the window. "But it's delicate, and I need to handle it without dragging you into the chaos."

"Chaos is my middle name," I shot back, my heart pounding. "You know I can handle it. You don't have to face this alone."

He met my gaze, searching for something—trust, perhaps? Or maybe a sliver of understanding? "This isn't just about me anymore. If things go sideways, it could affect you too."

"Then let's face it together," I insisted, my resolve hardening. "I'm not backing down now, Ethan. You may think you're protecting me, but all you're doing is pushing me away."

The vulnerability in his eyes flickered again, and for a moment, I thought I saw a glimmer of hope. "Okay, but you have to promise me one thing," he said, his voice barely above a whisper.

"Anything," I replied, my heart racing at the weight of his request.

"Promise me you won't do anything reckless. This is dangerous territory, and I can't lose you."

"Reckless? Me?" I feigned shock, but inside, the gravity of the situation wrapped around me tighter than I'd expected. "I make it a point to stay on the straight and narrow. We're in this together, right?"

His lips twitched, a flicker of a smile creeping back in, yet the worry still etched in his features reminded me of the storm that loomed ahead. And as I stared into those eyes, the walls around us began to feel less like a barrier and more like a promise—a promise that together we could navigate the treacherous waters, even if we didn't yet know where they would lead.

In the days that followed, a strange dance of avoidance and curiosity enveloped our home. I found myself scrutinizing every exchange, every touch, as if the very fabric of our relationship had become a puzzle I desperately needed to solve. I wondered if he could see the tension in my shoulders or hear the frantic thrum of my heart whenever he entered a room. It was as if we were two actors lost in a scene without a script, each searching for the right moment to break character.

The mornings were the worst. The sun would stream through our kitchen window, bathing the space in golden light, yet the warmth felt distant, as if the universe was mocking my unease. I would brew coffee, the rich aroma promising comfort, but when Ethan would wander in, his eyes clouded and guarded, I felt like I was standing in the eye of a storm. "Morning," I'd say, forcing a smile that didn't quite reach my eyes. "Ready for another day of adulting?"

"Always," he'd reply, his tone casual but lacking the usual lilt that made my stomach flutter. I craved the playful banter that used to flow between us like an effortless melody. Instead, our conversations felt like a series of sharp notes, discordant and strained.

One evening, I decided to break the cycle. After a long day filled with distracted meetings and the pressure of unspoken words, I invited him for a walk along the river. The path was a haven, lined with blossoming cherry trees that cast soft pink shadows against the ground. The air was sweet with the scent of spring, promising renewal, but even the beauty of our surroundings couldn't lift the weight on my chest.

As we strolled, I stole glances at Ethan, his profile etched against the fading light. "You know, it's easier to talk when you're not in the middle of a hostage negotiation," I said lightly, hoping to spark some laughter. He turned to me, the hint of a smile flickering before the shadows reclaimed his expression.

"I appreciate the attempt at humor," he replied, his voice low. "But I can't—"

"Ethan," I interrupted, stopping in my tracks. "This isn't just about you anymore. I can feel the distance growing. Talk to me. Let me in."

He paused, his shoulders stiffening as he absorbed my words. "I wish I could," he finally said, a flicker of something dark crossing his eyes. "But this is bigger than both of us. I don't want to drag you into it."

"Guess what? I'm already dragged in, whether you like it or not," I shot back, exasperated. "You've left me hanging, and the longer you wait to tell me, the more I'll imagine the worst. You think I'm worried about a little chaos? Try me."

His gaze turned to the river, where the water shimmered under the moonlight like a thousand scattered stars. "What if I told you it involves people who don't play by the rules?" he asked, his voice barely above a whisper.

I felt a chill creep down my spine. "What does that mean?"

He opened his mouth to answer, but just then, a loud shout broke through the quiet evening. A group of people nearby had erupted into laughter, their carefree energy a stark contrast to the tension enveloping us. Ethan's expression shifted again, becoming even more guarded, and my heart sank as I realized he was slipping away from me once more.

"Let's just head back," he said abruptly, turning on his heel and beginning to walk. The warmth between us felt like a distant memory, replaced by an icy dread that settled deep within me.

The walk home was silent, our footsteps echoing against the pavement, each sound amplifying the gap between us. I struggled to keep my emotions in check, the tightness in my chest threatening to choke me. As we entered our apartment, I felt like I was stepping into a battlefield, one filled with unsaid words and unresolved issues.

"Ethan, please," I urged, watching as he dropped his jacket on the chair, his back still turned to me. "We can't keep doing this. You have to let me help you."

He turned slowly, his expression softening for just a moment. "I know, but this isn't something you can fix with a pep talk and a cute smile."

"Watch me," I replied, my voice firm. "You underestimate how much I can handle. I'm not afraid of a little chaos. You've seen me in action."

"Maybe you don't understand the stakes." His voice wavered, the facade cracking as the vulnerability seeped through. "This could put you in danger."

"Danger? From what? A pesky client or a nasty coworker?" I asked, trying to keep the conversation grounded in humor, but the joke fell flat in the tense atmosphere.

"It's not that simple," he said, frustration lacing his tone. "It's... it's about a deal that went south. There are people involved who don't take kindly to mistakes."

"Then you have to tell me everything," I said, determination flooding my voice. "I can't be left in the dark, wondering if the next knock on the door is going to change everything."

He sighed, rubbing his forehead as if the weight of the world rested there. "I just—"

Suddenly, there was a loud knock at the door, and we both froze, the air thickening with tension. I glanced at Ethan, whose eyes widened in alarm, and my stomach dropped. The knock came again, more insistent this time. "Who is it?" I called out, though a knot of dread twisted in my gut.

"I don't know," Ethan whispered, his expression shifting to one of fear. "Stay back."

Before I could respond, he moved toward the door, the uncertainty weighing heavy in the air like a thunderstorm about to break. My heart raced as I watched him reach for the knob, my mind racing with a thousand possibilities. Who could it be? Was it someone from his secret?

The door creaked open just a crack, and the world outside remained hidden from view. "Ethan," a voice called out, low and menacing. "We need to talk."

My breath caught in my throat as the tension crackled between us, each heartbeat echoing the unspoken dread that hung heavy in the room. Ethan's face paled, and in that moment, I knew we were standing at the precipice of something I couldn't have anticipated, something that could change everything forever.

Chapter 14: The Confrontation

The air was thick with unspoken words, curling around us like the delicate tendrils of smoke from the candle flickering on the coffee table. Ethan sat across from me, his profile softened by the warm glow of fairy lights strung haphazardly across the walls, illuminating the cozy room with a golden hue that felt almost enchanted. The couch cradled us in its embrace, a sanctuary from the world outside, where reality often intruded with its unforgiving edges. Yet, here, nestled among cushions and a scattering of throw blankets, my heart raced with an urgency that felt as tangible as the evening breeze drifting through the open window.

"Ethan," I began, the name lingering in the air like a promise. I drew a breath, summoning the courage that had evaded me all week. "We need to talk." The words felt heavy, each syllable tumbling out with the weight of the unvoiced thoughts that had kept me awake at night, turning in my mind like restless shadows. His eyes, deep pools of uncertainty, met mine, and I could see the flicker of tension there, the way his brow furrowed just slightly as if he were bracing himself for something monumental.

"Okay," he said, the single word rich with implications, as if he knew this conversation was a dam poised to burst. He leaned forward, elbows resting on his knees, his fingers intertwining in a nervous dance. I envied his calm demeanor, the way he always seemed to find his center even when I felt as though I was spiraling.

"I've noticed you've been... distant lately," I ventured, feeling a twinge of discomfort at the admission. "You've been working late, and I can't help but wonder what's going on." The honesty of my words hung between us, uncomfortably naked.

He sighed, the sound heavy with the weight of unspoken burdens. "It's not what you think," he finally said, his voice low, almost hesitant. "I didn't want to worry you." His admission sent a shiver of apprehension skittering down my spine. The dim light of the room seemed to dim further, as though the shadows themselves were leaning in to listen.

"Ethan, just tell me. Whatever it is, we can face it together." I leaned closer, my heart racing as I sought to bridge the gap of uncertainty that had widened between us. The silence stretched, and in that moment, I could see the internal struggle play out across his features, the flicker of vulnerability crossing his eyes.

"I took a second job," he finally confessed, the words tumbling out like stones dropped into a still pond, sending ripples of surprise and concern cascading through me. "My family... we're facing some financial difficulties." The honesty of his revelation hit me like a wave, washing over my initial fears with a tide of relief and guilt.

"Oh, Ethan," I breathed, feeling the warmth of empathy surge within me. "I'm so sorry. I had no idea." Guilt pinched at my insides, a tight knot in my stomach as I recalled the myriad of doubts that had plagued me, the sleepless nights where I had let my imagination run wild, constructing elaborate scenarios of betrayal and distance.

"I didn't want you to worry," he said, his voice softer now, the tension in his shoulders easing ever so slightly. "I thought I could handle it on my own. But it's been harder than I expected." The honesty in his admission tugged at my heartstrings, a melody of vulnerability that resonated deeply within me.

As the truth settled between us, the atmosphere shifted from one of suspicion to a shared understanding. I reached across the coffee table, my fingers brushing against his, a silent gesture of solidarity. "You don't have to face this alone," I said, my voice steadying with conviction. "We're in this together, remember? Whatever it takes, we'll find a way."

His gaze softened, and the corners of his mouth twitched upward in a tentative smile, the kind that spoke of hope amidst uncertainty. "I didn't want to burden you," he admitted, a hint of embarrassment coloring his cheeks.

"Burden? Please. You're my best friend, Ethan. That's not a burden; it's a privilege." I let the words flow freely, a gentle tide meant to soothe the jagged edges of his worry. "You can talk to me about anything. I want to help."

The atmosphere lightened as we shared a knowing smile, the connection between us deepening, fortified by this new layer of honesty. I could see the relief wash over him, a slow exhale that seemed to lift the weight from his shoulders, allowing his laughter to bubble up like a brook breaking free of winter's grip.

"You know," he said, a playful glint returning to his eyes, "I might need you to manage my finances then. I could use a financial advisor who works for cookies and coffee." The warmth of his humor melted away the last remnants of tension, and I chuckled softly, feeling the lightness return to my chest.

"Absolutely. Let's make it a deal," I replied, rolling my eyes with a grin. "But you owe me a lifetime supply of chocolate chip cookies for my services."

"Deal," he agreed, a playful grin stretching across his face. "Though I'll need to check with my accountant first. I can't afford to go broke in the cookie department."

As we bantered back and forth, the shadows that had loomed so large moments ago receded into the background, replaced by the comfortable intimacy that had defined our friendship for years. We made a pact that night, not just to share our burdens but to celebrate our victories, however small they might be.

In that cozy glow of fairy lights, surrounded by laughter and a renewed sense of trust, I realized that vulnerability was indeed a strength. In sharing our truths, we had carved out a sanctuary where honesty could thrive, and I felt a sense of liberation, a breath of fresh air blowing through the remnants of our previous fears. Together, we would navigate whatever challenges lay ahead, fortified by our newfound honesty, ready to face the world with open hearts and open minds.

The next few days were an unexpected rollercoaster of emotions. After our heart-to-heart, I thought I'd feel lighter, as though a weight had been lifted. Instead, I found myself immersed in a peculiar blend of sympathy and worry. I caught myself staring out the window more often, watching the world go by while I wrestled with my thoughts. The streetlamps outside cast long shadows, and the chill in the air felt like a constant reminder of the uncertainties that lingered, both in Ethan's life and mine.

One evening, as the sun dipped below the horizon, painting the sky in hues of pink and orange, I made my way to Ethan's place. It was our usual hangout, the safe haven where laughter bounced off the walls, but today, it felt different. As I stepped inside, the familiar scent of his homemade pasta filled the air, inviting and comforting. I could almost forget the reason I was here, but a flutter of anxiety settled in my stomach.

"Hey, you!" he greeted, his smile brightening the room even more than the overhead lights. He wore an apron emblazoned with a cartoonish chef, which somehow managed to be both charming and ridiculous. "I was just about to serve dinner. Hope you're hungry."

I chuckled, shaking my head. "I could eat a horse, especially if it's drowning in marinara sauce."

"I'll take that as a compliment," he quipped, his eyes sparkling with mischief. "Dinner is my specialty. Let me know when you want the secret ingredient: my famous extra-virgin olive oil."

As we settled at his small kitchen table, filled with bowls of pasta, garlic bread, and a fresh salad, I felt a sense of normalcy wash over me. We dug into our meal, the conversation flowing easily, punctuated by playful banter. Yet, beneath the surface of our lightheartedness, the weight of his struggles loomed large, a quiet specter hovering just out of sight.

"I've been thinking about the second job," I ventured cautiously, probing the depths of our earlier conversation. "Are you sure you can handle it? I mean, I don't want you to burn out."

Ethan paused, his fork hovering mid-air. "It's not just about me anymore. I've got to help my parents. They've sacrificed so much for me. This is the least I can do." The resolve in his voice was palpable, and I admired his dedication even as my heart ached for him.

"I get that," I replied, leaning in closer. "But if it's taking a toll on you, you have to let me know. You can't be a superhero all the time, you know."

He chuckled, the tension in his shoulders easing just a bit. "And yet, here I am, donning the cape and all." He struck a mock pose, arms akimbo, a hero in his own kitchen. It was a moment of levity that I cherished, a reminder of the Ethan I knew and loved.

After dinner, we curled up on the couch, the remnants of our meal forgotten as we settled in for a movie. The warm glow of the screen illuminated Ethan's features, and I felt a swell of affection. He was more than just my friend; he was family. As the plot unfolded on screen, my mind wandered to the uncharted territory we had traversed, and I felt the urge to dig deeper.

"Ethan, I really want to help you. Have you thought about what your parents need? Maybe we could brainstorm some ideas together."

He turned to me, a flicker of uncertainty crossing his face. "It's complicated. They're proud, you know? Asking for help isn't easy for them."

"Pride can be a double-edged sword," I said softly, searching for the right words. "Sometimes, letting others in can be the most courageous thing you can do."

"I appreciate that," he replied, his gaze softening. "It's just tough. I want to carry my weight, but I also don't want to lose sight of what's important."

The movie played on, but I could feel a shift in the atmosphere. "What if we set up a family meeting? Just to talk it through, see where they're at?" The suggestion hung in the air, a delicate thread woven into our conversation.

"I'll think about it," he said, though the hesitation in his voice was unmistakable.

The rest of the evening passed in a comfortable haze, laughter punctuating the air as we bantered over movie quotes and snack preferences. But as I said my goodbyes, an inexplicable heaviness settled over me, like a storm cloud rolling in to obscure the stars.

The following days turned into a blur of work and worry. I found myself constantly checking my phone, waiting for a message from Ethan, hoping to hear that he had reached out to his parents. When he finally texted, my heart raced with anticipation, but the message was cryptic. "Can we talk?" it read, and the gravity behind those four words sent my pulse racing.

We met at our favorite coffee shop, a cozy little nook adorned with vintage posters and the scent of freshly brewed espresso swirling in the air. I arrived early, my heart a thrum of apprehension as I ordered a large cappuccino, needing the comfort of caffeine to bolster my nerves. When he walked in, the bell above the door chimed cheerfully, but the look on his face was anything but.

"Hey," he said, sliding into the seat across from me, the weight of the world etched into his features. "Thanks for meeting me."

"Of course," I replied, sensing the undercurrent of tension that swirled between us. "What's going on? You look like you've seen a ghost."

He let out a breath, a mixture of frustration and relief. "I talked to my parents last night."

I leaned in, the tension in my shoulders rising. "And?"

"They don't want my help. They refuse to accept it." His voice cracked slightly, the hurt clear as day.

My heart sank, a wave of sympathy crashing over me. "Ethan, I'm so sorry. That must be really tough."

"It is," he said, running a hand through his hair in frustration. "I thought it would be a relief to finally have that conversation, but it only made things worse. They're stuck in their ways, and I can't just watch them struggle."

His pain echoed in my chest, and I felt a surge of determination. "Maybe they just need time to process. You've always been there for them; they might just be scared of changing the dynamic."

Ethan shook his head, his brow furrowed. "But at what cost? I can't keep pretending everything is okay while they're struggling."

"Then don't pretend. Show them you're there for them. You don't have to take everything on yourself. You can lean on your friends too, you know."

"Like I'm leaning on you right now?" he shot back, his words sharp but laced with an undeniable affection.

"Exactly," I replied, holding his gaze steady, a flicker of mischief lighting up my eyes. "I'm like a support beam—just don't expect me to lift heavy things. I'm all about emotional labor, not physical."

A hint of a smile broke through his solemnity, and I felt a rush of relief. Even in his darkest moments, I knew he could find a glimmer of light. "Okay, maybe I won't be lifting heavy things, but I could definitely use a sidekick in this whole mess."

"You've got it," I said, the spark of hope igniting in the pit of my stomach. "Together, we'll figure this out. And who knows? Maybe your parents will surprise you."

As we finished our coffee, the storm clouds above began to part ever so slightly, revealing a hint of blue sky. In that moment, I realized that while the path ahead was fraught with challenges, it was one we could navigate together—hand in hand, ready to face whatever life threw our way.

The days that followed were a strange dance of hope and uncertainty, and as the weekend approached, I felt an electric buzz in the air. It was a bittersweet mix of excitement and dread, like the moment before a roller coaster drops. I had invited Ethan to a small gathering at my place, a distraction from the heavy conversations we had been navigating. My apartment was a canvas of color—vivid throw pillows strewn across the couch, fragrant candles flickering to life, and the rich aroma of homemade chili simmering on the stove. I wanted this to be a night of laughter, a refuge from the worries that had begun to take root in both our lives.

As guests began to arrive, the atmosphere shifted from somber to vibrant. Friends filled the room, each one a piece of the puzzle that was our shared life. Laughter mingled with the clinking of glasses, and for a moment, I felt the weight of our earlier discussions dissolve like sugar in warm water. I caught sight of Ethan across the room, his dark hair slightly tousled, his smile bright as he engaged in a conversation with Jenna, our mutual friend. I felt a flutter of warmth in my chest; his laughter was like a melody, cutting through the tension of the week.

"Hey, you!" I called out, approaching him with a playful smirk. "Is Jenna stealing you away, or do you have room for a partner in crime?"

Ethan looked at me, mock horror in his eyes. "I'm not going anywhere! Jenna just has this ridiculous idea that I should consider being a chef instead of an accountant. Can you believe that?"

"Why not? You're practically a culinary genius!" I retorted, stealing a chip from the bowl on the table. "But if you do decide to swap spreadsheets for soufflés, remember who your biggest fan is."

Jenna laughed, leaning against the wall with an exaggerated sigh. "Oh, please. The only thing you've ever successfully cooked is instant ramen. But maybe I should have you both audition for a cooking show. The comedy factor alone would be priceless!"

As the night wore on, the banter flowed easily, yet a part of me remained hyper-aware of Ethan's quiet moments, the flickers of worry that still danced behind his eyes. I was determined to create a safe haven for him tonight, a brief escape from the realities that had begun to crowd in around us.

Just as I was about to refill our drinks, the door swung open, and in walked Max, a childhood friend of Ethan's whom I had only met once or twice. He had an air of mischief about him, a twinkle in his eye that suggested he was always up to something. "Hey, everyone!" he boomed, instantly drawing attention as he clapped Ethan on the back. "Did I hear something about a cooking competition? Because I'm ready to judge!"

I rolled my eyes playfully. "If you're judging, then this might be a very short competition. We'd lose before the first dish is served."

Ethan grinned, his earlier tension seeming to dissipate like mist under the sun. "I've got my trusty recipe book, so I think I'll be okay."

As the evening unfolded, I watched Ethan grow more animated, the sound of laughter pushing the shadows further back. It was moments like this that reminded me why I cared so deeply for him; he had an innate ability to lighten the mood, to make the world seem less daunting.

But just as I began to relax, the doorbell chimed again, cutting through the laughter. "I'll get it!" I called, curious who else might join our little celebration. As I opened the door, my heart sank. Standing before me was Ethan's younger sister, Mia, her face pale, eyes wide. The warmth of the party faded into a distant memory.

"Mia?" I asked, concern lacing my voice. "What's wrong?"

"Ethan, I need to talk to you," she said, glancing past me into the room, her demeanor heavy with urgency. Ethan caught my eye, and the playful atmosphere turned tense in an instant.

"I'll be right back," he said, his voice steady but tinged with something I couldn't quite place. He stood, a sense of foreboding hanging in the air like an impending storm. As he stepped toward the door, I felt an uncomfortable twist in my stomach.

"What's going on?" I asked, my voice low as I followed him. But Ethan was already out the door, the conversation fading as they moved to the hallway.

I watched, a growing sense of dread washing over me, as they spoke in hushed tones. Mia's hands were animated, gesturing urgently, while Ethan's expression morphed from confusion to concern. I couldn't hear their words, but the intensity was palpable.

"Hey, what's happening?" I asked, stepping outside to join them. The night air was cool against my skin, the distant sounds of laughter from the party echoing in my ears, a stark contrast to the tension that crackled between us.

Ethan turned, a flicker of frustration crossing his face as he ran a hand through his hair. "It's just some family stuff. I'll handle it."

But Mia shook her head, her voice barely above a whisper. "You don't understand. It's bad. We need you."

I felt a knot tighten in my stomach. "What do you mean 'bad'? What's going on?"

Ethan shot me a look that was equal parts pleading and protective. "It's fine, really. I can take care of this."

"No, it's not fine!" Mia snapped, her frustration bubbling over. "We can't keep pretending everything's okay. Dad needs help, and it's getting worse."

My heart raced, the pieces of this puzzle clicking together in a way I hadn't anticipated. The weight of unspoken truths loomed over us, an invisible wall. "What kind of help?" I asked, unable to mask the worry in my voice.

Ethan shifted, his eyes darkening. "Mia, we don't need to—"

"Don't protect me, Ethan!" she interrupted, her voice shaking. "This is serious. If you don't come home now, things might change for us forever."

In that moment, the room fell silent, the laughter and chatter from inside fading into a distant memory. The world felt heavy, the air thick with unspoken fears and the gravity of impending decisions. I stood frozen, the truth settling heavily in the pit of my stomach.

Ethan looked at me, his expression caught between the urge to shield me and the undeniable reality of his family's struggles. "I have to go," he finally said, his voice low and resolute.

"Wait—" I began, but the words caught in my throat. I knew that whatever this was, it would change everything. And as Ethan stepped back, the door swinging shut behind him, I felt the weight of uncertainty descend like a thick fog, wrapping around me as I was left standing in the doorway, utterly unprepared for what lay ahead.

Chapter 15: The Support

The scent of coffee wafted through the air as I set up my favorite study corner in the library, an unassuming nook with worn leather armchairs and a table that bore the scars of countless late-night sessions. Sunlight streamed through the tall windows, casting warm golden beams over the pages of my textbooks. I'd claimed this spot as a sanctuary of sorts, where I could retreat from the cacophony of campus life. Today, however, it was more than just my refuge; it was a battlefield in the war against the relentless tides of time and responsibility.

Ethan had been pushing himself harder than ever, juggling classes and two part-time jobs like a circus performer spinning plates. I watched him from across the table as he hunched over his notes, his brow furrowed in concentration. There was a vulnerability in him that tugged at my heartstrings. The casual charm that usually lit up his features was dulled, the shadows of fatigue lurking beneath his eyes. I could only imagine the weight he carried, but I was determined to lighten the load however I could.

"Did you eat today?" I asked, sliding a steaming container of homemade pasta toward him. I'd whipped it up during my last free afternoon, a small gesture meant to sustain him through the onslaught of academic demands.

He looked up, surprise flickering in his eyes, a hint of a smile threatening to break through. "You're going to feed me like a stray cat now?"

"Only the finest homemade lasagna," I quipped, pretending to be offended. "This recipe is a family secret, you know. My grandma would roll over in her grave if she knew I was serving it to someone without proper Italian seasoning."

He laughed, a genuine sound that cut through the weight of our shared worries. "As long as it's not just tomato sauce, I'll take it." He dug into the pasta with an enthusiasm that made my heart swell, each forkful a victory against the pressures of his day.

As the minutes ticked by, the conversation shifted seamlessly from mundane topics—like the best places to grab a quick meal on campus—to our dreams and ambitions. The way Ethan talked about his future made my heart race. He envisioned a world where he could combine his love for technology with his passion for art, designing spaces that merged functionality with beauty. I could see it in his eyes: the fervor, the hope, the limitless possibilities that stretched before him like an open road.

"You're going to do amazing things, you know," I said softly, watching him light up as he animatedly described his ideas. "I believe in you."

Ethan paused, his fork hovering mid-air. "And what about you? What's your dream?"

I hesitated. My aspirations felt so much less tangible, a fluttering whisper in the wind compared to the roar of his ambition. I had always envisioned a life filled with words—writing stories that danced off the pages and resonated with readers in the way that the stories of my youth had shaped me. But those dreams seemed far away, overshadowed by the reality of bills and responsibilities.

"Honestly? I just want to create something beautiful," I admitted, my voice barely above a whisper. "To share pieces of my heart with the world."

Ethan leaned back, studying me with an intensity that made my skin tingle. "Then do it. Don't let anything stop you."

His unwavering confidence sent a spark of determination through me, igniting the dormant embers of my dreams. I wanted to believe that I could carve out a space for my writing, even in the chaos of life.

As the evening wore on, we moved from the library to a nearby café, the kind that stayed open late and served pastries that melted in your mouth. The warm glow of hanging lights created a cozy ambiance, a stark contrast to the cold, hard world outside. We settled into a booth, and I watched him savoring every bite of a chocolate croissant, his eyes momentarily closed in bliss.

"Okay, let's brainstorm," I said, excitement bubbling within me as I grabbed a napkin and a pen. "What if we made a pact? I help you with your projects, and you help me with my writing? You can be my first reader."

He raised an eyebrow, a playful smirk tugging at his lips. "So you're telling me I'll get to critique your heartfelt prose?"

"Don't make it weird," I shot back, grinning. "I'm not asking for a harsh critique; I just need a sounding board. Plus, who better to help me shape my characters than someone who's practically a work of art himself?"

"Flattery will get you everywhere," he replied, leaning in closer, his voice dropping to a conspiratorial whisper. "But seriously, I'd love to help. Maybe we can hold each other accountable? You know, keep the creative juices flowing while we navigate this chaos together."

Our laughter filled the air, a buoyant melody against the backdrop of clinking dishes and hushed conversations. I felt a rush of gratitude for these moments, these simple exchanges that tied us closer together.

As the night wore on, our conversation dipped into deeper waters, exploring fears and failures. I revealed my insecurities about pursuing a career in writing, about the nagging voice that whispered I'd never be good enough. He shared his own struggles, the pressure of expectations weighing heavily on his shoulders, and how sometimes he felt like he was just treading water.

"What if we fail?" I asked, a flicker of doubt creeping into my voice.

"Then we get up and try again," he said resolutely, his eyes steady on mine. "It's not about perfection; it's about the journey. And I'd rather fail trying to reach for something than sit back and wonder what could have been."

His words resonated within me, weaving a thread of courage through the tapestry of my fears. I wanted to believe him. I wanted to grasp onto that belief like a lifeline in a stormy sea. With every shared story, every laugh, I felt the weight of my worries lift, replaced by a sense of possibility.

As we finally left the café, the night air wrapped around us like a warm embrace. The stars shimmered above, each one a promise of new beginnings and uncharted adventures. I walked beside Ethan, a sense of purpose blossoming in my chest. Perhaps love was not just about the moments of passion but also about standing shoulder to shoulder, each step taken in support of one another's dreams. With him by my side, the future felt a little less daunting, a little more like the beginning of something beautiful.

The following week blurred into a chaotic mix of study sessions and stolen moments, each day presenting new challenges as Ethan balanced his heavy workload. He became a master of juggling obligations, dashing from one commitment to another with a tenacity that left me in awe. I, on the other hand, transformed into his unofficial assistant, a cheerful, albeit slightly exhausted, cheerleader in his corner. Our cozy library evenings morphed into a ritual, a haven where we plotted our futures over shared meals and laughter.

One afternoon, as I sat at our usual table, I noticed a couple of students nearby engrossed in a debate about the latest campus scandal. Their raised voices mingled with the sound of pages turning and the soft tap of fingers on keyboards. I was mildly intrigued by their intensity but mostly focused on the scribbled notes in front of me, crafting ideas that would give life to my next story.

"Do you think they ever get tired of yelling about nothing?" Ethan mused, glancing at the pair with a bemused expression as he took a sip of his coffee.

"Maybe it's just a cover for their unfulfilled dreams. I'd like to think they're really just passionate about life," I replied, trying to sound philosophical.

"Passionate about drama, you mean?" He raised an eyebrow, and I couldn't help but laugh.

"True. But isn't there a certain charm in all that noise? It's like they're auditioning for their own reality show."

Ethan leaned back in his chair, his expression thoughtful. "I'd watch that. 'Campus Chaos: The Real Lives of Overdramatic Students.' It has a ring to it."

"Only if you promise to star as the dashing protagonist who saves the day," I quipped, leaning forward. "Otherwise, I'm not interested."

"Dashing, you say? I'll bring the charm; you bring the witty comebacks," he replied, his smile infectious.

Just then, a loud crash interrupted our banter. The couple had knocked over a tower of textbooks, sending papers and pens scattering like confetti. Ethan and I exchanged amused glances, and the tension in the air dissolved into laughter.

"Looks like they just lost their 'best supporting actors' status," I chuckled.

As the chaos settled, I noticed Ethan's laughter fading into silence. He turned his gaze to the window, watching the sun dip lower in the sky, casting long shadows across the library floor. There was a flicker of worry in his eyes, and I could sense that familiar tension returning.

"What's on your mind?" I asked gently, wanting to pull him back from whatever shadow loomed in his thoughts.

"It's just... with finals coming up and work, I'm starting to feel overwhelmed," he admitted, rubbing the back of his neck, a habit he had when he was stressed. "Sometimes I wonder if I can really keep this up."

I reached across the table, placing my hand over his. "You're not alone in this. We're a team, remember? We'll find a way to tackle everything together."

He smiled, but I could see the worry still lingering. "What if I drop the ball? What if I fail?"

"Then we'll figure it out together, just like we always do," I assured him, squeezing his hand for emphasis. "And hey, failure is just a stepping stone to success, right? If anyone can bounce back, it's you."

His eyes softened, gratitude flooding through them. "Thanks for being here. I honestly don't know what I'd do without you."

The conversation lingered in the air like the sweet aroma of the cinnamon rolls we had shared. Each moment between us felt charged with the promise of something greater—a connection deepening beyond mere friendship.

As we wrapped up our study session, I made a point to remind him of our pact, to hold each other accountable for our dreams. We could harness our individual struggles into a shared momentum, lifting each other as we climbed.

Days turned into a rhythm of late nights and early mornings, punctuated by laughter and heart-to-heart conversations. But soon, as the final exams loomed larger, our sanctuary began to feel more like a battleground.

One evening, while I was editing a short story, I glanced up to see Ethan pacing around the library, a frown creasing his forehead. It wasn't just the usual stress; there was an urgency in his movements that set my heart racing.

"Ethan, what's wrong?" I asked, pushing aside my laptop to give him my full attention.

He stopped abruptly, running a hand through his hair in that familiar gesture of frustration. "I just got an email from my boss. They want me to cover a shift this weekend, right before finals. I can't keep saying yes. I need to focus."

"Maybe you could talk to them?" I suggested, concern etching my features. "Tell them you're balancing too much right now."

He shook his head, a mix of disappointment and resolve in his expression. "It's not that simple. They're already short-staffed. I can't leave them hanging."

"Ethan, you're not a superhero. You can't save everyone," I said softly, trying to inject some reason into his spiraling thoughts.

"I know, but I hate letting people down. I've seen what happens when I don't pull my weight," he replied, his voice strained. "I just don't want to be that person."

A silence settled between us, thick with unspoken fears. "You're not that person," I insisted, standing firm. "And what about your well-being? You can't be there for everyone if you're running on empty."

He looked down, the weight of my words sinking in. "It's just hard to say no."

"Maybe it's time you learned how to. Saying no isn't a weakness; it's a strength," I encouraged, hoping to spark that flicker of confidence within him. "You need to prioritize your goals. Remember, you've got a future to fight for, too."

He met my gaze, and in that moment, I saw a spark of realization flicker in his eyes. "You're right. I need to make space for what matters."

"Exactly. And I'm here to help you find that space," I said, my voice steady.

As the night stretched on, the tension between us eased. Together, we plotted a course of action. He would draft an email to his boss, a firm but respectful request for balance. I would help him study for finals, ensuring he was prepared without burning out. It felt like a small victory, but in that moment, it was monumental.

By the time we left the library, the stars had returned, twinkling brightly in the night sky. I walked beside Ethan, my heart lighter, each step in sync with the pulse of newfound hope that coursed between us. The world felt expansive, ripe with possibilities, and I knew that together, we could navigate whatever challenges lay ahead. Our bond was growing deeper, turning those fleeting moments into a sturdy foundation for everything yet to come.

The days turned into a blur, a whirlwind of coffee-fueled nights and hurried conversations. Each stolen moment with Ethan became a treasured fragment of my life, glimmering like the stars that peeked through the library windows. We were two ships navigating a stormy sea of responsibilities, but somehow, we found an anchor in each other. As finals approached, the pressure began to mount, and I could sense the weight bearing down on Ethan even more.

One evening, we were ensconced in our usual corner of the library, a fortress of books around us. The comforting scent of old pages mixed with the sharp tang of fresh coffee. I was bent over my laptop, trying to fine-tune a short story that had stubbornly resisted my every attempt to mold it into something cohesive. Across from me, Ethan was immersed in his notes, the glow of the desk lamp highlighting the deep furrows in his brow.

"Do you think the universe is trying to tell me something?" I muttered, half to myself, my fingers dancing over the keyboard in frustration. "Like maybe I should stick to writing grocery lists instead of stories?"

Ethan looked up, a grin breaking through the clouds of stress that shrouded him. "If the universe wanted to be helpful, it wouldn't have given us these ridiculous assignments right before break."

"Right?" I laughed, the sound easing some of the tension in the air. "I mean, who needs sleep when you can spend nights crying over literary analysis?"

He shook his head, chuckling. "At least you have a solid reason to get all dramatic. I'm just trying to figure out how to build a database that won't crash and burn during my presentation."

"Oh, the thrill of tech support! I can see the excitement in your eyes," I teased, leaning back in my chair. "You're practically glowing."

"Yeah, well, if I crash and burn, it won't just be my grades that take a hit," he replied, the laughter fading from his tone. "I need this job. It's my ticket to internships and, hopefully, a real career."

"Ethan," I said gently, "you are more than your grades. You're talented, driven, and—dare I say—charming." I flashed a playful smile, trying to lift his spirits. "The world is not just a spreadsheet."

He let out a breath, the corners of his mouth twitching as he tried to mask the seriousness of his thoughts. "Sometimes, it feels like that's all there is. A series of numbers and deadlines. It's exhausting."

"It is," I agreed. "But remember, you're not alone in this. We're a team, remember?"

He nodded, gratitude lighting his features for a moment before the worry crept back in. "I just wish I could get a break."

As if the universe was listening, a loud crash resonated through the library, jolting us from our conversation. A student had knocked over a stack of books, sending them cascading to the floor.

"Maybe that's a sign," I quipped, trying to inject humor back into the moment. "The universe saying, 'Enough with the studying; go out and live!'"

Ethan chuckled, but I could see the weariness returning. "If only it were that easy."

The atmosphere shifted, the library's dim lighting suddenly feeling too heavy. I felt a surge of determination. "Okay, how about this: We take a break. Right now. I'll grab us some snacks, and then we can find somewhere fun to unwind for a bit."

He hesitated, the internal struggle playing out on his face. "I really should keep studying..."

"Not a chance! You've been working yourself to the bone, and it's time for some reprieve. Besides, I'm pretty sure chocolate is scientifically proven to improve academic performance."

With a reluctant smile, he relented. "Fine, but only if you promise not to judge my snack choices."

"Deal!" I said, already plotting our escape.

We stashed our things and headed out into the crisp evening air. The campus felt alive, students milling about, their laughter ringing through the night. I led Ethan toward a little café I loved, a place with fairy lights strung across the patio and a menu that boasted everything from decadent desserts to savory treats.

As we approached, the familiar sight brought a sense of comfort. The café's warm glow beckoned us inside. I was already envisioning the hot chocolate piled high with whipped cream, a concoction that could erase even the most daunting of days.

Once inside, we ordered our drinks and settled at a table tucked in a corner. As we sipped, the warmth seeped into our bones, and I could see the tension beginning to melt away from Ethan's shoulders.

"You know," I said, breaking the comfortable silence, "I've been thinking about your presentation. What if we did a practice run? I could be your audience, and you could wow me with all your database wizardry."

He raised an eyebrow, intrigued. "You'd actually want to sit through that?"

"Absolutely. I'll bring popcorn and everything. Consider it a private screening of 'Ethan the Great: Database Defender.'"

"Now that sounds like a blockbuster hit," he said, chuckling. "I'm in. But I might need you to bring your best 'wow' face."

"Don't worry. I'm a professional 'wow-er,'" I replied, puffing up my chest in mock seriousness.

As our conversation flowed, I noticed the evening sky darkening outside, the stars twinkling like tiny diamonds. It felt like a reprieve from the weight of the world, a brief escape that had been sorely needed.

But just as I began to relax, my phone buzzed on the table, the harsh sound cutting through the ambiance. I glanced down, my heart sinking as I saw the name on the screen: my mother.

"I should take this," I said, feeling an odd mixture of dread and obligation. "I'll be right back."

I stepped outside, the chill of the night air hitting me. "Hey, Mom," I answered, trying to keep my voice steady.

"Where have you been?" she demanded, her tone sharp. "I've been trying to reach you. We need to talk."

My stomach twisted. "Can it wait? I'm really busy right now."

"Busy? You think this is just about you? Your father has been asking about you. We all have. You can't just disappear," she shot back, frustration lacing her voice.

"Mom, I'm not disappearing. I'm in school. I have responsibilities," I said, forcing my tone to remain calm.

"You need to come home this weekend," she insisted, her voice softening. "We're worried about you."

A rush of conflicting emotions flooded through me—guilt, anger, sadness. "I can't just drop everything. I have finals and…"

"Your family needs you," she interrupted, the weight of her words sinking in.

"I can't," I whispered, my voice barely audible.

I hung up, my heart racing. Anxiety clawed at my insides. I returned to the café, where Ethan was waiting, an expectant look on his face.

"What's wrong?" he asked, the warmth in his eyes replaced by concern.

I tried to smile, but it faltered. "Just family stuff."

"Do you want to talk about it?" he offered gently, concern etched into his features.

"It's nothing," I replied, a little too quickly, hoping to brush it off. But as I caught a glimpse of his worried expression, I realized that it was anything but nothing.

The café seemed to close in around me, the laughter and chatter fading into a dull hum. "It's just... my mom wants me to come home this weekend. I don't know if I can."

He reached across the table, his fingers brushing mine. "You need to do what's best for you. Your family is important, but so is your mental health and your future."

"I know, but..." I hesitated, the weight of my decisions pressing down on me. "What if I go home, and they want me to stay? What if I can't handle it?"

His grip tightened slightly, reassuring. "You're stronger than you think. And whatever you decide, I'm here to support you."

Before I could respond, a loud commotion erupted from inside the café, shattering the moment. A group of students rushed out, their faces pale and frantic.

"Someone got hurt!" one of them shouted, panic lacing their voice.

Ethan and I exchanged glances, alarm creeping into my chest. I stood up, my instincts kicking in. "What happened?"

"There was an accident inside!" another student yelled, their voice shaky.

Ethan and I rushed inside, hearts pounding, as we pushed through the crowd gathering at the entrance. The atmosphere crackled with tension, and my pulse raced as I scanned the room, desperate to understand what was unfolding.

Then I saw it—a figure sprawled on the floor, surrounded by worried faces and the distant wail of sirens approaching. The world around me blurred as dread pooled in my stomach.

"Is that...?" My breath caught in my throat, and panic swelled within me.

Ethan turned to me, eyes wide with disbelief. "No, it can't be..."

The realization hit me like a freight train. Someone's life was hanging in the balance, and the consequences of the night had just escalated into something I never saw coming. My heart raced as I clutched the edge of the table, the chaotic energy threatening to spiral out of control.

"Ethan, what do

Chapter 16: The Snowstorm

The wind howled outside, a fierce serenade of swirling snowflakes that danced like lost spirits seeking refuge in the warmth of the cozy homes lining Cedar Hill's streets. Each gust seemed to whisper secrets of winter, pressing against the windows with a determined insistence, daring anyone to venture out. I peered through the frosted glass, watching the world transform into a canvas of white, each flake unique, yet together they formed an unyielding blanket that muffled the sounds of the town. There was something about this winter storm that felt like a harbinger of change, a promise of new beginnings cloaked in the chill of the night.

Ethan had been so tired lately, his shifts at the diner stretching longer than usual, the kind of weariness that seeped into the bones. When I called to suggest he come over, I could hear the fatigue in his voice, a melodic undertone of reluctant acceptance. I hoped the thought of a warm haven, filled with the aroma of cocoa and the soft glow of fairy lights, would pull him from the edges of his exhaustion. It was exactly what we needed—an escape from the demands of life, if only for a few hours.

When he arrived, the door creaked open, and a gust of cold air rushed in, wrapping around him like an unwanted embrace. He shook off the snow, his cheeks flushed from the cold, and for a fleeting moment, I marveled at how his presence could warm the entire room. "I didn't know you were inviting the Arctic Circle with you," he teased, shaking out his hair like a wet dog, sending tiny flecks of snow tumbling to the floor.

"Only the best for you," I quipped back, an impish smile tugging at my lips. The snowstorm roared outside, but inside, the world felt safe, cocooned in our little bubble. I quickly ushered him to the living room, where we began crafting a fortress of blankets and pillows, a fortress that would stand strong against the winter storm outside. It was a spontaneous project that sent us into fits of laughter, the kind that comes easily when you're surrounded by someone who feels like home.

"Do you think we can make it big enough to keep the snow out?" he joked, pulling another pillow from the couch.

"Only if you stop eating all the marshmallows," I shot back, stealing a glance at the pile of supplies we had gathered. I had promised hot cocoa, and the little bag of marshmallows was our secret weapon—little clouds of sweetness that would take our drinks from ordinary to extraordinary.

As we nestled into our makeshift hideaway, the world outside faded into a distant memory. The wind continued to howl, but inside, the atmosphere was alive with warmth and comfort. I could feel the tension easing from Ethan's shoulders, the weight of his long shifts slowly melting away in the glow of the fairy lights strung above us. We settled into a rhythm, trading stories and laughter as if we were old friends rediscovering each other in the glow of a shared adventure.

"What's your wildest dream?" I asked, curiosity piquing through the playful banter.

Ethan paused, his eyes narrowing in thought, a small smile creeping onto his lips. "I always wanted to be a chef," he said finally, a hint of vulnerability in his voice. "I just never thought I'd end up slinging burgers and fries instead."

"Why not? You make the best fries in town," I replied, teasing him. "Besides, every great chef starts somewhere, right?"

He chuckled, the sound rich and warm, and I couldn't help but feel a flutter in my chest at the way his laughter seemed to fill the room. "You're right, but I'm still trying to figure out how to get from here to there," he said, a flicker of determination in his eyes. "Maybe I'll surprise everyone and open a gourmet diner right here in Cedar Hill."

"Count me in as your first customer. I'll even bring the marshmallows," I promised, our eyes locking for a moment that felt like it could stretch into eternity. In that instant, something unspoken flickered between us, a delicate tension that held the promise of something more.

As the evening progressed, we settled into our shared silence, sipping cocoa while the snowstorm continued its relentless dance outside. With each sip, the world beyond the windows seemed to fade further away. I could see the exhaustion still lurking in the depths of Ethan's eyes, but with every smile, every laugh, he drew a little closer to the surface, closer to the warmth we were creating together.

"Tell me about your worst customer," I challenged, eager to hear a story that would blend laughter with the life he led at the diner.

Ethan grinned, leaning back against the pillows, his expression shifting into one of mock seriousness. "There was this one time a guy came in and ordered a 'diet burger'—I still don't know what that is. Do you want the bun or the burger? Pick one!"

His rendition of the scenario had me in stitches, his animated expressions bringing the scene to life. As he shared more stories—of bizarre orders and unexpected moments—his laughter echoed around the room, filling the air with warmth and comfort, making the snowstorm feel like a distant dream.

In the middle of his story about a flamboyant lady who insisted on changing her order six times, the lights flickered. For a brief moment, the room fell into darkness before the emergency lights kicked in, bathing us in a soft, eerie glow. Ethan looked at me, his expression a mix of amusement and feigned horror. "Looks like we're going to need a flashlight for our fort," he said dramatically, reaching for the makeshift ceiling of blankets.

"Or we could just embrace the darkness," I replied, my heart racing a little faster. "Let's see where this takes us."

With that, we pulled the blankets tighter around us, enveloping ourselves in the cocoon we had created. The world outside was lost to us now, the snowstorm a mere whisper against the warmth of our laughter and the glow of our shared stories. In that moment, surrounded by the glow of our little sanctuary, I could feel something shifting, an awakening of dreams yet to be realized, waiting just beyond the edge of the storm.

The flickering lights cast playful shadows across the walls, enhancing the whimsical atmosphere we had created. Laughter echoed between the blankets as I leaned into Ethan, eager to catch the twinkle in his eyes that danced like the falling snow outside. With each passing moment, I felt an undeniable pull toward him, a magnetic force drawing me deeper into the warmth of our makeshift fortress.

"Do you think this storm could actually be hiding something?" I mused, teasingly nudging his shoulder. "Like, maybe a polar bear or a long-lost snowman who finally got tired of standing still?"

Ethan laughed, shaking his head. "Please, if it were a snowman, it'd be wearing a Hawaiian shirt, basking in the winter sun." He paused, his eyes narrowing in thought. "Or maybe it's just a group of raccoons staging a mutiny because they're tired of living off leftovers. Imagine their little protests—'We demand more pizza!'"

I could barely contain my laughter, picturing a band of raccoons brandishing tiny protest signs, their little paws waving dramatically. "Honestly, I would pay to see that," I replied, wiping away the tears of laughter that threatened to spill over. "But let's be real—if we see anything out there, it's just going to be a stray cat judging our life choices."

Ethan leaned back, grinning at me. "You'd be surprised how many cats have opinions these days. I bet they're the ones orchestrating the snowstorm, demanding more cuddles and less cold."

With a smirk, I reached for my cocoa, the marshmallows floating atop like little clouds of sweetness. "If they're in charge, we're doomed. They'll have us all under house arrest, making sure we never leave our cozy forts again."

As the night unfolded, the storm outside raged on, but inside, we were wrapped in laughter and warmth. Ethan's stories flowed like the cocoa between us, a steady stream of anecdotes and dreams. I shared my own secrets, the aspirations I had tucked away, like fragile ornaments waiting for the right moment to shine. "I always wanted to travel," I confessed, letting my guard down. "See the world, taste the food, and maybe even get lost in a city where no one knows my name."

He studied me, the flickering light catching the gleam in his eyes. "What's stopping you? Just pack your bags and go. The world is waiting for you."

"It's not that easy," I sighed, the weight of my own doubts creeping in. "Responsibilities, bills, all that fun adult stuff."

Ethan chuckled, the sound like music in the air. "You know, bills are overrated. What's life without a little risk? You could be a jet-setting snow bunny by next winter."

"Snow bunny?" I laughed, shaking my head. "I'd probably freeze on the first flight. I can barely handle the cold of my living room!"

"Then let's build a career around staying warm," he shot back, his eyes twinkling. "You could be the official hot cocoa taster for the world. It's a solid plan."

I feigned a thoughtful expression, tapping my chin. "Ah, yes. 'Official Hot Cocoa Taster.' I can see it now—'Your mission: travel the world to find the best marshmallows and sprinkle them with joy!'"

With each whimsical suggestion, the walls of our fort became a canvas for our dreams. I could feel the possibilities swirling in the air around us, mixing with the sweet scent of cocoa and the laughter that felt like sunshine. It was easy to forget the world outside—the blizzard that raged on and the responsibilities that lurked like shadows in the corners of our minds.

Suddenly, a loud crack of thunder echoed through the night, startling us both. I nearly spilled my drink, and Ethan jumped, wide-eyed. "Is it just me, or did that sound suspiciously like a walrus?"

"Maybe the raccoons summoned the walruses for backup!" I exclaimed, my heart racing from the surprise. "You know, a strategic alliance to dominate Cedar Hill."

He chuckled, recovering from the sudden fright. "I can picture it now—a rebellion led by walruses and raccoons, uniting against the humans for their unfair treatment of leftovers."

In our laughter, I found comfort, yet a thread of tension lingered in the air. There was something deeper beneath the surface of our playful banter, an unspoken truth waiting for the right moment to surface. The energy shifted slightly as our eyes locked, the world around us fading into a soft blur.

"What if," Ethan began slowly, breaking the spell with his carefully chosen words, "what if there's more out there for us than just this?"

My heart raced as I contemplated his words, the weight of his question heavy in the air. "More?" I repeated, my voice barely above a whisper.

He leaned closer, the warmth of his body igniting the space between us. "Yeah. I mean, we've built this amazing little world here, but I can't shake the feeling that there's something bigger waiting for us. Something outside this storm."

I swallowed hard, the reality of his statement crashing over me like the snow piling against the windows. The connection between us was undeniable, yet the thought of stepping beyond this moment felt daunting. "You think so?" I asked, seeking reassurance in his gaze.

"Absolutely. I can see it in your eyes," he replied, his voice steady. "We both have dreams—yours of traveling, and mine of creating something more. What's stopping us from chasing them together?"

The question hung in the air, a thread of hope woven through the fear. Could we really step beyond this cozy fort and the comfort it provided? The thought excited me, but it also terrified me. It was one thing to dream, another entirely to pursue those dreams side by side with someone who had already begun to feel like an anchor in my life.

In the brief silence that followed, the wind howled outside, almost as if echoing my own inner turmoil. "Together?" I echoed, a mix of excitement and uncertainty swirling in my chest.

"Why not? We could be the raccoons leading the charge against mediocrity," he replied, a playful grin breaking across his face.

A laugh escaped my lips, easing the tension. "Raccoons with big dreams—now that's a story I'd pay to see." But as I spoke, I felt a twinge of something deeper—a spark of possibility igniting within me. What if we were more than just two friends seeking warmth from a storm? What if we could forge our paths together, hand in hand, unafraid of the challenges ahead?

"I want that," I admitted, my voice steadier now. "I want to chase those dreams. I want to explore the world, and I think... I think I want to do it with you."

Ethan's eyes widened in surprise, and the smile that broke across his face felt like the first rays of sunlight after a long, cold night. "So it's settled then," he said, his tone playful yet sincere. "Raccoons and walruses, here we come."

The moment felt charged with possibility, the storm outside now a mere backdrop to the excitement unfolding between us. We were at the precipice of something new, a whirlwind of dreams and shared laughter waiting to be explored. The snow continued to fall, but inside our fort, the world felt alive with endless possibilities.

The laughter hung in the air, buoyant and electric, weaving through the blankets and pillows that surrounded us like a protective cocoon. The chaos of the storm beyond felt far removed, almost unreal, as we shared snippets of our lives—those seemingly mundane details that suddenly felt monumental under the soft glow of our makeshift fort. I found myself leaning into the warmth of Ethan's shoulder, a comfortable familiarity settling between us.

"You know," he began, his tone teasing, "if we're raccoons planning a rebellion, we should probably come up with a strategy. I can't be the only one working on this."

"Oh, you mean like a detailed plan? Because I thought we were just winging it, pulling off a full-scale winter mutiny on the fly." I took a sip of my cocoa, the sweet warmth filling me with a sense of daring. "What do you have in mind? A rallying cry? I can see the poster now: 'Join Us in the Great Raccoon Revolution!'"

He chuckled, shaking his head. "No, no, I envision something more subtle. Perhaps an underground network of cocoa-loving raccoons ready to invade unsuspecting kitchens."

"Very sneaky," I replied, my mind racing with the imagery. "But we need a mascot—something that strikes fear into the hearts of our adversaries."

"Definitely a walrus," he said, a serious nod accompanying his words. "Think about it: they're huge, they have tusks, and no one wants to mess with a walrus on a mission."

"While I love the idea, I feel like a walrus would be more of a hindrance than a help," I said, biting back laughter. "Imagine trying to fit one in a kitchen to steal cookies. I think we need something a little more stealthy."

As we bantered, I felt the warmth in the room cocooning us, a stark contrast to the chaos outside. My heart raced, fueled by the sense of connection that was blossoming in ways I hadn't anticipated. Yet, beneath the playful exchanges, I sensed an unspoken weight—our dreams were tinged with uncertainty, a delicate thread that could easily fray.

We let the laughter fade into comfortable silence, our gazes drifting toward the flickering lights above us. It was in this quiet moment that I realized how much I yearned for the possibilities we had barely brushed upon. I wanted to step outside the fortress we'd built, not just for an adventure but for the chance to truly share my life with him.

"Ethan," I said, my voice barely above a whisper. "What if we actually went for it? What if we planned a trip together?"

His eyes lit up, and a smile broke across his face, his enthusiasm palpable. "You mean, like a real raccoon revolution? We could take the show on the road!"

"Exactly! We could start somewhere simple, maybe a weekend trip to the coast. Or even a road trip to the mountains. We'd be like those people who have their whole lives figured out."

"Or at least people who know how to drink hot cocoa while staring at mountains," he replied with a grin. "That counts for something, right?"

"Definitely more than a little something," I shot back, feeling my heart swell at the thought of planning adventures together. "But let's not forget our mission of culinary excellence along the way. There's bound to be local hot chocolate competitions we can enter."

"Now you're talking! I can picture it—a hot cocoa championship where we rule as the ultimate cocoa connoisseurs."

But beneath the surface of our playful exchange, I felt a tremor of uncertainty. What if this was just a fleeting moment, a temporary escape from reality? What if the world outside—the one full of bills, responsibilities, and uncertainties—intruded on our cozy sanctuary?

Just then, a loud crash echoed from outside, jolting us from our laughter. I froze, eyes wide as I exchanged a glance with Ethan.

The storm had intensified, and a sudden rush of wind rattled the windows, shaking the fragile walls of our fort.

"Did you hear that?" I whispered, the warmth of the moment suddenly replaced by a chill creeping in from the outside.

Ethan nodded, a furrow forming between his brows. "It sounded like something hit the house. Maybe a tree branch?"

I stood up, peeking through the window, the swirling snow obscuring my view. "I think it's time for a reconnaissance mission," I said, attempting to inject some humor back into the moment, though my heart raced with trepidation.

He pushed himself off the ground, and we moved cautiously to the window. The landscape outside was shrouded in white, the world reduced to shades of gray and blue, but I could just make out a silhouette against the backdrop of swirling snow. My stomach knotted as I squinted, trying to decipher the shape.

"What is that?" I asked, feeling a mix of curiosity and dread.

Ethan leaned closer, his breath fogging the glass. "It looks... like someone is out there."

I felt a shiver run down my spine, a dissonance breaking through the warmth we'd built. "In this storm? They can't be serious!"

"Let's grab a coat and see if we can help," he said, his expression shifting from playful to concerned. There was a determination in his voice that I found both reassuring and alarming.

We quickly bundled up, the weight of our blankets giving way to the chill of reality as we stepped outside into the howling winds. The snow whipped around us, a biting cold that seemed intent on seeping through every layer.

"Stay close," Ethan instructed, his voice barely rising above the roar of the storm. We trudged forward, the snow crunching beneath our feet, each step heavy with uncertainty.

As we approached the figure, my heart raced. The storm had obscured my vision, but I could make out the shape of a person half-buried in the snow.

"Are you okay?" I called out, the wind snatching my words before they could travel far.

There was a slight movement, and a muffled voice responded, barely audible. "Help... please."

My breath caught in my throat. "Ethan, we need to move faster!"

We reached the figure, pulling away the snow to reveal a woman, her face pale against the white blanket surrounding her. She shivered violently, and I felt panic welling inside me. "What happened? Are you hurt?"

"Stuck... my car..." she stammered, her voice trembling as much as her body.

"Stay with us," I urged, trying to provide comfort as Ethan quickly glanced around. "We'll figure this out. You're safe now."

But just as he turned, his expression shifted from concern to shock, his eyes widening as he stared past me. I felt a surge of unease ripple through the air, a weight that pressed heavily against my chest.

"What is it?" I asked, following his gaze.

Then, out of the swirling snow, emerged a shadow—a large figure, looming, moving with purpose through the storm. The figure was unmistakable, and my heart dropped as the realization crashed over me like the winter wind.

Ethan's voice broke through the mounting fear. "We need to get her inside! Now!"

I turned to grab the woman's arm, but before I could pull her to safety, the shadow stepped closer, revealing a face shrouded in mystery and intent. The snowstorm, once a cozy backdrop, had transformed into something much darker.

As the storm continued to rage, I realized we had unwittingly stepped into a moment that would change everything—a moment filled with secrets, shadows, and the weight of unknown choices hanging heavy in the air. The night felt charged with tension, and I could hardly breathe as the figure loomed closer, pulling us into a fate we had yet to understand.

Chapter 17: The Intimacy

The sun dipped low on the horizon, casting a golden hue over the apartment we had grown accustomed to sharing, a haven cluttered with textbooks, half-finished mugs of coffee, and a kaleidoscope of mismatched throw pillows. Outside, the world buzzed with the hurried pace of late-afternoon traffic, but inside, time seemed to still. I could hear the faint hum of the city, a backdrop to the quiet cocoon we had woven together. Ethan sat beside me on the couch, the fabric of his jeans brushing against mine, sending delightful sparks of awareness racing through my veins. He was lost in the pages of a book, his brow furrowed in concentration, yet I found myself utterly distracted by the way the light caught the golden flecks in his hazel eyes.

"Are you ever going to let me read that?" I teased, reaching out to tug at the corner of the book, but he effortlessly pulled it back, a mischievous grin spreading across his face.

"Not until I'm done with this chapter. It's getting really good," he replied, his voice low and smooth, like honey mixed with the faintest hint of a smirk. I couldn't help but roll my eyes, but a smile tugged at my lips.

"Oh, come on! You know I'm better at summarizing than you are," I countered, leaning closer, our shoulders brushing as I attempted to steal a glance at the text. It was a hopeless endeavor; I was far more captivated by him than the words on the page.

"Maybe. But I'm pretty sure you'd just turn it into a romance novel," he shot back, and laughter bubbled up between us, brightening the soft glow of the evening light filtering through the window.

"Guilty as charged," I said, mock-serious. "Can you blame me? Life is just begging for a little dramatization. Especially this chapter." I gestured around the room, and he chuckled, shaking his head.

"Fair enough. But I'd rather read about the complexities of this—" he gestured to our surroundings, the casual clutter, the warmth radiating from our shared space, "than anything about a love triangle."

With a sudden intensity, his gaze met mine, and the playful banter melted away, replaced by something deeper, something electric. My pulse quickened, and it was as though the air around us thickened with unspoken words. I leaned in slightly, caught in a moment where time ceased to exist. Just then, the moment was interrupted by the piercing ring of my phone. I recoiled slightly, frustration bubbling up as I glanced at the screen. It was a reminder, blaring insistently for attention, but my heart was still racing from the uncharted territory we had been tiptoeing around.

"Ignore it," Ethan urged, his voice a gentle command that washed over me, soothing my irritation. He set the book down, leaning closer. "It's just noise."

And it was. The phone fell silent as I placed it facedown on the coffee table, the weight of anticipation hanging in the air like a storm cloud ready to burst. "I don't want anything to break this moment," I confessed, my voice barely a whisper, feeling the weight of my own vulnerability spilling forth.

His eyes softened, and he reached out, tucking a loose strand of hair behind my ear, his fingers lingering against my skin, igniting a trail of warmth. "Then let's not. Let's just be here. Together." His words wrapped around me like a warm blanket, coaxing me to lean into the warmth of our connection.

With each heartbeat, I felt the layers between us dissolve. The tentative kisses we had shared before surged back to mind, but now there was an urgency, a need to explore the intimacy that had been quietly simmering beneath the surface. I tilted my head, allowing the silence to envelop us, every breath becoming a shared rhythm that pulsed with promise.

"I've been thinking," I started, my voice tinged with uncertainty, but Ethan leaned in, his expression encouraging, ready to dive deeper. "About us. About how everything feels different with you."

He nodded, his gaze never wavering, as if he were drawing strength from my words. "I feel it too," he admitted, his voice low and resonant. "It's like... we're finally stepping into something real."

With that, the air around us crackled with energy, a potent mix of excitement and fear, as if we stood on the edge of a precipice, ready to leap. I hesitated, grappling with the swirl of emotions, the trust that hung between us like a fragile thread, yet somehow unbreakable. "But what if—"

"Hey," he interrupted gently, cupping my cheek with his warm hand, his thumb brushing against my skin. "What if we just embrace the 'what ifs'? What if we let go of the fear?"

His words struck a chord deep within me, and I felt a surge of courage in the face of my uncertainty. "You're right," I breathed, leaning into his touch, surrendering to the truth we both understood. The journey toward intimacy wasn't a destination but a path, winding and full of unexpected turns, yet somehow worth every step.

With a newfound resolve, I reached for him, our lips meeting in a tentative kiss that slowly deepened, igniting a fire within. Each movement was a dance of exploration, our mouths melding together with the softest urgency, as though we were trying to memorize the taste of each other's hearts. I felt the warmth of his hands slip around my waist, pulling me closer, anchoring me in the moment. In that intoxicating blend of kisses and whispered confessions, I knew we were on the brink of something beautiful, and I felt myself falling deeper, ready to embrace whatever came next.

The following week unfurled like a vibrant tapestry, each day woven with threads of anticipation and quiet joy. I found myself stealing glances at Ethan between classes, our eyes locking in silent conversations that felt more profound than words. The familiarity of our connection settled comfortably around me, yet an undercurrent of tension danced just beneath the surface. It was as if we were holding our breaths, waiting for something unsaid to bloom into reality.

One evening, we decided to break the monotony of our routines. Ethan suggested a spontaneous adventure, his hazel eyes sparkling with mischief as he proposed we visit the new art exhibit at the gallery downtown. The idea ignited a spark of excitement in me. I could already picture us wandering through rooms filled with colors and shapes, our laughter mingling with the whispers of art enthusiasts.

"Art? You mean the place where people stand around pretending to be cultured?" I teased, raising an eyebrow as I slipped on my favorite pair of boots. "I thought we were going to do something wild, like skydiving."

"Let's save that for another day," he shot back, a mock-serious expression on his face. "I promise you'll love it. Besides, there's wine involved."

"Now you're speaking my language," I replied, grinning as I finished tying my laces. The prospect of an evening filled with art, wine, and Ethan's easy laughter felt like the perfect remedy for the week's stress.

As we strolled through the gallery, I was surprised by how much I enjoyed it. Each piece seemed to spark conversation, pulling us deeper into discussions that revealed layers of our personalities. We admired abstract paintings that captured emotions we couldn't quite articulate, and I found myself fascinated by Ethan's insights, his passion lighting up his features.

"See, art can be thrilling," he said, gesturing at a particularly chaotic painting splashed with wild colors. "This one speaks of chaos, the raw emotion of being human."

"Or it could be a toddler's finger painting gone rogue," I countered, stifling a laugh. He shot me a mock glare, his lips curling into an amused smile.

"Cynic!" he declared playfully, nudging my shoulder. "But I appreciate your perspective. It's refreshing."

We meandered through the exhibit, our hands brushing occasionally, igniting sparks of connection with every touch. The atmosphere was charged, the art serving as a backdrop to our evolving intimacy, layering our relationship with vibrant hues of trust and excitement.

As the night wore on, we found ourselves sipping wine in a cozy corner café nearby. The rich, bold flavors warmed my senses, and the soft glow of the candles flickered like fireflies around us. I could feel the heat radiating from Ethan as he leaned in, his voice low and inviting. "What's the most embarrassing thing you've ever done?"

I nearly choked on my wine, laughter bubbling up uncontrollably. "Oh, you're going to have to be more specific. I'm a treasure trove of embarrassing stories."

"Let's start with something relatable. Like that time you tripped in front of the whole class?" He grinned, mischief dancing in his eyes, and I felt the warmth of his gaze, electric and encouraging.

"Okay, okay! You got me. But you have to share one too," I said, a challenge lacing my tone. "I'm not the only clumsy one here."

He hesitated, as if weighing his options. "Alright, I'll go first. Back in high school, I thought I'd impress a girl by showing off on the basketball court. I ended up slipping on the floor and crashing into the bleachers. Not exactly the heroic moment I'd envisioned."

I burst into laughter, the sound ringing through the café, a shared moment of vulnerability and hilarity. "And I thought you were cool," I teased. "Now you're just a basketball disaster."

He chuckled, shaking his head. "Hey, at least I'm honest about my embarrassing moments. Your turn!"

I took a sip of wine, gathering my thoughts. "Fine, but prepare yourself. It was during a school play. I was the lead, and in my big dramatic moment, I forgot my lines and improvised. I ended up ranting about the merits of ice cream over pizza."

Ethan erupted in laughter, his eyes crinkling with delight. "You're kidding! That's amazing. I wish I had been there to witness that."

"It was mortifying," I admitted, rolling my eyes at the memory. "But I've come to terms with it. Ice cream is definitely superior, though."

"I'll remember that for our next date," he said, winking as he leaned back in his chair, a satisfied smile lingering on his lips. "So, what's your favorite flavor?"

"Mint chocolate chip, obviously," I replied, grinning. "It's the perfect balance of refreshing and indulgent."

His eyes sparkled with mischief. "You know, I've heard that people who love mint chocolate chip are adventurous and full of surprises."

"Oh, really? You must think I'm a wild card then," I shot back, my heart racing at the underlying implications of his words.

"Definitely," he said, leaning forward, his voice dropping to a conspiratorial whisper. "But I think we need to test that theory out. Let's find an adventure this weekend—something unexpected."

"Like what? More art?" I quipped, raising an eyebrow playfully.

"Or maybe we ditch the predictable and go camping. Just you and me, under the stars," he suggested, his gaze unwavering, and my heart skipped a beat.

"Camping? Seriously?" I replied, trying to hide my surprise. "You're just full of surprises tonight."

"Consider it a challenge," he teased, his eyes dancing with excitement. "You in?"

I hesitated, contemplating the idea. The prospect of being alone with Ethan, surrounded by nature, ignited a thrill within me. "Alright, I'm in. But you better bring a good tent, or I'm sleeping in your car."

"Deal!" he laughed, his grin infectious.

With every shared moment, I felt us edging closer to something beautifully raw and genuine. The chemistry between us crackled with possibility, each day revealing new depths to our connection. As we clinked our glasses, the world around us faded, leaving just Ethan and me, wrapped in laughter, wine, and dreams of adventures yet to come.

As the sun dipped beneath the horizon, the weekend loomed like a canvas waiting for us to splash it with memories. Ethan and I had spent the past few days preparing for our camping trip, excitement sparking in the air as we gathered supplies. I felt a delightful blend of anticipation and nerves, my mind racing at the thought of spending a night under the stars with him. The thrill of adventure surged through me, and I couldn't help but imagine how intimate and exhilarating it would be to be away from the noise of everyday life, stripped down to the essentials—just us and the great outdoors.

On the day of our trip, the morning sun poured through my window like liquid gold, coaxing me awake with promises of adventure. I dressed quickly, my heart fluttering as I thought of Ethan's smile, his laughter ringing in my ears. We had agreed to meet at the park, our starting point before heading to the campsite. I arrived early, the air fresh with the scent of pine and the distant sounds of chirping birds.

When Ethan pulled up, the world seemed to brighten, his familiar silhouette framed by the sunlight. He jumped out of his car, his laughter bubbling over as he hoisted our gear over his shoulder with effortless ease. "Ready to get lost in the woods?" he called, the playfulness in his voice sending a thrill through me.

"Only if you promise not to get us hopelessly lost," I shot back, feigning indignation, though I was already grinning.

"Come on, it'll be an adventure!" he insisted, winking as he tossed my backpack into the trunk. The thrill of spontaneity thrummed between us, a palpable connection that felt electric.

The drive to the campsite was filled with music and laughter, the kind of easy banter that solidified our bond. We took turns choosing songs, our voices blending in sweet harmony, sometimes off-key but always spirited. As the trees thickened around us, I felt my excitement grow, each twist of the road promising the unknown.

When we finally arrived, I stepped out, inhaling the rich, earthy scent of the forest. The sound of rustling leaves and the distant babble of a stream welcomed us, and I couldn't help but smile at the beauty of it all. "This place is perfect," I said, taking a moment to soak it all in.

Ethan grinned, the sunlight catching the strands of his hair, giving him an almost ethereal glow. "Told you! Now, let's set up the tent before nightfall. We wouldn't want to be the clueless campers fumbling in the dark."

We pitched the tent with laughter punctuating our efforts, our playful jabs at each other echoing through the woods. When we finally stepped back to admire our handiwork, the sun was already beginning its descent, casting an orange hue across the sky.

"Not bad for a couple of city kids," I said, placing my hands on my hips, pretending to inspect our work.

Ethan feigned a thoughtful expression. "I'd say we're ready for Survivor: Forest Edition."

As dusk settled, we settled down by a crackling fire, the flames dancing and flickering in the growing darkness. I could feel the heat radiating between us, the world outside our little circle fading away. The sound of the crackling fire mingled with the rustling leaves overhead, creating a symphony of nature.

"Do you remember the first time we met?" Ethan asked, his voice low, almost conspiratorial, as he leaned closer.

I couldn't help but chuckle at the memory. "Of course! You were the cocky guy who thought he could win the debate competition with zero preparation."

He laughed, a deep, rich sound that warmed my insides. "And you were the overachiever who had to save my sorry butt," he shot back. "I think I owe you one."

"Just one? I feel like it should be at least five," I retorted playfully, nudging him with my foot.

As we bantered, the connection between us deepened, the spark of intimacy flickering brightly in the shadows. With every shared glance, every laugh, it felt like we were carving out our own little world, separate from the demands of life back home.

The fire crackled as the stars began to pepper the night sky, twinkling like diamonds against the velvet backdrop. I leaned back, looking up at the vastness above us, feeling small yet comforted by the enormity of the universe. "It's beautiful out here," I murmured, lost in the moment.

"It really is," Ethan agreed, his tone softer now, laced with a tenderness that made my heart flutter. "I can't remember the last time I felt this free."

I turned to him, searching his gaze, sensing the shift in our conversation. "Isn't it funny how being away from everything can make you feel more connected?"

He nodded, his expression serious now. "I've been thinking a lot about that. About how much I've come to rely on you. Not just for fun, but for the real stuff."

The gravity of his words hung between us, drawing me closer, urging me to explore the depths of what lay ahead. "What do you mean by the real stuff?" I asked, my heart racing as the moment hung suspended in the air.

"Like... I don't want to lose this," he said slowly, his eyes locking onto mine, the sincerity etched on his face making my breath catch. "I want to explore whatever this is, you know?"

I felt a rush of warmth spread through me, the vulnerability in his admission igniting a fire of hope and possibility. "Me too," I replied, my voice barely above a whisper, the truth spilling out like a long-held secret.

Just as the words hung between us, a rustle in the bushes nearby jolted me from the moment. "Did you hear that?" I asked, suddenly on alert.

Ethan frowned, his eyes narrowing as he scanned the darkness. "Probably just an animal. Don't worry."

But I wasn't so easily reassured. The rustling grew louder, almost purposeful, and I felt the hairs on the back of my neck prickling with unease. "Maybe we should check it out," I suggested, my heart pounding.

"Or we could just stay right here," he countered, a playful grin creeping back onto his face.

"Very funny, but seriously. Something's out there."

Before he could respond, a shadow darted through the trees, fast and erratic, and my breath caught in my throat. "Ethan," I said, fear creeping into my voice, "that wasn't just a squirrel."

He stood up, tension radiating from him as he stepped toward the noise. "Stay here," he instructed, his tone shifting from playful to protective.

"Yeah, right. Like I'm going to let you face the unknown alone," I shot back, scrambling to my feet.

Together, we moved cautiously toward the sound, hearts pounding in sync, the firelight flickering behind us. As we reached the edge of the clearing, the rustling stopped, replaced by an eerie silence. My pulse raced, every nerve in my body on high alert.

"Maybe it was nothing," Ethan whispered, but I could see the uncertainty in his eyes.

Just then, a figure emerged from the shadows, half-hidden by the trees, and I froze. The air crackled with tension as the reality of the moment sunk in.

Chapter 18: The Setback

The sun had begun its lazy descent, draping the living room in a golden hue, transforming every ordinary corner into a soft, glowing memory. I watched Ethan from the kitchen, his silhouette hunched over the kitchen table, as if the weight of the news had pulled him down into a different world—one where dreams had suddenly dimmed and ambitions felt like distant echoes. My heart ached at the sight; the lines on his forehead deepened as he replayed the words from his boss in his mind like a broken record, the melody turning sour with each repetition.

"Hours cut," he had said, his voice a quiet storm of disbelief and worry. "They're restructuring. It's nothing personal." But how could it not feel personal? I longed to reach out, to hold his hand and share the burden, but a knot twisted in my stomach. My own insecurities whispered to me, clawing at the edges of my thoughts. What if this was just the beginning? What if this setback unraveled everything we had worked so hard to build?

"Want some coffee?" I called softly, the sound of my voice a faint anchor in the swirling chaos of our situation. I busied myself at the counter, pouring the rich liquid into our mismatched mugs, hoping the warmth would somehow seep into our strained silence.

Ethan's gaze flickered up, momentarily breaking through the fog of his thoughts. "Sure, I guess," he replied, his voice low, each word heavy with unshed emotions. I brought the steaming cups over, placing one in front of him before settling into the chair across from him. The mug felt warm in my hands, but the room was growing colder by the second, the chill of uncertainty creeping into our conversation like an unwelcome guest.

"What are we going to do?" I asked, letting the question hang in the air, heavy and thick. I could see the gears turning in his mind, his expression morphing between determination and defeat.

"I'll figure something out. I always do," he said, but there was a tremor in his voice, a hint of vulnerability that made my heart flutter with a mix of hope and despair.

"I know you will," I replied, forcing a smile that didn't quite reach my eyes. "But maybe we could talk about options? We could make a plan together."

He took a long sip from his mug, contemplating my words, and I could see the fight rising in him, battling against the tide of disappointment that threatened to pull him under. "You have enough on your plate, Sarah. I don't want you to worry about this too."

"Ethan," I said, leaning forward, my hands clasped tightly around the warmth of the mug. "You're not alone in this. We're a team, remember? It's okay to lean on me sometimes."

His eyes softened, and I caught a glimpse of the man I fell in love with—the one who could light up a room with a grin, who made even the mundane feel extraordinary. But the shadows flickered at the edges, and I could feel the worry wrapping its tendrils around us, a tightening grip that promised to squeeze the joy from our lives if we let it.

After a moment, he nodded slowly, as if accepting a challenge rather than a lifeline. "Okay. What do you suggest?"

I breathed a sigh of relief, grateful that he was willing to open the door to discussion. "What if we create a budget? Look at your expenses and see where we can cut back?" I could see him considering it, the gears of his mind shifting.

"Like when we tried to save for that trip to Italy?" He smirked slightly, and for a brief moment, the tension eased as we both recalled the ridiculous sacrifice of giving up coffee for a month.

"Exactly! We survived that," I said, feeling the corners of my mouth lift into a genuine smile. "And I'm still not quite sure how we managed to get through the month without espresso-induced meltdowns."

He chuckled, the sound a balm against the worry looming like dark clouds. "And you swore you'd never do that again."

"Desperate times call for desperate measures," I countered playfully. "I'd rather deal with my caffeine addiction than lose you to a corporate restructuring. I mean, I think I can live without caffeine for a little while longer."

"Not sure if I can survive you without caffeine," he teased back, a flicker of the old light sparking in his eyes.

We fell into a rhythm of laughter, navigating our way back to the surface, buoyed by shared humor and the faint glimmer of resilience. But the laughter didn't drown out the underlying tension completely; it simply masked it, like a beautifully painted wall hiding cracks underneath.

As the evening wore on, we crafted our budget, a series of numbers and ideas sprawled across the table, each line a commitment to face this challenge together. Yet, as I glanced at Ethan, the worry lines etched deep into his skin didn't quite fade away. I knew that even with plans in place, the fear of the unknown loomed like an ominous cloud, threatening to rain down on our parade.

Just when we thought we had a handle on things, the doorbell rang, pulling me from my thoughts and sending a jolt of unexpected energy through the room. "Who could that be?" I asked, glancing toward the door, our earlier discussions momentarily suspended in the air.

Ethan shrugged, his brows knitting together as he pushed back from the table. "No idea. Could be a neighbor or something."

As he opened the door, I caught my breath, the atmosphere shifting again as a stranger stood on the threshold. A man in a sharp suit, his expression unreadable, held a manila envelope in his hands like it contained the very fate of the universe.

The man at the door stood poised, like a statue crafted in sleek marble, his crisp suit perfectly tailored, and his hair slicked back with the kind of precision that suggested he was no stranger to high-stakes negotiations. I could almost hear the ticking of a clock echoing in the air, amplifying the tension that crackled between us. Ethan's brow furrowed in confusion as he opened the door wider, his expression a cocktail of curiosity and wariness.

"Can I help you?" Ethan asked, his voice steady yet laced with an underlying question that hung in the air.

The stranger stepped forward, the envelope clutched tightly in his hand, as if it were a secret he was reluctant to share. "Ethan Miller?" he asked, his tone polished and professional, like someone accustomed to commanding attention.

Ethan nodded slowly, a shadow of unease flickering across his features. "Yes, that's me."

"Good. I'm here on behalf of HR from your company," the man said, glancing at me with a fleeting look that suggested I wasn't supposed to be in this conversation. "We need to discuss your severance package."

A chill swept through the room, cutting through the warmth of the evening like a knife. I could see Ethan's posture stiffen, the flicker of confusion transforming into something darker, something that felt all too familiar. My heart sank as the implications washed over me like a tidal wave. "Severance package?" I repeated, the words slipping from my lips like ice.

"Yes," the man said, his gaze now firmly fixed on Ethan, ignoring my presence completely. "Due to the recent restructuring, they are making significant cuts. Your hours being reduced is just the beginning."

Ethan's mouth opened slightly, but no words came out, his thoughts clearly spiraling in a direction he hadn't anticipated. I could feel the walls of our world closing in, the laughter we had just shared now a distant memory, eclipsed by this unwelcome revelation.

"Look, I understand this isn't easy, but we need to discuss the terms," the man continued, glancing at the envelope in his hand as if it contained the keys to our future—or perhaps the shackles that would bind us in fear. "I'm here to ensure you're aware of your rights and what support is available moving forward."

"What support?" Ethan's voice was sharper now, a veneer of anger coating his confusion. "You're telling me I might lose my job entirely."

The man shifted slightly, a minuscule gesture, but it felt like he was repositioning himself in a war zone. "I can assure you, this is not a reflection of your work ethic. The decision has been made at the corporate level."

"That's comforting," I interjected, unable to hold back the sarcasm that bubbled up inside me. "It's always nice to know that faceless entities are pulling the strings while we're left to pick up the pieces."

Ethan shot me a grateful look, though his eyes were dark with anxiety. "What do you want from me?" he asked the man, his voice a low rumble.

"Just a few signatures and a discussion about what comes next. I understand this is overwhelming."

"Overwhelming? That's an understatement," I muttered, crossing my arms and leaning against the door frame. "You're coming here with bad news and expecting us to play along as if this is just another Tuesday. Where's the compassion in that?"

Ethan shifted his weight from one foot to the other, glancing between me and the stranger, clearly torn between wanting to be professional and needing to express the frustration that hung like a cloud over our heads. "Can we talk about this later? I need a moment to process."

The man nodded, his expression impassive. "Of course. Just know that the paperwork needs to be signed by the end of the week."

As he turned to leave, I caught a flicker of something in his eyes—perhaps guilt or an understanding of the upheaval he was leaving in his wake. It wasn't much, but it was enough to remind me that even in corporate machinery, humanity could still slip through the cracks.

Once the door clicked shut, the atmosphere in the room felt unbearably heavy, like a storm about to break. I turned to Ethan, who was running a hand through his hair, his breathing uneven. "What just happened?" he asked, his voice barely above a whisper.

"Honestly? I think we just stepped into a whirlwind of chaos," I replied, my heart racing as the reality of our situation settled over us. "They're taking away not just your job, but our stability. Everything feels uncertain right now."

He nodded, the fight visibly draining from him, replaced by a weariness that pulled at his features. "I didn't expect this. I thought I could manage the cutbacks, but this..."

"This feels like a body blow," I said softly, inching closer to him. "It's okay to feel overwhelmed. We can face this together, but we need to be honest with each other."

"Honest," he echoed, his voice thick with emotion. "Yeah, I guess that's the first step, huh?"

I reached for his hand, intertwining my fingers with his, the warmth grounding us amid the swirling uncertainty. "We'll find a way to navigate this. You're resourceful, and you've always been good at finding opportunities in the chaos."

"Maybe I need to take a few steps back and reassess," he mused, his gaze distant, as if looking through the wall and into a future we had yet to chart.

"What if we brainstorm some ideas? I mean, your skills are incredibly valuable. There are other paths we could explore."

Ethan looked at me, a hint of that familiar spark igniting in his eyes. "You really think so?"

"Absolutely. You're not just an employee; you're a problem solver, a creator. Remember how you transformed that entire project last year?"

He chuckled softly, the sound breaking through the tension like sunlight after a storm. "I thought that was just my usual stubbornness."

"Stubbornness is sometimes the secret ingredient to success," I said, teasingly nudging his shoulder. "And we both know you have enough stubbornness to fuel an entire army."

His smile grew, and for a moment, the weight of the world felt a little lighter. "Okay, let's brainstorm. I may not have coffee to fuel my creativity right now, but I think I can still come up with something."

"Let's start with the basics. What do you enjoy doing outside of work?"

Ethan leaned back in his chair, considering. "Well, I love teaching. It's what drew me to my job in the first place."

"Teaching!" I exclaimed, enthusiasm bubbling up. "You've always had a way of breaking things down so people can actually understand them. What if you explored that further?"

He leaned forward, a thoughtful expression on his face. "You mean like workshops or online courses?"

"Exactly! You have expertise that people would pay for. Plus, you could be your own boss, setting your own hours."

A flicker of hope crossed his features, and I could see the wheels turning in his mind. "I've never thought about it that way. It might actually be worth pursuing."

"Of course it is! Let's make a plan. We can map out what you'd want to teach and how to reach out to people who could benefit from your knowledge."

The tension in the room began to ease as we leaned into the idea, sketching out possibilities with laughter and light banter, our earlier worries fading, if only for a moment. The shadows that had threatened to consume us receded, revealing a path forward—one filled with uncertainty, yes, but also with potential.

As the night wore on, we moved through brainstorming sessions like explorers charting uncharted territory, the fear of the unknown morphing into a thrill of discovery. The world felt vibrant again, brimming with possibilities, and I couldn't help but think that even in the darkest times, we could still find a way to light the way ahead.

As we dove into the brainstorming session, I could feel the momentum shifting. Each idea we tossed around seemed to light a spark in Ethan, igniting a warmth that had been stifled by the cold reality of the earlier conversation. We spent the next hour sketching out plans, potential topics for workshops, and the logistics of how he could market his expertise. The kitchen table transformed into a battlefield of creativity, covered in a chaotic spread of papers, sticky notes, and coffee-stained mugs that told the tale of our burgeoning hope.

"Okay, so let's nail down your unique angle," I said, leaning forward with enthusiasm. "What makes your teaching style special? Why should people choose you over the myriad of options out there?"

Ethan chuckled, a lightness returning to his eyes. "Because I can make even the dullest corporate jargon sound like a thrilling adventure? Who doesn't want to experience the excitement of quarterly earnings reports?"

I laughed, the sound bright and airy, banishing the last remnants of our earlier gloom. "Exactly! You could title your course Corporate Adventures: The Quest for Understanding. Just imagine the marketing slogan!"

"Or, Join Me on the Boring Journey to Knowledge. That'll really draw them in," he quipped, rolling his eyes dramatically.

"Hey, if you can make a balance sheet sound like an epic saga, you might just create a new genre!" I shot back, my playful jab punctuating the laughter that filled the room.

The humor helped to create a rhythm, each idea spurring the next, and soon we had a rough outline of what could become a series of workshops. I could feel excitement building between us, an electric current that chased away the shadows that had lingered since the man at the door had left.

"So, what's next?" he asked, his voice tinged with anticipation, a flicker of determination igniting in his gaze. "If I want to do this, I need to move quickly. I don't want to be sitting on my hands while the clock ticks down."

"Then let's start with a website," I suggested, my mind racing with possibilities. "You could showcase your expertise, offer free resources, and even include a blog to attract attention."

"Are you volunteering to help me with that?" he asked, eyebrows raised playfully. "I wouldn't want to overextend your already jam-packed schedule."

"Oh, please," I waved my hand dismissively. "My schedule can make room for a project that'll keep us both sane through this chaos. Besides, you'll be the star. I'll just be the fairy godmother waving a wand and sprinkling some HTML pixie dust."

Ethan laughed again, and it felt like a balm to my own lingering insecurities. "Alright, let's do it! But you know this means you'll have to let me buy you dinner every night as a thank you, right?"

"Dinner? How about an entire week's worth of takeout? I have some serious cravings for Thai food," I shot back, unable to suppress the smile spreading across my face.

"Thai it is! Consider it a deal. But I get to choose the place," he grinned, and for a moment, it felt like we were no longer battling the uncertainty of our future but planning for a shared adventure instead.

We shifted seamlessly from one idea to the next, creating an outline for his first workshop titled Unpacking Corporate Jargon: A Beginner's Guide to Understanding Your Boss. It was so absurdly straightforward that it almost made me want to sign up myself, just to hear him deliver it.

Ethan leaned back in his chair, his fingers tapping a rhythm against the table. "You know," he said thoughtfully, "I used to think all this corporate nonsense was just a necessary evil. But now it feels like a puzzle that I can help people solve. I can empower them."

"Absolutely! And think about it—by helping them navigate the complexities, you'll also be building your own community. That's a powerful thing."

As the evening wore on, the energy in the room shifted from tense uncertainty to hopeful ambition. We laughed, debated the merits of different marketing strategies, and planned out a timeline. Every idea was met with enthusiasm, each word building a bridge from fear to possibility.

But just as I began to think that we might emerge from this storm stronger than before, the phone rang, shattering the fragile calm that had settled over us. The shrill tone cut through the atmosphere like a knife, causing both of us to jump.

"Who could that be?" I asked, glancing at the screen that flashed Ethan's mother's name. He hesitated, his expression faltering for a moment, the earlier joy in his eyes replaced by a flicker of apprehension.

"It's Mom," he said, his voice dropping to a murmur. "I'll take it."

As he answered, I resumed my seat, trying to shake off the creeping dread that curled around my thoughts. From the snippets of conversation I could hear, I could tell that something wasn't right. His voice was steady, but the tension in his body betrayed him. The playful energy we had created began to fade, replaced by the weight of concern as he moved to the far end of the room, talking quietly.

I turned back to our makeshift planning table, my mind racing with possibilities. What could she want? Had something happened? I could see Ethan's brow furrow in concentration, his free hand instinctively reaching for the edge of the table as he leaned forward, engaged in whatever conversation had suddenly demanded his full attention.

"Mom, just take a breath," he said, and my heart plummeted at the worry that etched deeper into his features. "What do you mean you can't pay rent? But we talked about this... Yes, I understand, but..."

I stood up slowly, the impending weight of something ominous pressing on my chest. Ethan's face had paled, and his voice grew more strained with each passing second. "I'll figure something out," he said, his tone clipped, his jaw tightening with determination.

I held my breath, torn between wanting to offer him comfort and needing to stay out of the fray, yet every instinct told me to step in, to help. Whatever news his mother was delivering had shattered the fragile peace we'd just crafted.

"Look, I need to talk to Sarah about this. We'll come up with a plan," he said firmly, and the air thickened around us, vibrating with the weight of uncertainty.

When he finally hung up, the silence that followed felt heavier than before. He turned slowly to face me, his eyes shadowed with a mix of determination and defeat.

"My mom needs help," he said quietly, the words barely escaping his lips. "She's behind on rent, and if we don't figure something out, she could lose her apartment."

The revelation hit me like a cold wave crashing over me, and suddenly our worries about his job felt minuscule compared to the tidal wave of uncertainty crashing down on his family. "What can we do?" I asked, my mind racing through the possibilities, heart pounding in my chest.

"I don't know yet. I'll need to talk to her again and see how much time we have."

"Maybe we can organize a fundraiser or something? We could reach out to friends and family," I suggested, though the weight of the situation gnawed at my optimism.

Ethan shook his head, the expression in his eyes a mixture of fear and fierce resolve. "It's not that simple. I can't just ask people for money. What if she loses her job too? This could all spiral out of control."

We stood there, the air crackling with an electric tension, the world outside moving on while ours felt suspended in uncertainty. The laughter and lightness we had just shared hung in the air like ghosts, fading into the reality of impending chaos. I could see the storm brewing in his eyes, the fear of losing not just his job but his family's stability intertwining with the growing shadows that loomed over us both.

As we stared at each other, the weight of our respective burdens loomed larger than ever, a reality neither of us could escape. And just when I thought we might have a plan, a solution to forge through the storm together, a loud knock echoed through the house, jarring us both and shattering the fragile calm once more.

"Who is it this time?" Ethan asked, tension creeping back into his voice, uncertainty threading through each word.

"I have no idea," I replied, my heart racing again, anxiety climbing back to the surface.

As Ethan moved toward the door, I caught a glimpse of dread pooling in his eyes. I could sense that whatever awaited us on the other side could either deepen our despair or shatter the remnants of hope we had just begun to stitch together.

When he opened the door, the figure standing there sent my heart plummeting to my stomach, a storm of possibilities swirling, each more chaotic than the last.

Chapter 19: The Decision

The bell above the door tinkled softly as I stepped into the familiar embrace of the bookstore. The air was thick with the comforting scent of old pages and fresh coffee, a heady mix that wrapped around me like a well-loved blanket. The dim lights cast a warm glow on the wooden shelves, each one teeming with stories waiting to be unearthed. I paused, letting the ambiance sink in, savoring the hushed whispers of characters trapped between covers, as if they were in on a secret I had yet to discover. My heart thrummed with a nervous anticipation; I was here not just as a customer, but as a person ready to rewrite my own story.

Ethan had always been my anchor, his laugh a buoy that kept me afloat in the turbulent waters of life. But lately, I'd seen him struggle, the weight of his responsibilities pulling at the corners of his smile. It was as if a storm cloud had settled over him, casting a shadow on the vibrant boy I had fallen for. I couldn't just stand by while he bore the burden alone. I had to act, to throw my own weight into the scale and tilt it back toward balance.

I strolled over to the counter, where he stood, running a hand through his tousled hair, a gesture that had always made my heart flutter. Today, however, his brow was furrowed, deepening the lines of worry etched on his face. "Hey, you," I said, injecting a brightness into my voice that I didn't quite feel yet.

"Hey," he replied, his smile faltering as his eyes darted around the shop. "It's a little crazy today. We've got a shipment of new releases, and the owner expects me to handle it all by myself."

His frustration was palpable, like a thick fog that lingered around him. I took a step closer, my fingers brushing against the counter. "I was thinking... maybe I could help out more? I could take on extra hours, help with the shipment, or even just manage the cash register."

Ethan's gaze snapped to mine, a mix of surprise and concern flooding his features. "I can't ask you to do that. You have your own stuff to deal with. Your classes, your writing... it's a lot already."

"But it's not too much for me if it helps you," I insisted, trying to keep my tone light despite the seriousness of my words. "You've been carrying this weight on your shoulders alone for too long. I want to share the load."

A beat passed, and I could see the battle waging in his mind. He wanted to protect me, to shield me from the chaos that had enveloped him. But I wasn't fragile; I was willing to step into the fray. "You really mean that?" he finally asked, his voice barely above a whisper.

"Of course I do. You know I've always got your back." I stepped closer, my hand covering his. "Let me in, Ethan. Let's figure this out together."

He exhaled a breath he didn't know he was holding, his tension visibly easing as a small, genuine smile broke through. "Alright, but if it gets too much, you promise me you'll speak up?"

"Scout's honor," I quipped, raising my hand in a mock salute. He chuckled, a sound that felt like sunshine breaking through clouds, and just like that, the heaviness that had weighed us both down began to lift.

We spent the rest of the afternoon surrounded by boxes and books, our laughter mingling with the rustle of packaging tape and the soft thud of new arrivals hitting the shelves. Each title we unwrapped felt like a new possibility, a story waiting to unfold, mirroring the narrative we were crafting together.

As we worked, our shoulders brushed, and I caught myself stealing glances at him—his focus, the way he bit his lip when he was deep in thought, and the kindness that radiated from him even in moments of stress. The thought that we were embarking on this journey side by side sent a flutter of excitement through me.

We took a break, sinking into a couple of well-worn chairs tucked in the corner. The distant hum of chatter faded into the background as we sipped our coffee, the taste rich and warm, much like the burgeoning sense of unity between us. "You know, I didn't think you'd actually go for it," Ethan admitted, leaning back, his arms stretched out lazily across the armrests. "You really are full of surprises."

"Maybe I'm just trying to keep you on your toes," I shot back playfully, my heart swelling at the sight of him relaxing. "Besides, this place is like a treasure trove. I can't believe I've been missing out on all this. And it's not just the books, you know? It's you."

He looked at me, his expression softening. "I've been a bit of a mess lately," he confessed, his voice barely above a whisper. "I didn't want you to see that side of me."

"But you're still you, mess and all. And I'm here for it." I smiled, hoping my words would tether him to this moment, where the chaos felt manageable and the possibilities felt endless. "I've got your back, remember?"

As we shared a quiet moment, I felt a ripple of something deeper than friendship shifting in the air between us, charged and electric. The way he looked at me, his gaze lingering just a moment longer, made my breath hitch. But before I could dwell too long on it, the sudden sound of the bell above the door jolted us back to reality, ushering in a few customers.

Our laughter faded as we returned to the task at hand, but a newfound sense of purpose lingered in the air, vibrant and alive. I could see it in Ethan's eyes, too; this wasn't just a decision to help out at the bookstore—it was a declaration that we were in this together, ready to tackle whatever life threw our way.

Days melted into weeks, the rhythm of the bookstore becoming a new heartbeat in my life. The smell of coffee mingled with the mustiness of old books, creating an aroma that felt like home. Each morning, I arrived earlier, eager to dive into the chaos of shipments and shelves, finding solace in the familiar disarray of cardboard boxes and the anticipation of fresh pages. Together, Ethan and I built a routine, each day layering our partnership with laughter and shared glances that lingered just a moment too long, thickening the air around us with unspoken words.

Ethan had a knack for turning mundane tasks into small adventures. One afternoon, as we tackled the seemingly endless boxes of newly released novels, he pulled out a vibrant book with an absurdly detailed cover featuring a dragon battling a robot in a neon-lit city. "What do you think? Should we add this to our 'absolutely not for children' section?" he teased, his eyebrows dancing playfully.

I snorted, unable to contain my laughter. "I think this one could go right beside the 'adventures in existential dread' titles. Let's give kids something to talk about at recess."

He chuckled, shaking his head. "I love that you have strong opinions about categorizing chaotic fantasy books. It's what makes you you."

There was a comfort in our banter, a rhythm that felt as natural as breathing. Yet, as the weeks passed, I sensed a shift in Ethan. He often stared out the window, his gaze unfocused as if he were searching for something just beyond the horizon. On particularly hectic days, when customers flooded the store, I would catch him lingering by the door, absently tracing the grain of the wood as though it held answers he couldn't quite grasp.

One evening, after closing up shop, I decided it was time to address the elephant in the room. We sat on the worn-out couch nestled in the corner, the remnants of our earlier laughter dissipating like steam from our cold coffee cups. I turned to him, the silence stretching uncomfortably between us. "What's going on in that wonderfully chaotic mind of yours?"

He hesitated, the flickering light from the lamp casting shadows across his face. "I've just been thinking... about what comes next for us. For me. This place is great, but I feel like I'm treading water."

My heart sank, realizing that despite our growing connection, he was wrestling with uncertainty. "You mean in terms of the store? Or... us?" I asked, each word feeling heavier than the last.

"Both, I guess," he admitted, running a hand through his hair in frustration. "I don't want to hold you back. You're... you're going places, and I'm still figuring out how to manage a bookstore and my life at the same time."

I leaned forward, my eyes locking onto his. "Ethan, you're not holding me back. You're a part of my journey. I can't imagine this place without you—without us."

He sighed, his shoulders sagging under the weight of the world. "It's just that I have dreams, but they feel so far out of reach. I keep wondering if I should take a leap or stay safe here."

"Tell me about your dreams," I urged, sensing the vulnerability lacing his words. "What do you really want?"

He took a moment, his expression softening as he began to open up. "I've always wanted to write. I have these ideas, stories buzzing around in my head, but I've never had the courage to put them down on paper. I'm terrified of failing, of making a mess of it all."

"Failure is just a stepping stone, you know," I replied, my voice steady, encouraging him to lean into his fears. "What if you started small? Just write a page a day, or even just a paragraph? You could do it right here, in the bookstore. I could help, we could find a quiet spot and make it part of our routine."

He looked at me, uncertainty mingling with a flicker of hope. "Do you really think I could?"

"Absolutely. You've got stories to tell, Ethan. And I'd love to be part of your process. We're a team, remember? Besides, how can I root for you from the sidelines when I'd rather be in the thick of it?"

A smile broke through the clouds shadowing his features, and it felt like a sunbeam piercing through fog. "You're incredible, you know that?" he said, his voice warmer than the coffee cooling on the table.

"Only because I've got you cheering me on too," I shot back, my heart swelling with warmth at the thought of us standing shoulder to shoulder in pursuit of our dreams.

As we discussed the nuances of storytelling and shared dreams, I felt a shift—not just in Ethan's perspective, but in our relationship as well. The tension that had lingered dissipated, replaced by an excitement that hung in the air like the sweet scent of summer rain.

But just as I was basking in this newfound energy, the bell above the door jingled, and a figure stepped inside. My stomach twisted as I recognized Claire, a former classmate who always seemed to have a knack for entering at the worst possible moments.

"Ethan! I didn't know you were working here!" she exclaimed, her voice a mix of surprise and something I couldn't quite place. "And look at you, still holding onto your dreams of being a writer?"

My heart dropped. Here she was, the embodiment of everything I didn't want to deal with, standing at the threshold of our cozy haven with an air of superiority that set my teeth on edge.

"Claire, hey!" Ethan replied, his voice cheerful but strained. "It's nice to see you."

"Nice to see you, too!" she chirped, her gaze darting between us, a glimmer of mischief in her eyes. "I was just passing by and thought I'd pop in. I see you've got a cute little book club going on here."

Her words hung in the air, sharp and taunting, a stark contrast to the warmth we'd just shared. I shot Ethan a glance, silently urging him to brush it off, but I could see the storm clouds returning to his face.

"Just helping each other out, that's all," he said, his tone dismissive but polite.

"Oh, is that all?" she mused, a smirk dancing on her lips. "I always knew you'd end up in a bookstore, Ethan. It's safe, isn't it? Don't have to worry about chasing dreams when you can just—"

"Excuse me, but I think you're mistaking this for a place to belittle others," I interjected, my voice stronger than I felt. "Ethan's more than just a bookstore clerk; he's an aspiring writer and a really good friend."

Claire blinked, clearly taken aback by my sudden outburst, and for a moment, I relished the startled expression on her face. "How cute," she finally replied, trying to regain control. "You're standing up for your friend. But let's be honest, Ethan. You could do better."

But the momentary thrill of confrontation didn't last long, and as I glanced at Ethan, I saw the familiar shadows creeping back into his eyes, the storm clouds swirling around him again. And just like that, the energy in the room shifted, leaving me feeling as if I were clutching at straws.

"Claire, why don't you go find your next 'better' thing?" I said, forcing a smile that felt brittle on my lips. "We're really busy here, and your interruptions are getting old."

She opened her mouth to retort, but I didn't wait for her to respond. Instead, I turned to Ethan, seeking his gaze, hoping to tether him back to the moment we had just created.

"Come on, let's get back to those dreams," I urged softly, the warmth between us flickering, but still holding strong against the chilly wind of Claire's presence.

Ethan hesitated, his expression unreadable, but I could see the embers of his resolve glowing beneath the surface. "You're right," he said, his voice low but steady. "Let's not let anyone pull us away from what matters."

And just like that, the world outside faded, the bookstore surrounding us again, filled with endless possibilities and stories waiting to be told.

With Claire's departure, the air around us crackled with an energy that felt both familiar and frightening. I could sense Ethan's tension beneath the surface; his usually bright demeanor had dimmed, leaving behind a haze of uncertainty. We both retreated into the comforting routine of stocking shelves and organizing books, but the remnants of that encounter clung to us like an unwelcome fog.

"Hey, let's do something fun," I suggested, desperate to break the thick silence hanging between us. "We could play the 'what book should this person read next?' game. It'll be like our version of a reality show." I grinned, hoping my playful tone would lighten the mood.

Ethan cracked a smile, though it didn't quite reach his eyes. "Fine, but if we get a customer who wants a book recommendation for their cat, I'm out."

"Challenge accepted!" I laughed, feeling a glimmer of the old spark between us. Just as we were about to dive into our little game, the bell over the door chimed again. I glanced up, half-expecting Claire to return with another jab, but instead, I was greeted by the unmistakable figure of Mrs. Henderson, the neighborhood's resident book enthusiast and fierce critic.

"Hello, darlings!" she exclaimed, her voice warm yet commanding as she waddled over, a floral scarf draped around her neck and a tote bag slung over her shoulder, practically bursting with newly acquired titles. "I need your expert advice. I simply must find something to sweep me off my feet!"

Ethan and I exchanged glances, a silent agreement passing between us. "Oh, we can definitely help with that!" I replied, putting on my best enthusiastic customer-service face. "What genre are we diving into today?"

Mrs. Henderson leaned in conspiratorially, lowering her voice as if sharing a secret. "I'm in the mood for something scandalous—perhaps a romance with a twist? Something that makes me sigh and giggle simultaneously."

Ethan raised an eyebrow at me, a glimmer of mischief sparking in his eyes. "You know, I think we have just the book for you," he said, stepping behind the counter to grab a well-loved paperback. "This one has more drama than a soap opera and enough swoon-worthy moments to keep you turning pages well into the night."

Mrs. Henderson's eyes lit up as she took the book from him, and I couldn't help but feel a pang of jealousy at how effortlessly he could charm our customers. "Oh, Ethan, you know exactly what I like! I'll take it!" she declared, handing him a crisp twenty-dollar bill.

As she ambled toward the door, she paused, turning back to us with a knowing smile. "You two are positively adorable together. Don't let anyone—or anything—come between you!" With that, she swept out the door, leaving us in the wake of her enthusiasm and unexpected affirmation.

"Adorable?" I muttered, a mix of embarrassment and amusement swirling in my chest. "I mean, sure, I guess it's better than 'awkward.'"

Ethan chuckled, the sound finally reaching his eyes. "I'll take 'adorable' any day. At least it means we're not completely failing at this whole relationship thing."

The lighthearted moment helped push aside the remnants of Claire's visit, but I could still feel the tension lingering in Ethan. After finishing up for the day, we walked to his car, the evening air cool against my skin, infused with the scents of distant blooming jasmine.

"Can we talk?" I asked, pulling the door shut behind me as we settled into the seats. "About earlier?"

He hesitated for a moment, and I could practically see the gears turning in his mind. "Yeah, of course."

"Claire was a total buzzkill," I said, my voice firm yet light. "Don't let her get under your skin. You're worth so much more than whatever insecurities she's throwing around."

Ethan turned to me, his expression serious. "It's not just her, you know. It's everything. I want to be more than just this guy who works at the bookstore. I want to create something, to share my stories. But every time I sit down to write, I freeze. I don't know if I have what it takes."

"Ethan, every writer feels that way at some point," I replied, reaching out to cover his hand with mine. "What if you started small? Just write about us—our crazy bookstore days, your dragon versus robot epic. You have so many ideas inside you; don't let fear keep you from sharing them."

He looked at me, a spark of determination igniting in his eyes. "You really think I can do this?"

"I know you can." My voice was firm, my heart swelling with confidence in him. "But you have to take that leap. I'll be right here, ready to catch you if you fall."

He smiled, and for a moment, the weight on his shoulders lifted. But just as quickly, the smile faded, and the uncertainty returned. "What if I'm not good enough? What if I let you down?"

"Then we'll figure it out together," I assured him, squeezing his hand. "It's a journey, not a race. Besides, who says the first draft has to be perfect? There's beauty in the mess, in the revisions."

Just as Ethan opened his mouth to respond, the sudden ringing of my phone shattered the moment. I fished it out of my pocket, glancing at the screen. It was my mother. "I should probably take this," I said, an uneasy feeling settling in my stomach.

"Of course." Ethan's smile faded into something more serious, and I could sense the tension creeping back into the car.

I answered the call, trying to maintain a calm facade. "Hi, Mom," I said, forcing a bright tone.

"Hey, sweetie. I hope I'm not interrupting," she began, her voice sweet but laced with an undercurrent of urgency. "I just wanted to check in and see how you're doing. Is Ethan there with you?"

I nodded, instinctively lowering my voice. "Yeah, we're just talking. Everything's good."

"Listen, I need to tell you something important," she said, her tone dropping a notch. "Your dad... he's been looking for you."

My heart raced, confusion spiraling within me. "Looking for me? What do you mean?"

"Just... please be careful. He's been asking around, and it doesn't feel right. I don't want you to panic, but you need to stay alert."

Ethan's eyes widened as he picked up on my unease. "What's going on?" he mouthed, concern etched across his face.

"Mom, I don't understand. Why is Dad looking for me?"

"He just wants to talk, but it's been a while since he reached out, and I don't trust him. Just promise me you'll be cautious."

As she spoke, a knot of dread twisted in my stomach. "I promise, but I'm fine, really. You don't have to worry."

I hung up, staring blankly at my phone. The sense of safety we'd created shattered, replaced by the echo of my mother's words. Ethan leaned in closer, his expression a mix of concern and curiosity. "What's wrong?"

"My dad... he's back in town. He's looking for me," I whispered, the weight of those words crashing down around us.

Ethan's grip tightened on my hand, his expression shifting from concern to determination. "You're not alone in this. We'll face it together."

I nodded, but as the shadows lengthened in the twilight, a feeling of dread began to settle deep within my bones. This was just the beginning, and I couldn't shake the sense that our lives were about to be turned upside down. The warmth of the moment slipped away, leaving a cold gust of uncertainty swirling in the air around us, foreboding and unrelenting. Just as I opened my mouth to voice my fears, the car headlights caught movement at the edge of the parking lot. A figure stood watching us, cloaked in the shadows, and my heart dropped, my breath catching in my throat.

Chapter 20: The New Opportunity

Winter's chill clung to the air like an uninvited guest, nipping at my nose and whispering secrets of the cold outside. The world beyond my window was a palette of grays and whites, a muted landscape where life seemed to slow, but inside, a wildfire burned bright. The news of the local art exhibit spread through me like warmth on a frigid day—a chance to step into the light, to finally share my story through my work. I could almost hear the chorus of my paintings calling me, their colors dancing in my mind, begging to be set free.

I found Ethan in his usual spot, hunched over the kitchen table, surrounded by a chaotic array of papers, sketches, and half-empty coffee cups. His dark hair fell over his forehead, and the corners of his mouth turned up slightly when he noticed my approach. There was something about his presence, steady and grounded, that made the storm of emotions swirling in my chest feel manageable. I stood there for a moment, summoning courage, watching as he pushed aside the mess to make room for me, like I mattered more than the chaos that enveloped him.

"Hey," I said, my voice barely above a whisper, betraying the tumult within. "I heard about the exhibit... and I want to submit my artwork." My heart raced at the words, each syllable tumbling from my lips like a daring leap into the unknown. I feared the implications—the failure, the judgment. But I couldn't back down now; the thought of leaving this part of me unexpressed felt like suffocating in the depths of winter.

Ethan looked up, his eyes brightening like the first rays of sunlight piercing through a cloudy sky. "You should absolutely do it! Your work deserves to be seen," he exclaimed, his voice a rich baritone that seemed to wrap around me, lending warmth to my confidence. I felt the tension in my shoulders ease, his belief in me sparking a flicker of hope that I clung to like a lifeline.

I grinned, buoyed by his encouragement. "You really think so?" I asked, a hint of disbelief dancing in my tone. My journey had been fraught with self-doubt and hesitance, each brushstroke a whisper of my struggles, fears, and dreams, tangled together in the vivid chaos of color.

"Absolutely," he said, leaning back in his chair, arms crossed over his chest in that confident way that made him appear effortlessly charming. "You've got a gift, and you owe it to yourself to share it. Besides, what's the worst that could happen? They won't like it? Who cares? You're not doing this for them—you're doing it for you."

His words ignited something deep within, a fire I hadn't realized I'd buried beneath layers of uncertainty. I could feel the creative energy bubbling within me, a potent mix of excitement and trepidation. I needed to let my art tell the stories I had been holding inside for so long, stories that were aching to break free.

For days, I immersed myself in a flurry of creativity, finding solace in the rhythmic motion of my brush against the canvas. The studio became my sanctuary, a haven filled with colors that whispered and laughed, canvases that welcomed my touch with open arms. Each stroke transformed not only the canvas but me, breathing life into my dreams, illuminating the shadows I had previously inhabited.

I poured my heart into each piece, reflecting moments of joy and pain, love and loss. The blues and greens swirled into storms of emotion, while fiery reds and yellows captured my fleeting moments of hope. Each painting was a testament to my journey—a beautiful, messy collection of everything I had faced and overcome. The very act of creation was cathartic, a reminder that I was not merely a passive observer of life; I was the artist, the author of my narrative, and I had the power to shape my own destiny.

Submission day arrived, and the gallery loomed before me like a magnificent beast, grand and intimidating. The sleek glass doors beckoned with the promise of possibility, but a wave of anxiety washed over me as I stood on the threshold, feeling both small and significant all at once. I could hear the faint hum of conversations drifting from inside, artists and enthusiasts mingling, each seeking connection through the language of art. My stomach churned, a relentless tide of excitement and fear.

As I stepped inside, the warmth enveloped me, wrapping around my shoulders like a comforting blanket. The air smelled faintly of fresh paint and polished wood, mingling with the aroma of coffee brewing nearby. My eyes darted around the room, taking in the diverse array of artworks displayed—each piece a world unto itself, waiting to be explored. A swirl of colors caught my attention, a vibrant mural that seemed to leap off the wall, filled with life and passion. I wanted to lose myself in its depths, to understand the heart behind it, just as I hoped others would do with my own work.

Ethan's voice cut through the crowd, his laughter a melody that steadied my racing heart. I caught a glimpse of him across the room, his presence like an anchor amidst the whirlwind of art and conversation. He was chatting with a group of artists, his hands animatedly gesturing as he spoke, a genuine enthusiasm radiating from him. I felt a rush of gratitude; he had been my beacon, urging me to embrace my creativity and share it with the world.

Taking a deep breath, I approached the submission desk, my palms sweaty and heart pounding as I handed over my portfolio. The woman behind the desk glanced at me, her expression unreadable, and I felt a knot tighten in my stomach. But before I could dwell on my apprehensions, Ethan appeared by my side, placing a reassuring hand on my shoulder. "You did it," he said softly, his gaze steady and warm, igniting the flicker of confidence still flickering within me.

"I did," I breathed, a smile breaking through the tension, as if the weight of my fears was finally lifting. For the first time in ages, I felt a sense of liberation, a flutter of hope that perhaps, just perhaps, this was the beginning of something extraordinary.

The gallery was alive with voices, a symphony of excitement mingling with the faint echoes of footsteps on polished floors. I found myself engulfed in the atmosphere, an intoxicating blend of creativity and ambition. Artists flitted from one piece to another, their eyes alight with passion as they discussed their inspirations and intentions. I marveled at the array of talent surrounding me, a colorful tapestry woven from countless narratives. Each brushstroke, each color choice, told a story; some whispered softly, while others shouted with fervor.

My pulse quickened, not just from the electric energy of the room but from the weight of my own creations pressing against my chest. I could feel the presence of my portfolio, thick with the fruits of my labor, resting under my arm like a secret waiting to be unveiled. As I scanned the walls adorned with mesmerizing works, a flicker of self-doubt crept in. What if my pieces didn't belong here? What if I was simply an interloper in a realm I wasn't meant to inhabit?

"Hey, you're not allowed to disappear into your head at an art exhibit," Ethan teased, sidling up next to me, his presence grounding and familiar. "Look at those colors! This place is practically begging for your work to join the conversation." His grin was infectious, and I couldn't help but smile back, even as my anxiety simmered beneath the surface.

"I just hope they're as vibrant as I imagined they'd be in this setting," I admitted, biting my lip. The weight of his encouragement was a double-edged sword; it bolstered me while simultaneously amplifying my fears.

"They will be. Trust me. You've got the goods, and you're here, so that's already half the battle won," he said, nudging me playfully. "Now, let's find some wine and toast to your bravery."

As we wove through the crowd, my senses sharpened, absorbing every detail—the laughter, the clinking of glasses, the scent of fresh paint mingling with a hint of aged wood. I couldn't resist sneaking glances at the other artists, each one a vibrant personality in their own right. A woman with cascading red curls was passionately discussing her large abstract piece, the colors of which resembled a sunset gone wild. Nearby, a bespectacled man was meticulously explaining the nuances of his detailed pencil sketches to a captivated audience, his fingers dancing through the air as if conducting an orchestra.

I felt a pang of envy but quickly reminded myself that this was my time to embrace my artistry, not to compare. "You know," I said to Ethan, "I've always envied people who can talk so eloquently about their art. I feel like I'd just stand there stammering about how I threw some paint at a canvas and hoped for the best."

Ethan chuckled, his laughter rich and warm. "You underestimate yourself. You'd be surprised how many people would find the phrase 'threw some paint' intriguing. It's about the passion behind it, not just the technique."

His words resonated with me, filling the spaces of doubt with possibility. Maybe it wasn't about being a grand orator but rather an authentic storyteller, sharing my experience and the emotions that led me to each piece.

With glasses of wine in hand, we found a quiet corner away from the bustle, and I took a moment to breathe. "Okay, I can do this," I said, raising my glass to Ethan in a mock toast. "To bravery and a little chaos."

"To a lot of chaos," he replied, clinking his glass against mine with a grin. "And the magic that comes from it."

As we sipped our wine, I felt the warmth of the moment settle over me, a blanket of camaraderie that soothed my nerves. I turned my gaze back to the exhibit, feeling a spark of determination igniting deep within me. This wasn't just about showcasing my art; it was about embracing who I was and the journey I had taken to get here.

"Let's find your portfolio," Ethan suggested, his eyes sparkling with mischief. "I want to see how you're going to knock their socks off."

I laughed, a genuine sound that felt foreign yet liberating. "Alright, but if I trip and spill wine on it, I'm blaming you."

"Noted. I'll just stand back and offer moral support while you wield your artistic prowess." He stepped back, pretending to raise a shield as we navigated through the crowd, laughter bubbling between us.

When we reached the submission desk, I was met by a woman with a sharp bob haircut and a clipboard that looked like it was ready to take on the world. Her gaze was piercing yet curious, as if she could see right through to my very core. "Name?" she asked, barely looking up as she jotted down information.

"Lila Bennett," I replied, my voice steadier than I felt. I handed her my portfolio, and she took it with a brisk nod, flipping it open as if she were inspecting a prized piece of fruit. My heart raced as I watched her eyes scan the pages, anticipation buzzing like electricity in the air.

"Hmm," she murmured, her brow furrowing slightly as she turned to the next piece. "Interesting use of color. You're capturing emotion quite well." Her comments sliced through my anxiety, each word resonating like a bell chiming in the stillness of my fears.

"Thank you," I managed, a smile breaking through my nervousness. "I wanted to express my journey—the highs and lows, the chaos of it all."

Her gaze shifted to meet mine, and for a moment, it felt like we were sharing a secret. "Art is meant to evoke feelings. If you can connect with people through your work, you've already succeeded."

Her words settled over me like a soft embrace, and I felt a rush of gratitude towards her. Maybe I was on the right path after all. As she continued to peruse my pieces, the weight of my insecurities began to lift, replaced by a flicker of hope.

But just as I was beginning to settle into the moment, a loud commotion erupted from across the gallery. A tall figure, arms waving animatedly, drew my attention. The crowd parted like the sea as a man with wild hair and paint-splattered overalls approached the desk, his presence unmistakably commanding. "You can't just hang that piece without context! It's a disservice to the artist!"

His voice boomed, carrying an energy that filled the room. I exchanged a glance with Ethan, my excitement dimming as curiosity piqued. What was happening? The sudden tension in the air was palpable, and I could sense the crowd's collective breath held in anticipation.

The woman at the desk shot the newcomer a quelling look. "This isn't the time or place for your theatrics, Marcus. We're here to appreciate the art, not to dissect it."

"Art is meant to be dissected!" he retorted, unwavering, and I felt a nervous flutter in my stomach. The atmosphere shifted; it felt like a rollercoaster that had just crested its peak, teetering on the edge of the unknown.

As the scene unfolded, I was caught in a whirlwind of emotion—curiosity, confusion, and a hint of excitement. Maybe the chaos that surrounded art was exactly what I had been searching for, an unpredictable rhythm that matched the vibrant strokes of my own creations.

The argument hung in the air, thick with tension, as Marcus—the man who seemed to thrive on chaos—continued to make his case. His voice was animated, punctuated by grand gestures that sent his paint-splattered sleeves flaring like wings. "Art doesn't just exist in a vacuum! It's a conversation! You can't simply ignore the context that birthed it!" His passion radiated through the gallery, and I couldn't help but feel a mix of admiration and apprehension at his audacity.

The woman at the desk, whose name I now guessed to be Clara, remained unfazed, her cool demeanor almost infuriatingly composed. "And I can't allow you to derail this exhibit with your theatrics, Marcus. The artists are here to showcase their work, not to dissect it in public."

"Maybe they should!" he shot back, pointing a finger as if accusing a shadow lurking in the corner. "We need to inspire thought, not complacency! It's our job to provoke! Otherwise, what's the point?"

The gallery buzzed with whispers and sidelong glances, a community of creators caught between appreciation for the art and the unfolding drama. I felt a sudden urge to step in, to quell the tension that threatened to consume the room, but I didn't even know how to begin. Would my voice matter amidst the tumult of established artists?

"Shouldn't we let the viewers draw their own conclusions?" a soft voice piped up from the back of the crowd. A petite woman with striking blue hair stood, her hands tucked nervously in her pockets. "Isn't that the beauty of art? It speaks differently to everyone."

"That's exactly the point!" Marcus exclaimed, swinging around to face her, his enthusiasm momentarily redirected. "But if we allow art to hang without context, we're robbing the viewers of deeper engagement. What good is a masterpiece if it's merely decorative?"

I exchanged glances with Ethan, who leaned in closer. "Looks like this is turning into a full-blown debate club. What's next? A panel discussion?"

"Let's hope not," I replied, stifling a laugh as Marcus's fervor grew. "I'd hate to see the art pieces get dragged into it. They're already trying to be stars."

As the discussion continued to swirl around me, I realized I was grappling with more than just the drama unfolding before my eyes; I was wrestling with my own insecurities. The thought of stepping onto that stage and sharing my art now felt monumentally more daunting. What if my work didn't evoke the same passion, the same outrage? What if it was simply... forgettable?

Marcus was relentless, his words weaving through the crowd and rallying support like a charismatic leader. "Every stroke tells a story! And those stories matter. They should be heard and understood. Artists owe it to themselves to explain the heart behind their work." His intensity lit a fire in some, while others remained skeptical.

"Sure, but isn't the viewer's experience equally important?" Clara shot back, crossing her arms defiantly. "We can't control how they perceive our art, and that's what makes it magical!"

The crowd murmured in agreement, and I found my pulse quickening. There was a magic here, a raw energy that pulled at my heartstrings. Maybe this was exactly what I needed—a jolt of inspiration, a reminder that art was more than just a personal expression; it was a bridge connecting souls.

"Okay, fine," Marcus relented, lifting his hands in mock surrender, though the fire in his eyes remained. "Let's take a vote. How many of you believe that context is crucial in understanding an artwork?"

A chorus of voices filled the air, some passionately affirming his stance while others sided with Clara's perspective. I remained silent, my heart racing as I considered my own feelings about my work. Would my art speak for itself, or would it need me to breathe life into it with explanations?

Before I could settle on an answer, a sudden commotion erupted at the entrance. The gallery doors swung open with a crash, and a figure burst in, their silhouette striking against the bright lights. "I need to speak!" a voice called out, filled with urgency that silenced the room in an instant.

Everyone turned, curiosity painted on their faces. A woman with wild curls and wide eyes stood before us, her breath coming in quick bursts, as though she had run a marathon. "I've come to deliver a message," she said, her voice trembling slightly.

"From whom?" Clara asked, raising an eyebrow, the earlier tension replaced by intrigue.

The newcomer took a deep breath, gathering her composure. "From Marla Jennings—the curator for this exhibit. She's been following your work, and she believes it's time for a new perspective."

The room buzzed again, but this time with excitement. Whispers of Marla's name danced through the crowd, and I felt my heart drop, then leap. What did this mean? Was this about me?

"She wants to meet you, Lila," the woman continued, her gaze locking onto mine. "She believes your work could be a centerpiece in the upcoming showcase."

A shocked silence settled over the gallery as every eye turned to me, a thousand questions swirling in the air. I could feel the weight of their expectations pressing down on my shoulders, an electric charge igniting the air around me. "Me?" I finally managed to stammer, disbelief creeping into my voice. "She wants to meet me?"

"Absolutely," the woman affirmed, a smile breaking across her face, lighting up her features. "She sees potential in your work that resonates with her vision."

My mind raced, heart pounding like a drum in my chest. What did that even mean? Did I have the skill? The talent? The confidence to step up to the challenge? The thrill of opportunity danced on the edge of my consciousness, but the shadows of doubt clawed at me.

Ethan leaned closer, his voice a soft encouragement, "This could be everything, Lila. You have to take it."

Before I could respond, Marcus interjected, "Isn't this a bit too sudden? A curator's interest is not something to take lightly. We should question her motives."

"Stop!" Clara snapped, her patience clearly fraying. "This is a huge opportunity, Marcus. Lila deserves to hear what Marla has to say."

The debate reignited, but I was only half-listening, caught in a whirlwind of emotion. It felt surreal, like a page torn from a dream. All the fear, the struggles, and the determination—it was all leading me to this moment. Yet, beneath the excitement lurked the very real possibility of failure.

What if I wasn't ready? What if my art couldn't hold its own against the giants in the room? I could feel the weight of my insecurities creeping back in, threatening to snuff out the spark ignited within me.

But before I could spiral further into doubt, the woman who brought the message stepped forward. "Marla's waiting outside. You need to decide quickly. This could be your moment."

The urgency in her voice propelled me into action, and I glanced at Ethan, who nodded encouragingly. I took a deep breath, heart racing, my gaze drifting back to the door, where the world beyond felt tantalizingly close.

With a final glance around the room, I made my choice. This was my chance to break free from the shadows, to embrace my voice in a way I never thought possible. Just as I was about to step forward, my phone buzzed in my pocket, a sharp reminder of the life waiting outside this art-filled whirlwind.

I pulled it out, and my heart sank. The message on the screen was not what I expected, not at all. A single line, chilling in its brevity: "We need to talk. It's urgent."

The weight of uncertainty crashed down around me, the exhilaration of opportunity overshadowed by a sudden wave of dread. I glanced up at Ethan, who wore a look of concern, and then back at the door. What awaited me on the other side? My heart pounded as I stood at the crossroads of fate, poised to make a choice that would alter the course of my life forever.

Chapter 21: The Setback

The moment the email landed in my inbox, its subject line stark and unyielding, my heart plummeted. I sat at my cluttered kitchen table, a half-finished mug of lukewarm coffee cooling beside me, the steam that had once danced upward now replaced by a dull resignation. The words on the screen swam before my eyes, mocking me with their crisp, unyielding clarity: "We regret to inform you that your submission has not been accepted." A heavy sigh escaped my lips, an audible surrender to the weight of disappointment that pressed down on my chest. I had envisioned this moment as a celebration, a victory parade for the countless hours I had spent hunched over my laptop, spilling my heart onto the pages. But now, it felt like a funeral march for my dreams.

I glanced around my kitchen, a haphazard collection of mismatched chairs and well-worn utensils, all echoes of a life lived in pursuit of creativity and connection. The walls, splashed with an array of vibrant colors, seemed to close in around me, a cacophony of vibrant memories that suddenly felt tainted. My trusty corkboard, adorned with scraps of inspiration and to-do lists scrawled in my chaotic handwriting, loomed overhead, the sticky notes now fading reminders of my ambitions. I had always believed in the magic of storytelling, the way words could transform the mundane into the extraordinary. Yet here I was, a solitary figure surrounded by the detritus of failed aspirations.

Ethan's presence filled the room like a warm breeze, his footsteps a steady cadence that drew my gaze from the abyss of my despair. He hovered at the edge of my kitchen, his expression a blend of concern and determination. I could see the wheels turning in his mind as he took in the scene—a battle-scarred writer wrestling with defeat. "You okay?" His voice was soft, laced with the kind of gentleness that always made me feel safe, even when the world seemed intent on kicking me down.

"Yeah, just peachy," I replied, my voice dripping with sarcasm. "I've officially mastered the art of rejection."

Ethan stepped closer, his brow furrowing in that endearing way that made me want to roll my eyes and hug him all at once. "Hey, it's not the end of the world. It's just... feedback. Maybe a rough draft." He grinned, his confidence like a beacon of hope piercing through the fog of my disappointment. "Think of it as an opportunity. You're a writer. You can fix this."

His unwavering belief in me felt like a balm on my bruised spirit, and I couldn't help but let out a watery laugh. "Opportunity? It feels more like a cosmic joke at this point. I thought I had finally found my voice, and now it's like I'm stuck in the back of a noisy café, shouting into the void."

"Voices can be tricky," he replied, leaning back against the counter, arms crossed as if to anchor himself against the tide of my swirling thoughts. "But maybe you just need a little more time in the café. Take a break, clear your mind. Let's brainstorm together."

I glanced at the mess of papers strewn across the table—scenes and characters, dreams and desires entwined in a chaotic symphony. Ethan was right; perhaps what I needed was to step back, to look at the pieces with fresh eyes. "Okay," I conceded, wiping away the remnants of my tears with the back of my hand. "But only if you promise to help me figure out what went wrong."

"Deal," he said, his smile a warm sunbeam cutting through my lingering shadows. "Let's take a look at your outline and see what we can salvage."

We settled into a rhythm, a dance of ideas and inspirations as Ethan began to sift through my notes. His brow furrowed in concentration, and I found myself captivated by the way he lost himself in the world I had created. "You've got a strong premise here," he mused, tapping a finger against a particular line in my manuscript. "But what if you deepen the conflict? Make it messier? Readers love a good twist."

I leaned closer, my heart quickening at the thought of injecting a new layer into my work. "You mean, like throwing a wrench into the protagonist's plans? Making it more complicated?"

"Exactly. Let's make it so that every time she thinks she's figured it out, life throws her a curveball."

Ideas began to flow between us, weaving a tapestry of possibility that lifted my spirits higher with every exchange. Each suggestion he offered sparked a flicker of excitement in my chest, reigniting my passion for the story I had poured my soul into. "What if," I proposed, "instead of the villain being a shadowy figure in the background, they become someone she trusts? Someone close to her?"

"Now we're cooking!" Ethan exclaimed, his eyes lighting up like fireworks in the night sky. "That's the kind of twist that keeps readers on their toes."

The more we brainstormed, the more I could feel the tendrils of doubt slipping away. It was exhilarating, as if we were crafting a new world together, one where setbacks were mere stepping stones, and every rejection was a chance to rise stronger. "You really believe this can work?" I asked, half-hopeful, half-fearful that he might call my enthusiasm misguided.

"Absolutely. But remember, every masterpiece starts as a rough draft," he replied, his confidence wrapping around me like a warm blanket. "It's all part of the process. You just have to trust yourself."

As we sat surrounded by the remnants of my failed submission, I realized that my setback wasn't the end of the road. Instead, it felt like a pivot point, a chance to dig deeper into my creativity. And with Ethan by my side, I felt ready to dive back into the fray. The world outside my kitchen may have felt dreary, but within these walls, new life was brewing, waiting to be unleashed.

The morning sun streamed through the kitchen window, casting a golden glow on the chaos of papers and coffee mugs strewn across the table. It was a new day, a canvas yet to be painted. The taste of yesterday's tears still lingered in my throat, but the flicker of hope ignited by Ethan's presence had turned into a steady flame. I stared at the jumble of notes before me, feeling both exhilarated and anxious. What lay ahead was uncharted territory, and I was both the captain and the crew of this ship, bracing for a storm that might just be the catalyst for my greatest journey.

Ethan leaned against the counter, arms crossed, a patient smile playing on his lips as if he were holding a secret. "Okay, what's next? You've got a premise that can turn heads; now let's dive into those characters." His enthusiasm was infectious, a buoy that kept me afloat in the turbulent waters of my mind. I shuffled through my notes, the remnants of my past effort whispering disapproval, but I shoved them aside. It was time to sculpt something new from the clay of my dreams.

"Right, characters," I murmured, running a hand through my disheveled hair. "I think my protagonist needs to be a little more... relatable, you know? I want readers to see parts of themselves in her."

Ethan nodded, his eyes narrowing thoughtfully. "So, what's her biggest flaw? Everyone has one. The more real she is, the more readers will connect with her."

I bit my lip, pondering this. "Maybe she's a bit too trusting. She believes in the goodness of people, and that leads her into tricky situations. It's like she has this instinct to see the best in others, which is great until it's not."

"Now that's a gem," Ethan replied, his excitement palpable. "It creates conflict and tension, especially when her trust is betrayed. Who doesn't love a good betrayal?"

The thought sent a shiver down my spine. There was something deliciously wicked about betrayal, like chocolate cake laced with a hint of salt. "And it could be someone close to her. A best friend, perhaps? Someone she's relied on throughout her journey."

"Or a romantic interest," he suggested, his eyebrows raising in playful challenge. "Imagine the drama when the person she's falling for turns out to have a hidden agenda. That would really up the stakes."

My heart raced at the prospect. The idea of weaving romance and betrayal into the narrative felt like tossing a lit match into a barrel of gasoline. "I like where you're going with this. It adds layers to the story and keeps the readers guessing."

Ethan leaned closer, a spark of mischief in his gaze. "What if, as she starts to unravel the truth, she realizes that she's been the puppet in a much bigger game? Maybe her idealism makes her blind to the reality around her, setting her up for a grand reveal that's both heart-wrenching and exhilarating."

"Okay, but how do we keep readers engaged during that twist?" I asked, furrowing my brow. "I don't want them to see it coming from a mile away."

"That's the beauty of the buildup," he said, waving his hand like a conductor leading an orchestra. "You sprinkle in clues along the way—innocuous conversations, fleeting glances—things that seem irrelevant at first but start to make sense once the truth is revealed."

"Like a breadcrumb trail," I mused, a grin spreading across my face. "Leading them into a dark forest of intrigue."

"Exactly! But don't give them all the breadcrumbs at once. Just enough to keep them hungry for more."

Our brainstorming session turned into a whirlwind of ideas, each one building upon the last, creating a vivid tapestry of possibilities. The atmosphere shifted, my kitchen transforming into a sanctuary of creativity. Ethan's laughter bounced off the walls, igniting a spark within me that I hadn't felt in ages.

"Okay, but let's talk about the love interest," I said, leaning back in my chair, considering the canvas of my story. "What kind of guy would she fall for? Someone charming and sweet, or a brooding type with a dark past?"

"Why not both?" Ethan suggested, a grin dancing at the corners of his mouth. "Make him the charming, brooding type. He charms her, but there's always an undercurrent of danger—something that keeps her on edge."

I chuckled, the image of a dashing rogue flickering to life in my mind. "A bad boy with a heart of gold? How original!"

Ethan feigned shock, clutching his chest. "Hey, originality is overrated! It's all about how you twist those tropes to make them your own."

As laughter spilled from my lips, I felt lighter, like a weight had been lifted from my shoulders. The connection between us was electric, charged with the thrill of creation. We bounced ideas back and forth, a volley of creativity that seemed to know no bounds.

But just as I was starting to lose myself in the joy of it all, a sudden pang of doubt sliced through my exhilaration. "What if I mess this up again? What if I pour my heart into this new version only for it to be rejected again?"

Ethan stepped closer, his eyes steady and unwavering. "Then you learn. Rejection isn't the end; it's just a part of the process. It's how you grow as a writer and as a person. Every great author has faced their fair share of rejection."

I let his words sink in, feeling the warmth of his conviction wash over me. It was comforting, grounding, and I couldn't help but wonder how many writers had thrived because they refused to give up. "You really believe that, don't you?" I asked, a hint of vulnerability creeping into my voice.

"Absolutely. You're not just a writer; you're an artist. And artists thrive on pushing boundaries, testing limits. Besides, what's life without a little risk?"

His words hung in the air, a challenge and a promise all at once. The idea of risk felt like a double-edged sword, both terrifying and thrilling. "You make it sound so easy," I said, shaking my head with a smile.

"It's not easy, but it's worth it," he replied, his voice earnest. "And I'll be right here, cheering you on, no matter what. We'll turn this setback into something spectacular."

With that, I felt the shift within me, a determination blossoming alongside the nagging fears. There was something undeniably potent about having someone believe in you, and it filled me with an energy I hadn't realized I was missing. Together, we could turn my disappointment into a symphony of creativity, each note resonating with the trials and tribulations of life. And as I looked at the vibrant mess surrounding me, I knew we were only just beginning to compose the melody of my next adventure.

The hours slipped away in a haze of creativity, the kitchen buzzing with the kind of energy that feels almost magical. As Ethan and I delved deeper into the world we were building, I found myself rediscovering the joy that had drawn me to writing in the first place. Each new idea felt like a pebble dropped into a pond, sending ripples across the surface of my imagination. I could practically see the characters coming to life, their stories intertwining in ways I hadn't dared to consider before.

"I think we need a backstory for her," I said, my fingers tapping the table as I gathered my thoughts. "Something that explains why she's so trusting."

"Great idea," Ethan replied, his gaze fixed on the corkboard now dotted with colorful sticky notes. "How about a childhood experience? Maybe her parents always encouraged her to see the good in everyone, even when they shouldn't have."

I nodded, the wheels in my mind turning faster. "Yes! It gives her depth and makes her choices more relatable. But it also sets her up for a dramatic fall when she realizes that not everyone shares that perspective."

"Exactly! And think about how she'll react when that trust is shattered. Will she become bitter, or will she dig in her heels and fight back?"

"Definitely the latter," I said, enthusiasm bubbling over. "I want her to rise from the ashes, not retreat into herself. That's how growth happens, right?"

Ethan grinned, his eyes brightening. "That's the spirit! You're building a character that readers will root for, and that's no small feat."

The momentum was intoxicating, and for the first time in days, the specter of rejection felt like a distant memory, a mere footnote in the unfolding story of my creative journey. Ideas continued to flow, each one layering complexity onto my protagonist's arc.

"So, if we're introducing this childhood trauma, maybe we should also explore her relationships with the people around her," I suggested. "How does her trust—or lack thereof—affect her friendships and romantic entanglements?"

Ethan leaned back, stroking his chin as if pondering a grand philosophical question. "Let's give her a best friend who challenges her perspective. Someone who's the opposite of her—cynical and street-smart. That way, you can have some great back-and-forth dialogue that showcases their differences."

"Oh, that would be fun!" I laughed, picturing their banter. "She'd roll her eyes while her friend reminds her that rainbows don't always lead to gold. It's the perfect foil for her character."

"Plus, it opens the door for some witty exchanges. You know, the kind that keeps readers chuckling while they ponder life's deeper meanings."

"Like the ones we have?" I shot back, a teasing smile on my face. "Except maybe with more sarcasm and fewer kitchen disasters."

"Hey, those disasters make the best stories!" he quipped, raising his mug in mock salute. "Besides, who doesn't love a good metaphor for life's unpredictability?"

As we continued weaving ideas together, the warmth in the kitchen grew more vibrant, filling the air with the aroma of coffee mingling with laughter. For the first time in a while, I felt like I was regaining control of my narrative, and the exhilaration surged through me like caffeine.

But amidst our creative revelry, a shadow of doubt lingered in the corner of my mind, whispering warnings of another potential failure. I shook my head, determined to banish the negativity. "You know," I began, glancing up from my notes, "I've realized that even if this story doesn't turn out the way I hope, I can still find value in the process. The lessons learned and the friendships forged along the way are priceless."

Ethan's expression softened, his eyes reflecting an understanding that went deeper than words. "Exactly. It's like life itself. We plan, we dream, but it's the unexpected twists that make the journey worthwhile."

Just as I was about to add another layer to my character's backstory, my phone buzzed insistently on the table, interrupting our creative flow. I glanced at the screen, my heart skipping a beat. It was a notification from the submission platform. "Oh no, not now," I muttered under my breath, dread creeping in like a cold breeze.

"Don't let it get to you," Ethan said, his voice steadying me. "Whatever it is, you can handle it."

I hesitated, my fingers hovering over the screen. With a deep breath, I opened the notification. The message was short but stung like a bee: "We regret to inform you that your appeal for reconsideration has also been rejected."

A sickening twist of disappointment twisted in my gut. I had naively thought that once I refined my work, the rejection would fade away, replaced by the sweet sound of acceptance. Instead, I felt the familiar weight of despair settle in my chest.

"It's just a setback," Ethan said softly, stepping closer. "This doesn't define you."

"It sure feels like it does," I replied, my voice trembling. "What if this is it? What if I'm just not good enough?"

"Then you keep going," he insisted, his resolve unwavering. "Every artist has faced this moment. You have to dig deeper, find a way to turn this into fuel for your fire. Don't let them extinguish your spark."

I nodded, biting back the surge of emotion that threatened to spill over. "I know you're right, but it's hard to see that right now."

The sound of my phone buzzing again caught my attention, drawing my gaze back to the screen. Another notification flashed—a message from the same platform, this time from an editor I hadn't expected to hear from. My heart raced as I opened it, my pulse quickening with anticipation and anxiety.

"Dear [Your Name], we appreciate your perseverance and would like to discuss your work further. Please contact us to schedule a meeting."

The words blurred as a rush of emotions washed over me. Hope mingled with disbelief, and suddenly, the walls of my kitchen seemed to pulse with possibility. "Ethan, look!" I exclaimed, holding up the phone as if it were a winning lottery ticket.

His eyes widened, a mix of excitement and curiosity dancing across his face. "What does it say?"

"An editor wants to meet! They want to discuss my work!"

A grin broke across Ethan's face, his joy infectious. "That's amazing! See? This is the universe telling you that you're on the right path!"

But as the thrill of newfound hope coursed through me, another notification chimed, stark and ominous. The name of my closest friend flashed on the screen, and I felt an icy knot tighten in my stomach. The last time we'd spoken had been during the early days of my writing journey, a time filled with promises and dreams yet to unfold.

"Wait, I need to take this," I said, my heart pounding in my chest as I answered the call. "Hey, what's up?"

Her voice came through the line, strained and urgent. "We need to talk. It's important."

The light in the room dimmed as the weight of her tone settled in, and I realized that whatever news she had to share could shatter the fragile excitement building within me. A chill ran down my spine, a premonition whispering that this conversation would change everything.

"Okay," I replied, my pulse quickening. "What's going on?"

The silence stretched between us like a taut wire, and just as I braced myself for whatever storm was about to hit, I caught Ethan's eye across the room. His expression mirrored my concern, a quiet strength and determination intertwined.

"Just meet me," she said finally, her voice a fragile thread that sent ripples of anxiety through me. "We need to discuss something about your submission. It's... complicated."

"Complicated how?" I pressed, my heart racing as dread settled in.

"You're not going to believe it," she replied, her words hanging in the air like a weight.

In that moment, I realized I was standing on the edge of a precipice, the ground beneath me shifting unpredictably. With a heart full of both hope and dread, I braced myself for the leap into the unknown, wondering if I was truly ready for what lay ahead.

Chapter 22: The Revelation

The sunlight streamed through the attic window, casting a warm, golden glow over the dust motes dancing in the air. I had clambered up the creaky wooden ladder with the singular intention of organizing the chaotic mess that my childhood memories had become. Instead, I found myself surrendering to nostalgia as I pulled an old, dust-covered box from the shadows. The label was faded, but I recognized my youthful scrawl. It read: "Dreams & Things."

As I opened the box, the familiar scent of musty paper wafted out, wrapping around me like a comforting embrace. Inside, crumpled sketches peered out, vibrant pastels fighting for attention against the dull, faded pages. I gingerly unfolded the first drawing—a landscape splashed with color, where the ocean met the sky in a swirl of blues and greens. It felt like a lifetime since I had lost myself in the colors of the world, trading my paintbrush for the practicality of adulthood. My fingers brushed against the paper, and it sparked something deep within me, a memory of when art was not just a hobby but a lifeline.

Ethan, with his easy charm and keen eye for beauty, had been my anchor through this stormy sea of self-doubt. He was downstairs, likely experimenting with yet another recipe that would either be a culinary masterpiece or a kitchen disaster. The thought made me smile, yet my heart felt heavy with the weight of unrealized ambitions. I could almost hear his voice, teasingly encouraging me to embrace the chaos. "What's life without a little mess?" he'd say with that mischievous grin.

With newfound determination, I settled down on the attic floor, surrounded by the remnants of my past. Each page revealed a facet of the girl I used to be—dreamer, poet, artist. The lines of verse I had once written breathed life back into the silent corners of my mind. "In the whispers of the ocean, I found my heart's reflection," one poem read, echoing the sentiments I had buried under years of practicality and doubt. Each stanza unfolded like a wave crashing against the shore of my consciousness, a reminder of the dreams I once cherished.

Ethan's footsteps creaked up the stairs, interrupting my reverie. He poked his head through the door, curiosity etched across his face. "You're not having a meltdown up here, are you?" he quipped, his eyes twinkling with mischief.

I glanced up, laughter bubbling to the surface. "Just a stroll down memory lane. Care to join?"

He stepped fully into the attic, brushing off dust from his jeans. "What do you have? The remnants of your childhood aspirations?" His teasing tone was affectionate, a gentle reminder that he had always supported me, even when I faltered.

I gestured towards the scattered sketches and poetry. "More like the remnants of my creativity. I think I'm ready to dust off these dreams."

Ethan knelt beside me, examining the contents of the box. "This is brilliant," he exclaimed, picking up one of the sketches—a swirling sunset over a quiet beach. "Why did you stop?"

I shrugged, the question hovering in the air like a delicate soap bubble, ready to burst. "Life happened, I suppose. Responsibilities took over. I forgot how to be... me."

His gaze softened, understanding flickering behind his eyes. "You haven't lost her, you know. She's still there, waiting for you to bring her back."

The weight of his words hung between us, wrapping around the moment like a soft blanket. He was right; somewhere beneath layers of self-imposed limits, the artist I once was still pulsed with life. In that attic, surrounded by the ghosts of my past, an ember ignited. The desire to create, to blend art with the poetry of my youth, surged through me.

"What if…" I began, my voice barely a whisper. "What if I combined my art with these poems? What if I let them dance together again?"

Ethan's eyes widened, excitement shimmering in their depths. "Now that's a brilliant idea! The world needs to see that side of you."

I could feel a smile creeping onto my face, a tentative blossom amidst the weeds of uncertainty. "You really think so?"

"Absolutely," he replied, a spark igniting in his expression. "Your art has always been about more than just pretty pictures. It tells stories, captures emotions. Pairing it with your words could create something truly magical."

As we sat there, the attic transformed into a sanctuary for my rebirth. The sketches, once forgotten, now felt alive, each line begging for a touch of color, each word yearning for a canvas. The prospect of rediscovering myself through this fusion of art and poetry filled me with exhilaration, pushing aside the fog of doubt that had lingered for too long.

I dove deeper into the box, pulling out fragments of my former self, allowing the memories to wash over me. I could hear the waves lapping at the shore, feel the warm sun on my skin, and the salty breeze tousling my hair. Those days spent sketching by the water's edge, reciting poems to the sea, felt like a dream, distant yet achingly familiar.

Ethan watched me, a soft smile gracing his lips. "You're glowing, you know that? Like you've been recharged."

I glanced at him, heart fluttering like a nervous bird. "Maybe I have. It's incredible how a little dust can reveal so much."

As the sun dipped lower in the sky, casting a golden hue through the attic window, I could feel the tide of change rising within me. It wasn't just about the art or the poetry; it was about reclaiming a piece of myself I had long surrendered to the pressures of adulthood. I felt as if I was standing on the cusp of something profound, the world bursting with possibility and vibrant colors just waiting to be captured on canvas.

With Ethan by my side, I knew I was ready to embrace this journey back to myself, the thrill of exploration mingling with the sweet anticipation of discovery. I could already envision the first painting, how it would breathe life into the words that had remained silent for so long. The canvas beckoned, and I was finally ready to answer its call.

The next morning dawned with the soft light filtering through the curtains, illuminating the corners of my studio like a secret promise. The remnants of yesterday's revelations danced in my mind, nudging me toward a new path I hadn't realized I was yearning to follow. I could feel the pulse of creativity thrumming beneath my skin, an electric current urging me to dive headfirst into the vibrant chaos of art and poetry intertwined.

Ethan was already bustling around the kitchen, the aroma of freshly brewed coffee wafting through the air, mingling with the scent of his latest culinary experiment. I could hear the gentle clinking of pots and pans, the rhythm of his morning routine like a comforting soundtrack to my own thoughts. When I wandered into the kitchen, I found him at the stove, focused intently on a bubbling pot of what appeared to be an ambitious combination of herbs, spices, and—was that chocolate?

"Morning, Picasso," he called over his shoulder, a teasing grin breaking across his face. "I was just about to add some cinnamon to my savory chocolate stew. What do you think? Too much?"

I raised an eyebrow, crossing my arms as I leaned against the doorframe. "What's next, a hint of lavender? I think the flavor profile is flirting with confusion."

He turned, feigning horror, his hands clasped to his chest. "What a tragedy! I might need to hire a flavor consultant."

"Lucky for you, I know a good one," I shot back, moving to pour myself a cup of coffee. As the rich liquid swirled into the mug, I felt a rush of anticipation. "By the way, I think I'm ready to get started on that art project we talked about."

Ethan's eyes lit up, a spark igniting within him. "Really? That's amazing! What's your vision?"

I took a sip of the warm brew, savoring the bold flavor. "I want to blend my sketches with some of the poetry I unearthed yesterday. It feels like the perfect way to reconnect with that part of myself."

He nodded thoughtfully, stirring the pot with renewed enthusiasm. "Sounds like a match made in artistic heaven. We could even host a little showcase when it's done. Invite friends over, share your work. You know, make it a thing."

The idea hung in the air, tantalizing and terrifying all at once. "A showcase? That sounds a bit... ambitious, don't you think?"

"Ambition is just confidence in a new outfit," he said, winking at me. "Besides, you've got the talent. It's time the world saw it. And, of course, they need to taste my chocolate stew."

Laughter bubbled up within me, a soothing balm to my lingering apprehension. "Well, if your stew can convince them to appreciate art, then maybe it's worth it."

We spent the rest of the morning bouncing ideas off one another, a playful dance of words and creativity. With each brushstroke I envisioned, each stanza I recalled, my heart felt lighter, a weight lifting as I embraced the artist I once was. Ethan was relentless in his encouragement, gently coaxing my ideas into tangible forms.

"I see you surrounded by your art, your sketches and poems woven together like a tapestry," he mused, stirring the pot with a flourish. "Imagine the colors, the textures—an explosion of everything you've held inside."

"Okay, now you're getting a bit too poetic," I teased, but his words resonated deep within me, striking a chord that had long been silent.

By noon, I had gathered my old sketches, laying them out on the dining table. The sunlight streamed through the window, casting intricate patterns across the pages. I felt a heady mix of nostalgia and excitement as I sorted through them, each piece igniting memories of laughter, heartache, and dreams yet to be realized.

Ethan wandered in, a plate of toast in hand, and plopped down beside me. "What's the plan, artist?"

"Let's see how these can meld with my poetry," I said, my voice barely concealing the thrill of the challenge. "I want to create something that feels like a conversation between the two forms."

He took a bite of toast, chewing thoughtfully. "How about starting with that sunset piece? I can see it paired with the poem about finding reflection in the ocean."

I grinned, feeling the adrenaline rush through me. "Yes! That could work perfectly."

As I picked up my favorite sketch, I felt an unexpected flutter in my stomach. The vibrant colors seemed to call out, begging for attention. I took a deep breath, ready to dive into the swirling chaos of my creativity, when my phone buzzed on the table.

I picked it up, my heart sinking slightly as I glanced at the screen. It was a message from my sister, Elise, a well-meaning but often overzealous curator of our family expectations. "Hey, I'm coming by later! Can't wait to see you and what you're working on!"

My stomach twisted in an unexpected knot. While Elise meant well, her presence often brought a wave of unspoken pressure that dampened my creative spirit.

"Something wrong?" Ethan noticed my change in demeanor, his brow furrowing with concern.

"My sister is stopping by later," I said, trying to keep my voice light. "She's... excited to see what I've been working on."

He grinned knowingly, the corners of his eyes crinkling. "Sounds like a perfect opportunity to dazzle her with your newfound artistic brilliance."

"Or to have her question my life choices," I countered, trying to mask my unease.

"Just remind her that Picasso didn't always paint masterpieces on the first go."

I chuckled, appreciating his lightheartedness. "Yeah, but I don't think she'll settle for anything less than perfection."

"Just be yourself," he advised, placing a reassuring hand on my shoulder. "You don't need to impress anyone but yourself."

With his words echoing in my mind, I pushed aside the anxiety that threatened to creep in. "Okay, you're right. It's just one visit. I can handle it."

The doorbell chimed just as I was finding my rhythm again, the unexpected sound cutting through the air like a sudden gust of wind. I shot Ethan a glance, a mixture of dread and determination swirling within me. "Here goes nothing."

He offered a reassuring smile, squeezing my shoulder gently. "You've got this."

I opened the door to find Elise standing there, her auburn hair pulled back in a neat bun and a smile that could brighten the darkest day. "Surprise!" she exclaimed, bursting through the threshold, a flurry of energy and excitement.

"Hi! What a surprise," I managed, trying to keep my voice steady.

"I couldn't wait to see you! And I brought a little something!" She held up a brightly wrapped package, the paper shimmering like a beacon.

As I took the gift, I felt the familiar tug of family expectations, the weight of their love layered with the pressure to conform. What was it this time? A book on corporate success? A guide to the perfect life?

"Open it!" she urged, eyes sparkling with anticipation.

With hesitant fingers, I peeled back the wrapping to reveal a sleek, leather-bound planner, embossed with gold letters. "It's for organizing your creative ideas!" she beamed, unaware of the way my heart sank.

"Wow, thanks! I'll definitely use it," I said, forcing a smile as I internally grappled with the reality of her well-meaning but constrictive gift.

"Are you working on something new? You look different, by the way," she remarked, glancing at the dining table scattered with my sketches.

"Just a little project," I replied, heart racing as I considered how to navigate this conversation without revealing too much.

Her gaze drifted to the sketches, her expression shifting from curiosity to scrutiny. "Oh, this is interesting. Are you still painting, or is this just a hobby?"

As she asked the question, I felt a flicker of rebellion ignite within me. "Actually, I'm exploring a blend of art and poetry. It's… liberating."

"Really? That sounds lovely! But what about your career? You have so much potential to do great things in the corporate world."

The weight of her expectations felt suffocating, yet somewhere deep inside, I clung to the new spark of creativity that had awakened. "This is great too, you know. Art can be a career."

Elise hesitated, a flash of disappointment crossing her face before she quickly masked it with a smile. "Of course! I just want you to succeed."

The conversation hung in the air, tinged with unspoken words. In that moment, I realized that while Elise's intentions were rooted in love, my journey was mine to navigate. With Ethan's encouragement echoing in my mind, I felt the resolve strengthen within me.

As Elise continued to probe with questions, a plan began to form—a way to showcase my new direction, to embrace my artistic self unapologetically. Perhaps the upcoming showcase would be the perfect opportunity to share my journey, to redefine success on my own terms.

With each sketch, each poem, I felt a renewed sense of purpose, a chance to redefine not just my art, but the very essence of who I was. The waves of creativity were crashing against the shore, and I was finally ready to ride the tide.

The afternoon light poured through the kitchen window, bathing the room in a warm, golden hue, and Elise's probing questions hung in the air like a cloud of steam from Ethan's bubbling pot. She had finally shifted her attention from my sketches to her phone, scrolling as if searching for a distraction that could fill the growing tension between us. I could almost hear the gears turning in her mind, assessing and recalibrating her approach.

"Look at this!" she exclaimed suddenly, shoving her phone in my direction. "There's an art festival in town next month. You should enter your work. It could be a great platform for you!"

I felt my stomach twist, half thrilled and half terrified at the thought. "Elise, I'm not sure I'm ready for that kind of exposure. What if people don't like it?"

"Or what if they love it?" she countered, her enthusiasm undeterred. "You'll never know unless you take the plunge! You can't keep hiding your talent."

Ethan interjected, his voice smooth as the stirring of his culinary concoction. "She's got a point. Sometimes, you have to leap before you can look."

I shot him a grateful glance, feeling buoyed by his support but still grappling with the reality of putting my heart on display. The thought of standing before a crowd, unveiling pieces of myself that I had only recently begun to reclaim, was daunting.

Elise continued, oblivious to my internal struggle. "And I could help! I could arrange a little gallery showing at my office. We could invite clients, friends, everyone! It would be perfect!"

I tried to suppress the dread rising within me. "Clients? Are you sure that's the right audience for my work?"

She waved her hand dismissively, a motion that said I was overthinking things. "Art is art! They'll appreciate it, trust me. Plus, it could bring in new business for me. It's a win-win!"

Her eagerness made me squirm; I didn't want my art to be a marketing strategy. I wanted it to breathe freely, without the constraints of business jargon or expectations.

"Maybe we can focus on one thing at a time?" Ethan suggested gently, nudging me closer to the edge of decision-making. "Let's see how you feel about showcasing your work after you've created it."

"Exactly," I agreed, feeling bolstered by Ethan's calm demeanor. "I think I need to take a step back and just create for now."

Elise crossed her arms, a slight frown forming on her lips. "You know I only want what's best for you, right? I just don't want you to waste this talent."

"Trust me, I won't," I replied, a note of firmness in my voice that surprised even me. "I appreciate your support, but I need to find my own way back into this world."

She sighed dramatically, her fingers tapping rhythmically against the table. "Fine, but just promise me you'll consider it. I think you'd be amazing, and I'd love to show off my sister's work!"

I laughed lightly, but inside, a whirlwind of anxiety churned. "Okay, I'll consider it, but no promises."

With the tension slightly eased, I focused on the sketches, feeling the creative spark reigniting within me. The afternoon turned into a playful brainstorming session, with Ethan tossing ideas into the mix as I sketched furiously.

"Here's a wild idea," he said, leaning over my shoulder. "What if you created a series? Each piece reflects a different phase of your journey—like chapters in a book."

My pencil paused, a flicker of intrigue sparking within me. "That could be interesting... like a visual representation of growth."

"Yes! And we can call it 'Reclamation' or something equally artsy," he said, a grin breaking across his face. "You know, the kind of title that makes you sound profound and mysterious."

"Or the kind that leaves everyone wondering what the heck it means," I teased back, the playful banter lightening my heart.

We tossed around ideas until the shadows began to lengthen, and my sketches started to take shape. Each stroke of the pencil felt like a step toward reclaiming not just my art but my identity. I could almost hear the whisper of my younger self, urging me forward, inviting me to dance with the colors again.

Elise eventually gathered her things, her enthusiasm palpable despite the earlier tension. "I'll let you two lovebirds get back to your artistry. Just remember, I'm still waiting for that showcase proposal!"

I nodded, grateful for her support but eager to close the door on her expectations. As she left, I turned back to Ethan, who was now cleaning up the remnants of lunch.

"Thanks for backing me up," I said, leaning against the counter. "It's hard to navigate all of this."

"Anytime," he replied, smiling. "You're a force of nature, you know. I'm just here to help you find your way."

With a newfound determination, I settled into my work, diving into the rhythm of creation. The hours slipped by, and soon the remnants of sunlight faded into twilight, the room glowing with a soft ambiance as I painted.

It was liberating, the way colors merged and flowed, the way my poetry found its place on the canvas. I felt more alive than I had in years, an artist rediscovering her voice.

As the day wore on, I paused to take in what I had created. Each piece told a story, a raw reflection of my journey, a blend of colors and words that harmonized in a way I hadn't anticipated.

Suddenly, the doorbell rang again, breaking the spell. My heart raced, caught between excitement and apprehension. Was it Elise again, ready to dissect my art before I'd even had a chance to share it?

I opened the door, and to my surprise, it wasn't Elise standing there but a tall figure cloaked in shadows. The dim light cast a haunting glow around him, obscuring his features.

"Can I help you?" I asked, the uncertainty in my voice evident.

He stepped closer, and as the light caught his face, I recognized him—a name, a memory, a ghost from my past that I had never expected to see again. "It's been a long time," he said, his voice low and laced with familiarity.

A rush of emotions crashed over me, filling the air with tension. "What are you doing here?" I barely managed, my heart pounding against my ribs.

"I came to see you... and to talk about your art."

The air thickened between us, a charged current that sent shivers down my spine. This was not how I had envisioned this moment, not like this. The echoes of my past were colliding with my present, and I could feel the walls I had so carefully built begin to tremble.

"What do you mean?" I whispered, dread and curiosity mingling, leaving me on the edge of something I couldn't yet define.

He stepped closer, and for a fleeting second, the world seemed to hold its breath. "You have no idea what you've stumbled upon."

Chapter 23: The Conflict

The diner buzzed with the familiar clatter of dishes and the low hum of conversation, yet tonight, the warmth that usually enveloped the room felt stifling. I perched on a barstool, a slight distance from the counter where Ethan worked his magic with a spatula and an unfaltering smile that seemed to flicker and fade as the minutes passed. I could see the tension curling around him like smoke from a dying fire. It wrapped around his shoulders, hunched and tight, whispering secrets of frustration and worry that seemed to seep into the air, mingling with the scent of greasy fries and burnt coffee.

The news of a new management regime had rippled through the diner like a shockwave. Customers noticed the subtle changes—menu items disappearing, the staff growing quieter, and a pervasive unease settling in like an unwanted guest. I could hardly remember a time when the diner felt like home to us, a haven of laughter and late-night conversations over shared slices of pie. Now it was a battleground, and Ethan, with his kind eyes and easy laughter, was caught in the crossfire.

He wiped the counter with a rag, the gesture a bit too harsh, as if he were trying to scrub away the mounting pressure. I wanted to reach out, to comfort him, but words felt inadequate, trapped behind the fortress of my own insecurities. I was just beginning to find my own creative voice, a tentative whisper that was so easily drowned out by the chaos surrounding him. I had my own battles to fight, my own doubts about my writing gnawing at me. But watching Ethan bear the weight of his workplace like a heavy yoke made my heart ache.

I leaned forward, resting my chin on my hand, my eyes fixed on him. "You seem... different tonight," I ventured, keeping my tone light, though my heart raced beneath the surface.

Ethan paused, the spark in his eyes dimming further. "Just tired," he replied, the weariness in his voice betraying him. "You know how it is."

"No, I don't," I countered, my own frustration bubbling to the surface. "It's not just tired. You look like you're about to crack."

"Great observation, Sherlock," he shot back, but the sharpness in his tone felt like a desperate defense rather than genuine annoyance.

I pressed my lips together, anger mixing with concern. "Ethan, I'm just trying to help. You can't keep bottling this up. It's not good for you."

He straightened, a flicker of anger sparking in his gaze. "And what do you know about it? You're busy playing the tortured artist while I'm drowning here."

His words struck like a slap. I felt my heart lurch, a painful twist of betrayal and longing. "I'm not 'playing' anything. I'm trying to figure out who I am in all this chaos, just like you!" I couldn't keep the edge from my voice; the walls of my composure began to crumble. "You're my best friend, Ethan, and I hate seeing you like this. But you won't let me in!"

He inhaled sharply, and for a moment, the storm brewing in his eyes faded into something softer. "It's just... I don't want to burden you with my problems. You have enough on your plate."

"Since when did sharing burdens become a bad thing?" I pressed, the heat of the moment propelling me forward. "I thought we were supposed to lean on each other. Isn't that what friends do?"

"Friends, yes. But this... this is different." He stepped back, as if creating a physical space between us would somehow shield him from the truth. "I don't want to drag you down with me."

"Ethan!" I could feel my pulse quickening, each word punctuated by the tension simmering between us. "I want to be here for you. Can't you see that?"

He looked at me then, really looked, and I could see the war waging behind his eyes—the desire to confide in me battling against the instinct to keep me safe from his turmoil. "It's just a lot right now. New management means new rules, and they don't care about us, about how long we've been here or what we've built. They're ruthless. They're... they're going to ruin this place."

His voice trembled, and it shattered something in me. "You've worked too hard for that. We both have," I murmured, the reality of our lives crashing around us. The diner wasn't just a job for him; it was a lifeline, a part of his identity. "You can't let them take that from you."

"Easy for you to say. You have your writing, your dreams. What do I have if they destroy this?" His frustration boiled over, his fists clenched by his sides. "This is my world, and I can't just stand by and watch it burn."

The weight of his words settled between us, heavy and suffocating. I wanted to scream that he wasn't alone, that I would stand by him no matter what, but instead, the words tangled in my throat, caught up in the swell of emotions threatening to overflow. "Ethan, you have to fight back. You can't just let them walk all over you."

He turned away, a defeated gesture, and I felt the chill of his retreat. "It's not that simple. You don't know what it's like to feel powerless."

My heart cracked open at his admission, the raw honesty resonating deep within me. "But you're not powerless. You're one of the strongest people I know." The words slipped from my lips, carrying a fervor I hadn't intended, but as they hung in the air, I realized their truth. I believed in him, even when he didn't believe in himself.

For a moment, the air felt thick with unsaid things, the silence wrapping around us like a fragile thread, waiting to snap. I stepped closer, my voice softer now, laden with sincerity. "Please, let me in. Don't push me away. I'm here for you."

The tension hung in the air like a storm cloud ready to burst, but I refused to back down. The weight of Ethan's struggles pressed heavily on my heart, and I could no longer stand idly by, pretending everything was fine. "Ethan, you can't just push me away," I insisted, my voice softening but resolute. "You matter to me, and I'm not going anywhere."

He turned slowly, his brow furrowed, and for a moment, it felt as though he was searching for words to fill the chasm that had opened between us. "You're right. You're my best friend. But..." He hesitated, the 'but' hanging between us like a fragile balloon ready to pop. "I can't help feeling like I'm dragging you down with me. I don't want that."

The hurt in his eyes twisted something deep within me. "Ethan, I'm already down here with you," I said, trying to infuse a sense of levity into the moment. "We're both floundering, but that's why we're a team. I promise you, I won't drown."

He chuckled softly, the sound like a warm breeze cutting through the tension. "You say that now, but wait until I start throwing tantrums in the middle of a dinner rush."

"Please, I'll just dodge the flying plates," I teased, trying to inject some humor into the dark space we found ourselves in. "You know I've got great reflexes. I've saved more than one soufflé from certain doom."

His lips quirked up into a smile, and for a fleeting moment, the heaviness lifted, revealing the Ethan I adored—the one who could turn the simplest of moments into something extraordinary with just a flicker of joy. "Fine, but if I lose my job because of a melty chocolate cake, I'll hold you responsible."

"Deal," I replied, feeling a surge of warmth spreading through me. This was the connection we'd always shared, and I was determined to nurture it despite the pressures that threatened to suffocate us.

Just then, the door swung open with a jangle of bells, cutting through our moment of levity. A familiar figure stepped inside—the diner's new manager, a slick-haired man named Tony, with a permanent scowl etched into his face. He strode across the floor, his eyes scanning the room like a hawk on the hunt. The vibrant atmosphere of the diner dimmed as he approached the counter.

Ethan's body stiffened, the ease he had just found evaporating in an instant. "Speak of the devil," he muttered under his breath, his gaze flitting nervously to me. "Time to put on my happy face."

"Or a mask," I suggested, trying to keep the mood light. "You could always pretend to be a robot. Just beep and serve."

"Good plan," he replied with a tight grin, but I could see the worry etched in the lines of his forehead. As Tony loomed over the counter, I felt the shift in the room's energy—a palpable anxiety that rippled through the diners and settled heavily on Ethan.

"Listen up, people!" Tony's voice boomed, slicing through the murmurs of the diners like a knife. "From now on, we're revamping the menu. No more cutesy specials. We'll focus on quick, profit-driving items. That means no more experimentation, and certainly no more late-night desserts. This is about efficiency, people!"

The collective gasp from the staff echoed my own horror. I glanced at Ethan, his expression a mask of disbelief mixed with fury. "He can't just—" I began, but Ethan cut me off.

"He can and he will. It's his way or the highway," he said, his voice low and simmering.

"Why doesn't he see that the charm of this place is the warmth we create?" I blurted, the indignation spilling from my lips. "This is more than just a job; it's a community!"

Ethan's eyes met mine, and there was a flicker of something there—something that suggested he was wrestling with a decision. "You're right, but this is a fight I can't win. He's got the upper hand."

"Not if you rally your coworkers. If they're feeling the same way, maybe you could present a united front," I urged, my heart racing at the thought of him standing up for what he believed in. "You can't let him dictate what this place means to you. Not after all the blood, sweat, and fries you've put into it."

He let out a humorless laugh. "And what happens if I stand up and he decides to fire me on the spot? I have bills to pay."

"Then you keep fighting," I pressed, my frustration bubbling over. "Because I'd rather see you standing tall with your dignity than slinking away under his thumb. I'll help you!"

Ethan stared at me, the storm in his eyes momentarily calmed by my words. "You really think we can change his mind?"

"Not just you, but all of us. We're in this together," I declared, the confidence swelling within me. "We can brainstorm ideas, create a presentation. Show him the heart and soul that makes this diner a second home."

"God, you make it sound easy." He sighed, running a hand through his hair, which seemed to be getting thicker with worry. "What if he doesn't care?"

"Then we'll find a way to make him care. We can't just roll over and let him erase everything we love about this place," I insisted, the determination coursing through me. "Let's make a plan."

With a newfound resolve flickering in his eyes, Ethan nodded, a hesitant smile breaking through the clouds of doubt. "You're insane, you know that?"

"Only when I'm inspired," I quipped, flashing him a grin. "Besides, you wouldn't have me any other way."

Just then, the bell jingled again, and a familiar voice called out from the entrance. "There's my favorite diner! Hope you've been saving a piece of that chocolate cake for me!"

It was Mel, my best friend and Ethan's self-proclaimed number-one fan. She sauntered in with a wide smile, completely oblivious to the tension that had just permeated the air. The atmosphere lightened as she bounded over, her contagious energy filling the space.

"What's this? A secret meeting? Are you two plotting world domination without me?" she joked, her eyes sparkling with mischief.

Ethan and I exchanged a glance, a silent agreement passing between us. Maybe, just maybe, we could face the chaos together, armed with laughter and an unshakeable bond.

Mel's presence was like a splash of bright color on a drab canvas, an instant antidote to the tension that had settled like fog in the diner. "Okay, I might have slightly overdosed on caffeine today," she admitted, bouncing on her heels, her ponytail swinging in rhythm. "But I can take the hint—are we doing the 'let's save the diner' thing again?"

Ethan exchanged a glance with me, and I could see the flicker of hope igniting in his eyes. "More like plotting our revenge on Tony," he said with a grin, his voice warmer. "You in?"

"Absolutely!" Mel clapped her hands together, her enthusiasm palpable. "This Tony guy sounds like he needs a good talking-to. What's the plan?"

I leaned forward, excited to include her in our mission. "We need to gather the crew, brainstorm ideas, and maybe even put together a presentation. Show him why this diner isn't just about profits; it's about community."

"Sounds like we need a war room," Mel said, her eyes sparkling with mischief. "And I have just the right place in mind. My apartment has a comfy couch, a fridge stocked with snacks, and enough coffee to fuel an army."

Ethan laughed, the sound a welcome relief, as he glanced toward the kitchen, where the smell of frying onions wafted through the air. "As long as there's chocolate cake involved, count me in. I need some sweetness to balance this bitter mess."

"Consider it done." Mel winked, her excitement infectious. "But first, I think you should let off some steam. We need to do a little team bonding before we dive into the serious stuff. How about karaoke night at Gertie's Pub?"

My heart raced at the idea. Karaoke had always been our unofficial way to escape reality, a glorious mix of laughter and off-key singing. "Are you sure that's a good idea? I mean, we have serious issues to tackle here!"

"Exactly!" Mel replied, her hands on her hips. "What better way to prepare for battle than to warm up our vocal cords? Plus, who wouldn't want to hear Ethan belt out some '80s power ballads?"

Ethan looked momentarily torn, but a reluctant smile began to form. "I can't sing for the life of me. It's like the universe decided I should only cook."

"Then it's settled! We're going!" Mel declared, pulling us both toward the door. "A night of laughter will do us good. And besides, if we're going to convince Tony that this diner is worth saving, we need to channel our inner rock stars first."

As we stepped out into the brisk evening air, the world felt brighter. The streetlights flickered to life, casting a warm glow on the pavement, and laughter drifted from nearby cafés. I couldn't remember the last time I felt this lighthearted, and as we made our way to the pub, I found myself caught up in the infectious energy of my friends.

Gertie's Pub was a cozy haven, its walls adorned with photographs of local legends and neon beer signs that buzzed cheerily. The moment we stepped inside, the air thick with the smell of hops and fried food, I felt a wave of nostalgia wash over me. It was the kind of place where everyone knew your name, and the bartender never forgot your favorite drink.

We claimed a booth near the back, and I watched as Mel ordered a round of drinks, her voice bubbling with enthusiasm as she relayed the plan to the bartender. Ethan sat across from me, his demeanor much lighter than it had been earlier in the evening.

"Okay, I'm officially declaring this a no-stress zone," I announced, raising my glass when Mel returned with our drinks. "To good friends, and to taking down tyrants one karaoke song at a time!"

"To friendship!" Mel cheered, and we clinked our glasses, the sound ringing through the din of the bar.

As the evening progressed, our laughter echoed through the pub, the tension of the past days slowly dissolving into the night. Ethan finally agreed to sing, albeit under the condition that he would have the backup of Mel and me. We chose an upbeat song that had everyone swaying, the energy infectious.

"Okay, I know I'm not supposed to sing the high notes, but let's just pretend I'm a rock star for one night, alright?" Ethan quipped, glancing at us with mock seriousness.

"Deal!" Mel shot back, nudging him playfully. "Just channel your inner Freddie Mercury and we'll be golden!"

As the music started, we launched into our performance, our voices blending in a chaotic harmony. The crowd cheered, and for a moment, the weight of the world lifted, replaced by the pure joy of living in that moment. We danced, we sang, and for the first time in a while, I felt truly free.

But just as I thought we had escaped the chaos, the door swung open, and in walked Tony, flanked by a couple of his cronies. My heart sank as he strode in, surveying the room with an air of authority that sent a shiver down my spine.

"Are they really singing 'Don't Stop Believin'?" he scoffed, shaking his head in mock disbelief. "Pathetic."

Ethan's expression hardened, the carefree spark extinguished as he caught sight of his boss. "Just when I thought we could have some fun," he muttered, a storm brewing in his eyes.

"What a buzzkill," Mel whispered, her gaze darting nervously between Ethan and Tony. "What are we going to do?"

"Act natural," I replied, my heart racing as I forced a smile, determined not to let Tony ruin our night. "Let's keep singing."

But as the chorus swelled and we belted out the lyrics, I could feel Tony's eyes boring into us, an oppressive weight threatening to crush our lighthearted moment. I could sense Ethan's discomfort growing, the tension curling around him like a dark cloud.

Just as we finished the song, Tony approached our table, a smirk playing on his lips. "Well, well, well. Looks like the talented staff is more interested in karaoke than in saving their jobs," he sneered, his voice dripping with condescension.

Ethan straightened, his expression hardening into something resolute. "We were just blowing off steam, Tony. It's been a tough week."

"Blowing off steam?" Tony echoed, his voice a low growl. "That's the problem with this place. No one takes anything seriously anymore. You think this is a game?"

"Actually, we were just trying to remind ourselves why we love this diner," I interjected, my voice steady despite the turmoil inside me. "We're a family here, and that means something."

"Family?" He scoffed, his gaze narrowing. "All I see is a bunch of employees who don't care about their future."

Ethan stood, the fire of determination igniting in his eyes. "You know what? Maybe it's time we show you just how much we care."

Tony raised an eyebrow, his smirk faltering. "Oh? And how do you plan to do that?"

Ethan took a deep breath, his voice firm. "We're going to fight for this diner. We're not going down without a battle."

I held my breath, the air thick with tension as the challenge hung in the space between us. Tony's expression shifted, a flicker of something dangerous crossing his face. "I'd think twice about that. You don't want to test me."

"Try us," I said, my heart pounding. I had no idea where this newfound courage was coming from, but it felt electrifying.

But just as Tony opened his mouth to respond, the power suddenly flickered, and the entire pub plunged into darkness. Gasps filled the room, and I felt Ethan's hand close around mine in the pitch-black chaos.

"What the hell?" Mel exclaimed, and I could hear the frantic murmurs rising around us.

In that moment, the stakes felt impossibly high, a thread of uncertainty weaving its way into the fabric of our plans. I clung to Ethan's hand, our breaths mingling in the dark, the palpable tension rising as we faced the unknown.

Suddenly, a loud crash echoed from the back of the pub, and I could hear the unmistakable sound of shattering glass. My heart raced as fear crept in, weaving through the electric air.

"Ethan, what's happening?" I whispered, barely able to hear my own voice above the chaos.

He squeezed my hand tighter, his determination unwavering. "We're going to find out," he said, his voice steady even in the dark.

But as we moved towards the source of the noise, I couldn't shake the feeling that this night was only just beginning—and that the real fight was yet to come.

Chapter 24: The Apology

The door creaked open, and there he stood, tousled hair falling over his forehead, eyes shadowed with the weight of the world. A fleeting moment passed, suspended in the crisp morning air, where everything felt impossibly fragile. I could almost hear the distant echoes of our argument, swirling in the air between us like a thick fog, blurring the outlines of who we were just days ago. My heart thudded in my chest, each beat a reminder of the tension that had knotted itself around us like an unwelcome vine.

"Hey," he said, his voice a mere whisper, as if speaking louder might shatter the uneasy silence. The distance between us felt infinite, a chasm carved by misunderstandings and harsh words. I held the letter tightly in my hands, its edges crinkling under my grip, a physical representation of the turmoil roiling inside me.

"Ethan, I..." The words tangled in my throat, sticky and reluctant, but I pushed them out with a determined breath. "I came to apologize."

His gaze flickered to the letter, then back to my face, and in that moment, I could see a flicker of hope, quickly overshadowed by uncertainty. "You didn't have to do that," he replied, his tone neutral, but the tremor in his voice betrayed him. He stepped aside, and I took that as my cue, entering his apartment as if crossing a threshold into a world I wasn't sure I belonged in anymore.

The familiar scent of his cologne mixed with the faint aroma of coffee lingered in the air, a bittersweet reminder of the countless mornings we'd spent together, lost in laughter and shared dreams. Yet, today, the atmosphere felt charged, like the air before a storm, thick with unspoken words and unresolved feelings.

I stood there, letter in hand, awkwardly shifting my weight from one foot to the other as I glanced around his living room. The cozy chaos of his space felt different now—books piled haphazardly, a half-finished puzzle sprawled across the coffee table, and an empty mug that still bore the remnants of his last caffeine fix. This was our sanctuary, a haven where we had spun our tales, and yet, it felt tainted, as if the ghosts of our argument were hovering just out of sight.

"Can I read it?" he asked, his voice breaking through the silence.

"Of course," I replied, my heart racing. I watched as he carefully unfolded the letter, the very words I had penned with such care and anguish now exposed before him.

I had spent hours crafting those lines, pouring every ounce of regret, love, and longing into each stroke of my pen. "I didn't want to hurt you," I had written, "but I realize now that I let my fears get the best of me. You mean more to me than I can put into words."

As he read, I studied his face, searching for any signs of understanding, any glimmer of the warmth that once radiated between us. His brow furrowed, the lines deepening as he absorbed my words. I could see his defenses crumbling, piece by piece, but the air was still thick with hesitation.

Finally, he looked up, his expression softening. "You're right, you know," he said, his voice steadier now. "We both let things spiral out of control."

"I didn't want to add to your stress, Ethan. I just wanted you to know how much I care." My voice cracked, but I held his gaze, refusing to back down. "I don't want to lose what we have."

He stepped closer, and I could feel the warmth radiating from his body, melting some of the ice that had formed in the corners of my heart. "I don't want to lose it either," he admitted, the honesty in his eyes disarming me.

We stood there, inches apart, the unsteady ground beneath us shifting like the autumn leaves swirling outside. I could see it—the flicker of a shared understanding, a glimmer of hope that perhaps, just perhaps, we could navigate this storm together.

"Can we start over?" I asked, my voice barely above a whisper, the question hanging between us like a fragile thread.

"I'd like that," he said, the corners of his mouth lifting slightly, a tentative smile beginning to take shape. "But let's make a pact to be honest, even when it's uncomfortable."

I nodded, relief washing over me like a warm breeze, a sensation I had almost forgotten. "Agreed."

In that moment, the tension shifted, morphing into something lighter, something hopeful. The remnants of our argument lingered, but instead of suffocating us, they began to weave a new tapestry of understanding.

"Let's grab coffee," Ethan suggested, his tone lightening as if a weight had been lifted. "I need caffeine to celebrate our newfound honesty."

I laughed, the sound bubbling up from somewhere deep inside, chasing away the lingering shadows. "You just want to distract me with pastries," I teased, the banter rekindling a spark that had dimmed during our argument.

"Maybe a little," he admitted, his grin widening, "but let's be real, who doesn't love a good croissant?"

As we stepped out into the cool morning air, I couldn't shake the feeling that we were embarking on a new chapter, one filled with laughter, warmth, and a renewed commitment to each other. The sun broke through the clouds, casting golden rays that danced on the sidewalk, illuminating the path ahead.

In that moment, I realized that while the scars of our past argument would take time to heal, we were armed with honesty and a willingness to embrace whatever came next. As we walked side by side, I felt a sense of anticipation, a flutter of excitement in my chest. This was a beginning, and I was ready to embrace it wholeheartedly, no matter what twists and turns lay ahead.

The coffee shop bustled with energy, the kind that seemed to swirl around us like the rich aroma of freshly brewed beans, enveloping every corner and crevice of the quaint little place. The sound of laughter mingled with the low hum of conversation, creating a symphony of life that made my heart flutter with renewed hope. I watched as Ethan stood in line, his casual stance giving off an aura of ease that belied the tumult of emotions we'd just navigated. He was the kind of person who wore his heart on his sleeve, and even now, as he examined the pastry display with a look of feigned seriousness, I couldn't help but smile at the sight.

"Decisions, decisions," he muttered under his breath, glancing back at me with mock seriousness. "Do I go for the blueberry muffin or risk it all with a chocolate croissant? I'm telling you, this is a matter of life and pastry."

I leaned against the counter, a teasing grin spreading across my face. "Isn't life all about taking risks? I say go for the croissant; it's the daring choice."

He raised an eyebrow, his expression turning mockingly pensive. "You're right. I should embrace my inner pastry adventurer. What kind of man would I be if I played it safe?"

We both chuckled, the sound brightening the space between us, as though a spell had been cast to banish the shadows of our earlier argument. When it was his turn, he ordered with a flourish, theatrically waving his arm like a game show host. "One chocolate croissant, please! And a small black coffee—keep it strong; I need all the caffeine I can get to fuel this newfound adventurous spirit."

I couldn't help but admire the way he approached even the simplest decisions with a flair that could light up the dimmest of rooms. A warmth bubbled in my chest, filling the void of uncertainty that had hovered between us. The barista, a cheerful woman with vibrant pink hair, handed over our drinks and pastries with a wink, as if she sensed the magic crackling in the air around us.

"Here's to new beginnings," Ethan said, lifting his coffee cup with a boyish grin.

"To new beginnings," I echoed, clinking my cup against his, the sound of porcelain ringing like a promise.

We settled at a small table near the window, sunlight pouring in and dancing across our faces. As we took our first bites of the flaky croissant, I savored the delicate layers melting on my tongue, a rich delight that mirrored the warmth spreading through me. "This was definitely the right choice," I declared, pointing to his croissant as if it were a trophy.

"See? You're the voice of reason in my culinary adventures." He took a sip of his coffee, and for a brief moment, we existed in our own little bubble, a world where laughter and comfort overpowered the weight of our previous misunderstandings.

"Are you free this weekend?" he asked, his gaze earnest as he leaned forward, elbows resting on the table.

"Depends," I replied playfully, feigning nonchalance as I took another bite. "Are you planning another risky pastry expedition, or is it something more thrilling?"

"Much more thrilling," he said, his eyes sparkling with mischief. "I was thinking we could explore the new art exhibit downtown. I heard it's interactive, and you know how I love to make a fool of myself in public."

"Interactive, you say? Is this your clever way of telling me you plan to touch all the paintings?"

"Maybe," he laughed, raising his hands in mock surrender. "But I promise I won't get us arrested. Well, at least not on this outing."

We continued our banter, each quip fueling the laughter that echoed between us, until I felt a sense of normalcy returning. Yet, beneath the lighthearted exchanges, I sensed a current of vulnerability still lingering, waiting for its moment to surface. As we finished our pastries, I decided it was time to address the lingering doubts in my heart.

"Ethan," I began, my voice growing more serious, "about what happened between us... I know we're trying to move past it, but I need you to understand how deeply it affected me."

His expression shifted, the lightness dissipating as he leaned back, eyes searching mine. "I know, and I'm sorry too. I shouldn't have raised my voice; I let my frustrations take control. But it's hard sometimes—my work, the pressure..."

"I get it," I replied, leaning in to close the distance. "We both have our pressures, and I shouldn't have added to yours. I just felt lost and scared."

He nodded, a thoughtful look crossing his face. "Scared of what?"

"Of losing you," I admitted, the words spilling out before I could second-guess myself. "When we argue, it feels like we're teetering on the edge of something that might break us. And the thought of that scares me more than anything."

"I never want you to feel that way," he said, sincerity radiating from him. "I value what we have too much to let it slip away over misunderstandings."

I took a deep breath, the tension in my chest easing slightly. "It's a learning process, right? Figuring out how to communicate better? I mean, it's not like they offer courses in 'How to Navigate a Relationship' when you're signing up for life."

A smile broke through his seriousness, and I couldn't help but chuckle. "Maybe we should start a seminar—how to avoid arguing about who forgot to do the dishes."

"Exactly! We could charge a fortune for our expertise," he replied, his eyes twinkling. "And we'll throw in a bonus session on pastry selection strategies."

The laughter returned, flooding the space between us, filling the cracks of uncertainty with warmth and light. And just like that, I knew that while our path might not always be smooth, we were willing to navigate the rough patches together. Each shared laugh and vulnerable moment stitched us closer, binding our hearts in a way that felt both thrilling and terrifying.

As we prepared to leave, I felt a newfound determination. The road ahead was still uncertain, but with Ethan by my side, I knew I was ready to face whatever came our way, one croissant and laugh at a time.

The rest of the day flowed by in a haze of caffeine and laughter, the kind that wraps around you like a favorite sweater, warm and comforting. Ethan and I wandered through the streets, our footsteps echoing in the crisp autumn air, surrounded by trees blushing in shades of crimson and gold. Each moment felt like a little victory, a piece of the fractured puzzle between us sliding back into place. We strolled hand in hand, sharing stories and silly jokes, rekindling the spark that had flickered dangerously close to being extinguished.

As we approached the art exhibit, my stomach fluttered with excitement, and not just from the prospect of the colorful installations awaiting us. Ethan, with his easygoing charm, was already engaging in lighthearted banter with the security guard at the entrance. I stood back, marveling at how effortlessly he connected with others, his innate ability to draw people in like a moth to a flame. It made me realize how much I cherished that part of him—his laughter was a melody that resonated in the corners of my heart.

"Are you ready for some interactive art?" he asked, wiggling his eyebrows as we stepped inside the gallery, the air thick with the scent of paint and fresh canvas.

"I hope it's not too interactive," I replied, feigning seriousness. "I don't want to end up in a giant pile of paint like a living Jackson Pollock."

Ethan chuckled, nudging me gently. "What's life without a little mess? Besides, I'll be your trusty paint-wiping assistant."

As we meandered through the gallery, vibrant colors and dynamic shapes danced before us, pulling us into a world of creativity. We explored exhibits that encouraged us to touch and engage, to immerse ourselves in the art rather than merely observe it. I lost track of time as we experimented with different installations, leaving traces of our laughter and playfulness in our wake.

At one point, we found ourselves in front of an enormous canvas filled with swirling colors and bold strokes, a riotous explosion of creativity. "This one looks like it's begging for interaction," Ethan declared, his eyes sparkling with mischief. "What do you think? Should we add our own touch?"

"Only if you're prepared to ruin your precious jacket," I teased, but the playful challenge lingered in the air.

Ethan's smile widened, and with a flourish, he pulled a set of paintbrushes from a nearby station. "Oh, I dare you. Let's create a masterpiece."

With laughter bubbling up inside me, I joined him, the colors mixing beneath our strokes, blending into a chaotic symphony. The canvas quickly became a riot of purples and greens, our shared laughter echoing as we dabbed paint on each other's noses, transforming the act of creating into a delightful game.

Just as I was about to add a bold stroke of orange, I felt a familiar shiver of warmth flood through me. The way Ethan looked at me—his gaze warm, attentive, as if I were the only person in the room—sent a jolt of electricity coursing through my veins. In that moment, nothing else mattered.

As we stood back to admire our creation—a vibrant explosion of color that looked suspiciously like a joyful mess—Ethan leaned closer, a glimmer of something more than friendship dancing in his eyes. "You know," he began, his voice low and intimate, "I've missed this. Just being here with you, creating something together."

"Me too," I admitted, my heart racing. "It feels good to reconnect."

But just as I was about to suggest we celebrate our 'masterpiece' with some more pastries—because really, what was art without snacks?—a sudden commotion near the entrance pulled my attention away.

A group of people had gathered, their voices rising in a crescendo of concern. "What's happening?" I asked, straining to hear as Ethan stepped closer to me, our previous moment suspended in the air, thick with anticipation.

"It looks like someone's in trouble," he said, his expression turning serious as he squinted towards the crowd.

Curiosity piqued, we made our way closer, weaving through the throng of bodies. The murmur of voices crescendoed into alarm as we reached the front of the crowd. A tall man, his face flushed with anger, was arguing animatedly with a gallery staff member, gesturing wildly at the artwork behind him.

"—this is absolutely unacceptable!" he shouted, pointing at a portion of the exhibit, where a few small paint splatters marred the pristine display. "Do you see this? This is vandalism! How can you allow this?"

My heart sank as I realized what he was pointing at: our chaotic artwork, our playful masterpiece, was being accused of destruction.

Ethan's grip tightened around my hand, and I could feel the tension radiating from him. "That's our painting," I whispered, a wave of panic surging through me. "What are we going to do?"

"Stay calm," he replied, his voice steady. "We can explain."

But as we stepped forward, ready to defend our spontaneous creation, the man's voice rose again, drowning out the crowd's murmurs. "This is an outrage! Who would dare deface such a work of art?"

Before I could take a breath, the staff member looked our way, a mixture of confusion and concern painted across her face. "Excuse me, are you responsible for this?" she asked, her tone laced with uncertainty.

Ethan opened his mouth, but my mind raced ahead. "No, wait!" I blurted, caught between wanting to take responsibility for our actions and the dread of being in the spotlight. "I mean, yes, but it was an accident. We thought we were participating!"

The man's eyes darted between us, disbelief etched on his features. "You thought you were participating? You can't just mess with someone else's work!"

"Wait, what are you saying?" Ethan shot back, his voice growing more defensive. "We were told this was interactive art!"

As the tension in the room thickened, I felt a knot tightening in my stomach. This was not the joyful day of creativity I had envisioned, and I could sense the murmurs around us shifting from playful to accusatory.

In that moment of chaos, a sudden realization struck me—a chilling thought that sent shivers down my spine. "Ethan, we're not in trouble, are we?" I asked, panic creeping into my voice.

Before he could respond, the gallery manager stepped in, a stern look on her face. "I think it's time we get to the bottom of this. Everyone, please remain calm."

As the crowd shifted uneasily, I glanced at Ethan, my heart pounding. Something was off, and the weight of uncertainty settled like a heavy blanket over us. Just then, the man pointed an accusing finger at us, his voice sharp and clear above the din. "These two need to be held accountable for their actions!"

My breath caught in my throat as all eyes turned toward us, the playful atmosphere evaporating like morning mist, replaced by a storm of accusations and unease. The weight of the moment pressed down on me, and I knew—this was only the beginning of a confrontation that could change everything.

Chapter 25: The Healing

The sun was just beginning to dip below the horizon, casting a golden glow over the city, as I stood in front of the easel in our sun-drenched living room. The warm light filtered through the sheer curtains, illuminating the canvas with soft hues of orange and pink, mirroring the vibrant chaos of my emotions. Each stroke of the brush was a revelation, a blend of colors that flowed like the words I etched onto the pages of my poetry journal. It felt like a silent dialogue between my heart and soul, where every color expressed feelings I sometimes struggled to articulate. Art had become my sanctuary, a place where I could pour out the tangled threads of my heartache and hope.

Ethan, his silhouette framed by the doorway, watched with an intensity that made my heart race. I felt exposed, like a flower blooming for the first time after a long winter, but his presence grounded me. He leaned against the doorframe, arms crossed, his dark hair tousled and eyes lit with admiration. "You know, if I didn't know better, I'd say you were channeling Van Gogh with that explosion of colors." The hint of mischief in his voice made me smile, even as I felt the flutter of self-doubt creep in.

"Ha! Van Gogh had his own demons. I'm just here trying not to paint them," I shot back, mixing vibrant greens and yellows on my palette, feeling emboldened by our playful banter. There was something comforting about the way we could slip back into this rhythm, a melody woven from shared laughter and a few inside jokes that still made the corners of our mouths twitch.

"I mean, isn't that what art is about? Capturing the chaos?" he replied, stepping closer, his voice lowering into that familiar cadence that made my stomach do flips. "I think you're doing a beautiful job at it."

The praise washed over me like a gentle tide, reminding me of all the moments we had built together, brick by brick, even when the storms threatened to tear them down. I turned my focus back to the canvas, layering the colors with precision, crafting a landscape of emotions that only I could decipher. With every brushstroke, I breathed life into our healing journey, the struggles we faced crystallizing into a vivid representation of hope.

"You've been pretty quiet about your work lately. What's going on in that brilliant mind of yours?" I asked, glancing at him from the corner of my eye. The question hung in the air, heavy yet inviting, and I watched as he rubbed the back of his neck, a telltale sign of his internal conflict.

He hesitated, a flash of vulnerability crossing his features. "Honestly? I've been feeling like I'm in a rut. The projects are good, but I want something more... something that actually excites me." His voice trailed off, and I could see the flicker of ambition spark in his eyes—a flame yearning to break free from the constraints of routine.

"Then go for it, Ethan. Remember how we used to talk about your dream of working on sustainable architecture?" The words flowed easily, igniting a sense of urgency in my heart. "You're more than capable. You should chase what lights you up."

He looked at me, his gaze steady. "You really think so? I mean, it feels so far away."

I placed my brush down and stepped toward him, closing the distance that had felt like miles in the past. "No dream is too far away when you're willing to take the first step. You have the talent and the vision. Don't let fear hold you back." My voice was earnest, laced with the hope I had cultivated through my own artistic journey.

His expression softened, and I could see the wheels turning in his mind. It was as if my words had peeled back the layers of doubt, allowing the essence of who he truly was to shine through. "You're right. I've been too comfortable," he said finally, a determined spark igniting in his eyes. "I need to push myself, just like you do with your art."

We stood in the glow of that sunset, the air thick with unspoken dreams and promises, as our laughter mingled with the gentle rustle of the leaves outside. In that moment, the room felt alive, pulsing with the vibrant energy of renewed hope. I could sense the shift between us, like the turning of a page, an exciting anticipation brewing in the air.

Ethan reached out, taking my hands in his, grounding me in a shared resolve. "Let's make a pact, then. We'll push each other, explore new horizons, and refuse to let comfort box us in." His grip was firm, his gaze unwavering.

I nodded, my heart racing with the exhilaration of possibilities. "Deal."

Just as we sealed our promise, the doorbell chimed, jolting us from our moment. I exchanged a curious glance with Ethan. "Who could that be?"

As I crossed the room, a sense of trepidation nestled in my stomach. I swung open the door, and my breath caught in my throat. Standing there, with a sheepish grin, was my younger sister, Lily, arms loaded with colorful grocery bags.

"Surprise!" she exclaimed, beaming like a ray of sunshine. "I thought I'd come brighten your day with some of your favorite snacks!"

Her enthusiasm was infectious, and I couldn't help but laugh. "You're a little ray of chaos, you know that?"

"Hey, someone's gotta keep you two in check." Her eyes sparkled mischievously as she pushed past me, her energy filling the room.

Ethan chuckled, a knowing smile playing on his lips. "I think you're just jealous of our profound artistic discussions."

Lily rolled her eyes, rummaging through the bags. "Artistic discussions? Please. I came here for snacks and a dramatic reading of whatever it is you've been working on."

I grinned, grateful for this unexpected twist in the evening. It was a welcome interruption, a reminder that amidst the serious talk of dreams and ambitions, there was joy in the little moments, in the laughter and chaos of family.

As we settled in, the room filled with lighthearted banter and the scent of buttery popcorn. I caught Ethan's eye, and we exchanged a silent understanding: our journey of healing and growth was just beginning. And now, it felt like we had an ally in our corner, a reminder that we didn't have to navigate it alone.

The popcorn was barely settled in its bowl when Lily launched into her latest escapade, recounting the misadventures of her latest job as a barista. "You wouldn't believe it! This guy came in demanding a triple-shot caramel macchiato with a sprinkle of pixie dust," she said, her eyes wide with delight. "I mean, I thought he was kidding, but he was dead serious. I had to look him in the eye and say, 'Sir, I can do two out of three, but pixie dust? That's reserved for fairy tale lattes.'"

Ethan chuckled, and I couldn't help but smile at her theatrical flair. "Did you really tell him that?" I asked, trying to stifle a laugh.

"Of course! He just blinked at me like I was the one with the problem." She leaned back, crossing her arms with a satisfied grin. "But he did order a regular one after that, so I guess I saved his caffeine fix."

I felt a rush of affection for my sister, this bright spark who could turn even the dullest moments into something entertaining. "You might have a future in stand-up comedy," I teased, knowing full well she had a flair for dramatics.

"I'll leave that to the professionals. But hey, speaking of futures—" she glanced between Ethan and me, mischief dancing in her eyes. "What are you two planning? Any big, artistic collaborations on the horizon?"

Ethan shot me a look that was half-exasperation, half-amusement. "We're working on it, but I think we might need to brainstorm some actual ideas first."

Lily's grin widened. "Brainstorm? Or just eat popcorn and stare at each other like lovesick fools?"

"Who says we can't do both?" I chimed in, tossing a piece of popcorn at her.

As we indulged in a playful back-and-forth, I felt the tension from earlier slip away, like sand through my fingers. We spent the next hour immersed in laughter, swapping stories that wove a rich tapestry of our lives, each thread vibrant and colorful. In the midst of the light-hearted chaos, I noticed how Ethan's demeanor had shifted, his laughter growing freer and his eyes brighter, mirroring the warmth that enveloped the room.

Eventually, as the bowl of popcorn dwindled to a few stray kernels, Lily's laughter began to fade into contemplative silence. "So, really, how are you two doing?" she asked, her tone shifting to something more serious, more probing.

"We're getting there," I replied, my voice steady as I met Ethan's gaze, a silent affirmation passing between us. "It's been a process, but we're learning to communicate better."

"And he's finally realized that I'm not just a crazy artist," I added with a wink. "I'm a crazy artist with a plan."

Ethan laughed softly, his fingers brushing against mine. "And I'm finally learning to share my fears, rather than bottle them up like a soda that's been shaken too long."

Lily nodded, her expression shifting to something softer, almost proud. "That's really great to hear. Relationships are all about being brave enough to be vulnerable, even when it feels risky."

"It's definitely a work in progress," I said, feeling a rush of gratitude for her insight. "But every day feels like a step forward."

Just then, the clock on the wall chimed, its deep, resonant notes echoing through the room, marking the hour. A pang of regret struck me as I glanced at the time. "Oh, no. I didn't realize it was getting so late. I've got to finish up my painting before I lose the light entirely."

Lily stood up, dramatically placing a hand to her forehead. "Oh, the tragedy! The artist must complete her masterpiece before the sun sets!"

"Perhaps I should take my act on the road," I quipped back, pulling out my brushes.

As I began to paint again, I could feel Ethan's gaze on me, a comforting presence that grounded my creative spirit. The sound of my brush swishing against the canvas mingled with the ambient noise of the city outside, and I lost myself in the rhythm of creation. Each stroke became an expression of our healing journey, the colors swirling together to form something beautiful and chaotic.

Lily picked up her phone, scrolling through it with a distracted air. "While you do your artsy thing, I'm going to catch up on social media. You won't believe the ridiculous things people are posting these days."

Ethan chuckled. "Yeah, because that's a shocking turn of events."

"Hey! This is serious business," she retorted, throwing a crumpled napkin at him. "You know how important it is to keep up with the Kardashians!"

"I think they'll survive without you," he replied, shaking his head with feigned seriousness.

I laughed, feeling lighter than I had in weeks. It was moments like these that reminded me of the strength in our connections, the way laughter and love could weave through the heaviest of burdens, binding us together even when life threatened to pull us apart.

As the sun slipped lower, casting the room in an amber glow, I became aware of a nagging worry. My fingers hesitated on the brush, and I stole a glance at Ethan, who was still engaged with Lily's antics. Beneath the laughter, I felt a swell of concern—what if the fragility of our progress was just that? Fragile.

"Hey, Ethan?" I called, my voice steady despite the sudden weight on my chest. "What do you want to do about your career? I mean, really?"

He looked up, surprise flickering across his face. "What do you mean?"

"I know you mentioned feeling stuck, but we can't just talk about dreams—we need to chase them, right?" I pressed, my heart pounding. "I want to help you take those first steps."

Lily's playful demeanor shifted into supportive enthusiasm. "Yeah! If you're thinking of taking a leap, I'm totally on board. I'll be your number one cheerleader, complete with pom-poms."

"Or maybe a slightly less embarrassing version of a cheerleader," Ethan replied, a hint of laughter in his tone, but his expression was serious.

I stepped closer, placing my hand on his shoulder. "Seriously, you've got talent. What if we set up a plan together? Like, you could reach out to some local firms or start a portfolio site. We can brainstorm ideas for projects that showcase what you love."

His eyes narrowed, a thoughtful expression crossing his face. "You'd really help me with that?"

"Of course," I replied, my resolve strengthening. "We're a team. Remember?"

He smiled, a slow, genuine smile that warmed my heart. "I do remember. And maybe you're right. I need to take that leap, but it feels daunting."

"Then let's leap together."

As the three of us began to outline a plan over scattered popcorn and laughter, I felt a rush of determination settle in my chest. No longer would we be bound by fear or uncertainty. We were creating our paths, igniting our dreams with each shared idea, each supportive word. Together, we would explore the potential of tomorrow, crafting not only our individual destinies but also a future woven tightly with hope and love.

The planning session morphed into a whirlwind of ideas, with Ethan, Lily, and me tossing around possibilities like confetti at a parade. The room buzzed with excitement, our laughter echoing off the walls as we scribbled notes on a large whiteboard, which had become a colorful collage of dreams and inspirations.

"What if we created a community project? You know, something that brings sustainable architecture into the neighborhood?" I suggested, my heart racing with the thrill of our shared energy. "We could host workshops, get people involved, and maybe even partner with local schools!"

Lily's eyes sparkled. "Yes! You could inspire a whole new generation of eco-warriors! And I could design the promotional materials! I'm thinking vibrant colors, catchy slogans—'Building Tomorrow, Today!'"

Ethan chuckled, shaking his head with a playful grin. "You're really leaning into this, huh? If we go with your slogan, I might need to wear a cape while I build."

"Only if it's green," I interjected, grinning. "You can't save the world without looking fabulous while doing it."

Lily feigned exasperation. "As if capes are the worst of your ideas! I'll have you know that I once designed a dress that doubled as a tent. Fashionable camping, anyone?"

Ethan burst out laughing, and I joined in, the sound ringing through the air like music. "You're ridiculous, but I love it," he said, his eyes meeting mine, a warmth blooming in his chest that mirrored the playful chaos around us.

The brainstorming session continued to spiral into ever more elaborate schemes, our ideas ranging from ludicrous to downright brilliant. We plotted out everything, from art installations in local parks to hosting an open house showcasing Ethan's designs. With each proposal, I felt a swell of hope, not only for Ethan's career but also for the life we were building together—a life filled with laughter, creativity, and purpose.

As the evening wore on and the snacks dwindled, Lily leaned back in her chair, her expression turning contemplative. "So, if you two are really serious about this, when's the first workshop happening?"

Ethan and I exchanged a glance, a silent conversation passing between us. "How about next month?" I suggested, my heart racing at the thought. "That gives us time to prepare, spread the word, and get the community involved."

"I can get the logistics in order and handle the social media," Lily offered, excitement bubbling in her voice. "I'll turn this into the biggest event of the year!"

"We need to make sure we're ready, though," Ethan said, a serious edge creeping into his tone. "If we're going to do this, we have to commit fully. I can't half-ass it anymore."

"Then we won't," I assured him, sensing the gravity of the moment. "This is our chance, and we're doing it together."

With a determined nod, Ethan turned to me. "And this isn't just about me, you know. Your art has a voice, too. We need to showcase that alongside the architecture."

I felt a flush of warmth spread through me at his words. "You really think so?"

"Absolutely," he said, his gaze steady. "You've always had this incredible way of capturing emotions in your work. Let's not just inspire the community; let's move them."

The air shifted, thickening with a mix of excitement and nervous energy. Just then, a loud crash echoed from the kitchen, breaking the spell we had woven around ourselves. We all jumped, exchanging startled looks.

"What was that?" Lily asked, her voice dropping to a whisper as she exchanged nervous glances with us.

"I have no idea," I said, a sinking feeling settling in my stomach. "I'll check it out."

Ethan stood up immediately, his protective instincts kicking in. "No, let me. You stay here."

"Not a chance. If it's something dangerous, we both need to go," I insisted, already moving toward the kitchen with Lily following closely behind.

As we entered the kitchen, the sight before us sent chills down my spine. The back door swung open, its glass shattered, and the remnants of a broken vase scattered across the floor.

"What happened?" Lily gasped, her eyes wide as she stepped over the debris.

"I don't know," I said, moving cautiously toward the door, scanning the dimly lit patio beyond. The wind whistled softly, but it carried an eerie quietness that set my heart racing. "Ethan, can you check the other rooms?"

"Stay close," he replied, his voice low and steady. He moved away, his presence a calming force, but I felt the tension rising in the air, an unspoken worry binding us together.

As I stepped outside, the moonlight cast ghostly shadows across the yard, making the familiar space feel foreign and frightening. The world felt suspended in a heavy silence, as if holding its breath, waiting for something to happen.

"Do you think someone broke in?" Lily whispered, her voice trembling slightly.

I shook my head, trying to dispel the unease creeping into my thoughts. "Maybe it was just the wind? Or an animal?"

Just as I spoke, a rustle in the bushes nearby sent my heart into overdrive. I turned sharply, my pulse racing as I squinted into the darkness, trying to discern a shape lurking just beyond the light.

"Ethan?" I called, my voice strained.

"I'm here," he replied, rejoining us. "What's going on?"

"Something moved over there." My hand trembled slightly as I pointed toward the bushes, fear gnawing at the edges of my mind.

"Stay back," he instructed, positioning himself between us and the darkness. "I'll check it out."

"No!" I said, panic flaring in my chest. "We should call the police. This isn't just an accident anymore."

Before Ethan could respond, a figure emerged from the shadows, cloaked in darkness but unmistakably human. The breath caught in my throat as recognition flashed through me—someone I hadn't seen in years, a ghost from my past that I had hoped never to encounter again.

"Hello, stranger," the figure said, a smirk playing on their lips as they stepped into the light. "Miss me?"

My heart raced, and in that moment, everything shifted. The laughter, the warmth, the dreams we had just built—all of it hung precariously in the balance as the reality of my past collided with the fragile future I was trying to create. The air crackled with tension, an unpredictable storm gathering on the horizon, and I could only hold my breath as I faced the unexpected truth standing before us.

Chapter 26: The Surprise

The cabin stood proudly at the water's edge, its rustic charm woven seamlessly into the surrounding landscape, as if nature itself had crafted it from the very trees and earth. Weathered wood, softened by years of sun and rain, enveloped us as we stepped onto the porch. Ethan, with his unruly hair tousled by the gentle breeze, held my hand tightly, a warm reassurance that this weekend would be unlike any other.

I had spent countless late nights hunched over my easel, lost in the colors and shapes that danced in my mind, but here, in the embrace of the wilderness, inspiration crackled in the air like the fire we would later kindle. The scent of pine filled my lungs, mingling with the faint whiff of smoke from the old fireplace inside the cabin. My heart raced with excitement, and an unbidden smile crept across my lips.

"Just wait until you see the view from the dock," Ethan said, his voice rich with anticipation. "It's supposed to be breathtaking at sunset."

I couldn't wait to see it. I could already picture the palette of oranges, pinks, and purples blending seamlessly across the horizon, a perfect backdrop for the rest of the weekend. We unloaded our bags, tossing them haphazardly in the cozy living room, where a well-loved couch and an old plaid blanket beckoned us to curl up and bask in each other's company.

Ethan, always the energetic one, darted out the door, leaving me momentarily alone with my thoughts. I watched him disappear down the path to the dock, his movements effortless and free, a reminder of how often I felt tethered to my work. My fingers itched to capture the scene—the way the sunlight glinted off the lake like a thousand diamonds, the birds flitting overhead in search of the evening's supper.

Settling onto the porch steps, I pulled out my sketchbook, the paper slightly weathered from travel, and began to draw. I lost track of time as the world around me transformed into lines and shapes. Each stroke was a reminder of the joy I found in creation. The soft rustle of leaves provided a soothing rhythm, punctuated by the occasional splash of a fish breaking the surface of the water.

"Are you planning to draw me too?" Ethan's voice pulled me from my reverie, a teasing lilt in his tone. He stood at the edge of the dock, hands on his hips, water shimmering behind him like a mystical backdrop.

"Oh, you're a hard one to capture," I replied, grinning as I looked up from my sketch. "Too much charm for mere paper."

"Charm?" He laughed, a deep, rich sound that echoed through the trees. "I prefer to think of it as rugged good looks."

I rolled my eyes, though my smile lingered. "Rugged, huh? Maybe you should try modeling instead of all that construction work."

"Only if you promise to be my artist." He sauntered over, the sun casting a halo around his head as he joined me on the steps. "What are you working on?"

I showed him my drawing, a rough sketch of the lake and the distant mountains, and watched his face transform from playful banter to genuine admiration. "This is beautiful," he said, his voice softer now. "You have such a talent for capturing the essence of a place."

"Thanks," I said, warmth flooding my cheeks. "I just hope I can get it right before the sun sets."

"Then we better make the most of it," he declared, jumping to his feet and extending a hand to help me up. "Let's go explore the trails before we lose the light."

We wandered into the dense forest, where towering pines stood sentinel over a carpet of wildflowers. The path was narrow, winding between trees that whispered secrets to one another in the soft breeze. Ethan's laughter was a melody that floated through the air, mingling with the songs of birds overhead.

"This place is incredible," I marveled, my eyes darting between the vibrant colors of blooming flowers and the breathtaking view that unfolded around each bend.

He smiled, his gaze filled with admiration. "It's even better with you here. You make everything more vibrant."

As we hiked deeper into the woods, our conversations meandered like the trail itself, shifting from dreams and aspirations to the ridiculous antics of our friends back home. The laughter spilled from us effortlessly, brightening the air around us. With every shared joke, every playful nudge, I felt the tension of city life dissolve into the serene backdrop of nature.

We eventually stumbled upon a clearing, where the sunlight broke through the canopy like a spotlight, illuminating a small, sparkling pond. "This is perfect!" I exclaimed, dropping my backpack and rushing toward the water's edge.

Ethan followed, a teasing grin on his face. "You're like a kid at a candy store."

"Can you blame me?" I dipped my fingers into the cool water, marveling at how clear it was. "It's like a hidden treasure!"

"Then let's treasure it." He joined me, and we sat at the water's edge, our feet splashing playfully. I felt the world shrink, leaving just the two of us, the sunlight dancing across the pond, and the gentle rustle of leaves in the trees.

"Tell me something," he said, his voice suddenly serious, breaking the comfortable silence that had enveloped us. "What's your biggest dream?"

I paused, the question hanging between us like a fragile glass ornament, beautiful yet precarious. "I want to share my art with the world, to inspire others the way nature inspires me."

His eyes sparkled with understanding. "You will. I believe in you."

I turned to him, feeling a swell of gratitude. "Thank you for believing in me."

He reached out, tucking a stray hair behind my ear, the intimacy of the gesture sending a shiver down my spine. "Always."

As we sat in that sun-dappled moment, I knew this weekend was destined to be a pivotal chapter in our story—a breath of fresh air in the canvas of our lives, painting it with laughter, love, and boundless inspiration.

The cabin stood proudly at the water's edge, its rustic charm woven seamlessly into the surrounding landscape, as if nature itself had crafted it from the very trees and earth. Weathered wood, softened by years of sun and rain, enveloped us as we stepped onto the porch. Ethan, with his unruly hair tousled by the gentle breeze, held my hand tightly, a warm reassurance that this weekend would be unlike any other.

I had spent countless late nights hunched over my easel, lost in the colors and shapes that danced in my mind, but here, in the embrace of the wilderness, inspiration crackled in the air like the fire we would later kindle. The scent of pine filled my lungs, mingling with the faint whiff of smoke from the old fireplace inside the cabin. My heart raced with excitement, and an unbidden smile crept across my lips.

"Just wait until you see the view from the dock," Ethan said, his voice rich with anticipation. "It's supposed to be breathtaking at sunset."

I couldn't wait to see it. I could already picture the palette of oranges, pinks, and purples blending seamlessly across the horizon, a perfect backdrop for the rest of the weekend. We unloaded our bags, tossing them haphazardly in the cozy living room, where a well-loved couch and an old plaid blanket beckoned us to curl up and bask in each other's company.

Ethan, always the energetic one, darted out the door, leaving me momentarily alone with my thoughts. I watched him disappear down the path to the dock, his movements effortless and free, a reminder of how often I felt tethered to my work. My fingers itched to capture the scene—the way the sunlight glinted off the lake like a thousand diamonds, the birds flitting overhead in search of the evening's supper.

Settling onto the porch steps, I pulled out my sketchbook, the paper slightly weathered from travel, and began to draw. I lost track of time as the world around me transformed into lines and shapes. Each stroke was a reminder of the joy I found in creation. The soft rustle of leaves provided a soothing rhythm, punctuated by the occasional splash of a fish breaking the surface of the water.

"Are you planning to draw me too?" Ethan's voice pulled me from my reverie, a teasing lilt in his tone. He stood at the edge of the dock, hands on his hips, water shimmering behind him like a mystical backdrop.

"Oh, you're a hard one to capture," I replied, grinning as I looked up from my sketch. "Too much charm for mere paper."

"Charm?" He laughed, a deep, rich sound that echoed through the trees. "I prefer to think of it as rugged good looks."

I rolled my eyes, though my smile lingered. "Rugged, huh? Maybe you should try modeling instead of all that construction work."

"Only if you promise to be my artist." He sauntered over, the sun casting a halo around his head as he joined me on the steps. "What are you working on?"

I showed him my drawing, a rough sketch of the lake and the distant mountains, and watched his face transform from playful banter to genuine admiration. "This is beautiful," he said, his voice softer now. "You have such a talent for capturing the essence of a place."

"Thanks," I said, warmth flooding my cheeks. "I just hope I can get it right before the sun sets."

"Then we better make the most of it," he declared, jumping to his feet and extending a hand to help me up. "Let's go explore the trails before we lose the light."

We wandered into the dense forest, where towering pines stood sentinel over a carpet of wildflowers. The path was narrow, winding between trees that whispered secrets to one another in the soft breeze. Ethan's laughter was a melody that floated through the air, mingling with the songs of birds overhead.

"This place is incredible," I marveled, my eyes darting between the vibrant colors of blooming flowers and the breathtaking view that unfolded around each bend.

He smiled, his gaze filled with admiration. "It's even better with you here. You make everything more vibrant."

As we hiked deeper into the woods, our conversations meandered like the trail itself, shifting from dreams and aspirations to the ridiculous antics of our friends back home. The laughter spilled from us effortlessly, brightening the air around us. With every shared joke, every playful nudge, I felt the tension of city life dissolve into the serene backdrop of nature.

We eventually stumbled upon a clearing, where the sunlight broke through the canopy like a spotlight, illuminating a small, sparkling pond. "This is perfect!" I exclaimed, dropping my backpack and rushing toward the water's edge.

Ethan followed, a teasing grin on his face. "You're like a kid at a candy store."

"Can you blame me?" I dipped my fingers into the cool water, marveling at how clear it was. "It's like a hidden treasure!"

"Then let's treasure it." He joined me, and we sat at the water's edge, our feet splashing playfully. I felt the world shrink, leaving just the two of us, the sunlight dancing across the pond, and the gentle rustle of leaves in the trees.

"Tell me something," he said, his voice suddenly serious, breaking the comfortable silence that had enveloped us. "What's your biggest dream?"

I paused, the question hanging between us like a fragile glass ornament, beautiful yet precarious. "I want to share my art with the world, to inspire others the way nature inspires me."

His eyes sparkled with understanding. "You will. I believe in you."

I turned to him, feeling a swell of gratitude. "Thank you for believing in me."

He reached out, tucking a stray hair behind my ear, the intimacy of the gesture sending a shiver down my spine. "Always."

As we sat in that sun-dappled moment, I knew this weekend was destined to be a pivotal chapter in our story—a breath of fresh air in the canvas of our lives, painting it with laughter, love, and boundless inspiration.

The following morning, the sun peeked through the cabin's window, casting a warm golden glow that danced across the wooden floor. I stretched luxuriously, the remnants of sleep still clinging to me like a cozy blanket. Ethan was already awake, his silhouette framed against the bright light, busy brewing coffee in the small kitchenette. The rich, earthy aroma wafted through the air, promising a perfect start to the day.

"Good morning, sleepyhead," he called over his shoulder, his voice teasingly soft. "I was starting to think I'd have to launch a search party."

"Please," I chuckled, pushing myself up from the bed. "You'd probably just make a coffee run while I was out there, deep in the woods, searching for treasure."

"You know me too well." He turned, a mug in hand, his smile widening at the sight of me. "But I'd at least throw a granola bar in your direction for sustenance."

"Such a gentleman," I replied with mock seriousness, accepting the steaming cup he offered. The heat seeped through the ceramic, warming my hands, and I savored the first sip, the bitter richness a perfect complement to the tranquility of the morning.

After a leisurely breakfast of scrambled eggs and fresh fruit, we decided to explore the area further. Ethan led the way, his energy infectious as he bounded ahead, each step stirring up the earthy scents of damp soil and blooming flowers. The sunlight streamed through the trees, creating a mosaic of shadows that danced along the path.

As we trekked deeper into the woods, I found myself captivated by the symphony of sounds surrounding us—the distant call of a woodpecker, the rustle of leaves in the gentle breeze, and the soft chirps of hidden creatures. The world felt alive, vibrant with possibilities.

"What if we stumble upon a hidden waterfall?" Ethan suggested, his eyes sparkling with mischief. "Or maybe a family of bears just waiting to befriend us?"

"Or a bear that thinks we're dinner," I shot back, the playful banter rolling off my tongue. "If that happens, I'm throwing you to it as a distraction."

"Brave of you," he laughed, feigning mock offense. "I'll remember that when it's time to escape."

The playful mood propelled us forward until we reached a clearing that opened up to a stunning view of the lake, glittering under the mid-morning sun. "Now this is what I call a backdrop," Ethan exclaimed, arms wide as if embracing the landscape.

"Absolutely breathtaking," I breathed, feeling a surge of inspiration course through me. The stillness of the water contrasted sharply with the chaotic beauty of the trees, and my artistic mind raced, desperate to capture the moment. I pulled out my sketchbook, eager to immortalize the scene.

"You and your sketches," Ethan said, leaning over my shoulder to peek at the page. "You know, one of these days, I'll have to convince you to create a mural or something on one of the cabin walls."

"Only if you promise to model for me," I shot back playfully, eyes twinkling as I sketched the curves of the landscape.

"Deal. I'll rock a hat and sunglasses. Very artsy."

As the sun climbed higher, I lost myself in the rhythm of my pencil on paper, while Ethan entertained himself by tossing rocks into the water, each splash a small reminder of his playful spirit. It felt like a scene plucked straight from a dream, a lazy afternoon suspended in time.

Suddenly, a loud crash echoed through the woods, jolting me from my focus. I glanced up, my heart racing, to see Ethan frozen mid-throw, his expression shifting from carefree to concerned. "What was that?"

"I don't know," I replied, my pulse quickening as I scanned the tree line. The tranquil beauty of our surroundings began to feel ominous, shadows stretching longer, the rustling leaves carrying an eerie undertone.

Ethan moved closer, his eyes narrowing as he scanned the area. "Stay close," he whispered, the playful tone vanishing. The warmth of the sun now felt distant, overshadowed by an unsettling chill.

We approached the source of the noise, and with each cautious step, the underbrush crunched beneath our feet, amplifying the tense silence. "Maybe it was just a fallen tree," I suggested, attempting to lighten the mood, though my voice wavered slightly.

"Or something more," Ethan murmured, his brow furrowing as he spotted movement just beyond the trees. My heart skipped a beat as I strained to see through the foliage.

Suddenly, a large figure burst from the thicket—a massive stag, its antlers majestic against the backdrop of the green foliage. It paused, staring at us with intelligent, wary eyes, and for a moment, time seemed to stand still.

"Wow," I whispered, awe washing over me as I took in the creature's beauty. The stag held my gaze, a moment of connection sparking between us, before it bounded away, disappearing into the depths of the forest.

"Okay, that was both terrifying and amazing," Ethan said, his breath coming out in a rush as he leaned against a tree, a grin creeping back onto his face. "Nature sure knows how to put on a show."

"I didn't know whether to scream or applaud," I replied, my heart still racing but with a newfound excitement bubbling beneath the surface. "Did you see those antlers?"

"Pretty impressive, right? Maybe we should hang out with nature more often." He chuckled, the tension easing from his shoulders.

Just as we were about to head back, my gaze fell upon something on the ground. My heart sank as I knelt down, brushing away leaves to reveal a small, silver locket, tarnished with age but undeniably beautiful. "Ethan, look at this!"

He joined me, curiosity piqued. "What is it?"

"A locket," I replied, flipping it open to reveal a tiny, faded photograph of a couple, their faces frozen in time, surrounded by a silver filigree that hinted at a story waiting to be uncovered. "It must have belonged to someone."

"Maybe it's a sign," he mused, an adventurous glint in his eyes. "A treasure hunt?"

I laughed lightly but then felt a weight settle in my chest. "What if it belongs to someone who's still out there?"

"Then we'll return it. How hard can that be?" His confidence buoyed me, even as a sense of unease washed over me.

As we stood there, the woods around us seemed to grow still, holding its breath, and the air thickened with unspoken secrets. I tucked the locket into my pocket, a weighty reminder that our getaway had just taken a turn into something unexpected.

"Let's get back to the cabin," I suggested, my voice low. "We can figure this out later."

Ethan nodded, but just as we turned to leave, the sound of snapping twigs echoed behind us, sharp and distinct, sending a chill down my spine. The forest felt alive again, but not in the way it had moments before. Something was watching us.

Chapter 27: The Moment of Truth

The air was thick with the scent of pine and the faint smoke from the crackling fire, each note mixing into a symphony of the wild, rustic ambiance that enveloped us. Nestled in our cozy cabin, tucked away from the bustling world outside, we had found our sanctuary—an escape where nature whispered secrets and the stars shone like diamonds scattered across an indigo canvas. As I gazed up, a shiver of exhilaration ran down my spine, the kind that danced with anticipation. It was the kind of night that felt pregnant with possibilities, each twinkling star a silent witness to the unfolding of dreams.

I turned my head to look at Ethan, whose face was illuminated by the flickering flames, the light casting playful shadows that danced across his cheekbones. He was utterly captivating in this moment, with tousled hair and a softness in his gaze that melted my heart. In that stillness, I felt as though we were suspended in time, a tiny universe that belonged solely to us. The faint crackle of the fire was the only sound that punctuated the silence, urging me to let go of the reservations I had been clutching like a security blanket.

"Ethan," I began, my voice almost a whisper, as if speaking too loudly would shatter the delicate magic that surrounded us. He turned to me, his dark eyes wide with curiosity, an encouraging smile urging me on. "I've been thinking a lot about the future... my future." My heart raced, a wild animal desperate to break free. "About pursuing my art full-time."

His brow furrowed slightly, a flicker of concern threading through his expression, but it was swiftly replaced with something deeper, something that ignited a spark of hope within me. "What do you mean? You've always talked about your art like it's this beautiful, ethereal thing. Why not chase it?" His voice was steady, a solid foundation that calmed the storm within me.

I took a deep breath, the crisp night air filling my lungs and carrying my fears away with it. "I want to create, to pour myself into my work, to make something that resonates with people. But there's this fear, this nagging thought that says I'm not good enough, that it's impractical to leave everything behind."

Ethan leaned closer, his sincerity wrapping around me like a warm blanket. "But what if you are good enough? What if you leave behind the doubt and take a leap? You could paint the world in colors only you can see."

His words ignited a flicker of courage within me, a flame that flickered in sync with the fire before us. "I just want to feel like I'm really living, you know? I don't want to wake up one day and regret not chasing my dreams. I've watched you with your food, the way you create something magical from simple ingredients. It's inspiring."

At the mention of food, Ethan's eyes lit up, and I could see the familiar gleam of passion in his gaze. "Well, speaking of dreams," he said, leaning back slightly and crossing his arms, "I've been doing a lot of soul-searching myself. I want to dive into the culinary arts, really dig my heels in and see where it takes me."

The weight of his confession hung between us, mingling with the warmth of the fire. My heart soared at the thought of two dreamers, side by side, daring to leap into the unknown. "You?" I chuckled, incredulous. "A chef? That's brilliant! You have the hands of an artist; you just paint on plates instead of canvases."

Ethan's laughter rang out, bright and infectious, echoing through the night. "I mean, I do have a knack for transforming burnt toast into... well, at least edible toast." His eyes sparkled with mischief. "But seriously, it's what I love. I want to create dishes that tell stories, that make people feel something. Just like your art."

Our dreams wove together like threads in a tapestry, forming a rich narrative of ambition and desire. It was as if the universe conspired to align our paths, guiding us toward a future that shimmered with the potential of shared journeys. "So, what if we both pursue our passions?" I suggested, emboldened by the firelight and his unwavering support. "What if we challenge each other to grow, to create?"

Ethan's smile widened, revealing a warmth that made my heart flutter. "Imagine a world where your paintings hang in a gallery while my culinary creations delight palates in a bustling restaurant. We could inspire each other, push one another toward greatness."

"I can already see it," I said, laughter bubbling up inside me. "You in a chef's coat, swaying to music in the kitchen while I sip wine and critique your dishes."

"Critique?" He raised an eyebrow, a playful challenge in his tone. "I'll have you know I expect nothing less than rave reviews from my favorite art critic."

"Only if you promise to paint with flavors," I shot back, the banter flowing effortlessly between us, each quip like a brushstroke on a shared canvas of laughter and dreams.

As the fire crackled and the stars shimmered, we made a pact that night—not just to follow our dreams, but to be each other's anchors in the chaotic sea of uncertainty that lay ahead. With each promise we exchanged, I felt the weight of fear lift slightly, replaced by the exhilaration of shared dreams and the belief that together, we could weather any storm.

The night unfolded like a beautiful melody, each moment a note in a symphony of hopes and aspirations. Wrapped in the warmth of our camaraderie, I knew we were on the brink of something extraordinary. It was a moment of truth, a moment where the boundaries of possibility stretched wide, beckoning us into a future painted with the hues of our deepest desires.

Chapter 28: The Return

Returning home felt like stepping into a long-lost dream, the walls of my sanctuary alive with the echoes of laughter and creativity. The scent of fresh paint and varnish mingled with the sweet aroma of lavender wafting from the window boxes, creating an intoxicating blend that made my heart race with excitement. Each inch of my studio whispered stories of struggle and triumph, the splattered canvases telling tales of late nights fueled by coffee and desperation. With every brushstroke, I had poured pieces of my soul onto the canvas, a kaleidoscope of emotions that reflected my journey and the love that propelled me forward.

Ethan's unwavering support had been my anchor in this sea of uncertainty. He had witnessed my transformation from a timid artist hesitant to show her work to someone finally ready to embrace the vulnerability of exposure. Together, we had embarked on this exhilarating quest to find a local gallery willing to showcase my art. The thrill of it coursed through me, electrifying every nerve as I envisioned my pieces hanging on the walls, illuminated by soft golden light.

"Okay, Picasso," Ethan teased as we set up the display, his fingers deftly adjusting the placement of one of my favorite pieces—a swirling representation of a tempestuous ocean, rich with cerulean and emerald hues. "Let's make sure they don't accidentally think this is a high school art project."

I shot him a mock glare, a smile creeping onto my lips. "Careful, or I might just replace your beloved coffee with decaf."

"Now that's a low blow," he replied, chuckling as he stepped back to admire the arrangement. "But seriously, this is stunning. You've outdone yourself."

The night of the exhibit arrived with a rush of anticipation that tightened my chest. The gallery space was a canvas in itself—white walls stretched toward the ceiling, adorned with warm lighting that cast a welcoming glow over the polished wooden floors. As we arrived, the energy thrummed around us, vibrant and alive. The laughter and chatter of art enthusiasts filled the air, creating a tapestry of sound that made my heart race.

"Remember to breathe," Ethan whispered, his eyes sparkling with mischief. "And if you see anyone staring too long, just assume they're deeply moved by your genius, not plotting to steal your art."

"Right, because that's definitely a common occurrence in the world of local art shows," I replied, rolling my eyes but unable to suppress a grin. "I'll just have to fend them off with my incredible wit and charm."

As I stepped further into the gallery, the vibrant colors of my artwork seemed to come alive, swirling and dancing in the ambient light. Friends and family began to arrive, their faces lighting up like stars against the dim backdrop of the gallery. I felt their warmth enveloping me, their presence like a sturdy cloak that fortified my nerves. The laughter of familiar voices intertwined with the excited murmur of newcomers, each conversation a thread woven into the fabric of this beautiful evening.

I caught sight of my parents, their expressions brimming with pride as they approached me. My mother enveloped me in a hug, her perfume—an intoxicating blend of jasmine and vanilla—filling my senses. "You've done it, darling! Look at all these people," she beamed, her eyes glistening with unshed tears.

"They're here for the art," I said, waving a hand toward the crowd. "Or maybe just the free wine."

"Oh please," my dad chimed in, a twinkle of humor dancing in his eyes. "If they're anything like your mother, they're definitely here for both."

As the evening progressed, I mingled with the crowd, buoyed by their enthusiasm. I was introduced to fellow artists, local influencers, and even a few critics, each conversation punctuated by laughter and genuine interest in my work. I felt a sense of connection blossoming, each compliment a delicate brushstroke adding depth to my canvas of self-worth.

Yet, amidst the whirlwind of joyful chaos, a pang of anxiety lingered in my chest. What if they didn't truly appreciate my art? What if they were simply being polite? I had poured my heart into each piece, and the thought of rejection loomed over me like a storm cloud threatening to burst.

"Hey," Ethan said, appearing at my side as if he could sense my unease. He held a glass of red wine, offering it to me with a knowing smile. "You look like you need this more than I do."

"Thanks," I murmured, taking a sip that flooded my senses with rich, bold flavors. "I'm just worried about how they're reacting. What if they think it's all rubbish?"

"Then they clearly lack vision," he countered with a playful roll of his eyes. "But let me remind you—these people are here for you. Look around. They're intrigued, they're engaged, and they're excited. You're the star of the show."

I followed his gaze, my heart fluttering as I noticed a group of people gathered around my favorite piece, the tempestuous ocean, their expressions animated and thoughtful. I caught snippets of their conversation, the words washing over me like a soothing wave.

"This is breathtaking," one woman said, her voice a melodic whisper. "The way she captures the chaos of the sea—it's like you can feel the water crashing against the shore."

"Absolutely," another chimed in. "There's a rawness to it that makes it feel alive. I've never seen anything quite like it."

As their words seeped into my consciousness, a rush of warmth spread through me, obliterating my fears. My heart soared as I exchanged glances with Ethan, who raised his glass in a silent toast. In that moment, I understood that this night was more than just an exhibit; it was a celebration of my journey, a testament to the struggles I had overcome, and a beautiful reminder of the people who stood by my side through it all.

The evening unfolded in a blur of laughter, wine, and artistic discussions, each moment a stroke of vibrant color painting the canvas of my memory. I felt like a phoenix rising from the ashes of my past, ready to embrace the future that lay ahead, bright and full of promise.

A wave of warmth enveloped me as laughter echoed through the gallery, a symphony of voices blending with the soft music that floated from hidden speakers. I leaned against the cool wall, letting the ambiance wrap around me like a well-worn blanket. The excitement in the air was palpable, shimmering like the fairy lights strung from one corner to the other. I spotted familiar faces among the crowd, each one a thread in the tapestry of my life, interwoven through the art that had become my voice.

"Do you see that?" Ethan said, nodding toward a small group clustered around my depiction of a sunset—the colors bleeding together like a watercolor dream. "They're utterly captivated."

"Or they're trying to decide if it belongs in a gallery or a toddler's playroom," I quipped, attempting to mask the flutter of nerves that twisted in my stomach.

He chuckled, his deep voice a grounding presence. "Trust me, you're no Picasso, but that piece is definitely not child's play. You've got the soul of a true artist, and these people see it."

Just then, a woman in a sleek black dress approached us, her eyes alight with curiosity. "Excuse me," she said, her voice smooth as silk. "I'm sorry to interrupt, but I couldn't help but overhear your conversation. I just wanted to say that your sunset piece is stunning. The way you blend the colors is extraordinary."

"Thank you!" I replied, my voice catching slightly. "It's meant to represent hope—the idea that even after the darkest days, the sun still rises."

"Beautiful sentiment," she said, nodding appreciatively. "I'm Claire, by the way. I'm a curator at the Downtown Art Collective. We're always looking for fresh talent, and I think you have something really special here."

My heart raced at her words, a thrilling mix of disbelief and possibility. "Really? Thank you, I—"

"Would you be open to a chat about potentially showcasing some of your work in our space?" Claire interrupted, her enthusiasm infectious.

Ethan elbowed me gently, a knowing smile on his lips. "That sounds like a no-brainer. You'd be mad not to consider it."

"Absolutely," I managed to say, trying to contain the excitement bubbling up inside me. "I would love to discuss it further."

"Perfect! I'll give you my card," Claire said, rummaging through her sleek black handbag. "We can set up a time next week."

As she handed me her card, my fingers tingled, the weight of potential resting in my palm. I turned to Ethan, whose eyes sparkled with unrestrained pride. "Can you believe this? It's like my art is finally being recognized!"

"More than recognized, darling," he said, his voice thick with warmth. "This is your moment."

Before I could respond, another figure caught my eye—a tall, familiar silhouette emerging from the crowd. My heart sank. Of all the people to show up tonight, it had to be him.

"Is that—" Ethan started, but I waved him off, my stomach twisting in knots.

"Just...don't."

Jack, my ex, was sauntering over with an air of confidence that sent a jolt of anxiety coursing through me. His presence felt like a sudden storm, darkening the vibrant atmosphere of the evening. He flashed a charming smile that had once made my heart flutter but now felt like a cruel reminder of the past.

"Look who we have here!" he exclaimed, his voice smooth as molasses. "The artist of the hour! I didn't know you had it in you."

"Nice to see you, Jack," I said, forcing a smile that didn't quite reach my eyes. "What brings you here?"

"I heard there was an exhibit and thought I'd check it out. You know how I love a good piece of art." He looked over my shoulder at my paintings, his expression feigning interest. "I must say, I'm surprised. This is...well, impressive."

"Thanks," I replied, trying to keep my voice steady. "I've been working hard on it."

"It shows. Really, it does," he said, a glint of something I couldn't quite place in his eyes. "And I see you've found yourself a lovely partner to support you. How's Ethan treating you?"

"Better than you ever did," I shot back, surprised by the sharpness in my tone. It was a moment of boldness I hadn't expected to seize.

"Touché," Jack replied, raising an eyebrow. "So, is this what you've always dreamed of? Showing off your little paintings?"

The jab stung more than I wanted to admit, but I stood my ground. "Actually, it's exactly what I've dreamed of. Art is my passion, not just a hobby."

Ethan's presence felt like a fortress beside me, a silent reminder that I wasn't alone in this confrontation. He stepped forward, his expression firm but friendly. "Hey, Jack. It's great to see you, but I think we're busy celebrating a milestone here. If you'll excuse us?"

Jack's gaze flickered between us, the surprise evident on his face as he processed the shift in the atmosphere. "Oh, of course. Don't let me intrude on your precious moment." His tone dripped with sarcasm as he stepped back, but I felt a sense of relief wash over me.

"Thank you," I murmured to Ethan, who turned to me, his eyes reflecting a mix of concern and pride. "You handled that beautifully."

"Just protecting my girl," he said with a wink, but I could sense a tension lurking beneath his playful demeanor.

"I appreciate it," I said, squeezing his hand. "But I didn't expect him to show up. Not tonight."

"Not surprising, though," Ethan replied, leaning closer as if to shield me from the lingering shadow of my past. "He probably thought it would rattle you."

"Too bad for him, I'm not that easily shaken anymore," I said, my voice gaining strength. "This night is about me, not him."

"Exactly!" Ethan's smile was infectious, his confidence washing over me like a tidal wave. "Let's focus on the good vibes. You've got a potential opportunity and a room full of people who genuinely admire your work. Let's celebrate that!"

With a newfound determination, I turned back to the crowd, where Claire was now engaged with another attendee, her animated gestures creating a ripple of laughter. I approached them, ready to dive back into the joyous chaos of the evening.

As the night wore on, the tension from my encounter with Jack faded into the background, replaced by a rush of adrenaline and excitement. Every compliment felt like a spark igniting a fire deep within me, each praise a reminder of why I had embarked on this journey in the first place.

"Do you want to go and mingle?" Ethan suggested, his eyes bright with enthusiasm.

"Absolutely," I replied, taking a deep breath to center myself. "Let's see who else is captivated by my genius tonight."

Together, we navigated the sea of art lovers, our laughter blending with the joyous chatter that filled the room. Each moment felt like a brushstroke in my masterpiece—a collection of connections, compliments, and courage that I was finally beginning to embrace. I could feel the colors of my life shifting, brightening, transforming as I stepped further into the light of my dreams.

The laughter around me swelled like the tide, pulling me into its warm embrace as I relished the energy thrumming through the gallery. Each interaction felt like a brushstroke on the canvas of the night, a vivid testament to the connections I was forging. I spotted familiar faces—old friends, supportive family, and even acquaintances from my past—each one reflecting a piece of my journey. The thrill of this moment resonated deep within me, a feeling I had almost forgotten amidst the whirlwind of self-doubt and hesitation.

Ethan remained my steadfast companion, his presence a reassuring anchor in this sea of celebration. He expertly navigated conversations, introducing me to new faces while seamlessly blending humor into every interaction. "This is my talented partner," he would say, his voice carrying a hint of pride that made my heart swell. "She's basically a modern-day Van Gogh—just without the ear business."

I laughed, shaking my head at his antics. "I'm not sure I can handle the pressure of being an artistic genius. Besides, I like my ears just fine."

As the night wore on, I found myself drifting from group to group, each conversation igniting new sparks of inspiration. I discussed the emotional intricacies behind my pieces, and I felt each shared story resonate within me. It was like a dance of creativity, where each interaction contributed to the rhythm of the evening, bringing the art and the audience together in a shared experience.

Then, just as I began to relax into the joyful atmosphere, a familiar voice sliced through the revelry, sending a shiver down my spine. "Well, well, if it isn't the artist of the hour."

I turned slowly, dread curling in my stomach as I faced Jack again, his presence looming like a storm cloud. The confident smirk on his face felt like a betrayal, his eyes glinting with an energy that made my heart race—not with excitement, but with the rush of past memories flooding back.

"Jack," I managed, forcing a smile that felt more like a grimace. "What a surprise."

"Surprise indeed. I had to see for myself what all the fuss was about." He stepped closer, the crowd parting like waves around him, drawn by his magnetic energy. "And I must say, you've done quite well for yourself. Very...impressive."

I couldn't help but notice the way his eyes flickered to Ethan, a flash of something—jealousy?—passing over his features before he masked it with an indifferent smile. "You must be Ethan," Jack said, extending his hand, but his gaze lingered on me like a dark cloud threatening rain.

"That's me," Ethan replied, his tone steady but firm. "And you must be the shadow from the past she's trying to shake off."

I couldn't suppress the chuckle that escaped me, the tension momentarily easing. "Well put. I could use a good umbrella right about now."

Jack's smile faltered, and the air between us crackled with unspoken words. "I just wanted to say that it's good to see you're thriving," he said, his voice smooth yet tinged with an undertone of something else—mockery, perhaps? "I didn't think you had it in you, honestly."

"Guess I'm full of surprises," I shot back, my resolve hardening. "Just like the one where you show up uninvited. Quite the move, really."

"Touché," he replied, his expression shifting into something unreadable. "But I'm here now, and you should know that I can appreciate art, even if I didn't think much of it back then."

"What do you want, Jack?" I asked, unable to hide the irritation seeping into my voice. "Is this just another attempt to poke fun at my life choices?"

He stepped back, hands raised in mock surrender. "Relax, I'm not here to fight. Just curious about your newfound success."

Before I could respond, Ethan intervened, a firm yet gentle grip on my shoulder. "You've made your point, Jack. But this night isn't about you or your past. It's about her."

"Right. A night to remember," Jack said, a hint of sarcasm coloring his words. "Well, I'll leave you two to bask in the glow of your triumph. Just remember, every artist has to confront their past eventually."

The words hung in the air like a bitter aftertaste as he turned to leave, but something compelled me to call after him. "Jack, wait! What do you mean by that?"

He paused, his back to me, and I could feel the tension in the air shift. "You'll find out soon enough," he said, without looking back. "Just make sure you're ready for it."

And with that, he vanished into the crowd, leaving a void behind that seemed to pull at my insides. The celebration around me felt muted, like a once-vibrant painting washed out by an unexpected rain. I turned to Ethan, searching for reassurance in his steady gaze. "What was that about? Did he really just drop a cryptic bomb and walk away?"

Ethan's brow furrowed, the warmth in his eyes clouded by concern. "Don't let him get to you. He's just trying to stir the pot."

"But why now? After all this time?" I said, my heart racing. "I thought I had left him behind."

Ethan squeezed my hand, grounding me. "You have, but he's still a part of your story, even if you don't want him to be. You're stronger now. Don't let him ruin this night."

I nodded, but the unease lingered like an unwanted guest. As the festivities continued around us, I found it increasingly difficult to shake off the feeling that Jack's words held more weight than they should have. My thoughts spiraled into a whirlwind of possibilities, each more daunting than the last.

Ethan attempted to steer the conversation back to lighter topics, regaling me with tales of how he once attempted to paint a wall in his apartment, only to end up with more paint on himself than on the surface. Laughter bubbled up between us, but the warmth it brought felt fragile, a thin layer over the storm brewing inside me.

Just as I was beginning to relax again, I noticed a commotion near the entrance. A group of people had gathered, murmuring in hushed tones, their expressions a mixture of shock and curiosity. My heart raced as I glanced toward the scene, the atmosphere thickening with tension.

"What's going on over there?" I asked, trying to peer through the crowd.

Before Ethan could respond, a familiar figure stepped into view—a woman with long, flowing hair and a presence that radiated confidence. It was Lily, a fellow artist and friend, her face pale as she pushed through the throng of spectators.

"Lily!" I called, rushing toward her. "What's happening?"

She turned to me, her expression serious. "You need to come quick. There's been an accident. It's... it's bad."

An icy knot tightened in my stomach as I followed her gaze. The vibrant celebration faded into the background, the reality of her words sinking in like a stone. My breath hitched as I turned back to Ethan, uncertainty flooding my thoughts.

"Stay here," he urged, his voice steady but his eyes wide with concern. "I'll go check it out."

"No! I'm coming with you." The urgency in my tone surprised even me, but I needed to be part of whatever was unfolding.

Together, we pushed through the crowd, my heart pounding like a drumbeat echoing in the chaos around us. Each step felt heavier than the last as the murmurs grew louder, the atmosphere thick with an unshakable sense of dread.

As we reached the front, I could see a figure lying on the floor, surrounded by a ring of people, their faces masks of shock and disbelief. My breath caught in my throat, panic threatening to engulf me as I grasped Ethan's arm.

"Who is it?" I whispered, fear curling around my heart like a vice.

But as we moved closer, the figure came into focus, and the world around me seemed to tilt. There, amidst the chaos, lay Jack, the breath knocked from my lungs, a haunting reminder of the past I thought I had finally escaped.

Chapter 29: The First Showcase

The gallery buzzed like a hive, each laughter and whispered admiration weaving together a vibrant tapestry of celebration. I took a moment to breathe it all in—the gentle clinking of glasses, the soft rustle of silk dresses, and the warm glow of ambient lights reflecting off the polished floors. My heart raced, not from anxiety but from sheer exhilaration. I was finally here, in this moment, standing beside my art as it found its place in the world.

As guests mingled, I stood by my favorite piece, a large canvas sprawling like a sunrise across the wall, the colors blending into one another as if they were a story unfolding. Each brushstroke told a tale of my journey through doubt and discovery, an exploration of the shadows that had once engulfed me. The crimson hues symbolized my struggles, while the bright yellows and blues embodied the hope that had pulled me through. I thought of how I'd stared at this canvas countless nights, pouring every ounce of pain and joy into its surface, and now, it was finally being appreciated.

Ethan moved gracefully among the crowd, effortlessly drawing people into conversations about my work. His enthusiasm was infectious, and I could see the way he lit up when he spoke about my journey. "You have to understand," he said, his voice rising above the gentle hum of chatter, "each piece represents a chapter of her life. Look at how she plays with color and form—it's nothing short of magic." I felt a warm blush creep up my cheeks, gratitude bubbling within me. It wasn't just my art he championed; it was my story.

"Magic?" I echoed teasingly as he approached, a sly smile dancing on my lips. "You're laying it on a bit thick, don't you think? Just because I let the paint run wild doesn't mean I'm the next Picasso."

"Ah, but you have that spark, my dear," he replied, his eyes twinkling with mischief. "If Picasso had your flair for dramatics, who knows what masterpieces would have emerged?"

As I laughed, I caught sight of my mother standing a little distance away, her smile both proud and slightly anxious. She had always been my fiercest supporter, and yet, I could sense her apprehension about my artistic career. "Just remember," she had said earlier that day, "it's all about balance. Don't let the whirlwind of success sweep you away."

I shifted my gaze back to the guests, each one absorbed in my work, their faces reflecting curiosity and intrigue. The evening air thickened with the scent of fresh flowers and the soft hint of paint, creating a cocoon of inspiration. Suddenly, the doors swung open, and a chill swept through the gallery, drawing my attention. A figure lingered in the doorway, silhouetted against the light. My heart skipped a beat. It was Jonathan.

I hadn't seen him in years, and the sudden appearance sent a rush of memories flooding back. He had been my muse in college, the one whose laughter could ignite an entire room and whose presence was magnetic. But it was also a bittersweet reminder of why we had drifted apart—the unspoken words, the unresolved tension that had lingered long after we said goodbye. As he stepped inside, the crowd seemed to part for him, a silent acknowledgment of his charm.

"Is this what you've been working on all this time?" His voice, deep and familiar, cut through the noise, sending a shiver down my spine. He approached, and as he did, I could see the awe on his face as he examined my piece, his brow furrowing in concentration.

"Yeah, just a little something," I replied, trying to sound nonchalant, but the way my heart raced gave away my nervousness. "You know, the usual existential crisis laid out in color."

"Humility does not become you," he smirked, stepping closer. "You've grown so much since those late-night critiques in the dorms. I'd say you've turned your crisis into a masterpiece."

"I appreciate that, but you wouldn't know 'masterpiece' from 'messy splatter,'" I shot back, grinning.

His laughter danced through the air, but beneath it lay an undercurrent of something unspoken. I watched as he moved from piece to piece, occasionally glancing back at me, as if gauging my reaction.

"What brings you back?" I finally asked, my voice steadying despite the tempest of emotions swirling within me.

He paused, the question lingering like the scent of the jasmine blooming outside. "I heard about your show. I had to see it for myself. Your talent was always exceptional, and I guess I wanted to see if it was as vibrant as I remembered."

As he spoke, I felt the weight of those unshared moments, the nights we spent dissecting art and life, the laughter that felt like a lifeline. We had shared dreams once, both so sure of who we were destined to be. I realized I had missed that connection, the thrill of creation we once cultivated together.

The room was charged with a tension I could taste—sweet like the champagne flowing freely but tinged with an edge of uncertainty. In that moment, I felt the universe shift slightly, as if it was reminding me of all the roads I had traveled to reach this point. I turned back to the guests, reminding myself that I was here to celebrate, to embrace this triumph, regardless of the unexpected twist of Jonathan's arrival.

"Excuse me," I said, taking a breath and trying to shake off the thoughts of the past. "I need to go mingle." I offered Jonathan a polite smile and turned away, but not before catching the flicker of disappointment in his eyes.

As I stepped into the throng of admirers, I felt the energy of the night wrap around me like a warm embrace. This was my moment, a celebration of every brushstroke, every late-night revelation, and every tear that had fueled my journey. The night stretched out before me like an open canvas, full of possibilities, and for the first time in a long time, I was ready to paint my future.

The laughter and chatter filled the air like a rich tapestry, intertwining with the clinking of glasses and the soft strains of a jazz trio tucked in the corner. Each smile I encountered felt like a brushstroke of encouragement on the canvas of this moment. As I made my way through the crowd, my heart fluttered with a mixture of pride and disbelief. This was my art—the culmination of years spent in the dim light of my studio, wrestling with colors and emotions, and yet here it was, vibrant and alive, hanging boldly on the gallery walls.

Ethan had slipped away, probably engaging yet another enthusiastic guest with tales of my artistic process, and for a brief moment, I felt an exhilarating sense of freedom. The spotlight was no longer only on me; it was on the very essence of what I created. The guests moved from one piece to the next, their expressions shifting from curiosity to delight, their discussions animated, forming an invisible current that electrified the atmosphere. I overheard snippets of conversation that made me smile: "Did you see the way she captured that feeling?" and "It's like she's laid her soul bare for us to see."

I leaned against the wall, taking it all in, when a familiar voice broke through the din. "You're not hiding, are you?" It was Jess, my best friend since forever, with her curly hair framing her face like a halo of mischief. She was a whirlwind of energy, always bustling into my life with the perfect mix of support and chaos.

"Me? Hide? Never!" I replied, throwing my hands up in mock surrender. "I'm just admiring the view."

"Right, because there's nothing like watching your own art while pretending to be incognito," she said, arching an eyebrow. "You're the star of the show, darling. You should be front and center, soaking up every ounce of praise."

"Do I really have to?" I feigned a pout. "What if they only say nice things because they feel sorry for me? You know, the 'Oh, bless her heart, she tried' kind of praise?"

"Oh, please," she scoffed, her eyes sparkling with amusement. "You've poured your heart and soul into this. If they don't praise you, I'll hunt them down and have a word with them."

I chuckled, shaking my head. "You'd scare them into submission, that's for sure. But really, I'm just enjoying the moment." I gestured toward my work, watching as a couple of attendees leaned closer, their fingers hovering just above the canvas, as if afraid to touch what was so fragile yet so bold.

Jess followed my gaze, her smile fading slightly. "You know, you've come so far since those days when we'd critique each other's doodles in art class. I'm genuinely proud of you." She reached out, squeezing my arm, and I could feel the warmth of her support radiate through me.

"Thanks, Jess. That means a lot," I said, the sincerity of her words filling the small space in my heart that always ached for validation. "I just hope it resonates with people."

Before she could respond, a loud crash reverberated through the gallery. A ceramic piece teetered precariously on its pedestal before toppling to the floor in a shattering symphony of chaos. Everyone froze, gasps mingling with the music. I turned to see a young man, his face pale as a ghost, standing frozen with a half-empty glass in hand, looking utterly horrified.

"Oh no, that's not good," Jess murmured, her eyes wide.

I winced, watching the gallery manager dart toward the scene, her face a mask of composed urgency. "This is why we can't have nice things," I whispered, trying to lighten the mood. But the tension hung thick in the air, smothering the previous warmth.

Ethan returned just in time to see the commotion, his expression morphing from carefree to concerned. "What happened?" he asked, scanning the crowd for answers.

"Somebody's art appreciation got a little too enthusiastic," I replied, trying to find humor in the chaos, but my heart thudded uncomfortably. The night felt precariously balanced on a tightrope of excitement and disaster, and I wasn't sure which way it would tip.

As the gallery staff cleaned up the mess, I tried to refocus on the positive energy that had filled the room. I took a deep breath, reminding myself that this was still my night, my showcase. I caught Ethan's eye across the room, and he offered a reassuring smile, grounding me like an anchor in a turbulent sea.

"Let's find some champagne," Jess suggested, nudging me gently with her elbow. "You need a little liquid courage to push through this."

"Is that a euphemism for 'I need a drink'?" I shot back, grinning.

"Possibly," she admitted, her tone light. "But it also sounds like a perfect plan. Come on, let's celebrate the fact that you've made it this far. Crushed ceramics be damned!"

We wove our way through the crowd toward the refreshment table, and I could feel the adrenaline buzzing beneath my skin. The atmosphere slowly shifted back to its vibrant pulse as laughter returned, and people resumed their conversations. I filled my glass with champagne, the bubbles tickling my nose as I took a sip.

"Okay, now that's better," I said, leaning against the table. "Here's to overcoming artistic mishaps and turning them into stories."

"Cheers to that!" Jess clinked her glass against mine.

Suddenly, a shadow loomed beside us, and I turned to find Jonathan again, a grin playing at the corners of his mouth. "I didn't mean to disrupt your soirée," he said, a touch of mischief in his tone.

"But if you need a new piece for the gallery, I hear shattered pottery is all the rage."

I rolled my eyes but couldn't help the smile that broke across my face. "What's your expertise? An unintentional art critic or a one-man demolition crew?"

"Actually," he leaned closer, his voice low and conspiratorial, "I've always been a fan of abstract expressions—especially when they come with a side of chaos."

"Ah, the chaos artist strikes again," I teased.

"Guilty as charged," he replied, his gaze holding mine for a moment longer than necessary, the playful banter settling into something softer and more meaningful. There was an unspoken connection that stirred in the air, the kind that whispered of old memories and potential futures.

In that fleeting moment, the night expanded, filled with the weight of what was unsaid, and I felt an exhilarating thrill course through me. I had stepped into my own light tonight, but suddenly, I wondered what it would feel like to share that light with someone who had once held a piece of my past.

"Chaos artist, huh?" I replied, feigning seriousness as I looked Jonathan up and down. "Do you come with a warning label, or is that just implied?"

He laughed, a rich sound that cut through the remnants of tension still lingering in the air. "I think the chaos is what makes life interesting, don't you? Besides, if you ever need help breaking a few more ceramics, I'm your guy."

I raised my glass in mock salute. "To chaotic art! May it be ever in our favor."

"Let's just hope my fingers don't slip on the champagne," he quipped, his eyes gleaming.

The rhythm of the evening began to settle into a comfortable groove again, with guests returning to their mingling and laughter.

I leaned against the refreshment table, savoring the sharp fizz of the champagne as it danced on my tongue, while Jonathan shifted slightly closer, the warmth of his presence drawing me in like a moth to a flame.

"So," he said, taking a sip from his own glass, "what's next for you? More showcases? World domination? Perhaps an art installation featuring abstract chaos?"

"World domination sounds a bit ambitious," I mused, biting back a smile. "Maybe just a series of successful shows would suffice for now. You know, conquer the art world one exhibition at a time."

"Or you could become the star of an art reality show where everyone gets to critique your work while you try not to cry," he said, leaning in conspiratorially. "I think it could be a hit."

"Ugh, please, don't give me nightmares. I'm still recovering from my first showcase, thank you very much. Reality TV and I don't mix."

His laughter rang out, bright and infectious, and I felt the distance between us close in an effortless way. Each witty exchange felt like a puzzle piece snapping into place, the connection we once shared now reemerging with startling clarity.

Before I could respond, Jess swept in, her vibrant energy palpable. "What are you two plotting over here?" she asked, eyebrows raised in playful suspicion.

"Just discussing how to channel our inner chaos," Jonathan said smoothly.

"Ah, the usual," Jess replied with an exaggerated sigh. "As if the world doesn't have enough chaos already. Can't we have one nice night without the threat of artistic destruction looming over us?"

"Only if I can wear my 'Chaos Artist' badge," Jonathan countered, his playful demeanor never faltering.

"Fine, but keep the chaos away from my drinks," Jess shot back, winking at me as she picked up a glass of her own. "I can only handle so much excitement in one night."

As the three of us chatted, the energy of the gallery felt alive, the air rich with possibility and laughter. Yet, in the midst of our banter, I couldn't shake the feeling that something was brewing just beneath the surface. It was a strange sensation, as if the universe was holding its breath, waiting for the next twist in the night.

The gallery manager's voice echoed from the other side of the room, drawing attention as she attempted to restore order after the earlier incident. "Ladies and gentlemen, we apologize for the interruption. Let's raise our glasses to the talented artist behind tonight's showcase—"

At that moment, a loud gasp rippled through the crowd, cutting through her words like a knife. Heads turned, murmurs rose like a wave, and I felt a chill of unease prick at my spine. My heart raced as I followed their gaze to the far end of the gallery, where the light seemed to flicker momentarily.

"What's happening?" I asked, my voice barely above a whisper.

"I don't know," Jonathan replied, his brows furrowed as he squinted toward the commotion.

People began to shuffle, moving as if instinctively drawn to the source of the disturbance. I pushed through the crowd, curiosity propelling me forward, a mixture of excitement and dread bubbling within me. I had been basking in the glow of my accomplishments, and now it felt like a dark cloud was looming on the horizon.

As I approached, I caught sight of a small group gathered around one of my pieces, their expressions a mix of shock and disbelief. My heart plummeted as I recognized the artwork in question. It was my canvas—the vibrant one that had come to symbolize my journey. Only now, splashes of red paint had been smeared across the surface, obscuring my work, as if someone had decided to vandalize it in a fit of rage.

"What the hell?" I breathed, a wave of panic crashing over me.

"I didn't think it was possible to hate art that much," Jess said, her voice trembling with disbelief.

"No one hates it, right?" I protested, my pulse quickening. "It's supposed to resonate with people, to connect."

Jonathan stepped closer, his expression grave. "Maybe it's someone's misguided interpretation of your message? Art can be provocative, and not everyone understands the depths."

"But this is... this is destruction!" I stammered, feeling the world tilt on its axis. I fought against the rising tide of despair, desperately seeking clarity amid the chaos. My heart sank, not just for the canvas but for everything it represented—the late nights, the soul-baring emotions, the hope woven into every brushstroke.

As I stood frozen, the gallery manager approached, her face pale and drawn. "I'm so sorry, but we need to address this immediately. We can't let this continue."

The sound of murmuring grew louder, the crowd buzzing like a disturbed beehive. I felt the weight of their scrutiny, their gazes heavy with judgment. Would this one act of vandalism define my night? My journey?

A voice broke through the chaos, cutting sharply. "This is disgraceful!" An older woman with striking silver hair stepped forward, her tone scathing. "Who thought this was acceptable? This isn't art; it's a travesty!"

As I opened my mouth to respond, my heart raced, both from anger and disbelief. But before I could form a coherent thought, I felt a sudden tug at my sleeve. Turning, I found Ethan standing there, his face a mask of concern. "Are you okay?" he asked, searching my eyes for answers.

"I... I don't know," I stammered, the chaos swirling around us. "I don't understand why someone would do this."

Just as I was about to respond, the crowd began to part, revealing a figure standing at the back, hidden in shadows. As the light caught their face, my breath caught in my throat. It was someone I hadn't seen in years, someone whose presence was a ghost from my past. A storm of emotions crashed over me—anger, confusion, betrayal.

"Why are you here?" I breathed, feeling as if the ground beneath me had shifted entirely.

With a smirk, they stepped forward, and the tension in the room became a tangible thing, thickening the air around us. "Oh, darling," they said, their voice dripping with mockery, "I couldn't miss such a spectacular show."

Milton Keynes UK
Ingram Content Group UK Ltd.
UKHW032321221024
449917UK00001B/90